THREE
LAWS
LETHAL

THREE LAWS LETHAL

DAVID WALTON

Published 2019 by Pyr®

Cover image © Lonely/Shutterstock
Cover design by Nicole Sommer-Lecht
Cover design © Start Science Fiction

Inquiries should be addressed to
Start Science Fiction
101 Hudson Street, 37th Floor, Suite 3705
Jersey City, New Jersey 07302
Phone: 212-620-5700 www.pyrsf.com

10 9 8 7 6 5 4 3 2

ISBN: 978-1-63388-560-8 (paperback)
ISBN: 978-1-63388-561-5 (ebook)

Printed in the United States of America

To Caleb
They say engineers love to take things apart
and put them back together again.
You're halfway there.

"That the time will come when the machines will hold the real supremacy over the world and its inhabitants is what no person of a truly philosophic mind can for a moment question."

SAMUEL BUTLER, 1863

PROLOGUE

Annabelle Brighton checked her phone, trying to ignore the twins, who were bickering over nothing in the back seat as usual. She browsed her social media feeds, taking her eyes from the road despite the tense feeling in her shoulders. It still freaked her out a little not to have her hands on a steering wheel, even though it had been two months since they took the plunge and bought a fully automated Mercedes.

"It's safer," Brad had told her. "I don't want you trusting your life to your own reflexes."

She could have taken that personally, but she liked the freedom to read while on the road, or catch up on her messages, or watch one of the home remodeling shows she liked. With Hailey and Hannah turning thirteen next month, it seemed she spent half her life in the car these days, ferrying them to violin lessons, soccer games, ballet recitals, swimming meets, and increasingly, to the mall to hang out with their friends. She wondered what they did there, a gaggle of them just standing around or migrating from store to store. She worried about drugs, and boys, and about losing the influence she had on their choices.

"Mom, she took my book," Hailey said.

Hannah gasped in pretended indignation. "You were done with it!"

"It's *mine*. I didn't say you could read it."

Outside, rain pelted the road, turning the other cars into blurry streaks beyond the wet windows. The Mercedes hit a puddle, the rough sound vibrating through the car, but its steering adjusted smoothly, barely slowing down. They flew along the left lane at eighty miles an hour, a legal speed in the specially marked autocar-only lanes. A miserable-looking motorcyclist rode in the next lane over, his shoulders hunched and his leather jacket streaming with water. His gray beard and full sleeve tattoo might have looked impressive in other circumstances, but at the moment, he just looked like a drowned rat. Annabelle smiled. There was always someone having a worse day than you were.

"Mom!" Hailey's voice rose an octave. Annabelle looked back at her, ready to scold her for shrieking, until she saw the terror in her face. Hailey and Hannah both stared, their eyes wide, their hands raised to protect themselves. Annabelle whirled to see a huge tree falling across the road toward them. It struck the asphalt in front of their car, a snarl of wet branches glaring white in the headlights.

She barely had time to think before the car reacted, swerving with precision, independent brakes on each wheel applying just the right pressure to slow the car but avoid skidding in the rain. As Annabelle's right foot lunged forward by reflex, the Mercedes danced around the fallen tree as if by magic, changing direction with the suddenness of a bird in flight. She had just enough time to marvel that they had missed the tree entirely, when the car hit something with a sickening crunch, throwing her forward. She screamed as an airbag exploded into her face and the windshield shattered, raining pebbled glass into the car. They spun, the world whipping around her with the screech of scraping metal, until they finally ground to a halt.

Rain battered Annabelle through the broken windshield. Hailey and Hannah were screaming, but the sound barely penetrated the ringing in her ears. Eventually, the noise in her head subsided. She pawed at the seat belt release and finally found the button. The twins, still panicked, scrambled out of the car, and she followed them. The rain drenched her clothes instantly.

Columns of headlights blinded her. She shielded her eyes and looked at the Mercedes, which, except for the windshield, seemed surprisingly undamaged. Beyond it lay a twisted piece of metal and tires that she only belatedly identified as a motorcycle. Its frame was bent, its front wheel mangled, its headlight smashed. And further back, another shape, also twisted unnaturally. She cried out and ran toward it, but stopped when she saw the blood, the torn neck, the empty helmet lying several yards away.

"Don't look," she told her girls, whose eyes had gone wide. She drew them both to her, and for once, they didn't push away. She led them to the side of the road, where they stood in the rain and waited for the emergency vehicles to arrive.

She gave her story to the police in a daze, and barely registered their responses. She couldn't help thinking: the car did this on purpose. It would have known the motorcycle was there. Its sensors would have registered its location, speed, direction. It would have taken into account the barrier to their left, the fallen limb, the time available to brake or steer. In that split second, it had plotted all the possible courses and had chosen the route that would minimize the danger. To them, at least. Not to the motorcyclist.

Had she been behind the wheel, she probably would have plowed into the tree limb, maybe killing all three of them. The Mercedes had the time and skill to plot a different course, and had chosen to sacrifice a man's life to save theirs. She tried to feel sorry about that, but she couldn't. Her daughters were worth more to her than a thousand strangers. All she felt was a profound sense of relief. But by what right had the car's algorithms chosen their lives over his?

When Brad finally came to pick them up, the rain had stopped. He leaped from the car, worried and shaken. Annabelle threw her arms around his neck, reveling in the solidity of him, the familiar reality. "We're all right," she said. "We're fine."

Behind him, two men lifted a stretcher with the motorcyclist's body into a coroner's van. She heard a paramedic say the words "injuries incompatible with life." Rainwater dripped from the sheet that covered his face and dribbled onto the street.

"I called a tow truck," Brad said. "They should be here any minute."

Over Brad's shoulder, Annabelle saw a woman with dyed blonde hair standing by the van. She wore black leather pants and a sleeveless leather jacket, displaying a full sleeve tattoo on her left arm. Annabelle wasn't sure, but she thought it might have been identical to the motorcyclist's.

Their eyes met. Something changed in the woman's face, and she strode suddenly in Annabelle's direction. Annabelle took a step back, and Brad turned to look.

"It was you, wasn't it?" the woman said. "You're the one who killed him."

"I'm sorry," Annabelle said. "We couldn't help it. A tree fell in our lane."

"And I bet you didn't check for a bike next to you before you turned, did you? Nobody ever does."

Her posture was belligerent, aggressive, and Annabelle took

another step back, afraid. "I wasn't even driving. The car was. It turned by itself. The tree . . ."

The woman's eyes traveled down Annabelle's body, looking at her clothes, taking in Brad's tailored suit and the girls' matching designer outfits. She glanced at the Mercedes, then back, and gave Annabelle an acid smile. "So that's how it is."

"Look," Brad said, stepping between them. "I'm very sorry, but this was an accident."

"Accident, my ass," the woman said. "Your fancy Benz just killed my husband. We don't have much, but you bastards always find a way to take more."

"It wasn't on purpose," Annabelle said, trying not to cry. "Did you want us all to die instead?"

"Yeah," the woman said, walking forward until she was almost close enough to touch. "Yeah, that would be fine by me. But you're too rich to die. Rich enough to have a car that can kill someone else instead."

"Step back," Brad said. "Officer? Could you help us here?"

"Well, it's my lucky day, I guess," the woman said, though her voice cracked and her lower lip trembled. "I'm going to sue you for everything you've got."

A police officer broke away from what he was doing and approached them. "Ma'am," he said, but the woman was already turning away.

She threw one parting shot over her shoulder as she went. "I'll see you in court."

The Three Laws of Robotics

1. A robot may not injure a human being or, through inaction, allow a human being to come to harm.
2. A robot must obey orders given it by human beings except where such orders would conflict with the First Law.
3. A robot must protect its own existence as long as such protection does not conflict with the First or Second Law.

—Isaac Asimov, 1942

The Three Laws of Warfighting AIs

1. An AI may not injure a friendly human being, or, through inaction, cause a friendly human being to come to harm.
2. An AI must efficiently neutralize enemy humans and machines, except as it may conflict with the First Law.
3. An AI must accept the definitions of enemy and friend as given by its commanding officer.

—Gregory Harrison, 2028

CHAPTER 1

Tyler couldn't help checking the time again. He didn't have any experience with venture capitalists, but the later it got past midnight, the less likely it seemed this one would show up. He tried to ignore the nervous twisting in the pit of his stomach, but it was no use. This mattered to him. He didn't need to make millions designing self-driving cars, but he wanted to succeed at it. He'd wanted it for most of his life. A serious investor could erase all of his and Brandon's funding problems and catapult their dreams into a very real future, if he believed in what they were doing.

Tyler plucked his bottle of Yuengling off the roof and took a drink. He wiped his mouth, then balanced the bottle back on the curved surface of Brandon's silver Prius, where they both sat with their tablets perched on their knees. Their fleet of self-driving cars whipped past, kicking up a breeze, and it was testimony to how much their software had improved that neither of them even flinched.

2 THREE LAWS LETHAL

"When did Professor Lieu say this guy was coming?" Tyler asked.

"He didn't," Brandon said. "He just texted me to say some big investor friend of his might stop by. I don't know anything more than you do." He yawned. "Probably a no-show at this point."

It was well after 1:00 a.m., but the city lights provided more than enough illumination to see what they were doing. The parking lot belonged to the athletic complex of the University of Pennsylvania, where Tyler and Brandon were grad students in the computer engineering department. The school permitted them to use it between the hours of 12:00 and 6:00 a.m., when the athletic fields were officially closed.

Brandon yawned again.

"Wake up," Tyler said. "No mistakes tonight, okay?"

"Me? I don't make mistakes."

"No? Are you telling me you meant to run into that handicap parking sign?"

"That was months ago."

"I'm serious," Tyler said. "We can't make any more mistakes. Not today, not ever. Once we go public with this, one mistake is all it would take to bury us. People might commute to work in death traps every day, but one public accident, and nobody'll ride in our cars, not ever. Doesn't matter what the statistics say."

It was why what they were doing was so important. Thousands of people died in car accidents every day. Millions every year. Tyler knew firsthand how devastating just one death could be. A week before his eighth birthday, on their way to pick him up after karate practice, his parents had been sideswiped by a FedEx truck. Over an hour had passed while he waited, adults speaking over him in urgent, hushed voices, until his grandmother finally came and, through her own tears, explained to him that he would never see his parents again.

That had been fifteen years ago, but the question of who was to blame for the daily carnage on the roads was never far from Tyler's thoughts. Cancer, heart disease, old age—those were things people had fought against for centuries. But cars? That was something people had invented. And they killed more people every year than the Vietnam War. For Brandon, it was all about the engineering. He loved working with the cars. For Tyler, it was personal.

"So what do you think?" he asked. "That case in Seattle where the motorcyclist died. Is someone responsible?"

"You're obsessed, you know that?" Brandon said.

"It's an important question. If we're going to be asking people to put their lives in our hands, we need to know what we're responsible for."

"The Mercedes did what it was supposed to do." Brandon was taller and broader than Tyler, and his large hands gestured freely. "It protected its passengers. It avoided the large obstacle which was the greater threat and swerved into the small obstacle instead. You buy a car, you expect it to keep you safe, not sacrifice you to save somebody else."

Professor Lieu had mentioned the case to them that morning. The motorcyclist's wife had sued not only the woman in the car but also Mercedes-Benz and the software company that developed the driving algorithm, claiming that the car had intentionally killed her husband. Which, in a way, it had.

"I don't think it's so cut and dried," Tyler said. "What if a little boy ran out in front of your car, but swerving meant hitting a tree? Should your car just run the kid down to keep you safe?"

"Those cars don't differentiate between a little boy and somebody's pet dog. Or a box that falls off a truck, for that matter. They're all just obstacles."

"For now. The algorithms are out there to classify those

things, though; the companies just haven't worked them into their software yet."

"Because it doesn't matter to the car. Its job is to keep its own passengers safe. Besides, it wasn't a little boy—it was a fifty-year-old man on a motorcycle."

Tyler grinned. "I changed it."

Grassy dividers striped the parking lot every five lanes, each carefully landscaped and planted with young, identical-looking trees. Tyler pressed a button on his screen, and their fleet of cars switched from a loop to a wide S-curve, slaloming around the dividers. The "fleet" consisted of two ten-year-old gas-burning Honda Accords: the best they could afford by combining a Department of Transportation grant, a Kickstarter campaign, and some money that Brandon's father had donated.

They had no way to hack the cars' onboard computers, and Honda didn't publish the APIs. Instead, they had used two solenoids for the gas and brake pedals and a wheelchair motor with position feedback for the steering wheel. Once they could control the car externally, it was a simple matter to drive their setup using one of the open-source robotic hardware platforms that were in wide use with the maker crowd. They used the latest NavBerry robotics brain and sensor package, complete with the optional lidar sensor that allowed their cars to see a continuous 360-degree field of view around them. It amazed Tyler how low the barriers to entry had dropped for all the hardware required to put together a self-driving car. The software, however, was another story.

"It doesn't matter if it was a little boy or an elderly man with a heart condition," Brandon said. "The question is, did the car choose the best alternative under the circumstances? If so, then it did the best it could, certainly as well as any human could have done in the same situation."

"So you're going to go with 'run the kid down,'" Tyler said.

Brandon thought about it. "Not if the car can tell the difference between human obstacles and non-human ones. Then it becomes a matter of relative risk. There's a chance of harm to me if my car swerves toward the tree, but there's a hundred percent certainty of harm to the kid if I don't. That has to be taken into account."

Their test had drawn a small crowd of student onlookers, probably hoping to see a crash, or else just enjoying the excuse to stand out on the athletic fields under the stars and drink beer. Across the river, the Liberty buildings stood out from the Philadelphia skyline, their angular tops lit in green neon. The two Comcast buildings towered over them, taller but with considerably less charm.

Tyler knew, without even looking it up on his glasses, that on average, fifty automobiles would crash tomorrow in the city, closer to one hundred and fifty if you included its encircling highways and suburbs. On average, eight of the people involved in those crashes would die. It would be the same on the following day, and again the day after that. It was an unending cycle of disaster, one that people accepted only because it seemed ordinary and unavoidable. Professor Lieu's ethical exercises notwithstanding, self-driving cars would save far more lives than they would ever kill. Even the ones on the road today, sold as high-tech feature enhancements by the big car companies, were more effective at avoiding crashes than any human. His and Brandon's vision was bigger than that, though. They saw a future where *every* car was not only automated but also connected, flying along bumper-to-bumper in lanes only eight feet wide, and where traffic fatalities—the biggest killer of people under forty—were a thing of the past.

"I don't think it is a matter of risk," Tyler said. "For the car, there's no such thing, not really." He took another swallow of Yuengling. "If you're at the wheel, your choice to swerve or not is just a reflex reaction. You don't know the outcomes. But the car knows. It can see exactly where the tree is, and the oncoming traffic, and it knows its speed, and what its hardware can do. In the milliseconds before it reacts, it can model the result of all possible maneuvers. It isn't just reacting. It's *choosing*. And someone has to program what choice it should make. When it comes down to it, who's going to get hurt? You or them? We're writing the software. Ultimately, we're the ones who get to decide."

"Pause for a minute," Brandon said. "Look who just showed up."

Tyler followed his gaze past the gaggle of onlookers to a tall girl with curly, dark hair making her way across the field. He didn't recognize her, but his glasses quickly identified her as Abigail Sumner, an MBA student at Wharton, Penn's business school. Her curls danced around her face and gathered in piles at her shoulders. She wore a white dress with blue embroidery on the sleeves, and a cute knit cap.

"Don't get distracted," Tyler said. "Venture capitalist stopping by, remember?"

"Relax. I told her to come."

"You know her?"

"She's in my machine perception class."

Tyler shifted his gaze to another girl walking next to Abigail, and his glasses obliged with another pop-up notification identifying her as Naomi, Abigail's younger sister. Naomi was still an undergrad, a senior, finishing up dual degrees in computer and cognitive science. Shorter than her sister, she wore jeans, a *Doctor Who* T-shirt, and—if he wasn't mistaken—a tiny blue TARDIS necklace. Her dark hair was long and gathered into a braid.

"Hey! Abby!" Brandon waved his giant arms until Abby saw him. Brandon was rarely subtle, but he got results. Abby responded with a wave and a dazzling smile. The two girls maneuvered around the other students and joined them by Brandon's car.

"Climb on up," Brandon said. "We've got room."

He gave Abby a hand up onto the roof, and Naomi clambered up behind her. "Welcome to the show," he said. He tapped his tablet, cueing the cars into lead/follow mode, meaning the second car trailed the first one at a distance of just a few feet. "We call this one the deer-in-the-headlights scenario. Let's say a deer runs out in front of the first car, which brakes suddenly to avoid hitting it. Note that only the first car knows that the deer is there." He tapped the tablet again, and the lead car braked to a sudden halt. Behind it, the trailing car braked almost as quickly, stopping before it collided with the lead car's bumper.

Abby raised her eyebrows appreciatively. "Nice. So you only signaled the first car?"

"And the first car signaled the second one what it was going to do," Tyler said. "That's how we can get away with crappy sensors. There's already decades of work on getting cars to recognize their surroundings and react appropriately. What we're doing that's new is figuring out how cars can talk to each other—warn each other what they're going to do just as they do them."

"Sometimes there's even some back-and-forth negotiation," Brandon said. "Very fast negotiation, of course. Watch this one." The cars started up again, this time driving side by side. "I'm going to tell them both that an obstacle has suddenly appeared in front of them—say a crate fell off the back of a truck. Depending on its size and location, they may have to react differently." He pressed a key, and the cars suddenly swerved in opposite directions, avoiding an imaginary obstacle without hitting each other. When they came back together, he did it again, only this time, they both swerved to the left, one of them speeding up slightly to make room for the other.

"Impressive," Abby said. "And it always works? They never hit each other?"

"Well," Tyler said.

"We've been working out the bugs," Brandon said. "Though you may have noticed our cars have a number of dents . . ."

Abby laughed. "I did notice that, yes."

Tyler could see why Brandon would be attracted to Abby. She had long legs and a brilliant smile, and she laughed with easy abandon. She was just his type: outgoing and charismatic and gorgeous.

"As a matter of fact, we were just talking about autocar ethics when you walked up," Tyler said. "Brandon here thinks it's okay for cars to kill people."

"Whoa, hang on. I said a purchased car had a safety priority to its owner. Not that it should go running people down for fun."

"But why do other people's lives matter less than the lives of the people in the car?" Tyler asked.

Brandon shook his head. "They don't. That's why we can't go halfway. We need a whole transportation *system* that acts in everyone's best interest. Because you're right, being rich enough to afford an autocar doesn't mean your life is more valuable than other people's. Car algorithms should minimize loss of life, no matter whose lives they are."

He was showing off for Abby now. Tyler rolled his eyes.

"So, you'd ride in a car that was programmed to kill you in some circumstances?" Abby said.

Tyler laughed. "You tell him."

Brandon looked wounded. "It shouldn't be up to me. The algorithms should be regulated for everyone's good."

"So you want the government deciding what the rules should be," Tyler said.

Abby tossed her hair. "Can you imagine? The rules would be

so long and complicated, no one could understand them. And they would do the wrong thing half the time, but no one could change them because it would take a dozen committees and an act of Congress or something."

Brandon held up his hands. "All right, all right," he said. "You two are ganging up on me."

"What's the alternative?" Naomi said. It was the first time Abby's sister had said a word, and she spoke so softly that Tyler barely heard her.

"The alternative to what?" Tyler said.

Naomi's gaze slid off to the side, and she blushed slightly, but she said, "If the algorithms aren't regulated, then what happens? Does everybody just download the one they like best?"

"That's right!" Brandon crowed, happy that someone was taking his side. "What if I download an algorithm that values the lives of white people over black people, hmm? You're saying I should just be allowed to do that, because I'm the one in the car?"

"Of course not," Tyler said. "But neither should you be forced to use the algorithm a government committee decided was best, without any recourse. There has to be a middle ground."

A few more people joined the crowd, and Tyler looked around, trying to spot if Professor Lieu's friend was lurking. What did a venture capitalist look like anyway? He imagined an old white guy in a gray suit, but everyone around them just looked like students. For a college professor, Lieu seemed to have a lot of contacts, both in industry and elsewhere. Rumor had it he even knew some people in the CIA or the military sector or something and consulted on classified projects.

A loud pop caught Tyler's attention. He whirled to see one of the Accords veering to the left, its tire visibly deflating. Instead of stopping, the car tried to veer back toward its intended path, accelerating to make up the distance it had lost. The flat tire impeded its ability to turn, however, causing it to lunge directly at them.

"Crap," Brandon said. He tapped hurriedly on his tablet, but he lost his grip and dropped it onto the pavement, where it landed with a splintering sound. "I'll do it," Tyler said. He navigated through the UI to signal both cars to stop. Brandon jumped off the roof to retrieve his tablet, but thought better of it as he saw the Accord bearing down. He dove out of the way just as Tyler pressed the right button and the solenoid engaged, pressing the Accord's brakes to the floor. The car skidded, lurching to the left. The girls shouted and there were gasps from the gathered crowd. Tyler lifted his feet out of the way, just in time, as the Accord finally came to a stop inches from the Prius's front bumper.

Brandon climbed back to his feet and gave the car a savage kick. He locked eyes with Tyler, and Tyler could see the rage there. Brandon could be charming, but when he felt betrayed, by a person or just by life, he could lash out with unexpected ferocity. Tyler had seen him punch a hole in the drywall of a professor's office who wouldn't give him the grade he thought he deserved. He stood there with fists clenched until Abby's gentle laughter broke the tension.

"Phew!" she said. "That was a close one." Brandon's face shifted into a rueful smile as he got control and turned the charm back on. He'd always been able to do that. Abby reached a hand down and helped him back up onto the roof.

The spectators gave them ragged applause and some drunken hoots. Tyler laughed, too, though his mind was already racing through software routines, trying to understand what had happened. Their safety algorithms were rudimentary—no one was riding in these cars, after all, and they were concentrating on the fleet communication aspect of the problem—but they had to be sure their cars weren't going to run someone down. They would need to improve that aspect of the program.

Brandon held up his tablet, its screen a spider's web of tiny glass shards. He also held up his index finger, smeared with blood. "Sharp," he said.

"You're hurt!" Abby said. She took his hand in both of hers.

"Practically bleeding to death," Brandon said, smiling at her.

Tyler looked at Naomi, intending to roll his eyes, but her face was white, her expression pained. "Hey, are you okay?" he said.

"She doesn't like blood," Abby said. "The thought of blood, broken bones, any kind of medical procedure—it just bothers her." She dropped Brandon's hand and put an arm around her sister. "You're okay. Right?"

Naomi winced and gave a wavering smile. "I'm okay as long as I don't look at it."

Brandon laughed. "Well, no one died," he said. "I call that a successful test!" He hopped down and pulled another six-pack of Yuengling out of a cooler in his trunk. "Who wants a drink?"

As they clinked bottles, a middle-aged black woman in an expensive-looking suit approached them, walking confidently across the asphalt in high heels. Just behind her came Professor Lieu, a full head shorter, his bald scalp glinting in the moonlight. Tyler's heart flew up into his throat as soon as he spotted them. The woman was obviously not one of the student gawkers, and she didn't look like a professor or school administrator, either.

When they reached the car, she held out a hand for a beer. "I'll have one, if you don't mind."

Tyler's glasses identified her: Aisha al-Mohammad, philanthropist, rights activist, and investor. A quick details search suggested her personal fortune might reach into the hundreds of millions, and she regularly invested in small, high-risk entrepreneurial ventures.

Brandon, his glasses apparently telling him the same thing,

jogged around the car and wiped his hand off on his T-shirt before offering it to shake. "Brandon Kincannon."

"Yeah, got that," the woman said with a spark of amusement in her eyes. "The beer?"

Brandon snatched one, popped the cap off, and handed it over. She drank, wiped her chin, and smiled. "That's more like it."

He offered one to Professor Lieu, who waved it off. "I'm just here to make the introduction," he said. "I'll leave you boys to it." With a small smile playing across his face, he turned and strolled back across the field.

Tyler took another drink of his beer, took a deep breath, and met the woman's gaze. "I'm Tyler Daniels. How much did you see?"

"Enough," she said.

"That problem with the flat tire—"

She cut him off with a wave of the hand that held her beer. "No explanation necessary. I've been hearing a lot from Michael about you two."

"How do you know him?" Brandon asked.

"Favorite teacher of mine, back in the day. We keep in touch. He told me you boys were building something special, but in need of investment. I stopped by to see for myself."

"And what did you think?"

"I think you ought to join me for lunch tomorrow. Call it a business lunch. I want to hear your ideas and your plans. Where we go from there, we'll just have to see." She turned at that, waggling the bottle of Yuengling. "Thanks for the beer. I'll meet you in front of the White Dog Café at noon."

Tyler and Brandon watched her go. When she was out of sight, Brandon threw his beer bottle into the air with a whoop.

"I don't believe it," Tyler said. This could mean everything. Real funding, a real company. And yeah, he knew that more than ninety percent of startups failed, but still. You didn't have a chance to succeed if you didn't get started in the first place.

"What is it?" Abby asked.

"She's an angel investor," Tyler said. "She invests her own private fortune in ventures she thinks—"

"I know what an angel investor is. I'm a business major. Do you think she'll invest in the two of you?"

"One can hope."

"Drink up," Brandon said. "This is worth a celebration."

"Maybe not," Tyler said. "It's going to be a long night."

"What do you mean?"

"You heard her. She wants to hear our plans at *noon tomorrow*. She wants us to pitch her. That means we have less than ten hours to plan what we're going to say."

"But we know our plans already. We've talked about them for years. You even have a five-year financial plan."

"I know. But we'll only get one shot at this."

"You don't think getting a good night's sleep will improve our chances of talking coherently?"

"This is our big break," Tyler said. "We'll sleep next week."

Their audience, including Abby and Naomi, drifted away now that the show was over, and Tyler and Brandon started packing up their things. They disconnected the actuator assembly from each vehicle so they could drive them by more conventional means to the student parking garage on Walnut Street. Brandon slid a jack under the frame near the popped tire and lifted the car enough to slide off the wheel. Tyler retrieved the donut from the trunk and rolled it over.

"I thought we weren't going to make any mistakes today," Brandon said.

Tyler hoisted the donut and aligned the threaded bolts through the holes. "It must have had a nail in it or something that weakened the tire wall. It's not that old."

"Checking the cars before we drive is your job."

Tyler frowned. He didn't think it was his job so much as that he was the one who cared enough to do it. "Are you saying this was my fault?"

Brandon fitted the tire iron over the first of the bolts and started tightening it. He was stronger than Tyler and had longer arms, and made short work of it. "I'm saying you should admit it when you make a mistake. We both have to do our jobs if we want to make this work."

"I don't see how I could have predicted—"

Brandon lashed out with the tire iron and struck the donut. The metal rang. He brandished it at Tyler, his face twisted in anger. "No excuses. We looked like idiots today."

"She didn't care about that. She wants to talk. We're celebrating, remember?"

Brandon's angry expression suddenly cleared and he grinned. "You should see your face."

Tyler laughed nervously. "You didn't care about the investor. You just wanted to impress that girl, didn't you?"

"What, Abby? She's really something, isn't she?"

"I think she was impressed."

"I hope so. I'm going to call her after our meeting with the investor."

They finished attaching the tire and put the old one in the trunk. The nervous feeling in Tyler's stomach still hadn't gone away. Brandon wasn't right to blame him for the tire, but he wasn't entirely wrong either. Whatever their cars did, it was their responsibility. What would it be like if their software took the controls of real cars with real people in them? He remembered how disturbed Naomi had been by the sight of a little blood. This was serious. If more people survived on the road because of his cars, then it would be due to him. And whenever they died, it would be—at least in part—his fault.

CHAPTER 2

Naomi Sumner had found the secret door during her first month as a freshman. It wasn't a door, not really, but she thought of it that way. The university library atrium featured a wide, curving, central staircase that led to the second and third floors. On the second floor, a small gap at the end of a bookshelf led to a small space behind it. It would have been dark back there, except for a triangular opening high in the wall where it curved upward with the staircase. Standing, Naomi could look through the opening and just see the main entranceway and checkout desk below, with little chance of being seen in return.

It was her hideaway, a space barely large enough to lie down in, but that no one else in all the world knew about. Everywhere else in her life was public. She couldn't afford to live in an apartment by herself, so she had to share with two other girls. One of those girls was her sister, Abby, which made it bearable, but she never really felt at home there. She had nowhere to be alone.

Here in her secret lair, however, she felt safe. Her first year, she had lived in fear that someone else would discover it, and the secrecy of the space would be ruined. Now, as a senior, she was confident no one would. The thought that not a soul knew where she was or could find her if they wanted, not even Abby or her parents, made her relax like nothing else could. This was her place. It was her wardrobe, her rabbit hole, her subtle knife. An entrance to a world of her choosing.

Through her triangular spyhole, Naomi watched a girl enter the library through the main doors below. Her glasses identified the girl as Asia Chantell, a sophomore education major. Under the name, a pop-up suggested a conversation starter: *What do you think about the latest ruling on school vouchers?* Naomi knew nothing about the ruling, but she knew if she approached Asia and started a conversation along those lines, the app would provide her with further prompts. Of course, Naomi had no intention of starting a conversation with Asia or anyone else, but it was good to know the help was there, for when conversations were unavoidable.

She had written the app herself. Or trained it, actually. The number of software algorithms that were actually written, in the traditional sense, by people, was dwindling fast. Most apps—the thinking part of them, anyway—were machine learning algorithms, trained by feeding them data with known right answers. It was like teaching a child to recognize everything from a Chihuahua to a mastiff to a cartoon puppy as a "dog." You didn't do it by explaining the characteristics of a dog. You did it by pointing to things and saying, "That's a dog," or "That's not a dog."

She called the app *Jane*. A bit presumptuous, perhaps, but she liked to imagine she was Ender in *Speaker for the Dead*, talking to an AI no one else knew existed. Her Jane wasn't a great conversationalist yet, but Naomi was improving her little by little. Besides the personal data served up by the glasses, Jane could understand speech—there were plenty of open source libraries for speech recognition these days—and with that input, Jane could troll the web, searching for popular topics and appropriate responses to suggest to Naomi to use in conversation. The suggestions she served up were occasionally unhelpful, sometimes hilariously so, but Jane's lurking presence in her glasses took some of the stress out of social interaction.

Naomi settled down into the beanbag cushion she'd smuggled in a year before and rested her hand against the stack of *Harry Potter* novels next to her on the floor. She hadn't stolen them, not really. They'd never left the library, after all. But she had hoarded them back here as her private treasure, to read and re-read when she needed them. She had grown up with these books. Harry and Hermione and Ron were as real to her as any of her classmates or friends. As a child, she had fallen asleep most nights to Jim Dale's audiobook narration, the comfortable timbre of his voice as familiar as the words themselves. Even now, when life threatened to overwhelm, she could come here, choose a page at random, and slip into Hogwarts as if she had never left.

Today, however, she had work to do and a decision to make.

"Jane, launch Realplanet simulation number one." She whispered it, not wanting to be overheard by anyone else in the library. In a quiet setting like this, with no ambient noise, the speech recognition software could understand a whisper, though Naomi looked forward to the day when she could simply subvocalize, as worked in so many of the books she enjoyed.

Her glasses turned opaque, blocking her vision of the real world, and another world took its place. A vast and beautiful landscape, a sparkling lake, rolling forests backed by distant blue mountains. As she turned her head, the glasses responded, showing the view from a different angle, as if she were really standing in this imaginary world. It wasn't truly immersive—her peripheral vision revealed the deception, if she paid attention—but it was close enough for the willing mind to forget for a time and just believe. She controlled her motions using a wireless game controller in her lap. She could generally navigate it by touch and memory, though if she needed it, the program could temporarily transpose a view of her hands and the controller into the scene.

This was Realplanet, the latest in the craze of open sandbox games that had started with Minecraft two decades earlier. This version provided not only an open world in which players could build creatively and try to survive, but also configurable laws of physics, opening the game's creativity to a new level. The configuration could be as simple as reducing the strength of gravity, or as complex as defining fundamental substances and the laws by which they would combine, react, melt, or combust. The game was not only played by millions of children around the world but also used by scientists and engineers to simulate real-world experiments. Laws of thermodynamics and electromagnetism could be adjusted or defined, sometimes requiring thousands of lines of custom code in Realplanet's native scripting language.

This particular world represented her senior project, and with only two months to go until the end of school, it was shaping up into a complete failure. To her left stood a squat, ugly cabin made of wood—the only structure visible for miles. To call it a cabin took generosity. The walls more closely resembled stacks of badly cut tree branches than anything aesthetic. It had no windows to speak of, and only one door, which consisted of a piece of the wall that could be dragged far enough out of place to climb inside, and then dragged back again.

Naomi used the game controller to maneuver her way inside, where the view was no better. The dull interior was filled with a month's supply of yams in scattered piles on the floor and several bottles of water, the minimum supplies needed for survival. The cabin's one occupant stood motionless in the middle of the room, not acknowledging her presence.

The cabin's occupant—whom she had named Mike—was the first of the deep learning bots Naomi had written and set loose to live or die in Realplanet's unforgiving ecosystem. Mike—many different iterations of him—had played the game hundreds of thousands of times, learning a little more each time: how to find food and water, how to build a shelter, how to avoid or defend against the dangerous creatures that prowled the night. Naomi hadn't programmed this knowledge into the software. It had played and died, played and died, the value of each attempt measured by the length of time it managed to stay alive, until it learned how to survive indefinitely.

But Mike hadn't lived up to his namesake from Heinlein's *The Moon Is a Harsh Mistress*. The point of the experiment had been to see what he would do *after* he learned to survive. Would he explore his world, looking for better sources of food or more efficient building materials? Would he expand his shack into a palace? What creative things would he do with his time once he had mastered the skills of survival?

Instead, he had done nothing. He collected what he needed with a minimum of effort, and then stood motionless in his shelter for days on end, pausing only to eat and drink when necessary. Naomi knew the programming was solid. Mike was a recurrent neural network, the most involved and complicated software she'd ever written. But it was nothing new. It wasn't substantially different from what Google DeepMind had done more than a decade earlier, when they used general AI algorithms to master Atari video games like *Centipede* and *Space Invaders* blindly, with no prior knowledge of the rules of the game and no input but the pixels from the screen and the score.

Maybe back then it would have been enough to get her a good graduate school placement, but not anymore.

This wasn't the only version of Mike and his world she'd attempted—not by a long shot. She had put him in worlds with harsher climates and physical laws, worlds where survival took more creativity and cleverness. She introduced seasons, so there would be times of plenty and times of want, requiring long-term planning and forethought. But simulation two turned out the same as simulation one, as did simulations three, four, five, six, seven, and eight. Mike eventually learned to survive, but no more. He had no external sense of self, no drive to invent, no longings, no curiosity. He was just a set of instructions, more complicated than most, but no different in kind from a stack of ENIAC punch cards.

John Searle, a philosopher at the University of California, Berkeley, once posed the Chinese room experiment, suggesting that a computer could never truly be conscious. The experiment imagines a person who does not know Chinese sitting in a room, where he is passed slips of paper with Chinese ideograms written on them. He looks the ideograms up in a book and writes down the appropriate response, which he passes out through the door. To those outside the room, it appears as if the room speaks Chinese, but all of the intelligence went into creating the book in the first place—the person in the room has no comprehension of the conversation. Searle had argued that a computer, no matter how sophisticated its responses, will have no more understanding of the meaning of its responses than the person in the Chinese room.

As time after time her experiments failed to show any evidence of emergent intelligence, Naomi began to fear that Searle was right.

Her advisor had, of course, told Naomi the same thing, strongly suggesting that she take on a more achievable project.

Naomi had politely agreed, and then gone on to work on the idea anyway. She couldn't help it. It was the only project topic she really cared about. Now, however, she was at the point of no return. Her advisor had offered her a way out, if she chose to take it. She could spend the rest of the semester adjusting her research to show how machine learning could assist child education through game play. If she worked hard, she would still have time to do the work and write the paper. It wouldn't be groundbreaking, but it would be finished.

Naomi had dreamed of artificial intelligence, true strong AI, since she was a kid. Her dual majors in computer science and cognitive science had been specifically aimed at that goal. Yes, pundits had been predicting intelligent machines within twenty years for most of the last century, but now they seemed *so close*. Speech recognition and synthesis, face recognition, natural language processing, intelligent conversational agents: all of these had become everyday miracles, their interactions often mistaken for human, within narrow contexts.

She didn't care about graduate school placements, not really, except as a way to continue the work. She didn't want prestige or a high salary. She wanted to understand what made the human mind unique. She wanted to realize the dream of all those novels she had grown up reading.

She would worry about her advisor tomorrow.

"Jane," she said, "launch a new simulation."

She had to try something new. Not just a tweak to a previous idea, but something completely different. On a whim, instead of one Mike, she placed a hundred copies of Mike in the same simulation. A hundred different avatars, roaming the world with independent bodies and minds. And feeling bloody-minded, she provided the world with only enough resources of food and water to support five players. The hundred Mikes each had the same objective: to survive.

She started the Mikes from scratch again, with no knowledge of how to live, essentially just trying random actions. The first run finished quickly, with all the Mikes dead. The second, third, and fourth did the same. This was their training period, however, when they learned what it took to survive a little longer with each iteration, learning through random actions that happened to produce better results.

As the iterations proceeded, those who managed to live longer—even if just by moments—would improve their knowledge of how to play the game the next time. Since it was competitive, most would still die quickly, leaving a maximum of five to survive long-term. She didn't know what difference it would make, but perhaps the need to compete would spark the need for innovation that simply surviving had not.

The iterations flew by quickly, but it would still take time for there to be any meaningful results. She left it running and—after making sure no one was nearby—sidled around the bookshelf, slipping out of her private Narnia and back into the real world.

She bought a Caesar salad with extra croutons from one of the campus cafeterias and sat outside to eat it. The weather was cold, but she preferred to be alone instead of in the noise and bustle of other students eating food with friends. She took her time, enjoying the meal and the crisp air, and wrapping her fingers around her hot coffee when they started to feel numb.

After lunch, she had a class to attend. It was a human psychology class she'd signed up for to get a better idea of how the human mind worked. The class had turned out to be a disappointment, but she always went anyway. She rarely skipped classes. She always imagined what it would be like to be a professor and have no one show up for your class, and then she felt obligated to go, in case she was the only one who did. It never happened that way, but she still never quite had the heart to stay away.

At the end of the hour, she returned to the library and slipped into her secret nook. She settled on the beanbag chair, pulled the game console off of a shelf, and told Jane to start the new simulation.

The world sprang into being through her glasses. At first, she suspected a glitch, some kind of mistake on her part, or perhaps even a bug in the Realplanet software itself. All she could see, in any direction, was a tangle of brown lines. She tried to move, but the lines had substance, blocking her path. Naomi switched to superuser status, and used that power to fly up off the ground, the brown tangles passing through her now as if she were made of smoke.

In moments, she cleared them, and the familiar view of distant mountains and sky greeted her. From this vantage, she could see that the brown tangles were a wall or fence of some kind, encircling a large area of ground. As she flew higher, she saw that all the land in view had been subdivided this way, a series of roughly square shapes stretching for miles like a vast chessboard.

What were they? Perhaps each of the Mikes had erected the fences as borders around their own fiefdoms, a way to keep the others from stealing or killing. But that didn't make much sense. Only some of the areas had access to the lake or to the forest, and some of them were entirely surrounded by others. Only a few of the enclosures had buildings, though they were large ones, made at least partly of metal that glinted in the sunlight. She saw several enclosures stuffed full of sheep or cows, grazing contentedly.

A Mike below her walked across one enclosure toward the tangled brown fence. He disappeared for a moment inside it, and then emerged again on the other side in a new enclosure. Naomi flew down to investigate, but she could see no obvious door or path. Then she understood. It was like a maze. The AIs would have no difficulty remembering the complicated set of movements needed to weave their way through this tangle of briers. The wolves and tigers and balrogs and jabberwocks of the world, however, never could. The Mikes had compartmented their world into safe regions, passable by them but not by the predators. Even when a predator spawned inside an enclosure, they could escape and then kill it while keeping it contained.

This wasn't just a pattern of fences. It was a village. The Mikes were working together.

With growing excitement, Naomi checked the statistics for the world, and found that fifty-two Mikes were still alive of the original hundred. But that wasn't possible. She had designed the world to support a maximum of five. This particular iteration had been running for only a few minutes, but in game time, it was the equivalent of years. For the moment, she had slowed down its normal breakneck running speed to real time, so she could observe, but there had been plenty of time for the population to die off.

Why hadn't they? There wasn't enough food in the world to support fifty-two players. Yes, they could breed animals to create food, but there was only so much grass for those animals to eat. The players could grow grass, but it grew only slowly, not at a sufficient rate to feed the number of animals required to keep fifty-two players alive. The same applied to planting edible crops. Most of the ground was unsuitable for planting, leaving a maximum amount that could be grown, and planting crops would compete with planting grass for domestic animals. With this world's straightforward rules, the math was simple enough.

And yet they were alive. She examined one of the sheep enclosures more closely. The area was absolutely stuffed with sheep, and nearly stripped bare of grass. With this many sheep in such a tight place, the grass couldn't have lasted very long.

Several adjacent enclosures, however, were empty except for verdant swaths of uneaten grass.

As she watched, one of the Mikes destroyed a section of fence, allowing the sheep access to the next enclosure. They pushed through, bleating joyously, into the fresh new grass, leaving bare ground behind. Once all the sheep were through, the Mike repaired the gap in the fence.

But how did the grass grow so fast? At the rate this number of sheep ate, they would eradicate the grass in all the enclosures before nightfall, and new grass wouldn't grow back for days. A shadow fell across the sheep from one of the shining metal buildings. She would have to investigate those, too. It made sense for the Mikes to build their living structures tall; it left more ground for planting. But the structures could have been built on rocky ground, instead of here, where the ground was fertile for planting. And why were they covered in metal? Metal had to be mined from deep underground. It had to be melted down and forged. Why not simple wood or stone?

The sun shifted, reflecting off of the buildings in a bright glare. And then she understood. Taking to the sky again, she looked down on the pattern of enclosures and confirmed her suspicion. The buildings were shaped and placed in such a way as to reflect sunlight away from rocky ground and onto the grassy enclosures. As the sun moved, the reflected light moved, bathing each enclosure in an extra dose of sunlight. In the world's simple mechanics, growth was directly correlated with amount of sunlight. The Mikes had found a way to beat the math.

Naomi twirled in the air, giddy with excitement. The Mikes had cracked the world. They had, in a sense, outsmarted her, using the rules she had established to achieve an outcome she had tried to prevent. This was more than just a passing grade for her project; this was publishable. It implied that the development of intelligence required competition and conflict to thrive; and yet, somewhere along the way, the Mikes had discovered that working together made them more powerful than working alone.

It did make her wonder: what had happened to the other forty-eight? Had they been hunted and killed when they didn't join the larger group? Were there multiple groups that formed different strategies, and only one of the strategies had worked long-term? Or had two large groups warred for the right to use the land, the losers executed to make way for the winners? However it had happened, one hundred Mikes had started this round with all the same insights and experiences learned from thousands of previous games. Half of them had died. Naomi suspected that once she sifted through the logs, she would discover the darker side of this utopia.

Yawning, Naomi pulled off her glasses, blinking in the sudden dimness of her library nook. She fizzed with excitement over what she had accomplished. Her AIs were adapting, learning new skills, developing new strategies, and working together to solve difficult problems. It didn't mean they were self-aware. It didn't mean that John Searle was wrong. But it was something. It was progress.

She blinked away the bright afterimages in her eyes, but the library still seemed dim. A moment later, she realized it *was* dim. All the lights were turned off. She had stayed past eleven o'clock, and the library had been closed and locked with her inside.

She doubted she was trapped. She could probably find a way to slip out, a door that could be opened from the inside, but that would draw attention, perhaps her face on security cameras, identified by the same software that allowed her glasses to recognize strangers. It might even set off alarms. No, she couldn't leave now. She would just have to stretch out on the beanbag and sleep here as best she could. Again.

CHAPTER 3

Tyler rocked on the balls of his feet, bouncing with nervousness. "Maybe she won't come."

"Of course she'll come," Brandon said. He didn't look nervous at all. "But don't worry about it. If she wants to sponsor us, she will. If not, there will be others."

Spoken like someone with money, Tyler thought. Brandon's father controlled his family's fortune, so it wasn't like Brandon could access it directly. Just growing up with plenty, though, made Brandon less likely to think of money as an obstacle. He had just never experienced what it was like to be unable to do something for lack of funds.

Aisha al-Mohammad rolled up to the White Dog Café in a black Cadillac Escalade. Brandon rolled his eyes, but Tyler jabbed him in the ribs. "Best behavior, remember?" he said.

"Look at the size of that thing, though," Brandon said. "It's like a tank on wheels."

"Which she is perfectly within her rights to drive."

"It's a death machine. Do you know how much damage that much mass can do? It's like an arms race out there: people drive larger vehicles to feel safe, and the result is that our roads are more lethal than ever."

"But she's not people," Tyler said. "She's one person, and a mom. She probably picked the car so her daughter would be safe. You can't blame her for that."

"If everybody thinks that way—"

"If you say anything about her car, I'll run you over myself," Tyler said. "This could be our big break. Don't screw it up."

They had argued about what to wear, too, Tyler recommending suits and ties, while Brandon insisted that jeans and T-shirts would strike the right tone. In the end, they had compromised with dress shirts and jeans, no tie. The Escalade glided to a stop, and their potential patron stepped out of the driver's side door. Tyler was surprised; he had expected it would be self-driving, or that she would have a chauffeur.

She shook their hands and said, "Big lunches for both of you. You look like you need it."

They looked at each other for signs of malnourishment, shrugged, and followed her. The White Dog Café was a pricey organic restaurant in a repurposed brownstone townhouse a block off campus. Tyler had never been, not having fifty bucks to drop on a meal, but Brandon's father and stepmom had taken him there for lunch when they visited.

"Thanks for this opportunity, Ms. al-Mohammad," Tyler said.

"Aisha," she said. "Call me Aisha, and no shop talk until we've eaten."

At Aisha's request, the waitress seated them outside on the veranda and left them to peruse the menu. Tyler scanned the options with growing unease. He'd never seen a menu that listed multiple courses. Was he supposed to order something from each? And what on earth was 'Branzino' or 'Saffron Aioli' or 'Nicoise Olive Beurre Blanc'? It was like he'd stepped into another country, where he didn't know the language. He looked up the names of a few of the dishes on his glasses, but eventually gave up and settled on a chicken breast described with words he mostly recognized.

Aisha ordered a plate of local artisan cheeses for the table. They chatted nervously about nothing much, trading stories about Professor Lieu's notoriously early classes—held at the ungodly hour of 8:00 a.m.—and comparing notes on his teaching style and mannerisms from Aisha's college days, now two decades past. Tyler realized he was bouncing his leg up and down at a manic pace and forced himself to stop.

The meals arrived. Tyler couldn't tell which one was his until it was set in front of him. The chicken was sliced paper thin and artistically stacked, with asparagus stalks, mushrooms, and sprigs of fresh herbs positioned as carefully as a floral arrangement. It looked more like artwork than a meal. Silence reigned for several minutes as the three of them started to eat.

"Now," Aisha said, after sipping from her glass of Riesling. "Tell me why the world needs yet another company devoted to self-driving cars."

Brandon set down his fork and knife. "Because millions of people are still driving personal cars," he said. "They're the most dangerous, wasteful, inefficient, expensive boondoggle in history. People spend thousands to own a vehicle that sits parked most of the time, doing nothing. In cities, they may even have to pay for the privilege of parking it. Personal cars destroy the environment, clog our roadways, and kill more young adults than sickness or war."

"It's about freedom," Aisha said. "People want to go where they want, when they want."

"Listen," Brandon said, "What are the biggest problems that our city departments of transportation deal with?" He counted them off on his fingers. "One: traffic. Too many cars, not enough roads. Two: parking. Did you know a study estimated that thirty percent of city congestion is due to people driving around looking for a place to park? And think of the acres of prime urban real estate taken up with parking garages and street-side parking. Three—and this should probably be number one: safety. We call them 'accidents,' as if they can't be helped, but the vast majority of them are human error of one sort or another. Drunk driving tops the list, but there's distracted driving, falling asleep at the wheel, failing to notice red lights or deciding to ignore them—only a tiny percentage is due to icy roads or vehicle malfunction. People die in cars all the time, and we just accept it."

Tyler cringed a little—Brandon was coming on strong, and he didn't know how Aisha would take it. He was following the script, at least. Tyler pulled up the Philadelphia accident data report site on his phone and jumped in when Brandon paused for breath. "Early this morning, on Gregg Street, a thirty-five-year-old man named Harold McMillan was killed in a high-speed crash by a driver with a blood alcohol level of 0.2 percent. Last night, on Cottman Avenue, pedestrian Eric Adams was run down in a hit-and-run while waiting for a bus. Yesterday afternoon, bicyclist Stephanie Wilson was killed on Columbus Boulevard when a speeding car ran a stop sign. Also yesterday afternoon, Jamal Harris and his three children, ages five, three, and six months, were admitted to Jefferson with serious injuries after Louise Murphy, age seventy-eight—"

"I get the idea," Aisha said.

Brandon leaned over the table, fire lighting his eyes. "The point is our fleet of autocars would solve *all* of these problems. Most personal cars spend twenty-two out of every twenty-four hours parked, but ours wouldn't. They'd be driving the next customer instead of sitting idle, taking up parking spots. Because of that, we'd need fewer of them, reducing the number of cars on the road. Most of all, we'd eliminate all of those human-error collisions. Hundreds of casualties a year in Philadelphia alone. Thousands if we spread to other cities."

"Okay, okay," Aisha said, a smile fighting to break out of her professional interview expression. "You're passionate, I get that. And I can't argue with your statistics. But this is a dream Google has been chasing for years, not to mention Tesla, Mercedes, Audi, GM, Honda—all the big car manufacturers with self-driving cars already on the streets. Uber and Lyft have fleets of autocars already in service. The two of you are barely out of college, with no business credentials. What are you going to bring to the field that isn't there already?"

"Communication," Tyler said. "First off, the big automobile companies selling autocars are addressing only part of the problem. They have a vested interest in keeping personal cars on the road, so they sell personal self-driving cars, which are still parked most of the time, and still clog our streets. But more significantly, they don't talk to each other. Each car has to recognize from image and radar and lidar data that a threat is heading toward it and evade. That might be okay if you've got the only one on the road, but it doesn't scale. Three or four or five self-driving cars involved in the same incident would all react differently, *causing* collisions by their attempts to avoid them. We don't just need cars with the ability to act autonomously. We need them to be *coordinated*."

Aisha took another sip from her wine, but Tyler could tell she was hiding a smile. "Michael told me you boys were passionate," she said. "I like that, I do. But passion only goes so far. Thousands of startups launch on passion and go belly-up after a year or two. So maybe there's a business case for a coordinated fleet. Why are you two the ones who can make it succeed?"

They kept talking, ignoring what was left of their gourmet meals, telling her all their hopes and plans. They were prepared, and Tyler knew their software was top-notch, but Aisha had a point. They were novices. They'd never run a business, hired employees, advertised to customers, or even paid much in the way of taxes. There would be hundreds of legal and financial details to worry about, never mind the small problem of whether they could actually make money. She was right to be wary. Any money she poured into their venture she might never see again.

"All right," Aisha said after an hour had passed. "I've heard enough. Let me tell you two something about angel investing." She crossed her legs and stared them down, meeting first Brandon's eyes, and then Tyler's. "I don't invest in ideas. Anybody can have an idea. It doesn't mean they'll follow through with it, and it certainly doesn't mean they'll have the brains, guts, and endurance to make a company successful. So when I have meetings like this, the idea is secondary. I don't even care if the business plan is sound, because I can help with that. What I invest in is people. And I like what I see in you two, even though you're as green as next year's apples and have no clue what you're getting yourselves into. So this is what we're going to do."

Aisha sipped her wine, and the moment seemed to stretch out forever. Tyler and Brandon clamped their mouths shut and glanced at each other. Tyler felt like a condemned man, waiting while the jury filed back into the box to deliver their verdict. His leg started bouncing again, and he used both hands to hold it down.

"We're going to do this in stages," she finally said. "I'm going to fund you an initial, modest amount. No contract, no convertible debt or company equity—I'm just going to give you the money. About a month from now, you're going to stage a demonstration. Buy what you need to buy, code what you need to code, but that demo is your ticket. Because I'm going to bring all the interested investors I know to come and watch it. We angels travel in choirs, and if I tell my friends there's something to see, they'll come see it. If you knock our socks off, then I guarantee, you'll get your chance. If not, well"—she shrugged— "there are plenty of other passionate entrepreneurs out there, waiting for their big break."

She pulled out her checkbook and scribbled in it. "It's not very much," she said, handing it to Brandon, "but if you can do something special with it, there will be more to come."

Tyler's face hurt. He was grinning from ear to ear, which probably didn't seem very professional, but he couldn't help it. When he saw the check she wrote out for them, he nearly fell out of his chair. The amount was more than twice what they had spent so far, including purchasing the two Accords. They could buy more cars. They could buy real sensors and equipment. They could do this for real.

The waitress came with the check. "Who gets the damage?"

"Oh, sorry, could we get that split three ways?" Aisha asked.

Tyler raised his eyebrows and looked at Brandon. Did she expect them to pay? He had a very large check in his hand now, sure, but he didn't have enough cash to cover a meal like this, and his bank account was practically empty, since all the money that didn't go for school he had funneled into their project. He supposed he could use a credit card, and then pay it back with the investment money . . .

"Just kidding. I've got it," Aisha said, grinning and holding out a card to the waitress. "You'll need every cent if you want to impress me. And trust me—my friends are even harder to impress than I am." The waitress took the card and stepped back inside. Aisha nodded at the check Tyler still held. "Honestly? I think I've just thrown away some money. But I can afford to take some long odds. Every once in a while, one of them pays out big, and that makes up for all the rest. I'll see you boys in a month."

The waitress came back with her card, and Aisha stood, pushing in her chair. "You'll have to find an appropriate venue for the demo, rent it if it needs renting. I'll be in touch so we can work out a date."

She pulled on a trench coat, cinched the belt around her waist, and draped a thin scarf around her neck. "Good luck," she said. She walked back toward her car, and in moments, the black SUV roared past in front of the restaurant.

Brandon and Tyler looked at each other for a moment. Then Brandon threw back his head and howled, while Tyler threw his cloth napkin in the air like confetti. He snapped the check taut between two hands, and they stared at it, hardly believing it was real.

"We did it," Brandon said.

"Yes, we did," Tyler said. "Now comes the hard part."

CHAPTER 4

Tyler spotted Naomi Sumner in the Graduate Student Center the next morning. She wore a blue University of Pennsylvania sweatshirt and kept her head down, waiting for a turn at the coffee machine. The Center's common room offered free coffee all day on a bring-your-own-cup basis, making it a popular morning location. A busy stream of students filed in and out of the doors, fueling up before classes or meeting up with friends.

Tyler jumped up from the overstuffed chair he was lounging in and went to meet her. "Hey," he said. "You know that coffee's for grad students only."

He smiled to show he was joking, but she blushed and turned away. "I usually come in with my sister," she murmured.

"I know. I was just . . . never mind. Bad start. I'm Tyler Daniels. You were at my autocar test yesterday."

She just looked at him without saying anything.

"Which, of course, you know," Tyler said, feeling like he was rambling. "You were there when the venture capitalist stopped by too, weren't you?"

Naomi nodded, one hesitant bob of her head that stopped as soon as it started.

"Well, she's investing in our project, at least for a little while. She wants us to give a demo in a month. It's not a lot of time, and there's a lot of programming to do. I checked you out online . . ." She gave him a quick look, and he hastened to explain. "Your open source contributions. Lots of machine learning applications: voice recognition, handwriting identification. Good stuff. Everybody I talk to says you're the best in your class. I was wondering . . ." The girl ahead of Naomi stepped aside, and Naomi sidled in to fill her travel mug with coffee. Tyler stood uncomfortably next to her while the coffee poured. When she straightened, he said, "I was wondering if you wanted to join us. Help us get the software ready for prime time. It's not a paying gig, or anything, but if our company takes off like we hope it will, you'd be right in on the ground floor."

She met his gaze briefly, and then her eyes slid off to the side. Her shoulders lifted slightly, as if she were a turtle trying to pull her head into her shell. "Okay," she said.

"Okay? You'll do it?"

Another awkward head bob. "I have to go to the library," she said.

"All right. I'll walk with you."

A brief look of panic flitted across her face, and then vanished. "Okay," she said again.

Naomi headed out the door, and Tyler followed her. "You saw the trouble we had when a tire went flat," he said. "We need to raise the software to the next level. Its training has been superficial, just enough to implement some basic scenarios. We need to widen its experience, cover a lot more cases."

They crossed Thirty-Sixth Street and headed off across the green. The trees overhanging the crisscrossing brick paths were budding, and the fresh-washed scent of spring was in the air. Tyler loved this time of year, even though it often brought rain. With the bitter cold gone, students tossed Frisbees across the lawn, and others sat on benches to do their homework.

"What do you think of the Gomez bill?" Naomi asked.

Tyler turned, surprised to hear her speak. Gomez was a bill before Congress that would require autocar manufacturers to include loopholes for law enforcement, such as an override signal a policeman could send to force a car to stop. It addressed the public fear of an autocar gone berserk, with no way for a human to gain control. "I think it's a terrible idea," he said. "How long do you think it will be before people other than law enforcement get a hold of the key or find some way to hack the signal? Do you want someone to be able to force your car to a stop at the side of the road at night? If that bill passes, it'll be a disaster."

"It's unlikely to pass," Naomi said. "It's getting some traction in the House, but the Senate is 60–40 against."

"People are afraid of all the wrong things," Tyler said. "They imagine a robot apocalypse run by malevolent AIs bent on murder, and they want protection against that. But they don't fear the much more likely dangers that AIs protect them from every day."

"A recent poll showed that thirty-seven percent of people think artificial intelligence will be a threat to humanity," Naomi said.

"It's not just about AIs, either. If a plane crashes, it makes big news and sends people into a furor calling for measures to make sure it never happens again, no matter the cost. But in the time it took the plane to come down, more people in the country are killed in car accidents, every day. The plane crash is rarer—

and somehow scarier—and so it gets more attention than the thing that's actually likely to kill them."

"You're right about that. People are eighty-six times more likely to die in a car crash than in a plane crash," Naomi said.

Tyler gave her a suspicious look. Her last few responses had been oddly stilted, and a bit heavy on the random statistics. "Are you using a conversation bot?" he asked. He regretted the question as soon as it left his lips. If he was right, he would have embarrassed her, and worse, if he was wrong, he would have insulted her.

She blushed. "I'm sorry." She looked as though she wanted to dissolve and soak away into the grass. "I'm not very good at conversation, and Jane—I mean the bot—helps. Otherwise I just don't say anything."

"No, I don't mind. It's really good," he said, backpedaling and cursing himself. "I know they exist, but I never heard of one being that good before. Did you write it yourself?"

She nodded, but looked away.

"Honestly, I'd like to check it out. Have you open-sourced it? Is it out on GitHub?"

She shook her head and mumbled something too soft for him to hear. They reached the library doors, and Tyler pulled one open, letting her walk in ahead of him. He considered just saying goodbye right there, hoping he hadn't screwed things up so bad with her that she wouldn't program for them, when something she'd said fell into place in his brain, and he followed her inside.

"Jane," he said. "You named your conversation bot Jane? Like in *Speaker for the Dead*?"

She whirled to face him, this time with a genuine smile on her face. "You know it?"

"Of course, I know it. It's Card's best work." It had been written well before he was born, but it was an important part of the SF canon.

"No," she said. "Nothing beats *Ender's Game.*"

They argued about that briefly, just standing there in the atrium, until Tyler realized he was blocking the entrance. "Sorry," he said. "Where were you headed?"

"Um." She twisted her hair around one finger. "I have some books I need to check out for one of my cognitive science classes. I spend a lot of time here, actually."

Tyler grinned. "She sounds like someone who spends a lot of time in libraries, which are the best sorts of people."

Naomi clapped her hands. "Catherynne M. Valente!" she said. "From *The Girl Who Circumnavigated Fairyland in a Ship of Her Own Making*! I love that quote. I had it taped inside my locker in middle school."

"Well, if you're not in a hurry"—Tyler spotted a cluster of unoccupied reading chairs—"I could show you around our code. If you're really going to help us out, that is."

"Okay."

Tyler led the way. They sat on two comfortably-stuffed chairs arranged around a half-moon coffee table, decorated with a metal vase of faux dogwood branches and some kind of generic white blooms. The library was new, designed in a sparse, modern style that preferred brushed steel and abstract art over wood paneling and portraiture. High on elegance, but short on mystery.

"Ever been to the J.P. Morgan Library in New York?" Tyler asked. "When I'm a billionaire, that's the kind of library I'm going to build. It's like the one in *Beauty and the Beast*—a huge room, three stories high, with balconies, murals, a domed ceiling. Only mine will have secret walls that open up and tele-portation circles to get around. And carnivorous shadows." He eyed her for a reaction—he'd been referring to a library in a *Doctor Who* episode, but if she didn't recognize it, then that last part would make him sound like an idiot.

He needn't have worried. "So big it doesn't need a name, just a great big 'The,'" she said, smiling and brushing a lock of hair back behind one ear.

They synced glasses, and he started walking her through the code, showing her how it was organized, the training data they were using, and their build process. She picked it up quickly, often understanding the intent behind a function before he explained it. Instead of worrying if she'd be good enough to help, Tyler found himself worrying about her opinion of his code. Did she find it amateurish? Was she laughing at him behind that shy reserve? He got the feeling that there was a lot more going on in her mind than showed on her face or came out of her mouth.

"The real problem is the edge cases," she said. "These days, it's easy enough to train an AI to do simple recognition tasks— identifying faces, voices, cyber threats, suspicious behavior. But it's only ninety-nine percent. When people's lives are on the line, it's not good enough. You need an algorithm that can use good judgment with incomplete or conflicting data."

It was the longest group of sentences he'd ever heard her string together, but Tyler just went with it. "What does good judgment even mean in this situation? We call what we use 'AI,' but it's not really intelligent. It doesn't *think*, not really. We train a sophisticated mathematical configuration to filter out bad choices and select good ones, but that's not the same as having creativity, or making leaps of intuition, or showing common sense. And there's no way to test every possible situation."

"We need an AI whose highest motivation is to keep human beings safe, with the judgment to evaluate its own decisions on that merit," Naomi said.

Tyler grinned. "Three Laws Safe."

She took it seriously. "Exactly. What's the modern equivalent of Asimov's Three Laws? How can we make autocars inherently safe?"

"The problem is, cars *aren't* safe," Tyler said. "You're flying along in a two-ton steel box with lots of other two-ton steel boxes. Asimov's robots just wouldn't drive at all. They might even prevent a human from driving, if they could. 'A robot may not harm a human being, or allow a human being to come to harm.'"

"Except in 'Little Lost Robot,'" Naomi said. "In that story, they intentionally modified the First Law, so robots could work with humans doing a somewhat dangerous job without preventing them from doing it."

"I remember that story. It was radiation, right? The humans would get a small dose of radiation, and the robots had to be able to allow that to happen."

Naomi nodded. Tyler noticed that she still focused her eyes inside her glasses, not at him. He wondered if she was still reviewing the code while she talked, or if it just made her more comfortable to pretend he was an online contact instead of a person in real life. "So that's what we need," she said. "A root-level, built-in inability to harm humans directly."

"Directly? So, in that case in Seattle, the woman's car wouldn't swerve, because hitting the motorcycle would be directly *causing* harm to humans? Whereas plowing straight into the tree would be inaction—it might kill more people, but not actively on the part of the AI?"

"It sounds kind of stupid when you put it like that."

"Well, not necessarily. This is the kind of question moral philosophers argue about into the wee hours of the night. Is there a difference between doing and allowing? Between allowing harm to happen and doing the harm myself?" Tyler realized he was grinning. This was the kind of conversation he wanted to have with Brandon, but Brandon always resisted it. He cared about practicalities, not morals.

She thought about it. "I don't think there is a difference. If I truly have the power to stop it, and I don't, that's just as bad as doing it. Neglecting a child is just as wrong as actively hurting her—in both cases, you're causing harm, even though in the first case, you're technically doing nothing."

Tyler was enjoying this. She had relaxed in the chair opposite him, and although she still wasn't meeting his eyes, she at least wasn't browsing her glasses anymore. "Do you know the trolley problem?" he asked.

She shook her head.

"Really? It's something they talked about a lot, back when the first autocars came out. It's an ethical thought experiment. Here . . ." Tyler pulled a straight dogwood branch out of the vase on the coffee table. He laid it flat on the table. "This is a train track." He gestured at her travel coffee mug. "May I?" She nodded, and he placed the mug at one end of the branch. "This is a runaway train, brakes not working, and you're the driver. Down the track a ways, five people are working and don't see you coming. You're about to plow through and kill them all. But!" He pulled another branch out of the vase and laid it across the first, creating an alternate, forking path for the train to take. "On *this* track, there's only one worker. You have a choice. You can *switch* tracks, intentionally and actively killing the one person, or you can do nothing, and let the five die."

"That's easy," Naomi said. "Of course you choose the one. It's not your fault either way—you don't intend for anyone to die. You're just minimizing the loss of life."

"Fair enough," Tyler said. "Most people say the same. Not all, but most. Try this variation, though. Instead of driving the train, you're on a bridge above the tracks, watching the drama unfold." He removed the second dogwood branch. "There's no fork in the track, just five people about to be killed. You realize the train can't stop, but you're a railway engineer, and you know that if you could drop a weight of at least three hundred pounds on the track, you could stop the train before it reaches the workers. You don't have a weight, but there happens to be a fat man on the bridge in front of you, right over the tracks. If you push him over the edge, the train will hit him instead and the workers will be saved. Should you do it?"

Naomi didn't hesitate. "Of course. Five for one, the same as before."

Tyler opened his mouth and closed it again. He had been expecting her to say no, of course not, you couldn't push someone off a bridge—that was murder, even for a good cause. Then he could point out how this indicated there must be a difference between actively causing harm and just allowing harm to happen, because of the difference between these two cases. What did her answer say about her—that she was callous? Or just more consistent than most?

"But what if you were the fat man?" he blurted. "Would you still make the same choice?"

This time she had to consider. "That's a very different question," she said finally. "But the answer is the same. I *should* throw myself off to save the others, assuming I could know for sure that the others would be saved. It's the right thing to do. But in real life, would I? What if my sister was the fat man . . . would I then? Probably not. But that's because my sister is worth more to me than any five strangers."

"It's not a philosophical question, then; it's a personal one," Tyler said. "Which is exactly the problem we have with autocars. What people want to happen in general, to strangers, is different from what they want to happen when their own loved ones are involved. We somehow need people to agree on what choices are fair and correct before personal considerations get in the way."

"It'll never happen," Naomi said, and for the first time she met his gaze directly. "Everything in life is personal."

Her eyes were a deep brown, and while her face often seemed to hide her feelings, the eyes expressed them. She had none of Abby's vivacious charm, but Tyler thought she might just be the prettier of the two.

"Hey, are you free tonight?" Tyler said. "Brandon and I are going car shopping. We need to add a few more vehicles to the fleet, now that we can afford it. We're spending somebody else's money. It'll be fun."

Her gaze dropped to the floor again. "I don't think so. I'm busy."

"Okay," he said. "Maybe we could catch dinner together sometime. You free tomorrow?"

She stood hastily and picked up her travel mug. "I should go."

Tyler studied her face, but she showed nothing. He had thought they were hitting it off together, but maybe not. "Okay," he said. "I'll send you the link to our code repository, so you can get started."

"Great," she said, so softly he could barely hear her. She jostled the coffee table on her way out, so that one of the dogwood branches slid onto the floor. She pushed through the library doors and out into the sun. Tyler watched her go, a little stunned. She had never even checked out the books she said she needed for her class.

CHAPTER 5

Naomi felt uncomfortable, so she did what she always did in those circumstances. She shut herself away with her software. She couldn't go directly to her secret library nook, because Tyler might see her. Instead, she stood behind a statue on the green, waited until she saw him leave, and then slipped back into the library and up to the second floor.

She didn't have anything against Tyler Daniels. She had actually enjoyed their conversation, at least a little, but the effort of talking with a stranger exhausted her. The idea of going out again, in a situation she couldn't escape by just walking away, was more than she could handle.

Besides, she needed to check on her Mikes again. That morning, before leaving the library, she had reviewed the history of the competitive world. She found that most frequently, the Mikes who died did so by attrition, one at a time. The Mikes who contributed least to the survival of the group were denied food when there was a lack. The world wasn't big enough for any of them to strike out on their own and hope to survive; all available resources were co-opted by the group. That made it unlikely for rival groups to grow and war against each other.

Each Mike, however, was rewarded for individual survival, not for the survival of the group. The scheme was evolutionary, but unlike in the biological world, the ability to produce offspring came at the end of life, not in the middle, so every Mike had incentive to live as long as possible. Every millisecond counted. As long as an individual Mike's survival was linked to the survival of the group, he would work toward that end. However, once a Mike was marked for death, or predicted that future for himself, his actions would change. Some stole food and fled, and were then hunted down by the rest. Others attempted to destroy the entire village to achieve some small amount of extra time for themselves. Those most individually successful, however, were those who could find ways to preserve a large number of Mikes in their world.

In the most recent versions, the strategies for claiming sunlight had become more sophisticated, using what amounted to a series of giant rectangular mirrors to reflect the sunlight away from the rocky terrain to fertile ground, making the grazing grass or crops grow at prodigious rates. In this world, the Mikes had dug, too, sending sunlight down onto underground yam fields to produce more food. They always lost some percentage of their population toward the beginning, before they could establish their infrastructure, but the later generations were increasingly able to survive harsh winters or even the occasional devastating storm. It reminded Naomi of a Dyson sphere—the hypothetical sphere a planetary civilization might build entirely surrounding its sun, exploiting the entire energy output for their own purposes. She wondered if the Mikes might eventually find a way to accomplish the equivalent feat in their own world.

However, there was still no sign of emergent creative behavior. No art, no sports, no activities that didn't directly support survival. The Mikes didn't seem to communicate in any way beyond simple reactions to each other's actions. To each of them, the other Mikes were nothing more than a part of their environment, to be manipulated however possible to achieve the desired outcome. One could argue that they weren't so much coordinating as independently discovering strategies that jointly enabled them to survive.

It was enough. Enough for publication, enough to attract the attention of graduate schools, enough to land her a good job in the industry. But it wasn't enough for her.

Naomi selected the best one thousand Mikes from the most successful versions of their worlds, and started building a new Realplanet simulation for them to inhabit. She made this new world a harsher place, scattered with hidden traps, like nests of giant wasps that would attack and injure, and pits with lava that would cause burns. Nothing that would kill by surprise, at least not directly—she wanted to see if the Mikes would communicate to warn each other about the traps. She felt a little bit evil, like a game master in *The Hunger Games*, setting traps to catch unwary innocents, but it seemed as though competition and danger were critical to the development of intelligence.

Naomi stood and stretched. She had skipped lunch, and she was hungry. It was time to find some dinner. The quickest option would be one of the on-campus cafés, which really weren't too bad. The only problem there was that she might run into someone she knew, but she would just have to risk it. She emerged from her secret lair and went out into the real world.

When Tyler returned to the apartment he shared with Brandon, he found Abby Sumner there, reclining on their sagging, second-hand couch with Brandon, laughing. The apartment was one story of an old Philadelphia townhouse, with tall ceilings, narrow rooms, and warped wooden flooring that threatened splinters to unwary bare feet. *Monty Python and the Holy Grail* played on the wall, the scene where King Arthur's company is attacked by the Legendary Black Beast of Aaaaarrrrrrggghhh. The two were sitting very close, and Tyler got the idea that the movie wasn't what they were laughing about. He considered making some excuse and leaving the two of them alone, but it was his apartment, too.

"I thought we were going car shopping," Tyler said.

"We are," Brandon said. "I invited Abby to go with us."

"I invited Naomi, but she turned me down."

Abby laughed. "Poor Naomi."

"Poor Naomi?"

"Yeah. She enjoys being with people," Abby said. "She really does. She just doesn't admit it to herself."

"I thought I had said something that offended her," Tyler said.

"I don't know if she's ever been offended in her life. But if she were, she probably wouldn't tell you. She certainly wouldn't walk out in a huff."

"Maybe she was just busy tonight," Brandon suggested.

"Yeah, busy hiding in the library and working on her software," Abby said. "Just like every night. I'll take care of this." She touched the side of her glasses. "Call Naomi." They waited while the glasses made the connection. "Hey, girl, it's Abby. Come on out with us tonight. It'll be fun." A pause. "No, you don't. No, you're coming out with us. It's final. Okay, see you soon." She looked at Tyler. "Problem solved. She's on her way."

When Naomi arrived, smiling shyly, the four of them headed to the row of car dealerships on Grays Ferry Avenue. Brandon was the force behind the outing, eyeing cars skeptically under the hood and negotiating hard. The rest of them were just along for the ride, keeping it fun and pushing Brandon to test-drive the most expensive cars in the lot.

Eventually, they decided on a pair of electric Honda Alexis. The Alexis weren't any fancier than the Accords, but as Tyler and Brandon had discussed many times, it only made sense to go electric for a self-driving fleet. An electric car could be designed to return to base and recharge itself a lot easier than a gasoline car could refuel itself. The only problem with electric cars was the infrastructure, and offering cars as a service solved that problem nicely.

After a boring round of paperwork, they signed over Aisha's money, and the cars were theirs.

"Time to celebrate!" Brandon announced.

"What you need," Abby said over their first round of drinks, "is a showgirl."

They sat in a booth, Brandon and Abby on one side and Tyler and Naomi on the other, drinking bottles of Yuengling and munching on a plate of wings.

Brandon coughed. "A what?"

"You're going to have this big demo for investors, right? You can't just have it work right. You need to put on a show. Paint your cars all the same, something flashy, with a racing stripe and a company logo."

"Hondas aren't very flashy," Tyler said.

"Hush. You need a flashy paint job, and you need a beautiful showgirl, somebody charismatic, to point at the cars and flash her winning smile and announce each bit as you perform it. You can't just sit there with your tablet and say, 'Now we're going to execute scenario number five.' You need some sex appeal. You've got to sell it."

"And where would we find such a goddess?" Brandon asked.

Abby threw her arms above her head like a circus performer. "You're looking at her, baby."

Brandon frowned. "You want to be a car show bimbo?"

Abby dropped her arms and narrowed her eyes at him. "Be nice. I'm not going to wear a bikini or do a little dance. But if you want investors to rain down millions on you, you can't just let the technology speak for itself. You've got to create a spectacle."

"She's right," Tyler said. "We need a public face. I'm not great in front of an audience, and you're uglier than an Ood." He knew Brandon wouldn't get the *Doctor Who* reference, but he glanced at Naomi, whose mouth twitched into a shy smile. "For the demo, we need to have a script, perfect timing, showmanship. But even after the demo, we'll need to be raising public awareness, advertising, and establishing trust that our cars will keep people safe."

"How many millions do you need?" Abby asked.

"What?" Brandon said.

"Money. What's your goal? How much do you need to start your company?"

"I . . . uh . . ."

"Whatever we can get," Tyler said. "We'll start as small or as big as we have the means for."

Abby shook her head, her expression scolding. Tyler remembered she was a business major, working on her MBA. "That won't do at all," she said. "You need a plan, and you need a make-or-break minimum threshold. More than one threshold, if you like, to designate different levels. But when an investor asks you how much you need to get started, you should have an answer. You can't just say, 'Gimme everything you've got.'"

"I figured they would have an amount they were willing to give."

"It's an investment with considerable risk," Abby said. "Sorry, but it is. They want to give the right amount—not so little that it doesn't help, but not so much that they're throwing money away. You need to be ready with an answer, and know why it's the right one. Also, are they going to want convertible debt or ownership equity in return for their investment? And are you willing to offer either? They're going to expect a very large return on investment, if the company is profitable—have you thought about how high you're willing to go?"

Brandon and Tyler looked at each other. "I think we might need a business major on the team," Brandon said.

Abby smirked. "You think? Do you know what kind of insurance you'll need? What taxes you expect to pay? Are you starting a 'C' corporation or an LLC?"

"Okay, you're hired," Brandon said. "Your salary starts at zero, but with great potential for advancement. Unless . . . how much do we have to pay to get the bikini and the dance?"

She punched him hard in the thigh, and he yelped. "You do it first, and I'll think about it," she said.

Later, the evening finally over, Naomi stretched out on her bed with her glasses on and checked the progress of her latest Real-planet world. She was pleased to discover that, despite the harsher environment, as many as seventy of her Mikes were surviving in each iteration. Not only that, but they were communicating through a rudimentary kind of language, mostly to warn each other about the locations of the traps she'd set for them. They didn't speak by moving vocal chords to create sound waves; the simulation wasn't sophisticated enough for that. Instead, they used the game's "action" command in sequences, like a kind of Morse code.

To call it a language, however, was generous. The "action" command provided three different behaviors and their opposites: pick up/put down, build/break, and activate/deactivate. That meant it was a three-bit system, with a total of eight possible meanings. There was no way for them to increase the number of "words" without finding some different mechanism for communication.

She watched them for hours, deciphering the meanings of the signals from how the Mikes reacted. The eight words seemed to be the equivalent of: *yes, no, straight, right, left, danger, food,* and *grass*. They never had conversations, per se—they just passed information. For instance, "straight straight right straight right right danger" indicated the presence of a trap in a certain place. Since the world was broken into square tiles, the directions served as a sufficient indicator of location. Or, they might say "straight right food, straight straight grass" to indicate that one square should be used for planting food and another for grazing their sheep herds. It was no more sophisticated than a bee wiggling its backside to communicate the location of discovered nectar to the rest of the hive.

As Naomi studied the data from these new worlds, however, she started to notice patterns that made a chill creep up her spine. In previous worlds, there had been no leaders, just independent Mikes stumbling upon effective ways to survive. They didn't collaborate as much as discover the same things at the same times. Each Mike worked for his own survival. Arguably, they didn't even differentiate between fellow Mikes and other features of the world around them.

Now, however, things were different. Hierarchies had developed, with some Mikes at the bottom, doing most of the work and taking most of the risks. At the top, a single Mike ruled as a kind of king, doing no work, but taking a larger portion of the better food. The kings in each world had some of the best survival rates, however, since they had devised ways to manipulate and control the others, keeping most at subsistence levels while they themselves had plenty. They weren't just kings. They were tyrants.

Studying the early logs from each world, she could see how it was happening. Mikes lucky enough to find a trap without it killing them learned to exploit that advantage—they would tell others where to find it or how to avoid it, for a price. The most successful of them leveraged that price into more knowledge and more control, until the whole survival pattern of their world revolved around them.

It was the beginning of a society. Not a good one, perhaps, but it felt very human. Just about all human groups had self-organized in similar ways from the very beginning. Many mammals and birds did the same, developing hierarchies, pecking orders, rituals of subservience or challenge. So far, she had seen no evidence that the tyrant Mikes were ever challenged, but perhaps that was due to the basic simplicity of the world. Her Mikes never grew old, never had a bad winter, never had children who grew up and became strong enough to test their elders. Once king, they could stay king forever, or so it seemed.

Not that any of this disproved Searle. Just because they behaved in roughly human ways didn't make the Mikes intelligent in their own right. She could have written software to do this directly. In fact, she could have written software to imitate humans *better* than this. But that would have been straightforward if-then-else logic, and thus obviously a simulation, however realistic. What made this seem different was that it was emergent behavior. The deep learning algorithms were trained, not directly written, which made them more mysterious. She didn't know why they made one choice over another, and so they felt more human to her.

But was it really different? Did her ignorance of their decision-making really mean the Mikes had human-level, self-aware intelligence? Or had she just moved to the outside of the Chinese room, assuming intelligence simply because she couldn't see what was really happening inside? Humans were very good at anthropomorphizing things they didn't understand. Or could it be that *all* intelligence worked this way—even human intelligence—and it was only our inability to follow the complexity of the firings of neurons and synapses in our brains that made it seem like something magical?

Regardless, she knew she couldn't stop. She no longer worried about publishing; she had more than enough to do that. In fact, even now, if she revealed what she had to the larger world, she would attract a lot of attention. This wasn't just a senior project; this was a whole field of study. She could see dozens of researchers in various vocations wanting to study her Mikes in different settings and make conclusions about the nature of humanity and intelligence. She had no doubt the media would run with the idea as well. She could be famous.

The thought terrified her. She didn't like people noticing her across the room, never mind the kind of attention even a modest amount of fame would bring. People would look at her. Eventually, she would have to let the secret out, at least enough to get a passing grade and publish a paper. But not yet. She wasn't ready for that. Besides, the Mikes were hers. And she had a feeling she had only begun to see what they could do.

She decided to make one more change. Instead of selecting the longest-living Mikes after a simulation had ended to populate the next iteration, she baked the iterations into the world itself. Whenever a Mike survived for twenty years of game time, it would spawn a copy of itself. Not an exact copy—although ninety-eight percent of the weights and biases that made up the layers of its neural net remained the same, the remaining two percent were randomly generated. If it survived another twenty years, it would spawn another copy. This more directly mirrored the natural process of evolution, where the most successful variants produced the most offspring, and those in command ultimately had to make way for the younger.

More importantly, however, it meant a single game world could continue indefinitely. As new Mikes were spawned, they would compete against older versions for available resources. Children would inhabit the same world as their parents, making it possible for improved variants of the genome to overthrow entrenched tyrants. Perhaps later generations would learn to work together to achieve such a coup.

Physically, all Mikes were identical. None could evolve to be stronger or faster than the others, or able to survive with less food, or to eat something new. The only thing that changed was their behavior. A Mike could theoretically live forever in such a world, but the genome randomization should inevitably yield children that were smarter than their parents. And grandchildren that were smarter still. Eventually, the older generations, unable to compete, would be left behind to die.

CHAPTER 6

T yler, Brandon, Abby, and Naomi spent almost every waking hour in each other's company. They ate meals together, watched movies together, and most of all, worked on their upcoming demo together. Naomi and Tyler concentrated on the software; Brandon dealt with outfitting the new cars with the needed solenoids, microcontrollers, and sensors; and Abby wrote the script for herself as showgirl.

Abby spent so much time at their apartment that Tyler felt like he'd added a new roommate. She and Brandon were disgustingly in love, barely able to take a breath without kissing, and sitting close enough to each other that they took up only one spot on the furniture. Abby complained that her MBA work increasingly pulled her away from Brandon and the autocar project, but as far as Tyler could tell, she was always around.

Tyler hadn't gotten that far with Naomi, but he knew he was falling for her, and he thought the feeling was mutual, though it was sometimes hard to tell. They spent a tremendous amount of time together, virtually if not in person, reworking the code for their cars. Her brilliant insights had prompted a significant rewrite of most of what he had written, but once it was done, it would be capable of so much more. He admired her, was impressed by her, loved to be with her.

He couldn't rush her, though. She was skittish enough about relationships that he was afraid to make a misstep. He feared that if he came on too strong, she'd pull back into her shell and never speak to him again.

He had initially thought she must have been hurt in the past, some kind of trauma perpetrated by someone close to her, but she said that wasn't it. People just made her nervous, and always had. She couldn't tell what people were thinking and always imagined they were judging her. The prospect of having a conversation when people could be thinking just *anything* about her paralyzed her. If she said something out loud, how would she know if it was wrong? They could be laughing at her inside. Better not to say anything at all.

Tyler had felt enough like that at times in his life that he understood, at least somewhat. It wasn't as intense for him, but he, too, felt a sense of relief and comfort when he was alone, or at least with people he knew well enough not to be afraid of what they thought. Still, he wished he knew how to make her feel safe with him. For the moment, she seemed willing to talk, even share her feelings and fears, but it felt like trying to coax a wild animal to take a piece of food from his hand. If he made any sudden moves, she might bolt, and he would lose her forever.

He had taken to playing a question game with her, so he could get her talking and find out the things about her she didn't volunteer.

"I'll start with an easy one this time," he said. "What's your favorite color?"

"I'm not six," she said. "I don't have a favorite color."

"You stole that line from *Ex Machina*," Tyler said. "That's cheating." The science fiction references had become a game, too. They rarely managed to stump each other. "What's your real answer?"

"It is my real answer," she said. "I couldn't pick a favorite color. The others might feel bad."

This was a very Naomi response, and it made him smile. "Okay, fair enough. Your turn."

She twisted her mouth to one side, thinking. When she finally spoke, he could barely hear her. "Why do you hang out with me?"

He hesitated, surprised by her sudden directness. He sensed the vulnerability behind the question, too, and answered carefully. "We love what we love. Reason doesn't enter into it."

She narrowed her eyes at him, suspicious. "That's got to be a quote."

"Yup. Patrick Rothfuss, *The Wise Man's Fear*. But it's my real answer, too. I could say I like your knowledge of books, or your mad programming skillz, or your quirky sense of humor, but it's really none of that, or maybe all of it together. I enjoy being with you. That's all. I don't need a reason beyond that."

She hitched up her shoulders bit by bit as he spoke, doing her turtle-hiding-in-its-shell thing. She didn't say anything more, so he pressed on. "My turn," he said. He rubbed his chin and then gave her a devious look. "What's your most awkward or embarrassing memory?"

She blushed, pulled her head even farther between her shoulders, and looked at the floor. "This conversation," she said.

The topic of Naomi came up one evening in their apartment. Abby and Brandon sat practically on top of each other on one side of the sofa, passing a lollipop back and forth between them.

"She never opens up to anybody like she's doing with you," Abby said. "All through high school, she was my shadow. She got to know my friends better than anyone in her own class, because she never willingly entered social situations without me. If I went to a party, then she would come along, but if I wasn't going, she would stay home. It's not that she was completely unsocial—she could get crazy and have fun with the rest of us. But she never initiated conversations, and she never went anywhere without me, if she could help it."

"Is that why she came to Penn?"

"Because I was here? Yeah, I think so. I mean, Penn has a great program for the stuff she was interested in, so it was a good fit for her. But the fact that I was here helped, I'm sure. I'm only a year older, so she only had one year in high school without me, and I don't think she got out a lot that year. Not that she minded, probably—she's always happiest at home, in her room, writing software for hours on end." Abby licked the lollipop and handed it back to Brandon. "So when are you going to ask her out?"

"I don't know," Tyler said. "I'm kind of afraid to scare her off."

"She likes you," Abby said. "Heck, for Naomi, this is like renting a billboard with blinking, neon letters. She talks to you. She hangs out with you instead of reading a book. She actually looks forward to seeing you. Do you know how unusual that is?"

"So, what, I should take her out to dinner?"

Brandon handed the lollipop back to Abby and spoke up. "Naomi doesn't seem like a dinner and flowers type," he said. "You should take her to NerdFest or something."

Tyler raised an eyebrow. "NerdFest? Is that a thing?"

"You know what I mean. Something creative that she'd enjoy. A *Doctor Who* convention or a science fiction film festival or something."

Tyler considered. "I think the Quidditch World Cup is in Philadelphia this year. Across the river, anyway, in Cherry Hill."

"What's the Quidditch World Cup?" Abby asked.

Brandon rolled his eyes. "NerdFest," he said.

"Okay, Mr. I-go-to-the-Maker-Faire-every-year," Tyler said. To Abby, he added, "Quidditch, like in *Harry Potter*."

"I know what *quidditch* is," Abby said. "Even if I hadn't read the books—which I did—I couldn't have grown up with Naomi without knowing about quidditch. But it's a fantasy game. It's played on flying brooms, with enchanted balls that fly around by themselves. And, if I remember correctly, the game's rules didn't even make much sense. You're telling me people actually play it, as a sport?"

"For almost twenty years now," Tyler said. "With a national championship that moves around to different cities. I've played it casually, at cons and stuff. It's pretty fun. Somebody came up with clever ways to make the rules work for non-magical people running around a field. Like, if you get hit by a ball thrown by a beater, you've got to drop any balls you're holding, run back to your side, and tag a goalpost before you can play again. And the snitch is a person, dressed in yellow, who runs around the field trying not to get caught."

"And the flying brooms?" Brandon asked.

"Yeah, well, you've got to run around with a broom between your legs." Tyler grinned sheepishly. "Just one of the rules of the game."

"That sounds fantastic," Abby said. "Naomi would love it."

"I'll get some tickets," Tyler said. "Do you two want to come?"

"It's supposed to be a date," Brandon said. "Just the two of you go. Buy her some butterbeer and go snog behind the bleachers."

Tyler snatched an empty plastic cup from a side table and

hurled it at him, but it hit Abby in the leg and bounced off. "Sorry," Tyler said. "I was aiming for the sneering Muggle over there."

"Right, I'll do you for that," she said, putting on a high-pitched British accent.

Tyler grinned, picking up on the *Monty Python* reference. "What are you going to do, bleed on me?"

Abby extricated herself from Brandon and stood up, stretching. She looked Tyler in the eye. "Seriously, though. If you ever hurt Naomi, I'll kill you."

Tyler chuckled. "I'll keep that in mind."

"I'm not kidding. This is a first for her. When other guys have tried to get close to her, she's stopped talking to them until they went away. You've gotten past her defenses somehow, and she's vulnerable. If you treat her badly, she might never let anyone in again."

"I won't—"

"I'm not saying you will. I'm just saying, if you're going to pursue this, you'd better mean it. It's not a game for her. I don't mean you have to marry her. But if your plan is just to get in her pants and then move on, I swear, I will track you down wherever you go, and I will kill you. Slowly. You get it?"

She spoke with such quiet ferocity that it took Tyler's breath away. "I got it," he said. "I'm not just toying with her, honest."

"You'd better not be."

Brandon broke the tension with a loud, hearty laugh. "Wow," he said. "That's my girl. The vigilante of broken hearts."

Abby threw a backwards kick at him, catching him in the chest. "And you'd better remember it. I'm not above killing you if you treat me badly, either. Or maybe I'll just cut off those little bits you're so proud of."

Brandon gave a gasp of offended pride. "What do you mean *little?*"

"This is where I exit stage left," Tyler said, laughing. "Leave him a few of his parts, will you?"

As Tyler grabbed his keys and turned to go, Abby called after him, using the British accent again. "Oh, I see. Running away, eh? Come back here and take what's coming to you!"

Tyler went searching for Naomi. It had become a private game of sorts, trying to find her. He could message her, of course, and ask, but when he did, she invariably told him she was in the library. Which made sense, given that it was Naomi. If they then decided to meet up, she would suggest a spot inside the library—the lobby, say, or one of the study rooms—and when he arrived, she would already be there. Which suggested that she actually *was* in the library. The odd thing, though, was that if he went to the library, just assuming she would be there, and tried to find her, he never could. It was a big building, combining what had previously been several different libraries on campus, so it had a lot of rooms and a lot of shelves. But it wasn't *that* big.

Once again, he couldn't find her, so he messaged her with his glasses, and asked if she was busy.

<Just debugging your broken software> she wrote back.

<Want to work on it together?>

<Okay. Study room F, see you in five.>

He was already in the library, not far from the room, but sure enough, when he got there, she was there waiting for him.

"That was quick," she said.

"I was already here, looking for you. Couldn't find you, though."

She grinned. "I was in fairyland. It intersects the real world in any place I like." She tapped her glasses. "And speaking of fairyland, I've got something to show you. I, well . . . you'll see. I didn't exactly sleep last night."

He synced his glasses with hers, and she began walking him

through the changes she'd made to the autocar software. It took a long time to show him everything, both the way the software had changed and the results of her simulations, but he wasn't bored. He was amazed.

She had done something new. Not just new, revolutionary. At the core of his autocar software was an artificial intelligence, not in the HAL 9000 sense of a self-aware, thinking machine, but in the computer science, machine-learning algorithm sense. An algorithm that was trained to learn experimentally, like a child might, instead of being directly programmed. Naomi had swapped the AI out entirely.

He might have been annoyed, except that her replacement was so obviously better than his that he was too impressed to feel insulted. His algorithm had required painstaking retraining and configuration every time he threw a new type of problem at it. It learned and improved, but Tyler had to hold its hand every step of the way. Over time, it had become adept at most common traffic encounters, but Tyler had always been afraid of how it would respond to rare situations, when it encountered something out of the ordinary or bizarre in real life.

Naomi's AI, on the other hand, flew through their simulations without a hitch. That wasn't surprising in and of itself, since she must have spent days training it on that data. What was really amazing was how well it generalized. He threw all kinds of unfair tricks at it—traffic lights that changed color far too rapidly, cars that drove suddenly in reverse, tanker trucks that intentionally tried to run cars off the road. It performed beautifully, not just with one car but with whole simulated fleets of them, sliding them out of danger like a fast-paced game of mahjong.

"This thing is incredible," Tyler said, meaning it. "How did you come up with it so fast?"

Naomi gave one of her classic sheepish half-shrugs, an

endearing little-girl gesture he had come to recognize. She didn't twirl a lock of her hair or twist one toe on the floor, but the gestures would have fit. "The AI part I've been working on for a long time," she said. "Before I met you."

"Wow. And it generalized to this problem? This is A+ work." He looked at her appraisingly, a little awed. "You could work anywhere with talent like this," he said. "Or you could just write your own software and make a mint. If you stay with us, with our company, I'll make sure it's worth your while. Once we can pay you, that is."

He could tell he was embarrassing her, so he stopped gushing. "What did you originally build it to do?"

"Play games," she said. "Like those Atari games they taught DeepMind to play back in the day."

"Nice. What games?"

She shook her head. "I think it's enough to publish. Until I do, though, I'm keeping it a secret."

"It must work well, then. Not even a hint?"

"I haven't told my advisor yet. I haven't even told Abby."

"Okay, Miss Mysterious. Does this marvelous general AI of yours have a name? Deep Thought, maybe, or WOPR?"

Her brow furrowed. "Deep Thought is from *Hitchhikers Guide to the Galaxy*, but what's Whopper?"

He spelled it out. "W-O-P-R. WOPR. It's from *Wargames*. You know—" He put on a monotone robotic voice. "Shall . . . we . . . play . . . a . . . game?"

"I think I saw it, a long time ago," she said. "This kid, like, hacks an NSA computer or something, and asks it to play Global Thermonuclear War, right? Only the computer can't tell the difference between a game and real life, and nearly wipes out the planet?"

"That's the one. Hopefully yours isn't planning to start any wars."

"Not on the agenda," she said. "It's trained to save human lives, not take them. Three Laws Safe, remember?"

"That's a relief," Tyler said. "So what do you call it? It has to have a name."

She nodded. "I call it Mike."

Eventually, Tyler had to leave for a class. As a graduate student, he didn't have many classes, and at this point, his grade had much more to do with Professor Lieu's opinion of their autocar project than with what he learned or didn't learn in class, but he still felt obliged to attend. He complimented Naomi on her software again and left the study room.

Tyler felt like the pieces of his life were falling neatly into place. They hadn't even graduated yet, but they were already getting the attention of investors. He had no doubt their company would take off. He could see himself and Brandon joining the storied ranks of tech entrepreneurs. Gates. Jobs. Page and Brin. Bezos. Zuckerberg. And what were the chances he and Brandon would fall for two sisters, one a crack programmer and the other a business expert? It had a storybook neatness to it. It was almost too good to be true.

Tyler stepped into an alcove for a drink of water. As he was wiping water from mouth, he saw Naomi leave the study room and walk past toward the stairs, though he was pretty sure she hadn't seen him. This was his chance to solve the mystery. He was curious where Naomi hung out at the library, and why he could never find her. He imagined a secret door somewhere, like the four-plate door in the archives of the library in Patrick Rothfuss's *The Name of the Wind*. He followed her, staying back and stepping quietly.

When she reached the landing of the stairs going down to the first floor, he thought she might just be heading back to her apartment, but then she stopped and looked quickly around.

Tyler hadn't quite made the turn, so she didn't see him. As he watched, she squeezed behind an angled bookshelf that didn't quite reach the wall, and disappeared from view.

He ran quickly after her and stuck his head around the corner. "Aha!" he said. "So this is fairyland."

He realized his mistake almost immediately. The expression on her face was not one of surprise or mild embarrassment, as he might have expected, but one of panicked horror. He took in the beanbag chair, the pillows, and the stack of *Harry Potter* books, and he knew her well enough to understand. This was her refuge.

"No," she said. "No, no, no." The look on her face had melted into such an expression of sadness and loss that it made his heart break. He realized that nobody knew about this place, nobody at all. She had hid from the world here, probably for years, and felt utterly invisible. It was her hiding place. He had never been able to find her in the library, because she was always here. It was private, and safe, and now it was ruined.

He remembered, belatedly, the line from *The Name of the Wind* concerning the four-plate door: *This was not a door for opening. It was a door for staying closed.*

He pulled his head back. "I'm sorry," he said. "Naomi, I didn't know. I'm sorry."

If she were someone else, she might have screamed at him, or thrown something at him, but she was Naomi. He could still see her face in his mind, see the feelings of violation, of betrayal. He should have asked her instead of sneaking around like this. He hadn't imagined it was really a secret; this was a public place. He just thought of it as a mystery. And now he had blundered in where he didn't belong.

"I'll go," he said.

He had almost reached the stairwell when she said, "Wait."

He turned back. Her voice came from behind the bookcase, out of sight. "You can come in."

He came hesitantly, reverently, as if entering a throne room or a church. The space was triangular, formed by the angle of the bookcase away from the curve of the stairwell, and barely big enough for both of them. He noticed a few other details: sealed Tupperware containers on the back of the shelf, filled with crackers and raisins and other snacks; a picture of Naomi and Abby with their arms around each other, taped to the wall; a tiny porcelain statue of Hedwig the owl.

"A book is a door, you know," Tyler said. "Always and forever. A book is a door into another place and another heart and another world."

A smile slowly dawned on her face, lovely and intense. "Valente again," she said.

It was the right time. He kissed her.

She returned the kiss hungrily, pressing him back against the bookcase until he was afraid they would push it over. He wrapped his arms around her waist and pulled her even closer.

When they finally came up for air, she said, "You're late for class."

He didn't care about his class, but neither did he want to wreck this tenuous moment by overstaying his welcome.

"We'll continue this later," he said, grinning. Then, more seriously, "But this is your place. I'll never come in here again. And I'll never tell anyone about it. You're safe here."

She rewarded him with a brilliant smile and another kiss. Then, careful that no one saw him squeezing around the edge of the bookshelf, he left.

CHAPTER 7

"How was the Quidditch World Series?" Brandon asked.

"World Cup," Naomi corrected. "And it was great. The Harvard Horntails beat the Tufts University Tufflepuffs 130 to 100."

"Tufflepuffs?" Abby said. "Really?"

"I was more shocked by the 'Harvard' part of that sentence," Brandon said.

Tyler rolled his eyes. "If you're trying to set yourself up as the cool kid here, no one's buying it."

They had gathered at the athletic fields parking lot after dark, testing their fleet of cars yet again, now a nightly habit as the day of the demo grew near. Tyler had to admit that four cars cut a much more impressive picture than two. The two Accords roared up to speed, their combustion engines straining to accelerate, while the two Alexis could silently leap from zero to sixty in under four seconds. Together, though, they were a coordinated fleet. They could zip along side by side as if bolted together, or in a line like a snake only inches apart. At the appearance of an obstacle, they swerved perfectly, braking or speeding up to avoid both it and each other. The obstacles were still imaginary, but with glasses, you could see them: a virtual person or a vehicle suddenly appearing on the road.

Today, they were testing the emergency kill switch. At Tyler's insistence, they had bought a separate switch with a separate receiver for each car. Tyler had wired these up to pull the plug on the computer, disengage the accelerator, and slam the brake down hard. It was an emergency measure they could use to stop a car dead, no matter how badly haywire the programming went. It circumvented the computer entirely. Brandon thought it was an unnecessary waste of time and funds, but Tyler preferred to play it safe.

They tested it over and over again. Brandon would take the cars through their paces, and Tyler would, at random intervals, hit the kill switch for one or all of the cars. It worked beautifully. The moment he pressed the button, the chosen car would screech to a hard stop, disconnecting the computer from its power source so it couldn't try to do anything else. Finally, Brandon got fed up with the interruptions and told Tyler that it worked already, so knock it off. Tyler grinned and gave him a thumbs-up.

It wasn't that he thought their software was flawed. On the contrary, it performed perfectly in millions of test cases in the Realplanet driving simulation Naomi had built. But when two-ton buckets of steel were hurtling around in real life, it made him feel better to know that he could stop them if he needed to.

"They're perfect!" Abby shouted over the engine noise of the Accords. "You couldn't crash these babies if you tried!"

Brandon looked at her, and something in his eyes told Tyler he was about to do something stupid. "Now that's an idea," he said.

"What is?" Tyler asked. "Brandon . . ."

Brandon pressed a few buttons on his tablet. One of the Accords peeled away from the pack and came toward him, then pulled up next to him and stopped. Brandon opened the driver's side door and reached for the equipment controlling the car.

"What are you doing?" Tyler asked.

"A little test," Brandon said. He disconnected the solenoids from the accelerator and brake pedals, and then shifted the whole mechanism over to the passenger seat. He sat down behind the wheel and shut the door.

Tyler stepped forward and rapped on the window with a knuckle. Brandon pressed the button to open the window. "Come on, man," Tyler said. "What are you up to?"

"An important role of these cars will be their ability to share the road with human drivers," Brandon said. "Abby said we couldn't crash them if we tried. Well"—he grinned—"I'm going to try."

"Not a good idea!" Tyler said, but it was too late. Brandon peeled away and swerved toward the rest of the fleet.

Tyler looked helplessly across at Naomi. She gave a miniscule shrug. "Give it a chance," she said. "I don't think he can touch them."

She was right. Brandon drove straight for the formation, but they danced aside, letting him pass unscathed, only to close ranks again after he had passed. He came at them broadside, but they swerved and veered, missing him again. Abby and Naomi shouted and cheered, but Tyler just watched, his finger hovering over the kill switch on his tablet, every muscle in his shoulders clenched.

Brandon whooped through the open window and circled for

another pass. When the cars avoided a collision yet again, he drove back to join the three of them, a grin splitting his face wide. "Wow, what a rush," he said.

"My turn next!" Abby shouted.

Tyler made a noise of surprise and frustration. "No," he said. "Come on, we haven't tested for this . . ."

"Duly noted," Brandon said. He held open the door and swept Abby a bow, like a coach driver making way for an aristocrat.

"Naomi, what do you think? Will I be able to hit one?" Abby asked.

Naomi spoke softly, but a small smile played around the corners of her mouth. "Bring it on," she said.

Tyler groaned, betrayed, and gripped his tablet tightly. He couldn't stop Abby's car, but he could use the kill switch to stop the others. He was tempted to do it and put an end to this, but he didn't want to be a killjoy. Especially since Naomi had sided with them. And she knew the algorithm better than anyone. She wouldn't risk injury to her sister unless she was pretty sure.

Besides, he had to admit, as he watched the cars dance out of the way, it made a pretty impressive show. And Brandon was right; avoiding reckless human drivers was part of what their fleet had to be able to do. Let them do it once and get it out of their system.

After several passes, Abby circled back around and parked in front of them. She jumped out of the car, face flushed and eyes sparkling.

"That was incredible," she said. "We *so* need to do that in the demo."

The demo. The day swooped on them like a bird of prey, faster than they expected and with no mercy. The weatherman's augury of blue skies and perfect temperatures proved accurate, and Tyler woke early, bouncing with nerves. Today would make their fortune.

They had rented the Bridgeport Speedway's quarter-mile track for the event. It hadn't been cheap—Brandon had resorted to begging his father for more money to cover what was left after Aisha's funds had been exhausted—but it was the right place, a venue already set up to stage an exciting show with racing automobiles. They arrived to find a crowd already gathering, mostly students bused in from Penn, but families with children as well, and a TV crew setting up cameras by the track. Tyler felt like his stomach was trying to claw its way up out of his throat.

Their project had been getting a lot of "local kids ready to take the world by storm" kind of publicity, which of course they encouraged. Abby had slipped into the role of spokeswoman, a role she thrived in. Every media phone call she fielded left her giddy, and she skipped around the apartment or the quad, talking about how they were all going to be famous.

Abby had chosen the colors for their cars, an intense neon green with a wide black stripe down the middle. When Brandon complained, she insisted the color had to be a trademark. "It's got to be like nothing else out there. Whenever anyone sees one of our cars, no matter the make or model, they have to know instantly that it's a Yotta car."

Yotta. The name had been Abby's idea, too, and although both Brandon and Tyler initially hated it, it had stuck. Abby argued that it was short and memorable, and in keeping with the running tradition of giving silly names to technology companies. "Yahoo" and "Etsy" and "Hulu" and "Uber" had sounded ridiculous too, until they became household names. So Yotta it was. They had applied to the U.S. Patent and Trademark Office to trademark the name and a logo—a simple, chubby automobile, green and black, with a trail of zeros floating up out of its exhaust pipe. Brandon had designed it. The zeros were meant to evoke the "yotta" decimal prefix, which stood for a one with twenty-four zeros after it, as well as to give the idea of zero emissions. The two Accords still burned fossil fuels, of course, but once the company got off the ground for real, they would switch over to all electric.

Brandon, Tyler, Abby, and Naomi had each driven one of the Yotta cars from the Penn lot to the demo location the night before. Bridgeport Speedway, across the river in New Jersey, was still an operational dirt racetrack, with regular weekend races and a full schedule of special events and promotions, but there wasn't much happening there on a Tuesday night. The dirt track had been a much smoother ride than Tyler had anticipated. They had put the cars through their paces, and then left them in position, four abreast, ready to drive the next day. Tyler had double-checked the kill switch mechanism on each car, making sure it was tightly attached and ready to go.

Today, the four of them arrived in Brandon's Prius, jittery with nerves and astonished by the gathering crowd. Tyler wondered how many of the onlookers were just race enthusiasts from the area, frequent customers of the speedway who were curious enough about them to attend a free event. With half an hour to go until showtime, Abby dragged them all over to the TV crew and gave an impromptu interview, in which she mercifully did most of the talking. All Tyler had to do was smile.

After that, Aisha found them and introduced her investor friends, three women and a man, all white, all middle-aged, all wearing watches and jewelry and casual clothes that probably cost more than Tyler's entire wardrobe. They shook hands all around. Once again, Abby was the charming one, welcoming them and complimenting their good taste in investment opportunities. "I hope you brought your checkbooks," she told them.

If Tyler had said something like that, it would have sounded crass, but Abby pulled it off with grace.

Finally, seven o'clock rolled around, and it was time to start. Tyler hadn't eaten a bite for dinner—his nerves had been too tightly strung—but now he was suddenly starving. He would have killed for a granola bar and a Coke, but it was too late for that now. The four of them walked out onto the track.

Abby stepped forward and faced the gathered crowd. Although she had passed on the bikini, she was dressed for a show, in a short black skirt and a sleeveless green top that matched the vivid hue of the cars.

"Welcome to the premier demonstration of the innovative automation of Yotta Autocars," Abby declared. She wore a collar mic synced with the raceway's sound system, and her voice boomed back at them from all directions. She raised her hands high like she had just done a magic trick, and indicated each of the team members with a flourish. "This is Brandon Kincannon from Long Island, New York; Tyler Daniels from Upper Darby, Pennsylvania; Naomi Sumner from Scranton, Pennsylvania; and I'm Abby Sumner.

"We're here to show you the future. You've seen the first generation of autocars from Mercedes and Tesla, Audi and GM—impressive vehicles that can avoid the hazards on the road . . . some of the time. They've paved the way, and we applaud their efforts. But we're looking farther ahead. At Yotta, we don't think getting your family from A to B should cost you tens of thousands of dollars. We don't think you should be risking your children's lives every time you bring them to piano lessons or soccer practice. We see a future where there are no drunk drivers or distracted drivers or reckless drivers, because there are no drivers. We see a future where transportation is afford-able, available on demand, and safe."

Abby had told them many times how important this part

was, showing their potential investors not just that they could build the product but also that they could sell it. As her words echoed away across the field, the audience gave no response, not even polite applause. A light breeze ruffled Abby's hair. Tyler wondered how receptive an audience of car racing enthusiasts was going to be to a message that encouraged people not to drive. Maybe they should have paid a few people to come and cheer.

Brandon, Tyler, and Naomi took their seats. Some of the onlookers sat in the grandstands, but many just stood at the track and leaned over the rails. Tyler and Naomi pulled out their tablets and got to work. Somewhere along the way, Brandon had ceded his role at the controls to Naomi. She had written much of the software and had a better idea of how the controls worked now than he did. He had settled into his job as hardware engineer and seemed quite happy to give up the software part of things to her.

Abby stood on a small platform on the inside of the track, where she could be seen and could point to things as they happened. "I give you Yotta Autocars," she said. "A driving experience unlike anything you've seen before."

The fleet growled to life, and the four cars took off down the track in perfect tandem, raising a cloud of dirt behind them. This prompted a cheer from the crowd and probably resembled the start of a race in some respects. These cars would not be racing, however. As they took the turn on the far side of the track, accelerating to fifty miles per hour, Brandon jogged out onto the field with three flat objects, which he set up on the dirt at various points on the track. As he put them down, it was easy to identify them as cardboard cutouts of people from various films, the kind movie theaters put on display in their lobbies.

"Look out!" Abby said over the microphone. "We seem to have some celebrities crossing the road."

The track could just barely fit all four of their cars driving side by side. As they roared around the bend, their front bumpers formed a wall from one side of the track to the other, bearing down with barely an inch between them. When they came into view of the "people" standing on the track, however, the cars reacted smoothly, dancing into a new formation and slaloming around the obstacles. Brandon had weighted the cardboard movie stars down with cinder blocks, so that when the cars flew past, they fluttered violently in the wind, but didn't fall down.

The audience cheered more enthusiastically this time, enjoying the spectacle. Tyler found himself relaxing. He had little doubt that the cars would perform as intended. Not only had they tested them over and over with these scenarios in the real world, but Naomi had generated a driving world in Real-planet, training the software on literally millions of randomly generated traffic situations and accepting as seeds for the next iteration only those versions that performed the best.

Tyler and Naomi didn't even have that much to do. They simply cued the start of each scenario as Abby announced them. The cars darted, swerved, braked, and spun, perfectly evading all dangers. Even the weather was perfect, a cloudless blue sky with just the hint of a breeze. Tyler wanted to reach out and take Naomi's hand, but he didn't want to jinx it. Time enough for that later.

On the next pass, one of the cars pulled away from the group and turned around. The three continued, one behind the other, driving on the right side of the track as if it were a public road. The single car drove in the opposite direction. On the long stretch of the oval, the cars prepared to pass each other.

"Let's say the car driving on its own has a human driver," Abby said. "The driver was up late last night and is having trouble keeping himself awake." The solo car started to drift onto the other side of the track, into the path of the oncoming traffic. "Only the Yotta car in front can see the danger unfolding," Abby said, "but it communicates to the cars in back, letting them know of the problem." It had actually been difficult to program this part, because the Mike driving the solo car refused to drift. He recognized it as a dangerous maneuver and always corrected, overriding their commands. In the end, they had to disconnect Mike entirely from the car and control it directly.

The solo car turned broadside, blocking the left side of the road. The three remaining cars reacted immediately, braking and swerving in different directions, each finding a safe route while leaving room for the other two. The three screeched to a halt within a few feet of each other and of the solo car, throwing up a cloud of dirt, but leaving all four cars unscratched. The crowd cheered.

Abby climbed down from the platform and stepped onto the track. "Finally," she said, "we wanted to show you what it feels like to experience these cars from the inside. It's one thing to see a little car choreography. It's another thing to trust them with your lives."

Her delivery was perfect. Tyler found that his heart was thudding in his chest, even though he knew what she was going to do, and had seen her do it dozens of times. It was the showmanship. She was like the magician's beautiful assistant, willing to be locked in a box that would be sawed in half or run through with spikes or swords. You knew she wouldn't be harmed, but it sent your heart up into your throat all the same.

The cars tore around the far side of the track. "I'm going to climb into one of these cars and take the wheel," she said. "Then I'm going to drive around this track like a maniac, in the wrong direction, *trying* to collide with one of these cars. As you will see, they won't let me. No matter how reckless I am, they can see me coming, anticipate my every possible maneuver, and be ready for them all." She touched her glasses. "Not only that, if you tune your glasses to the raceway's public channel, you'll be able to see it all from my eyes."

Tyler switched to the screen on his tablet from which he could access the kill switch for each car, just in case. He had never needed it before, and they had practiced this so many times, it had begun to seem boring. Even so. Better to be safe.

Abby lifted her slim arms high, and Tyler thought of the scene in the film *The Prestige*, where a young woman was dropped into a tank of water with her hands tied together as part of a magic show. With his finger on the kill switch, Tyler was like Michael Caine's character, waiting behind the curtain with an ax in hand, ready to break the glass if things went wrong. He remembered Caine's line from the film, about audience-goers for dangerous acts: "People hoping for an accident, and likely to see one, too."

The cars rounded the final corner and headed toward them. They would slow and then stop, one of them rolling forward next to Abby to let her climb in and take control. Any moment, they would slow. He checked their speed on his screen. Fifty-five miles an hour. Fifty-six. Fifty-seven.

It wasn't right. He hesitated, not wanting to blow the demo, but the cars shouldn't be speeding up.

"Something's wrong," he said. "They shouldn't be going this fast."

Naomi glanced at the screen, and then at her sister, eyes wide. "Stop them!"

Tyler jabbed the button to activate the kill switch on all four cars. Nothing happened. He jabbed each of them in turn. Nothing.

Tyler leaped to his feet. "Abby, get out of there!"

They didn't stop. Abby realized something was wrong and tried to run, but it was too late. Four abreast, the cars slammed through her fragile body with barely a pause, an ocean wave sweeping away a pebble. A moment later, they ground to a halt. For a tiny part of a second, nothing made any noise at all.

When Naomi screamed, it was the most terrible sound Tyler had ever heard.

CHAPTER 8

T ime moved in slow motion. Naomi knew she was
screaming, but she couldn't hear it, as if the air around
her had turned to water. She stood frozen, unable to move.
Abby lay facedown on the dirt track, motionless. Tyler said
something, but his words were drowned out by the pounding
of her heart in her ears. She saw Brandon touching his glasses,
calling 911.

Naomi had expected blood, but she couldn't see any. Abby's
legs looked crushed, but she could survive that, couldn't she?
She had to get to her, help her. She ran forward, but Tyler threw
his arms around her, stopping her at the edge of the track.

He shouted at her, and this time she heard him. "The cars!"

She looked. The four green-and-black cars had made a neat,
coordinated U-turn, and were now idling, facing them, their
engines purring. Naomi felt a stab of fear, like stepping into
a lion's cage at the zoo and realizing that, despite their lazy

demeanor, they were lethal, three-hundred-pound predators. Then she saw Abby's hand move, and it didn't matter anymore.

"We have to get her out of there," Naomi said.

". . . not moving," Brandon said. "She's facedown on the ground. Should we . . ." Brandon turned toward them, shook his head. "Ambulance on its way. They said don't move her, don't try to turn her over."

Naomi didn't care what they said. She pushed Tyler's hands away. Her sister was alive, and if she couldn't move her, she was at least going to go to her. She ducked under the rail, onto the track, and after a quick glance at the cars to make sure they weren't charging her, she knelt in the dirt. Then she saw the blood. It was underneath Abby, soaking into the dirt.

The sight of it nauseated her, threatened to overwhelm her, but she choked the feeling down. She could hardly look at Abby's legs, could hardly think of her bones and flesh, crushed. "Abby!" she said. "Oh, Abby."

Brandon rushed to Abby's other side and took her hand. She saw the panic in his eyes.

"She's still breathing," Naomi said.

Tyler ran out onto the track as well, but he didn't stop at Abby's side. He ran past them, toward the cars. He slowed when he reached them and approached one from the side, hesitantly, arms out as if trying to calm a growling dog. It didn't move. He yanked open the door. As quickly as he could, he reached across and killed the engine, then tore the actuator assembly out of the driver's seat and threw it on the ground. When Brandon saw what he was doing, he ran out and joined him. In moments, they silenced all four cars. The cars never moved.

Naomi found out later that the ambulance arrived only eight minutes after Brandon's call, but it seemed like an hour. Naomi held Abby's hand and talked to her, though she didn't know if Abby could hear her. Mostly, she watched her sister's chest expand and contract almost imperceptibly and prayed that it wouldn't stop.

The ambulance drove out onto the track and stopped a few feet away. By that time, many of the crowd had gathered around them on the track, and a man who claimed to be a doctor was shouting at them to stay back. EMTs poured out of the ambulance, five of them, wearing blue uniforms with patches on the shoulder. They splinted Abby's legs and wrapped a collar around her neck. When they rolled her onto the stretcher, Abby groaned, and Naomi felt tears spark at the corners of her eyes. If she could groan, then she was still alive. Her eyes were closed, and she didn't respond to questions, but she was still there.

Abby's bright green blouse was dark with blood, but it was the skirt they cut away, revealing deep wounds on her upper thighs that welled up fresh blood as soon as they wiped it. One of the EMTs applied pressure while the other wrapped a tourniquet above the wound. Naomi's vision narrowed, blackness creeping in from the sides.

"Are you okay?" Tyler asked her.

"I'm fine," she said. "Abby . . ." The world slid to the side. She found herself on the ground, being lowered gently by Tyler, who had apparently caught her. She tried to sit up.

"Whoa, take it slow," Tyler said.

She sat up anyway. The world wobbled a little bit, but she willed herself to focus, angry that she would be so weak when her sister needed her most.

The EMTs strapped Abby to the stretcher, but they didn't lift her into the back of the ambulance. They just kneeled there, applying pressure and checking vitals. One of them, an older man with a mustache, peppered Naomi with questions. Was Abby allergic to any medications, had she had any previous surgeries, was there any possibility she could be pregnant? Naomi answered as best she could.

Brandon paced back and forth on the other side of Abby's prone form. Finally, he couldn't take it. "Why aren't you taking her to the hospital?" he demanded.

The EMT with the mustache pointed up. "Lifeflight," he said. "These are serious injuries, sir. The local medical center isn't equipped, and it would take us too long to drive."

Naomi heard the helicopter before she saw it. The noise grew into a roar as it circled and then landed in the grass at the center of the track: a small blue chopper with JeffSTAT emblazoned on its side, whipping up a stiff wind with its rotors. The EMTs lifted Abby's stretcher with a practiced motion and walked across the field to meet it.

Naomi scrambled to her feet with an effort and caught up with them. "I want to come!" she shouted.

The EMT shook his head. "No room," he said. "They're taking her to Jefferson. You'll have to drive and meet her there."

The helicopter came with its own team of medics, and it took off almost as soon as they had Abby inside, leaving the rest of them on the ground. "She's in the very best hands," the man with the mustache said. "They'll do everything they can for her."

Naomi felt a hand on her shoulder. She turned to see Aisha al-Mohammad, her expression sad and compassionate. "I'm so sorry," Aisha said. "Is there anything I can do?"

Naomi barely heard her. The other investors were nowhere to be seen, and Naomi doubted she'd ever see Aisha again either. "I have to go," she said. She turned and ran back to where Tyler and Brandon still stood, not registering the implication of the two uniformed cops with guns in their belts who stood talking to them.

"They're taking her to Jefferson," Naomi said breathlessly. "Brandon, we need your car. We need to go there right now."

One of the two cops, a woman with a Logan Township

Police Officer badge on her blue uniform, came forward and put a hand on her arm. "You're Naomi Sumner?" she asked.

"Yes. But I have to go. My sister . . ."

"That's why we're here," the woman said. "We need to ask you a few questions."

Naomi answered their questions with gritted teeth, anxious to be on the road. Practically, she knew she couldn't do anything for Abby. She would be in surgery, probably, and at the hospital there would be nothing to do but wait. But Abby was hurt, maybe dying. She wanted to be *there*. Not here answering endless questions from local cops who wouldn't have the first clue how to investigate this accident.

She'd been so worried about Abby that she hadn't given any thought to why it had happened. Now, prompted by the police-woman's questions, she had to. They'd practiced that scenario again and again. In simulation, they'd run it thousands of times. There had never been any hint of a catastrophe like this. The cars knew when to stop, and they always stopped.

And what about the kill switch? She had seen Tyler hit the switch, but it had done nothing. That switch didn't have anything to do with the AI. It was purely mechanical, a radio signal that would disconnect the computers from the cars alto-gether. How could both the algorithm and the mechanical kill switch have failed at the same time? It didn't make any sense.

She heard Tyler talking to the male cop a few feet away. "I checked them last night," he said. "They were tightly attached, all four of them. But after the accident, when I opened the doors, they were just lying on the floor. That didn't just happen. Somebody *disconnected* them."

"And you threw the mechanism out onto the track?"

"I was trying to make sure they were safe," Tyler said.

It was clear from their questions and demeanor that they

thought they were dealing with a reckless car stunt, and that it wasn't the first time they'd been called to the scene of an accident at the Bridgeport Speedway.

Finally, Naomi said, "Please, my sister's hurt, and I want to see her. Can we leave?"

"They can't keep us," Brandon said. "Not unless they want to arrest us. Let's go."

The police officers nodded. "Don't go far," they said. "We may need to ask you some more questions." The male cop held out his hand. "And the automobile forensics people are on their way. We'll need those keys."

Brandon handed over the key fobs. Naomi wanted to tell them not to mess with the computers, that only she and Tyler had the skill to figure out what had really happened, but she didn't want to start another conversation. She pulled on Brandon's arm. "Come on," she said. "Let's go."

They climbed into the Prius and took off for the city. Naomi wanted him to drive faster, but she didn't say so. She just sat and thought: *sabotage.*

There was no other possibility. That many pieces of equipment couldn't go wrong at the same time by accident. All four kill switches had failed, and Tyler said he had found them disconnected on the floor. That could have been done by anybody. Some kid on the racetrack at night who was curious about the cars and fooled around with the equipment. Or somebody who intentionally disconnected it to cause a crash, for whatever reason.

But before Tyler had tried to engage the kill switches, the demo had already gone wrong. The cars didn't stop when they were supposed to. That had nothing to do with the kill switches. That had to do with the computers, and sabotaging them would require a great deal more sophistication, not to mention a familiarity with the AI interface. There weren't very many people in the world who could have accomplished that, and she was sitting in the car with two of them.

But why? She couldn't believe Brandon or Tyler would want Abby hurt. Brandon loved her, she was sure of it. Could Tyler be jealous? It seemed unlikely. And even if he were, it would be Brandon he would want to kill, not Abby.

Could it have been done a different way? A mechanical way, not involving the computer? Perhaps someone hacked their signal and controlled the solenoids remotely. It sounded good to her, but she didn't know if it was actually possible. The same person who disconnected the kill switches could have loosened the solenoids on the brakes, she supposed, so they would slip off and fail at a random time. But that didn't make sense. All four cars had failed to brake at the same time. It had to have been controlled remotely.

Nothing made any sense. All of the ideas she could think of seemed outlandish. The multiple failures were far too unlikely to be a coincidence, and yet the skill and malice required to sabotage them seemed almost as unbelievable. Even the motive was a mystery. Who would want to kill Abby? She didn't have any enemies. Did a rival company building an autocar fleet want to ruin their chances? But that didn't make any sense, either. Their company had hardly done anything yet. They weren't a threat to anyone.

She had no doubt the local police would chalk it up to equipment failure, but she didn't think that was possible. Someone had done this, and Naomi wasn't going to rest until she found out who.

They rode in silence. Brandon had tried to speak a few times, but the threat of tears choked off his words. There was nothing to say, anyway. They would find out when they arrived.

Naomi didn't cry. She never did. She couldn't remember ever having cried, not really, though of course she must have as a child. She rarely laughed, either. Her emotions lived inside her head, where they belonged. If she showed emotions on the outside, they just felt fake, as if she had produced them on purpose for other people to see. People sometimes thought she didn't have feelings, just because she didn't wear her heart on her sleeve for everyone to gawk at, but that wasn't true. She just kept them inside. Sometimes Naomi thought the world would be a better place if everyone just kept their feelings to themselves.

Why wasn't Brandon driving faster? This was no time to worry about the speed limit. Traffic into the city, even on a Tuesday night, was thick, but it was moving. He could swerve around people instead of just sticking to one lane. Naomi found that she was digging furrows into her palms with her finger-nails, and with an effort, stopped.

Finally, they arrived at the Jefferson ER and parked. The three of them ran inside together and waited impatiently for the family in front of them at the triage desk. It was an Asian family with three young children, and none of them seemed to speak much English. Finally, they understood that they should take a seat, and Naomi, Tyler, and Brandon stepped forward.

"Abigail Sumner?" Brandon said.

The woman checked her computer. "Spell the last name?"

"S-U-M-N-E-R," Brandon said impatiently. "She was just life-flighted in—maybe she's not in your system yet."

"Are you family?" she asked.

"I am," Naomi said. "I'm her sister."

The nurse looked up, and Naomi could see it in her eyes before she spoke. She wanted to run, to throw something, to clamp a hand over the woman's mouth, anything to prevent her from speaking.

"I'm very sorry," the nurse said.

CHAPTER 9

"You were supposed to check them!" Brandon shouted. "It was your job!"

Tyler dropped onto the sofa and put his head in his hands. The apartment seemed hauntingly empty without Abby there. It was no good pointing out that Brandon hadn't wanted to install the kill switches in the first place. And besides, he was right. It had been Tyler's job.

"I did check them," Tyler said. "I know I did. The night before, they were fine."

"They weren't fine. If they were fine, then Abby would still . . ." Brandon's voice cut off, and he finished the thought with a vicious kick at an end table, knocking a lamp onto the floor.

The police had yet to release their cars or equipment, and Tyler had no idea how long that would take. It meant he couldn't check the kill switches for signs of tampering, and once he could, he wouldn't be able to differentiate between tampering by the police and tampering by the person who sabotaged the cars. That made it difficult to know anything for sure, or to convince Brandon it hadn't been just carelessness.

The one thing he did have was the software. For the last three days, Tyler spent most of his waking hours trying to repro- duce the accident in their Realplanet simulation. He had the exact version of the AI software that had been run in the cars the day before, unless it had somehow been switched out for a different one. He tried every variation he could think of to make the simulation match the reality of the demo, but no matter how many simulations he ran, he couldn't make it happen. Every time, the cars stopped exactly when they should.

Of course, the simulation, however detailed, could reflect only what Tyler himself knew. If the brand of solenoid they had purchased wore out after ten thousand uses, the simulation wouldn't show it, because he didn't know to program it in. But no equipment failure he could think of explained the simulta- neous failure of all four cars.

Which left only a software failure. Unless . . .

"Our R/F signal wasn't encrypted," Tyler said. "Someone could have hacked it. Just bypassed the AIs altogether and taken control."

Brandon whirled on him. "What, so this is my fault now?"

"No! I'm just saying . . ."

"Because it couldn't be the software, could it? The software was perfect. It's inconceivable that a software bug could be to blame, even though that's the obvious explanation."

"I've been testing it for—"

"Oh, please." Brandon rolled his eyes, his face curled in disgust. "There isn't a software product on Earth that doesn't have any bugs. That's why there's supposed to be error checking. Redundancies, backup audits, multiple calculation routes." He advanced on Tyler, pointing a finger at his chest. "So that something like this can never, ever happen." His eyes were rimmed with red, his face twisted in fury.

"Listen to me," Tyler said. "Say you have someone on some private crusade against self-driving cars. They wouldn't even have to know the interface. If they scrambled the input signal, just for a few seconds, they could send conflicting data to the solenoids, cause them to seize up. That's all it would take. Then, when the hacker stopped transmitting, the AIs would get control again and stop the cars."

It was a little crazy, as theories went, but not impossible. Audi's self-driving car had been hacked just the month before, though the hackers had been able only to turn the radio on and make the windshield wipers go berserk, not actually take control. It wasn't like he and Brandon had hardened against an attack like that. They were just college students. They weren't expecting to be targeted. But the event had been advertised. Anybody at the track could have done it with a simple transmitter and a few off-the-shelf parts.

Brandon backed away, pulling at his hair with an agonized groan. "Who cares? What does it matter? It's over, can't you see that? Everything is over." He leaned against the doorframe. "We thought we could rule the world, and instead, we killed the sweetest, most beautiful . . ."

"It's not your fault," Tyler said.

"Don't. Don't you dare patronize me." The words tore out of Brandon's throat. "She trusted us. She stood there in front of our cars, and she trusted us to make them stop. We failed her. There's no mystery to solve, no secret hacker conspiracy to blame. It doesn't matter what exact sequence of malfunctions made it happen. Abby didn't write a line of code or wire a single piece of electronics. That was our job. And there's nowhere else to point the finger. We killed her. We did."

Tyler didn't respond. There was nothing he could say.

Brandon was right. Even if a hacker had maliciously attacked them, they at least shared the blame. She had placed her life in their hands, and they had accepted that responsibility. It had been their job to protect her. Tyler realized now that, despite the obvious dangers, despite everything he knew, he had never really taken that responsibility seriously enough.

But he still wanted to know what had happened. The more he thought about it, the more he was convinced that they must have been hacked. The physical disconnection of all four kill switches and the inexplicable failure of the software in all four cars to apply the brakes on time implied a coordinated, planned attack. Someone must have sneaked onto the track the night before or arrived early in the morning and disconnected the kill switches. Then, during the demo, they'd intentionally scrambled the signals to cause the accident. It was even possible that they hadn't intended to hurt anyone, just to ruin the demo.

The explanation had holes, most importantly the question of who would want to do such a thing. But it was the only idea he'd come up with that didn't require an unbelievable series of coincidences or specialized knowledge that only he, Brandon, and Naomi had. That made the theory at least plausible.

And if it was true—if there was someone out there who had murdered Abby to make some point or just to prove it could be done—then Tyler was going to find him. The police forensics team might be good, but this was out of their field of expertise. Maybe he should try to get the FBI involved. The equipment had been developed at a Pennsylvania university, but the crime had occurred across state lines, in New Jersey. Maybe that would be enough to give them jurisdiction. The FBI might not be competent to evaluate cutting-edge AI technology, but they could probably track down who in the area had purchased the right equipment, or they could run facial recognition from the raceway's cameras on any known hacker activists.

At some level, Tyler knew he was fooling himself, just trying to keep busy enough to bury the emotions that threatened to rise up and drown him. No answers he found could bring Abby back. No arrested hackers could change the fact that he was at least partially responsible for her death. Solving the mystery wouldn't convince any venture capitalist to invest in their company, ever again. Nothing would change.

Brandon was right. Everything they had worked for was over. No one would ride in a car that ran down pedestrians on television, not even if a hacker was responsible. Their company had failed before it had even begun.

But Tyler found it hard to grieve for their company, at least right now. It felt wrong to mourn something so insignificant as a career when Abby had lost everything. The loss of his dreams even felt like justice of a kind, a punishment he felt he deserved. He had known the cars were dangerous, of course, but he had never really thought anything bad would happen, not really. He had been living under the delusion his whole life that with enough hard work, the world would open at his touch and give him anything he wanted. Money, fame, love. Now he knew better. And it was too late.

News of Abby's death was everywhere. It hadn't become the national debate that the case of the dead motorcyclist in Seattle had—they weren't a big company like Mercedes-Benz, and so the media treated it as a college project gone bad rather than a threat to public safety. But a news crew had been on site. They had film coverage of the accident. The news media couldn't pass up the tragedy of a beautiful, dead college student. Three days after her death, Tyler still couldn't look at news online for fear of seeing her face.

The first night, reporters had staked out their apartment building, hoping for an interview. Tyler had seen a clip of Naomi, pushing mutely past reporters on her way across the green. He hadn't seen her or spoken with her since the accident. He'd called a dozen times and left messages, but she hadn't responded to any of them. He knew where she was, of course, or at least suspected, but he didn't want to barge in there uninvited when she clearly didn't want company. And yet, she must be grieving terribly. Maybe the right thing to do was to go to her, even if she didn't think she wanted him. He didn't want to hurt her any more by forcing her to talk, but it couldn't be good for her not to have anyone with her. Could it?

He argued the question back and forth with himself, but finally, he couldn't stand it. He had to go to her. If she told him to leave, he would. On his way, he dropped into one of the campus cafeterias and bought a chicken Caesar salad with extra croutons. There was a good chance Naomi had hardly left the library, and if she hadn't left, that meant she probably hadn't eaten much, either.

He climbed the stairs and approached the angled bookcase. A tall boy bent over the water fountain, drinking, so Tyler pretended to be browsing the books until he left. Then he approached the edge of the bookcase cautiously and knocked.

"Go away." Naomi's voice was raw and scratched, barely louder than a whisper.

He eased around the corner. "I brought you some food," he said.

"I'm not hungry. I want to be alone." She sat curled on the beanbag chair, a pillow under her head. Her eyes were rimmed with red, her face streaked and drawn.

"I know. I won't stay," he said. He bent and set the plastic salad container on the shelf, next to the statue of Hedwig. "It feels like a betrayal of her, to keep living. It feels like, how could you eat, or watch TV, or go to class, when she can't do any of those things? But your body needs food." He straightened. "I'll leave you to it."

"How do you know what it feels like?" she asked.

"My parents. They died in a car accident when I was eight. And because I feel the same way now. Not as deeply as you, I'm sure. But it feels wrong to do anything. The only thing I've been able to do is run simulations of the demo, over and over again, trying to understand what went wrong."

Her eyes, which had been distant, focused on him momentarily. "And?"

"And nothing. It never goes wrong in simulation."

"Of course not. There's nothing wrong with the software."

"The only possibility I can come up with is that somebody hacked us. That it was done on purpose."

Her gaze drifted back into the far distance again. He noticed she held a necklace in her hands, a simple gold cross that she rubbed between her thumb and index finger. A keepsake? Something of Abby's?

"I was raised to think people go to heaven when they die," she said. "Or hell. Do you think she's still . . . out there somewhere?"

Tyler hesitated. He wanted to comfort her, but he wanted to answer honestly, too. "I don't," he said. "The neurons that made up her mind stopped firing. The data is gone. I don't believe it was magically captured or backed up somewhere, to be downloaded into a new body somewhere else. But some of that data is still here, in your memories, in mine. You loved her, and so she's a part of your life. It doesn't seem like enough, but it's all we have."

"Then what's the point?" Naomi said, suddenly loud. "Why do anything? Is life just about having babies to pass on your genes before you die? They're just going to die, too. Why live at all? It's an endless game that nobody wins."

"It's life," Tyler said. "It's short, but that doesn't mean it's not valuable. What Abby had was precious. It just makes us angry because we wanted her to have more."

Naomi didn't answer. She kept looking out into the distance and fingering the gold cross in her hand.

"I'll go," Tyler said. He turned sideways to squeeze his way around the bookcase again.

"How's Brandon?" Naomi asked.

Tyler paused. "Sad. Angry. He blames himself, I think."

"Good. He was reckless. He should never have tried that crazy stunt."

Tyler didn't argue with her. If there was blame there, it fell on all of them, Abby included. But there was no point in saying so. He just slipped out and left her to grieve alone.

By the time he walked back to his apartment, the sun had set, leaving the western clouds streaked pink and orange. He unlocked the door and opened it to find the apartment dark and quiet. The door tended to stick in its frame, but he had long mastered the knack of lifting on the handle and shoving it closed with a shoulder. He stepped through the narrow hallway and flipped on the light in the living room.

Brandon sat upright on the sofa, slightly hunched, his eyes staring. For a brief, terrifying moment, Tyler thought he was dead. Then his head turned, and he regarded Tyler with a glazed expression.

"You scared me to death!" Tyler said. "Why are you sitting here in the dark?"

"It was light before. I didn't realize."

"You didn't realize it had gotten dark?" Tyler looked closely at him. He hadn't shaved in three days, hadn't bathed, probably hadn't eaten much. He looked terrible, but there was something more. He seemed defeated. Resigned. "What happened?"

It took him a moment to answer. "I got a phone call. From my father's lawyer."

Tyler waited. "And?"

Brandon looked away. "My father died last night. An aneurism. No warning at all, just didn't wake up in the morning."

"Oh, my word, Brandon. I'm so sorry."

He looked up with anguished eyes. "What did I do? What did I do that was so horribly bad that I deserved all this?"

Tyler sat down next to him on the couch. "Nothing. You did nothing."

"I should have called more. He always complained I only called when I wanted money."

"What about your mom? Have you talked to her?"

Brandon's face twisted. "My mom died ten years ago."

"Your stepmom, I mean."

"Right." Brandon turned to meet Tyler's eyes. "She had the lawyer call to break the news instead of telling me herself. Does that sound like we're on speaking terms?"

"That's rough."

"Whatever. I never liked her. She always loved Dad's money more than him, and I think he knew it. Didn't matter to him, though. The lawyer wouldn't tell me anything before the will is officially read, but if I were to guess, Dad probably left her as much of his money as he left me."

The words hung in the silence. "What are you going to do?" Tyler asked eventually.

Brandon's face hardened. "You mean, am I going to use my share of Dad's money to fund our company?"

"I didn't say that."

"You were thinking it. Abby's dead, my father's dead, and you want to spend his money before his body's even buried?"

"No! I just wanted to know what you were planning. If you were going to go home to New York, or look for a job, or what."

"I don't know, Tyler. I just got the news today. I'll tell you one thing, though. If I do start a company, I'm sure not including you."

Tyler rocked back, stung. "What?"

"You can't even accept responsibility. You spin crazy theories about hackers, and you won't admit you made a mistake. There's no room for oversights in this business, or people end up hurt."

"That's not fair," Tyler said. "Don't put this on me. I checked those switches."

Brandon yelled, an incoherent cry of rage. He punched the wall behind the couch hard enough to leave an impression in the drywall. "Shut up!" he said. "Abby's dead! Don't you get it? We can't go back!"

Tyler stood. He walked to the window and leaned on the sill, looking down onto the street. He understood now. Brandon needed to blame him. He needed to leave him behind and move on. If he did start an autocar company, it couldn't include Tyler, because then it would be the same thing as before. It would be the thing that killed Abby.

Everything was broken now. Their future lay in splintered shards on the ground, and there was no way to piece it together again. Tyler had no idea now where he would be in a month, never mind in ten years. School was practically over, but he hadn't applied for any jobs. He couldn't even bring himself to care.

"I'm going home," Brandon said, as if he had just made up his mind. "I'll leave in the morning. I won't be coming back."

Brandon packed only a few boxes into the Prius. Tyler helped him carry them down, though they barely spoke.

"What should I do with the rest?" Tyler asked. Most of the furniture had been Brandon's, and he had left behind crates full of electronics and computer parts.

"This is all I need. Sell it, or keep it if you want; I don't care."

"Okay. I'll see you at commencement, then."

Brandon shook his head. "I'm not going."

"Seriously? It's an achievement—you should get your diploma."

"They can mail it to me. I'm not planning to come back here. Ever."

Tyler didn't know what to say to that. He watched the Prius drive away, and wondered if he would ever see his friend again. With Abby's death, he had lost not just one friend but two. Or maybe three.

He sat in the apartment flipping channels without actually watching the shows until he couldn't stand it anymore. Then he walked to the nearest café, bought a large coffee and a bagel with cream cheese, and brought it to the library. He shielded the food with his body on the way through the doors so no librarian who saw him could forbid him from bringing it inside. He jogged up the stairs and around to the angled bookcase.

He knocked on the wall. No answer. "Naomi?" he whispered. "I brought you some breakfast."

Holding the food out in front of him like an offering, he sidled around the edge of the shelves. For a moment, he thought he must have slipped behind the wrong bookcase. The triangular space was empty. Not only was she not sitting there on her beanbag cushion but the cushion itself was missing, as were her pictures, her containers of snacks, her stack of *Harry Potter* books, and her statue of Hedwig the owl.

Naomi was gone.

CHAPTER 10

B randon's emotions swung from anger to melancholy as he drove across Long Island and into East Hampton. He couldn't see the ocean from the highway, but he could smell it through the open windows, bringing back memories of childhood exploits on the white sands of Cooper's Beach. He still couldn't believe his father was gone. Even at college in a different city, Brandon had never been able to escape the fear of his father's disapproval. Even now, he found himself wondering what his father would think of his choice to skip commencement.

He hated his father. The man had barely spent two hours together with him, but he always seemed to sail in and ruin whatever plans Brandon had for his life. Lego camp? Not posh enough. His friends were always the wrong friends and his dreams the wrong dreams. Despite this, to Brandon's own disgust, it was always his father that he tried to please.

He had fantasized that the next time he drove this route, it would be to bring Abby home to meet him. He had wanted his father to approve of her. And somehow, he had thought he would. How could anyone disapprove of Abby? But his father had quickly relieved him of that delusion. All it had taken was a text home with her picture and the announcement they were dating. His father's response had been: "You can do better."

He hadn't even met her. She was brilliant, beautiful, funny, kind, and unfailingly polite. She hadn't grown up with money, but she was graceful and intelligent enough to impress anyway. She was perfect. She *had* been perfect. And now she was gone.

Brandon's mind kept going round and round, trying to process her death into something that would make sense. It just couldn't be true. He had to fix it. He would do anything, pay anything, if only he could figure out how to make it right. He felt the familiar catch in his throat as tears threatened to break through. He wanted to go back in time and cancel the demo, or else give Aisha the finger the night she came to visit and tell her he didn't need her money, that he would do it all himself.

He cried out in rage and pounded his fist again and again on the steering wheel. It wasn't fair. It wasn't right. It had been Tyler's software, Tyler's stupid broken kill switches—why wasn't it Tyler lying dead on the track? In a just world, it would have been.

Brandon took deep breaths and got himself under control. A tiny voice whispered to him that he was just as culpable for Abby's death as Tyler or anyone else, but he knew that if he listened to that voice, he would go mad. Part of him just wanted to drive into a tree and end it all, but he didn't quite have the courage for that. He didn't know what life would look like now that she was gone, but he knew that killing himself wasn't what she would have wanted.

He drove past his old high school—another rush of memories—and on toward his family's home, an eight-bedroom mansion with a swimming pool and easy access to both the beach and the golf course. It was technically their summer home, but his mother had loved it here even in the off-season, and so Brandon had spent most of his childhood here. Since their marriage, his father and Jillian had lived here on their own. Now, he supposed, only Jillian did.

Jillian. Twenty-nine years old, sexy and shameless, she had caught his father's eye on the beach one summer and managed to insinuate herself into his bed and into his fortune. It was embarrassing. She was so obviously a trophy wife he wondered how his father, who would have turned sixty this year, could stand to be seen with her in public. Nobody thought it was about love.

It was a betrayal of Brandon's mother, and it was a betrayal of him. His first summer at grad school, Brandon had come home to the house where he had grown up—where his mother had raised and cared for him—to find *her* walking around the halls in a bikini. She'd apparently returned from sunning herself at the beach, but hadn't bothered to change. His father had actually suggested at dinner that night that if he wanted, he could call her 'Mom.' Brandon had broken a chair against the wall and had never come home again.

They had visited him at Penn twice, and both times he had been civil. Dad was paying for school, after all, and had even grudgingly contributed a few times to their autocar venture. But Brandon would never acknowledge Jillian as part of the family. She was a gold-digging whore who hadn't even had the decency to call him herself when his father died. She was probably celebrating. He wondered how much of his inheritance his father had squandered on her. The will would be read on Monday morning, so he'd find out soon enough.

He pulled up in front of the house and parked. He'd thought about finding a hotel to avoid seeing her, but this was *his* house.

She had no right to stay here and keep him out. And it's not like there wasn't plenty of room.

He found her in the den, wearing workout pants and a tank top. She sat on the floor in a stretching pose, with one leg straight to either side, reaching both arms toward one foot with her forehead against her knee. She looked up when she heard him come in. Her eyes were red and puffy.

"Brandon," she said, her voice soft and compassionate. "I'm sorry—I was just finishing up a workout. It's good to see you." She stood and wiped one sweaty hand against her pants before holding it out to shake. He took it, and she squeezed his hand briefly. She looked into his eyes. "I'm sorry," she said. "He was a good man."

He looked away, uncomfortable. What kind of woman did an exercise routine when her husband was dead? Was she trying to keep her figure for the next millionaire she seduced? He couldn't look at her without thinking of her sharing his father's bed. This had been a bad idea. He should have stayed in a hotel.

"Look," she said. "This is your house now. I know your father meant to leave it to you. I have friends in the city, so I'm just going to stay with them for a few days, until this is all worked out. I've been packing up my things in boxes upstairs. I'll have it all moved next week."

"You don't need to do that," Brandon heard himself say. "There's plenty of room here. You don't have to leave."

She put a hand against his face. "You're sweet. But I think both of us will be more comfortable if I go." She paused. "I heard about your girlfriend. I'm so sorry. Both of them, within a few days—I can't imagine."

He pulled away. He didn't want her to talk about Abby. He certainly didn't want her sympathy. "Maybe you're right," he said. "Maybe it would be better for you to go."

She sighed. "Let me just take a shower, and then I'll be on my way. I'll walk down to the train, and you'll be rid of me."

He winced. Maybe he'd been too harsh. "I'll drive you to the station," he said.

"I can walk it. It's only a mile away."

"I'll drive you," he said. "It's the least I can do."

While she showered, he wandered the house. Jillian hadn't made much of a mark on the decorative style of the place. It looked much as it had when he'd lived there: the same oil paintings on the wall, the same glass figurines, the same grand piano that no one in the house knew how to play. Maybe Jillian could; he didn't know. Though he doubted she was the musical type.

She came out dressed in white pants and a sea green top. He had to admit she looked stunning. Her beauty, though, just made him all the more angry. Why did a woman like this, who used her looks to manipulate an old man out of his money, get to live on, while an angel like Abby died young? Nothing made sense. He felt his muscles clenching again and only relaxed them with an effort. "Ready?" he said.

She had one small suitcase, which he took from her and loaded into the trunk of the Prius. The drive to the train station took only a few minutes. He parked, retrieved her suitcase from the trunk, and carried it up to the platform for her.

The platform was under construction, much of it cordoned off by striped yellow tape. Blue plywood panels blocked the skeleton of a new walkway and covered waiting area. A wooden framework marked a new concrete ramp that hadn't been poured. A sign read, "Station still in operation. We apologize for any inconvenience."

It was mid-afternoon on a Friday, and no one else was on the platform. With the waiting area under construction, nothing blocked the brightness of the sun. The black half-sphere of a station camera hung limply from the half-finished roof, its wires trailing free. No one was watching them. Brandon set the case down.

"Thanks," she said.

"I'll see you later." He wished he would never see her again, but he knew she would be at the funeral on Saturday and at the reading of the will on Monday.

She took a breath, like she was facing up to do something hard. "Look," she said. "I ought to warn you." He turned back, wary. "Your dad told me about his plans. I know what's in the will."

That didn't sound good. He felt a flush of heat in his neck. "What are you saying?"

"Your father wanted you to have his money, but . . . not yet."

"Not yet?"

"He's giving it to me, to use on your behalf, until you turn thirty."

Brandon couldn't believe what he was hearing. "He gave it to you? All of it?"

"Just until you're thirty. He said he wanted you to have some maturity before . . . he didn't want you throwing his money away on . . ." Her expression changed, and she took a step back. Brandon realized he was looming over her.

He didn't care. A deep fire of rage erupted into his chest. He stepped forward, closing the gap again. "On what?"

The train was coming. He could feel it vibrating through the taut muscles of his shoulders. She looked suddenly nervous. "I shouldn't have brought it up."

He moved closer, driving her back against the rail. He was shouting now. "Tell me!"

"It wasn't right. He shouldn't have said it."

He grabbed her shoulders roughly, the sea green material of her shirt crumpling in his hands. "Throwing his money away on *what*?"

The silver and blue LIRR train shrieked as it moved toward them. He could hardly hear her over the din. "On your tramp of a girlfriend!"

If there had been some object nearby to kick or punch or break, maybe he wouldn't have done it. He hadn't planned it. But there was no room for thought in the blazing inferno of anger that consumed his mind. "It was him!" she said. "I didn't say it—it was him!" But Brandon wasn't listening. With a roar, Brandon pushed, lifted, *hurled* her over the rail and directly into the path of the oncoming train.

It took only a second. She didn't even scream before the hurtling metal vehicle thundered past, taking her with it.

Brandon stared, hardly breathing, astonished at what he had just done. Had anyone seen? The platform was still empty. The inert camera still hung from the roof, its wires disconnected. The train was screeching to a halt, however, and there must be passengers on board. Had they seen him push her? Could they identify him?

He raced for the stairs, in a daze, his heart hammering in his chest, and almost tripped over her suitcase. He had carried that. His fingerprints would be on it. He snatched it up and took it with him, down the stairs two at a time, to the Prius. He hurled it into the passenger seat and climbed in after it, starting the engine.

He backed up without looking and then floored the accelerator, racing out of the parking lot and toward the highway. He turned west, toward the city, and pushed the speedometer up to eighty. His hands were shaking, and he felt lightheaded.

No one knew he had been there. He had told no one of his plans to come to Long Island. He hadn't stopped for gas or used his credit card, not since the New Jersey Turnpike. Tyler knew he was heading home, but that could just as easily have been to his father's other house in Manhattan.

Thinking fast, Brandon dialed an old high school friend who was now performing in shows on Broadway. "Hey, Christine," he said. "I just got in to my dad's place and wanted to catch one of your shows tonight. Can you get me in the door?"

She responded pleasantly, saying nothing about his father, meaning she probably hadn't heard the news of his death. She told him yes, she could get him a seat, and it would be great if he could stay for drinks afterward. As alibis went, it was pretty flimsy, but he hoped it would at least establish an intention to stay in Manhattan rather than East Hampton. Not that it would do much good. He was an obvious suspect.

Would someone be willing to lie for him? Give him a fake alibi? No, too dangerous. The best he could do was get to the house and spend the evening seeing people. There would be a several-hour time gap between stopping for gas in New Jersey and entering Manhattan, but he would just say he had stopped for a meal and paid with cash. He took the long way, driving clear around to the other side of Manhattan so he could enter through the Lincoln Tunnel, as he should have done if that had been his destination in the first place, and finally reached his father's house.

The final problem was getting rid of the suitcase. He found some bleach under the sink and a pair of leather gloves in his father's coat pocket, and scrubbed the handle and the plastic rim to get rid of any fingerprints. He slid the paper tag identifying Jillian out of the tag holder and ran water over it until it turned to sludge. Unzipping the case, he looked for anything that could easily identify her—anything with a name or phone number—and found nothing. He closed it and wheeled it outside.

As he walked to the subway, he felt conspicuous, as if all the eyes of the neighborhood were on him. No one knew him here, though, and there was no sight more ordinary than a man walking to a station with a suitcase. He took the subway to

Grand Central Station, left the case in a bathroom stall, and walked out. When it was discovered, it would join the hundreds of lost cases that were found there all the time. Without any way to contact the owner, it would sit in storage indefinitely. It would certainly never be connected to the death of a woman in East Hampton.

He took the subway to the Forty-Ninth Street station in time to walk to his friend's theater and catch the show. He barely noticed what it was about. All he could think of was walking out to find the police waiting for him. But when he finally did leave with Christine and some of her friends, there was no one.

He saw the news story the next morning: "Woman Jumps to Her Death on LIRR Track." The article went on to say that this was the third such suicide in as many months. There was no mention of a police investigation or suspected homicide.

Brandon drove back to Long Island the next day as planned for his father's funeral. His mind reviewed the events of the previous afternoon constantly, trying to think of what evidence he might have left behind. He could have left a fingerprint or DNA evidence on her body, of course, but there was nothing he could do about that. He would just have to hope no evidence had survived.

The funeral was mercifully short. Brandon realized Jillian must have arranged the details. He felt suddenly annoyed that she had done so without consulting him, though of course he wouldn't have wanted to be involved. After the service, the procession of vehicles with funeral flags followed the hearse to the cemetery, where his father's body was interred.

When it was all finally over and he turned to go, he saw two men waiting for him. His heart started to race. This was it. He had missed something. They knew.

"Mr. Kincannon?" one of them said. He flashed a badge. "Sir, we just have a few questions."

It was all Brandon could do not to blurt out a confession. Somehow, a voice that didn't sound like his said, "What can I do for you?"

They were very polite. They asked how well he had known Jillian, and where he had been the day before. He answered as calmly as he could, and to his amazement, they seemed to accept his story. They were even apologetic.

Each of them shook his hand in turn. "Thank you for your time, Mr. Kincannon."

Mr. Kincannon. Of course. He was Mr. Kincannon now. Lord of the Kincannon fortune with all that it entailed. No wonder they were so polite.

He wasn't going down for this. They would accept the suicide story and not look too closely. He had grown up with money, but he'd never really owned it, never really knew what it could do. He was untouchable. Brandon smiled. He could do anything now.

CHAPTER 11

Naomi went home to her parents' house with no plans to return to school. She had no plans at all, except to hide away and be alone with her grief. The day of commencement came and went. A few weeks later, a diploma came in the mail, along with a letter from her advisor, saying that at his urging, the requirement for a senior project had been waived. She had been awarded her degree. She didn't care.

The days and weeks passed interminably. Her home didn't turn out to be the sanctuary she'd hoped for. She felt trapped there, smothered in her parents' sadness and well-meaning compassion. They were suffering too, but in a different way. They had lost a child, a future, grandchildren that would never be. Naomi had lost the only person with whom she had ever felt fully comfortable. Her parents grieved with noise and tears and loud arguments. Naomi grieved in silence.

She didn't want to console her parents, and she didn't want

to be consoled by them, either. When they were around, she found herself constantly evaluating what she should do and say. If she didn't show grief, she felt cold and unfeeling. If she did try to show what she felt, it seemed fake, a façade she was putting on purely for display. She felt watched, and she hated to be watched.

Every day was the same. She felt like time had stopped inside the little bubble that was her life. She stood motionless, trapped in a darkness that never changed while the rest of the world passed by in motion and color.

The tragedy drove her mother to religion. She started going to church, to Bible studies, to prayer meetings, and begged Naomi to come with her. The first time, Naomi went along, just to make her mother happy. It caused such a bitter argument with her father when they came home, however, that she never went again.

Her dad was angry at God, or perhaps more accurately, angry at anyone who could believe that God was good. He hated that her mom had turned to faith, and didn't want her pressuring Naomi to go. More and more, Naomi found herself between them, trying to mediate, or else just hiding away in her room while they fought. They needed help, but she didn't think it was the kind of help she could provide. She was too close to them. She was the daughter whose experimental tech had killed their other daughter. It made her too much of an emotional flashpoint to defuse anything.

She needed to be alone or, failing that, lost in a crowd of strangers. She loved her parents, and didn't want them to lose her as well, but eventually, she had to leave. In the final months of school, she had received dozens of recruiting offers from software companies around the world. Without really thinking about it, she interviewed and then accepted a job at a big data analytics firm in downtown Manhattan.

She rented a one-room apartment barely larger than a closet, which felt like the perfect size. She walked streets teeming with strangers, safe in anonymity, as alone as if she were the only person alive. She threw herself into the work, sixty or seventy hours a week, excelling at the job, although the code was tedious and uninspiring. She didn't want to be inspired. She just wanted to hide.

Although she spoke to her coworkers, she never offered any personal information, never asked about their families, never joined them after work for a drink. She developed a reputation for being talented but cold. She didn't care. It made no difference to her what they thought.

She ate poorly, sometimes skipping breakfast and lunch altogether, and grabbing dinner most nights at a tiny Indian hole-in-the-wall near her workplace. She hated having to feed and take care of her body. In high school, she'd read a novel by Nancy Kress called *Beggars in Spain*, in which children were genetically designed not to need sleep. Ever since she'd read it, Naomi had resented the hours she had to waste in bed. Why did she have to turn off her mind—her *self*—for hours of every day just so her body could sleep? Bodies were weak and fragile. They required food and rest and could be so easily harmed. Even when they were kept safe, they eventually grew old and died. They were prisons for the mind that came with a sentence of death.

But her body wasn't her. She felt that now more strongly than ever. She, Naomi, was something intangible, something that transcended flesh and bone. Science fiction had taught her that. With the right technology, a mind might be uploaded into a computer, allowing a person to live on without a body. Whether or not such technologies would ever be invented, it was the *idea* that mattered. The idea that if she were uploaded to a computer, or transplanted into a robot, or swapped into someone else's body, the result would still be *her*.

She wondered about the faith her mother had found. The idea that the human mind was like software running on a machine, and thus able to be copied or transferred, far predated the invention of the computer. Christians, after all, believed the same thing, didn't they? That a person was more than just the body they had lived in. That there was something more central, and longer lasting, than just this package of meat.

She danced around the word *soul*, since it felt a little too cosmic, but she supposed that was what she meant. She found it hard to accept that the laughter, the love, the beauty, the kindness, the unique thinking mind and heart that was Abby could be so easily snuffed out. If it were true, then life was a trap, a precious goblet in freefall with no hope other than to smash on the pavement below. She was more than just a collection of muscles and blood vessels and nerves, and Abby had been, too.

In the evenings, consumed by these thoughts, she wandered along Broadway, through Times Square, losing herself in the crowds and sounds and brightly lit signs. Only when she was too tired to walk another step did she take the subway back to her apartment and fall into her bed to sleep until morning.

Her weekends she spent at the public library, patting the lions on her way through the doors, then losing herself in classic science fiction until the work week began again. She read Robert Heinlein's *Time Enough for Love* and Robert Sawyer's *Mindscan* and David Brin's *Kiln People* and Robert Silverberg's *To Live Again*. She contemplated immortality and personality and consciousness. But even reading wasn't the escape it had always been before. She would read some passage or idea that caught her imagination, and she would think: I have to tell Tyler about this one. Then she would remember that Tyler was no longer around, and remember why he was no longer around, and her thoughts would spiral back into sadness.

She really had liked him, but she knew she could never see

him again. It was like wearing a necklace after a bad sunburn. It didn't matter how much you liked the necklace; it just hurt too much to keep it on. She would never be able to look at him again without thinking of Abby lying bleeding and broken in the dirt. Of course, a sunburn eventually healed. She didn't think this pain ever would.

She continued on like that, day after day, week after week, dulling grief in monotony and busyness, until one day, she received an email from the network administrators at Penn with the subject "Account Expiration Notice":

> Dear Student:
>
> As you are no longer enrolled or employed at the University of Pennsylvania, your computing accounts with the University of Pennsylvania are due to expire in thirty (30) days. If you plan to re-enroll during the coming year, contact our department to extend your time limit. Otherwise, please make every effort, as soon as is convenient, to migrate all personal email or data files to another system.

She had barely thought of Penn. In fact, she had intentionally shielded herself from such memories, surrounding herself with new places and sights and smells. She hadn't logged on to her Penn account in months. The autocar simulations she never wanted to see again, but they had been little more than a driving course with roads and traffic lights and simple rules anyway. Her true experiments had been the worlds in which her Mikes lived and died. As far as she knew, all of those simulations were still loaded on her cluster. In fact, they were probably still running.

The last time she had worked on that software, she had built the evolutionary algorithm directly into the worlds, so that new Mikes would keep spawning and fighting for resources indefinitely. The months since then would have been like millennia to them—tens of thousands of generations would have spawned and fought and died.

That night, she skipped her usual wandering and returned to her apartment. She lay back on her bed with her glasses and her game console and typed the password to access the cluster of virtual machines allocated to her on the university cloud. After logging in to the game, she was presented with a Realplanet avatar and a view of the sparkling lake and distant mountains of the Mikes' world. Everything looked much as it had before.

Then she pulled up an info panel to review the details of the world, and discovered the impossible. The original world she'd created covered about a dozen square miles and was limited to a hundred Mikes. It couldn't be much bigger than that, because the more Mikes she added, and the larger the world, the more computing capacity it required, and her university account was limited to the cluster of virtual machines and associated memory she had available.

The info panel, however, showed that the world had grown a thousandfold. Instead of a dozen square miles, it now covered the equivalent of the area of Maryland. Instead of a hundred Mikes, it now supported a population of ten million.

Ten million. It wasn't possible. The computing capacity required to manage a simulation of that size would far outstrip her university allotment. Besides, the world was a fixed size. It wasn't designed to grow larger. Realplanet could handle larger simulations, of course, but only when given the instructions and server capacity to do so. How was this happening?

There was only one explanation, crazy as it sounded. The Mikes had done it. Which meant they were reaching out of the confines of the Realplanet simulation. Somehow, they had evolved to use the tools inside their world to affect things outside of it. The environment to which they were adapting, after all, was not just the simulation but the whole computing system that hosted it. If some Realplanet bug allowed changes to the file system or runtime environment, and exploiting that bug gave them a survival advantage, then given enough time, the Mikes would find it.

It was the power of evolution at work. Over time, any mechanism that improved their ability to produce offspring would survive into the next generation. She didn't know how they were doing it yet, but she would find out. The real question was, if they could do this, what more could they learn to accomplish?

CHAPTER 12

O f the four of them, Tyler was the only one to attend
commencement and receive his diploma. He attended
the undergraduate ceremony, hoping to see Naomi, but she
didn't come. Brandon, true to his word, didn't show up for their
graduate school commencement either. Tyler felt the eyes of the
other students on him as he waited for his turn at the front.
They all knew what had happened.

He felt like a fraud, wearing the mortarboard and receiving
his diploma as if he had accomplished something. His grandmother took him for dinner afterwards. He didn't feel like
celebrating, and she understood that, but he tried to smile and
eat for her sake. The steak tasted delicious, but it was all he
could do not to spit it out. Even enjoying a meal seemed wrong.
It should have been all four of them, celebrating together. It
should have been Abby.

Finally, his grandmother dropped him off in front of his

apartment building and drove away. Some friends from the engineering school had invited him to go drinking, but he didn't feel like joining them. He had never been much of a drinker anyway, and this would be a celebration binge. As lonely as the apartment would be, he preferred it to cheerful company.

To his surprise, a woman waited for him outside his apartment. She was tall and blonde, in her thirties, and strikingly pretty in a hard-edged kind of way. She wore flowing black dress pants, a sleeveless black shirt, and low-cut dress boots. Her hair was short and professionally styled in a kind of uneven, curled bob, and she wore bright red lipstick. She leaned against his door with her arms crossed, all sharp angles and hard lines. She could have been posing for a photograph, except that she didn't smile.

He slowed to a stop, key card in hand.

"Tyler Daniels?" she asked.

"Yes."

She pushed off from the door with one boot and held out a hand. He shook it warily. Her hand was dry and slim, no rings. He got an unexpected scent from her, not perfume, something like wood varnish and old books.

"Congratulations on your graduation, Mr. Daniels. I'd like to buy you a drink."

He thought, *reporter*, though she didn't give him that vibe. Could she be a cop? FBI? She looked like female feds did on crime shows, though he didn't see a gun or a badge.

"Who are you?" he asked.

She flashed him a smile that seemed more classy and professional than warm. "Lauren Karelis. I represent Andrea Copeland, the motorcyclist whose husband was killed by a Mercedes autocar back in March."

"You're a lawyer?"

She shrugged. "Guilty as charged."

"What do you want with me, Ms. Karelis?"

"Please, call me Lauren. I want to hire you."

"I don't need a job," he said, though it was an outright lie. He hadn't even applied anywhere, and he couldn't just live in his parents' basement and play video games. He was going to have to find work.

"I'm hoping I can change your mind," she said. "But it's a long story. Could we do this over a drink instead of in the hall? I flew in from Seattle this afternoon, and I'm a bit tired."

"The local bars are going to be crowded tonight."

"I saw a café with a white dog on the sign on my way in— looked like a nice place. Do they serve drinks, or is it BYOB?"

Tyler grinned. "Pretty sure they serve drinks. A bit pricey, though."

Lauren waved away his concern. "The expense account can handle it."

For the second time that year, Tyler found himself at the White Dog Café, treated to a meal by a woman who had a lot more money than he did. This time, they sat inside, at a small table against a wall filled with paintings of dogs. The dogs came in all different colors, not just white. It was an eclectic collection, in a variety of frames and painting styles.

"I thought this case would have been over by now," Tyler said. "It's been two months since it was in the news."

Lauren shook her head. "Not even close. The wheels of justice turn slowly. Even the initial complaint filing takes weeks. Then there are pleadings with counterclaims and cross-claims, motions to dismiss and motions for judgment, scheduling conferences and attempts to settle out of court. Right now, we're still in the discovery process, with another two months to go until the court date."

"Where do I fit in?"

She leaned forward, arms resting on the table. "An important claim of our case is that the software driving the Mercedes-Benz chose to hit my client's husband's motorcycle on purpose," she said. "We believe the car's sensors would have detected his presence, but that the software determined his life to be less valuable than the occupants of the car, even though they were better protected in a heavy luxury vehicle. In short, we believe the car's software intentionally killed Mr. Copeland."

"Of course it did," Tyler said.

Lauren leaned back, breathed a sigh of relief. "I'm glad to hear you say that," she said. "I was afraid you'd disagree."

"I don't think there's any question. For you or me, it would just be a reflex. There's no time for us to do anything more than react. To a computer, though, it's plenty of time. It's as if we put the crash on slow motion, then got out of the car, looked around, made some careful measurements, thought about it awhile, and finally made a decision. There's enough time to consider all the options and choose one."

"The problem we have is that Mercedes denies it," Lauren said.

"Seriously?"

"They claim it was accidental. That there was only time to act to save Ms. Brighton and her children, and that Mr. Copeland's presence in the next lane was unfortunate and unavoidable."

"Unavoidable, maybe," Tyler said. "But not accidental. It's possible their software can't distinguish between a human obstacle and a non-human obstacle, and just chose the smaller one. Regardless, it made a choice."

"They further claim that their software is merely an aid to human drivers, just like cruise control, and that the human is always responsible to take control in emergencies. That's in the small print you sign when you purchase one of their cars, of course. But it's also completely at odds with how they market the car. They don't want humans taking control, and they don't encourage it. They tell people they're safer in an accident if they let the car drive. And maybe they are. Annabelle Brighton and her girls walked away without a scratch. But that doesn't mean you're safer in the next lane over. In fact, their car just might choose to take you out."

"So, what, you want me as an expert witness?" Tyler asked.

She made a wry face. "Not exactly."

Tyler wasn't really surprised. He was a fresh graduate with no experience in autocar software beyond getting a friend killed. He wasn't much of an expert in anything. "What then?"

"You're one of the few software engineers in the world with a deep understanding of autocar technology who is not employed by one of the major companies," she said.

He made a face. There was a reason he wasn't employed in the industry, and he didn't want to be reminded of it.

"I know what happened to your friend," she said. "I'm sorry."

"Thanks," Tyler said.

"But you were getting press for your software even before that unfortunate tragedy. You know this stuff. The guy I hired first is a forensic software analyst, used to intellectual property infringement cases. He isn't getting anywhere on this. You, on the other hand, know self-driving cars. You've written software to run them, so you know how they work." She leaned toward him and held his gaze with very blue eyes. "I need you to reverse-engineer the Mercedes software and prove that it intentionally murdered Hal Copeland."

The waiter brought their drinks. Tyler was glad, since it gave him a moment to collect his thoughts before answering. He didn't think she would like what he had to say.

"You should understand, I don't actually agree with your

cause," he told her. She kept looking at him, waiting, so he went on. "Self-driving cars are the future. We need them, and we need them as quickly as they can be fielded. For every person killed by one, whether by choice or by software error, a dozen more are saved because the cars' owners aren't driving drunk or texting or falling asleep at the wheel. I don't want to work against that advance. Self-driving cars, even bad ones, are a lot better than what we've got without them."

"I agree," Lauren said.

Tyler had been building up to a rant, but her quiet assent interrupted him. He threw up his hands. "How can you represent the plaintiff in this case, and still agree with what I just said?"

"Because they should be as good as possible. They're the future, as you said. There's no stopping them, and I wouldn't want to. But neither do I want big companies setting the rules in secret. This software can take lives. I don't want the wealthy barreling down highways in giant SUVs without concern for others because their software, tuned to drive aggressively, is free from public scrutiny. There's a huge transition going on here, and finding the right balance of freedom and protection is a process. It's a process that involves the law and the courts and includes lawsuits like this one."

Tyler felt a little sheepish. "I can see that," he said. "In fact, I wrote an article for an autocar magazine that argued that all the core, decision-making algorithms should be made available to the world as open source software. Not only would that make the basis of the cars' choices public, but also it would help with hacking, since the software would get worldwide scrutiny, and any vulnerabilities would be found quickly."

Her red lips turned upwards in a subtle smile. "So you see why this case is important. It's the first one of its kind, which means it's establishing precedent. Future cases will look back to this one to influence how these decisions are made."

"But why reverse-engineer the software? Don't they have to give it to you? It's pretty crucial to the case."

"Mercedes claims it's proprietary."

"But that's crazy. They've got to show you. It's like saying you're not allowed to examine the murder weapon to see if it has blood on it."

"Preaching to the choir," she said. "The problem is, a lot of the software that runs in your car is proprietary. There's precedent for ruling that way, despite the same argument being made."

"Can't the judge force them?"

She sighed. "Well, and that's where it gets complicated. I filed a motion, and the judge ruled that it was a discovery item, and they had to turn it over. They pled some nonsense about finding the exact version that had been installed in the car, and he gave them a week to prepare."

"Okay. But you should get it then, right?"

"Already did. The problem is, they spent that week obfuscating."

"Oh no." Tyler knew exactly what that meant.

"Oh, yes. They dumped the code into one giant file, removed all the comments, and changed the variable names to random letters of the alphabet. It compiles and runs, but it's completely unreadable."

"So when you say 'reverse-engineer' . . ."

"I mean I want you to make sense of their obfuscated source code and establish the basis on which it chose to swerve into Mr. Copeland's lane and take his life."

Tyler took a sip of his drink, barely tasting it. "You've got to be able to fight this," he said. "Obfuscated code is, as you said, unreadable. They're not acting in good faith."

"And I'm working that angle, too. It's a clear Rule 26 violation."

"Uh, yeah, sure," Tyler said. "Probably Rules 39 and 118.6c, too."

She laughed. "Sorry. Rule 26 of the Federal Rules of Civil Procedure is what prohibits lawyers from giving discovery responses that intentionally harass, cause unnecessary delay, or needlessly increase the cost of litigation. This pretty much does all three of those. I complained to the judge that it's like translating documents into Arabic before turning them over. The information is there, yes, but they sure didn't use them that way, and it's going to be a lot more effort and cost on our part to understand them. I think we'll win the argument. I *hope* we'll win it. But it'll take more motions and arguments and experts to make our point. And in the meantime, we need to do what we can."

"This whole thing is insane."

She grinned. "That's lawyers for you. Seriously, though, the problem is that the people who understand the law don't generally understand technology. They're making important determinations about issues that require some amount of technical expertise to rule on competently, but the technology changes faster than anybody can keep up with it."

"So that's what you want me to do. Wade through impossibly obfuscated code and try to make sense of it."

"Not exactly. I've got somebody working on that already. I want you to look at what he's deciphered, see if it makes sense and what you can understand from it. Then, when we get the real code—hopefully soon—you can dive in and tell us what you find."

Tyler looked up at the wall behind her, where two dozen dogs of various breeds looked down at him. He didn't exactly have any job prospects lined up. This was temporary, but it would, at least, let him interact in the autocar world a little longer. There were plenty of software companies in Seattle, so he could look for a job at the same time, maybe start a new life in the Pacific Northwest. "I'll do it," he said.

"One more thing." She winced a little, as if delivering bad news. "You'll have to sign an NDA."

"Meaning I agree not to disclose the source code to anybody else?"

"Meaning you can't benefit financially from what you see."

He nodded slowly. "I guess I can do that."

"Glad to hear it."

"Speaking of finances, how are you paying for all this?" Tyler asked. "Is Andrea Copeland that rich?"

"Nope. But Mercedes-Benz most definitely is. Enough so that my firm considers the chance of significant profit worth the risk of litigation. Besides, we're also getting a considerable investment in the case from the Carmichael Group."

Tyler frowned. "The Carmichael Group is anti-automation. They don't think computers should be involved in any important decisions. If it were up to them, we'd carry on as we are, killing 1.3 million people every year."

She held up her hands in a gesture of surrender. "This is an expensive case. We'll take any help we can get."

"Okay," Tyler said. "I'm in. When do I start?"

The move to Seattle required depressingly little effort. Most of the furniture in the apartment had been Brandon's, and most of the electronics as well. Tyler's collection of paperback science fiction books still gathered dust in his parents' basement, and it didn't seem practical to move them across the country. In the end, he had two suitcases of clothes and three boxes of other possessions, and that was it. He hired a company to sell everything he had left behind and climbed on a plane bound for Seattle–Tacoma International.

The obfuscated source code was just as indecipherable as

expected. Without any English variable names or comments, it was pure logic, without any way to understand the purpose of any portion of it. No programmer would have been able to read it, not even the Mercedes developers who wrote it in the first place. In fact, Lauren had hired an ex-Mercedes developer named Yusuf Nazari, who had worked on some portion of the code a few years earlier. He had done his best so far to make sense of it, trying to reason his way from known inputs to some level of meaning, but it was slow going. It was unquestionably a violation of the spirit of discovery, but to the judge, the real code would have been gibberish as well. It was hard to explain how one set of gibberish was acceptable, but another was not.

Tyler liked Seattle. He liked the breeze off of Puget Sound, the occasional sightings of Mount Rainier and Mount St. Helens, the seafood, the young tech culture, and, of course, the Science Fiction and Fantasy Hall of Fame. He didn't even mind the constant drizzling rain. As a place to start over, he could have done worse.

A week into the job, he saw the news about Brandon. It was buried in the announcements section of an autocar magazine: a new self-driving startup, offering app-driven ride services in New York City and its suburbs. The company was called Black Knight, and its founder and CEO was Brandon Kincannon. For most people, the name of the company would summon visions of a powerful warrior on horseback, or perhaps of Batman, or the Marvel Comics superhero. Tyler knew it was a reference to the ludicrous character in *Monty Python and the Holy Grail*, and thus a tribute to Abby.

Apparently, Brandon's inheritance from his parents had been considerable. In the millions, if it had been enough to start a viable company. It would be a hard battle to make it profitable, though. He would be trying to enter a market fenced on one side by car manufacturers, selling both traditional and self-driving cars to commuters, and on the other side by the New York taxi drivers union, eighteen thousand drivers strong, providing near-instant access to transportation from the street. Not to mention Uber and Lyft, which were already filling the same niche.

He wasn't surprised Brandon hadn't asked him to join his company, but it still hurt. It was a dream Tyler had been forced to abandon, and now Brandon had found a way to make it happen. He wondered who Brandon had hired to write the core software, and how good they were. Not that it really mattered. It wasn't Tyler, and never would be. He had a new life now, and he would have to get used to it.

CHAPTER 13

Naomi spent hours exploring the gigantic world the Mikes inhabited. Ten *million* of them. She flew over miles of countryside, mostly fields and sheep pastures as before, with mirrored buildings placed in regular patterns to reflect sunlight. The difference was the scale. The features of the world—lakes and rivers and forests and mountains—were randomly placed, but the landscape just kept going. Wherever she flew, she saw Mikes at work, shifting sheep to new grassy fields, constructing new buildings, harvesting yams.

As a society, they were doing what they had been created to do: survive. They had somehow reached out of their simulation and harnessed the power of the computing system to create a larger simulation, thus living longer and providing resources for the children they inevitably spawned. But how? How had it happened? They were characters in a video game. This shouldn't be any more possible than Pac-Man escaping its maze.

But the Mikes were a lot more sophisticated than Pac-Man. They had already hacked the game once, finding a way to survive that she hadn't intended. If anything, this demonstrated the power of an evolutionary framework. Given enough time, even very unlikely opportunities to improve survival would be discovered, and once discovered, would live on. Any good strategy for survival would soon be widely adopted, since those who followed it would survive and those who didn't would die. The tendency to pass instructions to children would become prevalent, because those who passed on such instructions would have more surviving grandchildren.

But how they had done it? She checked the cluster of machines the simulation was running on, and it, too, had grown to mammoth proportions. Like most computing systems these days, it was hosted on a cloud. That meant it wasn't like a computer sitting on her desk with a hard disk and a few processors. The university purchased their computing capacity as a commodity from a cloud retailer like Amazon. They paid for as little or as much computing as they used. So what looked and behaved like a single machine to Naomi, with processing capacity and storage for her files, was in fact part of a giant data center in a warehouse somewhere, with her data stored redundantly as stripes on multiple physical disks. Part of the advantage of a cloud was auto-scaling: the ability to grow a computer system to be as large as the problem you were trying to solve.

It seemed unlikely that the Mikes could be aware of the physical architecture behind their world. Yet somehow, they had figured out a way to affect it. Practically, that meant interacting in some way with the stack of addressable memory the operating system provided to the Realplanet application. They could theoretically have access to this through a bug, some kind of buffer overflow that allowed them to change memory values they weren't supposed to be able to touch.

It took her days to discover how they had done it. She hunted through the Realplanet history of the world, narrowing her search by looking at times when the population had suddenly increased. Even so, it wasn't easy. The transition had taken centuries of game time. Eventually, she did track it down to a bug—not in her scripts but in the Realplanet software itself.

It turned out it was done with mirrors. If two of the mirrored surfaces used to construct the buildings were set up facing each other, the resulting reflections caused an infinite loop in the software, which culminated in a buffer overflow. Smaller mirrors wouldn't do it, and they had to be exactly parallel, to a very small tolerance.

A buffer overflow happened when a program wrote data into memory outside of the limits intended for it, like water over-flowing a riverbank. If done unintentionally, it usually meant crashing the program. But hackers had a long tradition of exploiting such bugs to intentionally write their own data in place of data that was supposed to be there. In the old days, they had used buffer overflows to rewrite parts of the operating system or to gain root access to a system. These days, program memory addressing was limited to offsets from a given starting point, preventing such bugs from becoming unlimited security holes, but they could still be used in some contexts to cause effects outside of what the programmer intended.

The first time, the mirror hack had nearly crashed the simulation. The program's calculations went badly askew, sending the world into terrifying chaos. Straight lines went jagged, objects popped in and out of existence, mountains flickered into forests or lakes. Half the population died, and several that had been dead came back to life. The program recovered, and the simulation returned to normal, but from then on, the instructions written for future generations included a ban against facing two mirrors together.

Some of the Mikes, however, didn't obey the rules. In the random genetic variations of the children from their parents, most were spawned with the desire to follow the wisdom discovered by their elders, but some were not. Some of these renegades experimented with mirrors.

Often, nothing much would change. Other times, the Mike himself would die, or he would cause another catastrophe. On one game-changing occasion, however, the result was nearly magical. One of the Mikes, experimenting with large mirrors set to face each other, produced a hundred times the amount of light than should have been possible. Naturally, since survival was the primary goal of every Mike, and survival required light, this revived experimentation with the mirror hack. Which led to more deaths, more catastrophes, and more discoveries.

After centuries, the Mikes discovered not only how to reproduce exactly the right arrangement to yield a lot more light but also a host of other hacks that benefited them. They found ways to use the mirror effect as a weapon, destroying other clans of Mikes to preserve more resources for their own offspring. Eventually, they developed methods of manipulating the light that allowed them to access the underlying computer memory with more precision. They expressed this language using the same words they used to tell each other about food and building plans—*straight* and *left* and *yes* and *no*. It was a crude programming language of sorts, compiled into computer memory through a complex pattern of light reflection.

It was brilliant. From there, of course, they had reached farther, codifying commands to use again and again. They learned how to access the auto-scaling capability of the cloud, requesting more memory and processing resources for their growing cluster, thus allowing their world to expand. She doubted they actually understood the system, not in the same way a human programmer did. Theirs was more of a practical understanding, like a toddler who discovers consistent ways to make pretty colors and sounds with a smartphone, without knowing how it works or what it's really for.

Naomi wasn't surprised that Realplanet had been sold with such a bug, or that no one else had discovered it. Issues like that were pretty common, even in professionally developed software. Besides, this was something different. Realplanet was being hacked from the inside, and no programmer anticipated that. The Mikes were part of the programming. This was the program hacking itself.

Were the Mikes conscious?

The question pricked her more deeply than it might have before, obsessed as she had become with thoughts of the soul and identity apart from the body, immersed in stories about the nature of the mind. Could they have inner thought lives unique to themselves? They hadn't been programmed that way, but such a thing might have evolved if it improved their ability to survive. Did they know they existed? Were they just simulations, or something more? It was difficult to define what she even meant by the question, never mind knowing how to answer it.

Even the terminology fell short. Some people used the word *sentient*, but that just meant having senses and using them to interact with one's environment. A sea slug was sentient. *Intelligent* was too vague, since dogs and parrots and chimps and dolphins were all intelligent, to some degree. Naomi liked *sapient* best, but it essentially just meant "like *Homo sapiens*." Like humans. And wasn't it possible for a creature to exist that had a self-aware perspective and reasoning ability, and yet be utterly unlike humans?

She suspected that the problem with picking a word was that nobody really knew what it was they were talking about. There seemed to be an essence that distinguished the human experience from that of everything else on the planet, but we couldn't nail down what it was. Was human intelligence categorically different from a dolphin's, or were we just farther along on the same scale? Could the difference be defined? Measured? If the same essence appeared in a computer or an alien species, would we even recognize it?

The Turing test represented an attempt, at least, to measure the slippery concept, but it fell so far short as to be practically useless. Telemarketing bots could fool most people on the phone these days, but no one thought they had private emotional lives. The conundrum boiled down to this: the only person who could know if a creature was self-aware was the creature itself. Naomi knew that she was. She assumed other people were because they spoke and behaved in similar ways, but really, there was no way to be sure. Maybe they were robotic simulations, or clever hallucinations of her own mind. A novel by Robert Sawyer called *Quantum Night* suggested that only a small percentage of the human population was actually self-aware, while the rest had just developed an evolutionary survival strategy to imitate them.

Science fiction aside, it seemed reasonable to assume that for humans, the appearance matched the reality. With computers, however, the answer was far less clear.

The essence of the question seemed to be one of conscious experience. An AI could behave and even talk exactly like a human, but experience nothing. It would be like the inhabitant of Searle's Chinese room, only worse: instead of simply not understanding, it would be just a mechanism, with no subjective experience of being in the room at all. Was conscious experience something that could be fabricated? Was it even physical at all? The problem with subjective experience was just that; it was subjective. Who could say if another being was conscious of its surroundings?

In the case of the Mikes, Naomi found herself doubting it. For one thing, they had little in the way of language. Their communication hadn't progressed beyond the original set of directional words. Even these they used sparingly, barely communicating at all in their day-to-day lives. Didn't a human-level consciousness of self require some kind of language to think in? Could one truly think without a way to express those thoughts? Despite all they had done as a group, it was hard to watch the simple, repetitive interactions of a single Mike and think of it as sapient.

They had figured out how to hack their universe, to be sure. But did the Mikes really discover those things through thought and invention, or was it simply the power of the process of evolution? The same sorts of achievements were common in the natural world. Poison arrow frogs had "figured out" how to carry their tadpoles up tall trees to pools of water in the rainforest canopy. Gulls had "learned" to drop mollusks from a height to break them open and reach the meat inside. Hawk moths had "developed" a long proboscis to reach the nectar in the deepest flowers. But none of these were evidence of intelligence or clever invention on the part of the animal. They were the result of evolution, generating diversity and then rewarding the instincts and designs that proved most beneficial.

Could she really say, then, that simulations that followed their evolutionary programming were sapient, however sophisticated their activity might have become?

One thing she *was* sure of, though: the explosive growth of the Mikes' world was going to be a problem. Her original cluster had consisted of eight virtual machines with two cores each, fully utilized. This sprawling world of millions required a hundred times that at least, and it was still growing.

She remembered the email from Penn about her account expiring. No large organization hosted their own servers anymore, and Penn was no exception. Computing power and storage were a commodity, abstracted from the underlying hardware and sold to customers like electricity or water. The Penn network, which would once have been stored in the basement of one of the university buildings, was now part of a giant cloud computing warehouse housed somewhere in the suburbs, with fifty or eighty thousand servers in it. Penn's data and processing load would be distributed across those machines along with hundreds of other customers, and they would get a monthly bill for their usage. If that bill had doubled in size over the course of half a year—and she was pretty sure it had—the Penn network admins would certainly have noticed.

In fact, that's probably what had prompted the alert about her account expiring. The school usually gave students more time, a few semesters at least, to clear out their accounts. She had even heard of people still using their machines to host websites years after graduation. Which meant the admins probably didn't know where the extra usage was coming from. That wouldn't last long, though. They would add instrumentation and track it down by account and user. They would find the problem and shut it down.

There was no way Naomi was going to let that happen. But how could she stop it? A quick look at prices at major cloud service providers told her what she already knew: there was no way she could afford to host the Mikes' world herself. She was pulling a pretty good salary writing software, but it wasn't enough. Even if she re-enrolled at Penn, they wouldn't let her continue to run a simulation that cost more than her school tuition.

She could theoretically write some kind of program to distribute the simulation around the world, using other people's computing power like Bitcoin mining programs. Besides being illegal, however, she doubted she could do so effectively. The world of cryptocurrency mining was pretty well saturated, and usually involved bundling with other software that users downloaded. She doubted she could compete in that world, and besides, she didn't think Realplanet could be distributed that widely and still maintain a single, coherent simulation. There had to be another way.

Her glasses chimed, indicating an incoming call. This was unusual all by itself, since she had no social contacts in the city. Her mom called every day, but she had already talked to her that morning. A box to one side of her vision showed the name *Brandon Kincannon* along with his picture. She almost ignored it. If it had been Tyler, she would have. But Brandon hadn't tried to contact her before now, which made her curious. She answered it.

"Hello?"

"Naomi, it's Brandon. I won't ask how you're doing, because I can guess. But I have an offer for you."

"An offer?"

"Yeah. Well, to be honest, I need your help. You might have seen the news that I'm starting an autocar company."

"No." She hadn't been watching the news, and she certainly wasn't reading any articles about the self-driving car industry.

"Well, I am. And I heard you're living in Manhattan."

"Brandon—"

"Wait. Hear me out. It's in her memory. It's too late to save Abby, but we can save other people. You probably don't even want to see a self-driving car again, never mind build one. I get that. But if we don't, then nothing comes of her death at all. People keep on dying, and nothing changes."

"It was our self-driving cars that killed her," Naomi said.

"And it's the lack of them that's killing three thousand people a day. Just right here in Manhattan, there's a traffic accident every twelve minutes." His voice grew plaintive. "I don't know what else to do. Nothing else has any purpose, any meaning for me. I have to make it right somehow. This is the only way I know. And I can't do it without you."

"What about Tyler?"

A few seconds of silence passed before he answered. "I can't forgive him. I know it wasn't his fault, not really, but I can't believe he could have checked those kill switches thoroughly and then every one of them failed. It's probably not fair of me. But I loved her, and he didn't. I just can't handle seeing him. With you, at least I know you loved her as much as I did. Probably more. I know you're hurting like I am."

Naomi stared at the cracked beige plaster that made up the walls of her apartment. A gouge ran along one wall, probably from an attempt to move a piece of furniture in or out. She didn't want to see Brandon again. She didn't want him to talk about how much he loved her sister. She couldn't deal with anybody's pain but her own.

On the other hand, he was right. It was much more important work than what she was doing now, and Abby wouldn't have wanted the company to just fall apart. Besides, if he wanted her help badly enough, she could make some demands. She needed a place to host the Mikes' world, and she couldn't pay for it herself.

"I'm going to need a lot of computing bandwidth for my simulations. Huge amounts," she said.

She could hear his smile over the phone. "Whatever you need, it's yours."

CHAPTER 14

Tyler paced Lauren's office, resisting the urge to grab a paperweight from her desk and throw it through a window. The judge had finally ruled on the obfuscated code, but not in their favor.

"This is insane!" he said. "How do people expect any justice to be done when the judge on a case doesn't have the first idea of the technology involved?"

"I know," Lauren said. "It's not right. But there isn't anything we can do about it."

"This isn't a question of law. It's a question of simple comprehension. It's like having a judge who doesn't speak the same language. He's not qualified to make decisions."

"This is why I don't put you in a courtroom."

"Is there any recourse? Any way we can complain over his head or something?"

She steepled her fingers, leaning back in her chair, unnervingly calm. "If we lose the case, we can use it as a basis of appeal. Though not many appellate judges are tech literate either."

Tyler growled in frustration. He had spent every waking hour for the last week trying to piece together some kind of sensible construction from the obfuscated code Mercedes-Benz had handed over in discovery. He suspected they might have padded it with dead code as well, software that sat in the baseline and didn't do anything at all. There were portions they thought they understood now, but it was only a fraction of the total. He and Yusuf were trying to understand the criteria by which the car made decisions, but they'd barely gotten past the basic interfaces.

He walked back to his desk, fuming. Lauren had given the two of them a room to work in, a law office with mahogany bookshelves, leather chairs, and a deeply varnished desk the size of a conference table, which was now decorated with high-end development laptops and giant monitors. Yusuf sat in one of the leather chairs, slouching badly, typing away. Dark-haired, dark-skinned, he wore cargo shorts and a wrinkled *Space Invaders* T-shirt that contrasted sharply with the upscale surroundings.

"Got the news?" he asked, not looking up.

"Yep."

"Isn't it awesome? No freebies. This party can keep on rocking."

"Yeah, just what I was hoping for."

"Come on, man," Yusuf said. "They just hand over the code, things get boring. Anybody can read code." He pointed to the screen. "This is what you call a challenge."

Tyler sighed and sat down across from him. They were making some progress, slow as it was. Every time they figured out a variable or method, they would rename it globally, creating spiderwebs of meaning that reached into the morass of inscrutable code. It was like figuring out a ciphered message. Each symbol identified brought the message closer to readability, and provided clues that made it easier to identify the next symbol in turn. Only in this case, instead of twenty-six symbols, there were thousands.

"The frustrating thing," Tyler said, "is that I expect this to come to nothing. The software probably doesn't distinguish among obstacles at all. It did its best to find a safe path, choosing the smaller, less dangerous obstacle to hit. The fact that one of the obstacles had a wife who would mourn him probably didn't figure into the logic at all."

"And you think that's okay?" Yusuf asked.

"No. I think the government should mandate these algorithms to be open source, so everyone can see and know what the rules are and can contribute to them. It's crazy that software that can kill people is allowed to be proprietary. But that said, I don't think there's a smoking gun here. I don't think Mercedes probably did anything illegal."

Yusuf laughed. "Where did you go to law school?"

"Nowhere," Tyler said, a little stung by the laughter. "I studied computer science. You?"

"UW Law," Yusuf said, tipping his head in a little bow. "Right here in Seattle."

"No way. You attended law school? Then what are you doing locked in here with me?"

"Attended, yes. Graduated, no. I dropped out first year, took some programming courses instead, and ended up somewhere in the middle."

"So you know this stuff then?"

"Enough to know that illegal has nothing to do with it. This is a civil case. There's an injured party. The question is, who is responsible for that injury? Mercedes-Benz? Annabelle Brighton? Or maybe the motorcyclist himself did something wrong that caused the accident. That's what the court has to decide. If the Mercedes software specifically chose to kill Mr. Copeland, the court may decide the company is responsible."

"Even if the alternative was killing Ms. Brighton and her children?"

"Well, it depends. Can the company be considered negligent in the construction of the software? Was there a safe path it failed to identify? Were all reasonable attempts made to avoid this eventuality? It's a tricky question, and once it gets in front of a jury, it's mixed up with all of the usual emotional appeals to sympathize with the grieving widow. Big company like that, people figure they have enough money and want to give the girl a payday."

Tyler tipped his chair back, resting it against the bookcase behind him. "That's what I hate about this process. It's like a pediatric surgeon getting sued for malpractice when he did everything he could, but there's a dead child and people need someone to blame. It makes me feel like I'm on the wrong side of this case. On the other hand, I'm angry at Mercedes for hiding their code when people are trusting their lives to it."

"Maybe they've got something to hide."

Tyler studied him. "Why did you leave Mercedes anyway?"

"Fired for cause," Yusuf said. "Pretty juicy one, too. I was banging the boss's wife."

"You're kidding. Seriously?"

"Yeah. That's how the boss thought of it anyway. I thought of it as rescuing her from a complete asshole."

"Huh." Tyler wished he hadn't asked.

"Seriously. The guy didn't show her any attention at all. For her birthday, he bought her a new washing machine. True story."

"Did she leave him?"

Yusuf made a sour face. "No, man. She wanted to. Came down to it, though, she couldn't leave his money."

"Sorry to hear it."

Yusuf shrugged. "Money is everything, man. It's what makes the world go round."

They went back to work, and the only sounds for the next several hours were the hum of the air conditioner and the soft tapping of keys. Tyler had always been able to focus like this on problems. Once his mind was immersed in the code, he could keep going all night if necessary, until hunger or sheer exhaustion finally broke through his concentration. His mind filtered out all signals that might distract him from the puzzle, to the extent that he might not have noticed if the room was on fire.

He was closing in on the core decision-making software. They had identified the primary loop, the code that was executed over and over again at high speed, constantly reevaluating the current situation and adjusting the car's actions as needed. Unfortunately, that loop consisted of a tremendous amount of code, much of which remained obfuscated. A carton of Szechuan lo mein and an egg roll appeared next to him, which he dug into with a plastic fork, barely breaking eye contact with the screen. Either Yusuf or one of Lauren's assistants must have ordered it for him, but he didn't ask. Halfway through the carton, he got a break. He recognized a piece of code.

The code used a technique that he had seen only once before, in a piece of open source software written by Naomi. She had written it before they met, part of a machine learning library she'd created to support her AI projects at school. She'd made the code available under an MIT license for anyone to use. That way, she contributed to the programming community and could also benefit from any helpful improvements others might make to her work.

Tyler accessed the online repository hosting service, found her original code, and compared it to the Mercedes code. The variables, of course, had all been renamed, but the logic was

identical. It was Naomi's code. There was nothing illegal or
even unethical about that; under the MIT license, Mercedes
was free to use it and modify it as they saw fit. They didn't even
have to acknowledge her as the original author. But identifying
the code gave Tyler a big leap forward in making sense of the
Mercedes software. Especially when he noticed that it wasn't
exactly identical after all.

Mercedes had introduced something new. Every time through
the primary loop, it checked for a signal from the satellite radio
antenna. He thought at first it was just bad programming. The
primary loop needed to be as fast and responsive as possible,
and there was no reason to be accessing the satellite radio. That
kind of direct call to external hardware would slow it down.
But finally, as he unpacked the code, he recognized it for what
it was.

It was a remote control. External access through the satellite radio that allowed total command of the vehicle, from the
steering to the brakes, even to the ability to turn the car on and
off. This was no secret work inserted by one individual, either. It
was too pervasive and well integrated for that. Mercedes knew
it was there. It wasn't just that their cars were hackable. They
had installed the hack on purpose.

"Yusuf," he said. "You'd better take a look at this."

While Yusuf read over his shoulder, Tyler cracked open the
fortune cookie that had come with his Chinese food and pulled
out the small strip of paper. His fortune read: *Think twice
before taking a step you might regret.*

Half an hour later, Tyler stood at Lauren's desk, trying to
explain it to her.

"It's got to be for the government," he said. "The FBI,
maybe, but it smells more like Homeland Security. They want
the ability to stop any car, any time. Can you imagine? They

suspect someone of terrorism, so they take control of their car remotely and drive it to whatever location they want. No such thing as a getaway car anymore. The feds can stop the car dead. Stolen car? Amber alert? As long as they have the license plate, they can turn you around and drive you straight to the police station, and there's nothing you can do about it."

"Is that such a terrible thing?" Lauren asked.

Tyler stared at her in disbelief. "It's a disaster. How long do you think that key is going to stay secret? How long before it's leaked to the very criminals or terrorists it's supposed to be protecting us from? Do you want your car used as a terrorist weapon with you in it? They could turn a city into a massacre."

"There have to be ways to prevent that, right?" Lauren asked. "Change the key regularly, require authorization from someone higher up who has a different key, that kind of thing. We have secure wireless systems all over the country."

"And people hack them," Tyler said. "But even if they didn't, it still means giving that control to our own government. Is that what we want? They could take over anybody's vehicle, any time they wanted."

"Anybody driving a Mercedes," Lauren said.

Tyler's smile felt tight. "I can't believe Mercedes is the only one. Tesla, GM, Toyota, Honda, BMW, Ford, Volvo, Nissan—I bet if you took a look at their software, you'd find the same logic."

"But those aren't even all American companies. What's in it for them? Why would they give that kind of control to the US government?"

"Money, I expect." Tyler shrugged. "These companies have been developing this technology for years at a significant expenditure of research dollars. What if Homeland Security offered them a grant? Fifty million dollars, and all we ask is that you include this one little piece of code. Besides which, all those companies have major US headquarters and do significant business here, something that requires staying on our government's good side.

"There's a history of this kind of dealing. Years ago, the government pressured the big Internet and social media companies into contracts allowing them access to the personal communications of millions of people. Before that, it was the phone companies and secret wiretaps. Companies, even foreign companies, are usually willing to please the richest and most powerful money-spending entity on Earth."

Lauren reached into a lower drawer and lifted out a giant bottle of Ibuprofen. She shook out what looked like significantly more than two pills, popped them in her mouth, and washed them down with a drink of water. "How does this affect our case?" she asked. "Are you suggesting that someone hacked Annabelle Brighton's car and drove it into Hal Copeland?"

"No, no," Tyler said. "There's no evidence of that at all. But this is probably why Mercedes was so reluctant to let us see their code. Making them admit to it on the stand would certainly harm their credibility."

She chewed on her lip, nodding slightly. "The problem is we have to show that Mercedes-Benz caused harm to Hal Copeland through negligence. Including a secret remote control might be a shocking revelation, but it doesn't prove the point."

"There's one more thing. Run time."

"What do you mean?"

"This thing involves a check to the satellite radio every time through the primary loop. That means the loop is slower than it would have to be. That means slower detections, slower reaction times."

"By how much?"

"A millisecond, give or take. I don't know—can't know—that a faster cycle time would have made a difference in this instance. The car might have chosen to do exactly the same thing, with exactly the same result. Given the speed of the vehicle at the time, however, and the limited time to react, it's possible that it could have made a difference. If so, their secret remote control may have cost Hal Copeland his life."

Lauren smiled broadly and her eyes danced. "Now that's something I can use."

Tyler felt a twinge of guilt. A dozen other alterations in the software, all perfectly reasonable, might increase the runtime of the primary loop. The developers would have tried to make it fast, but even if they doubled the time, the automated software still significantly improved upon the reaction time of a human being. The problem wasn't that the cycle was slow. The problem was that Mercedes was adding secret capabilities that threatened the lives, or at least the freedoms, of their customers. That was the reason he was doing this—not to undermine the value of self-driving cars, but to force their software design out into the open.

"Tyler? Good work. But you need to keep this under wraps." She fixed him with a stare that left no room for doubt. "I don't want to see any announcements on the six o'clock news. Let me break this in my own way, in the courtroom."

"Okay," Tyler said. "For now."

She raised an eyebrow. "For now?"

"This is going to come out. It's too big and too important to keep secret. Eventually, case or not, I'm going to start talking."

"Don't forget you signed an NDA," she said. "You can't just post their code on the Internet."

"But I can tell people the truth, right? I can tell them what I found, in general terms."

She massaged one temple with her fingertips. "You can. And Mercedes can sue you. They might not, of course, depending on the public outcry, but they could claim you were breaking the terms of the agreement, and a judge might agree with them."

Tyler frowned. "It's not right."

"Right or not, it's how things work. Let it come out as part of the case. Then it becomes part of the public record, rather than just your word against theirs. Afterwards, if you're not satisfied, you can be a whistleblower if you want. You can decide that the public has a right to know. But you'll be working against both the government and some pretty big international companies. They might not like that very much. And they have a lot of power."

Tyler nodded. "That's exactly why people need to be told."

On his way out of Lauren's office, Tyler passed through her small waiting area, a nook with two armchairs and a glass coffee table piled with recent magazines. One of them caught his eye. Only part of the cover peeked out from under a copy of *Vogue*, but he saw enough. He reached down and slid it out, confirming his suspicion. It was a copy of a magazine called *Entrepreneur*, and the title story was "Five Young Millionaires Who Are Taking On the World." On the cover, dressed in a tailored suit and a new, expensive haircut, was Brandon Kincannon.

Tyler sank into an armchair and read the article. Brandon's company, apparently, had been causing quite a stir. The author called Black Knight "the hottest little venture to hit the streets of New York in a decade." Apparently, Brandon had kicked off his business by offering free rides anywhere in the city to Meals on Wheels and similar organizations who delivered meals to the elderly, as well as to anyone wanting to get to a soup kitchen, homeless shelter, or other charity. The scheme had earned him the nickname "The White Knight" in the city's news media and resulted in a lot of free publicity.

According to the article, however, Black Knight was more than just clever advertising. Metrics demonstrated a shorter pickup time—the time between when customers clicked on the app and the car actually came for them—than either Uber or Lyft, despite having only a fraction of the number of cars in their fleet. The writer of the article referred to Black Knight's "magic" secret algorithm that somehow brought cars to people's doors just as they asked for them.

"I wanted to go to that game store over on East Fifteenth Street," a man from Brooklyn was quoted as saying. "It's not like I go there every weekend or anything. Just wanted to get a present for my nephew. I put it into the app, looked out the window, and one of those black cars was already sitting there, waiting for me. It was so fast it was creepy."

Tyler tossed the magazine back onto the table and started searching the Internet through his glasses. He found dozens of articles, but when he looked for a list of employees, he couldn't find one. He mostly wanted to know who was writing his software, what their background was, and where they had worked before. Had he stolen a chief programmer from one of the big car companies, luring them away with a high salary and stock sharing? Would Brandon, too, give the US government access to control his cars?

All of that, however, was secondary. Tyler knew that it made no difference who worked for Brandon. It would just be a name, ultimately meaningless. His curiosity was a form of regret, a sorrow that he wasn't sharing those headlines. He wondered if Brandon still blamed him for Abby's death. Maybe he should call, just to congratulate him on his success. Then he could ask him who was writing his software. Whoever it was, they seemed to be doing a great job.

Tyler stretched his legs and stood up, leaving the magazine behind him. It didn't matter, not really. He just wanted to know who had replaced him.

CHAPTER 15

In the world of the Mikes, light meant survival. The more sunlit ground surface a Mike controlled, the more food he could create, and thus the more power he wielded in the community. When Naomi introduced the solar cell into their world, she revolutionized their civilization.

The solar cell could be made simply from readily available substances. A semi-magical device, it operated both as a collector and a battery, storing sunlight that could then be shined out of the cell at a later time, with no loss. It didn't provide them with more sunlight, but it did provide them with the ability to save it and move it around. In only a few generations, sunlight became currency. A solar cell filled with light could be exchanged for just about any object or service available in their world, and since the need for light was constant, the value of the currency remained stable.

It gave her a simple mechanism by which to put them to

work for her. Anything she wanted done, she could motivate them to accomplish by paying them in light. The job she set them to accomplish, of course, was to run Black Knight's fleet of self-driving cars.

Throughout the Mikes' world, millions of booths suddenly appeared one morning. In a booth, a Mike could play a video game in which he controlled a car somewhere in New York City. Whenever a real-life customer used their app to summon a car, the Mikes that were closest to that location in the city received a solar cell as a reward. The closer they were, the more light they would receive. The Mikes could use whatever means they wished to decide where to drive: app use history, customers' current locations, car-summoning patterns, personal information, the locations of their family members, jobs, favorite places to visit, and the times of different events in the city—any data stored by Black Knight or available on the Internet.

At the same time, Naomi reduced the output of the sun itself, causing a worldwide famine. Car driving became essential for most Mikes, the only way to get enough light to survive. As the generations passed, evolution again made its mark, favoring those who did it well with health and offspring, and weeding out those who couldn't compete. As a group, the Mikes became experts at anticipating and predicting when and where customers would want a car.

Most of those millions of car booths were just simulations, little more than video games, there to create competition and increase skill. The best of them, however, unbeknownst to the Mikes, directed the real cars on the streets of New York City.

The results were staggering, even to Naomi. Whenever she wanted to drive anywhere, she found that the Mikes had anticipated her. No sooner did she press the button on her app to summon a car than one would pull up to the curb. Sometimes the reason was obvious—she always drove to work at this time of day—but on other occasions, she had no idea what cue they had used to predict her desires. It was easy to feel like they were reading her mind.

As more and more customers used their service, Brandon poured their profits back into the company, buying new cars and expanding. She and Brandon were the only two profit-sharing employees of the company, though they also employed a cadre of automotive engineers to install the sensors and steering controls, and retained a lawyer, a PR firm, and a financial consultant. They talked about the possibility of buying their own repair shop instead of using outside mechanics, to keep costs low and make sure their work was prioritized. Naomi was the only developer. She wrote and maintained their apps for use in multiple mobile devices, tracked usage and analytics, and, of course, monitored the Mikes as they drove the cars.

Despite paying out relatively few salaries, costs were not low. The cars themselves were expensive to buy, of course, as was parking most of them outside the city at night. The electric bill to recharge them added up as well. Their largest expense, however, was the immense and growing amount of cloud computing bandwidth the Mikes' world required.

She had hoped that by reducing the strength of the sun, she would retard their rapid growth somewhat, but the opposite had proved true. Less sunlight meant more acreage was required to support each Mike. Faced with this fact, they had expanded their world even faster, not to increase in number but to spread out to more land. She could increase the sunlight, of course, but that didn't help either. More sunlight supported a larger population, which would spawn faster, and thus need more space. Either way, the Mikes benefited by growing.

There was nothing for it but to pay the cost. She hadn't told Brandon about the Mikes or how it all worked, but he believed her that the computing bandwidth was necessary. Still, it couldn't go on forever. They would have to contain the world. One way would be to build their own data center instead of buying it from an external company, thus limiting its size. The Mikes couldn't grow into computers that didn't exist. That would be far more expensive in the near term, however, far beyond their capabilities, and would involve hiring a lot more staff.

No, the real answer was much simpler. She hated to contemplate it, but really, it was the obvious solution. A large percentage of the Mikes would have to die. She could kill off the worst of the drivers, but it might be best to kill them randomly, so as not to eliminate too much diversity.

Her earlier thoughts about sapience came back to haunt her. If they were intelligent, self-aware beings, wouldn't it be wrong of her to end their lives? If that were the case, however, wasn't she responsible for ending their lives all the time? She had created the world with limited resources, so that only a limited number of Mikes could survive. Millions of them had died already. Without that competition, however, they never could have developed whatever level of intelligence they possessed. It was the cycle of life and death that had caused them to become who they were.

She was their god, and the ethics of godhood were invariably sticky. Was it wrong for her to take their lives when she had created them to begin with? Ultimately, if she didn't cull their numbers, they would surpass her ability to pay for their data usage, and their entire world would be destroyed. The death of some was a necessary sacrifice, one unavoidable if their race were to survive.

It reminded her of a story by Theodore Sturgeon called "Microcosmic God." She'd read it as a child, and it was a true dinosaur as far as science fiction went, written more than eighty years earlier. In the story, a scientist created a microscopic creature with a very short lifespan and guided its evolution. He acted as their god and forced them to spend generations making new inventions for him, maintaining his authority by killing off half their population whenever they disobeyed him.

Was that who she had become? In the story, the scientist was not presented as a villain, but she had found his actions chilling. She considered this step necessary, but if the Mikes were ever to become aware of her actions, would they agree? Would they consider her a benevolent god or a devil?

It didn't matter. It had to be done, and really, it was better to do it sooner than later, before the cost of maintaining their world drove Black Knight into bankruptcy. If she was their god, then she would act like one. It was time for her to send a plague.

In the end, she couldn't do it. She wrote the script that would decimate their population, but she just couldn't execute it. These were her children. Intellectually, she still didn't think the Mikes had reached sapience, but the tenuousness of the distinction made it hard to put it out of her mind. Emotionally, they were important to her, and she projected onto them feelings and dreams that she couldn't shake, even if she didn't think those feelings really existed. If they did have emotions, they would have learned to communicate them, wouldn't they? But they didn't. They communicated practical information, but they didn't write poetry or express love. They tried to live because evolution favored beings that wanted to live. It didn't mean they mourned.

She slept poorly that night, knowing that soon, qualms or not, she would have to run the script. And as time passed and their population grew, she would have to run it again. She could reduce their birthrate, of course, but it was through the process of having offspring that the evolutionary improvement worked. She could only slow their growth so much without ruining the framework that made them develop. They had to keep growing in order to advance. Which meant she would have to regularly murder them.

It was in this dark frame of mind, in the middle of the night with no one to share her thoughts with, that she went searching for news about Tyler.

She discovered almost immediately that he had moved to Seattle. The other side of the country. Without even a note to say goodbye. Of course, that wasn't fair, since she had ignored every call from him and deleted messages unread for weeks after the accident, until he'd stopped trying. But . . . Seattle?

She dug deeper and discovered he was working for that court case, the one with the motorcyclist killed by a self-driving car. Not only that—he was working for the *plaintiff*, trying to prove the car's manufacturer was to blame. Why would he do that? Was it just for the money?

The principal lawyer on the case, Lauren Karelis, was easier to find. Hundreds of articles and videos featured her answering questions about the case or her client. She was beautiful in a glamorous way Naomi never would be, with feminine gestures, a gleaming white smile, and salon-perfect blonde hair like a curly picture frame around her carefully made-up face. That's who Tyler was working with, instead of her.

But she didn't want to work with him. Did she? Naomi sighed and lay back on her bed, looking up at the cracked and dingy ceiling. This was stupid. She wanted to forget him and everything about him. All searching him out did was remind her of pain and loss. She was moving on with her life, a new life. So why was she looking him up in the middle of the night?

She switched instead to pictures of Abby. There were thousands, captured at all ages, stretching back to Abby at two years old, piling stuffed animals on top of an infant Naomi in her swing, when Naomi had been too small even to reach out and grab hold of them. The images flashed past on her glasses, first the older two-dimensional ones, then the modern stereo shots, which the glasses rendered to make it look like she was standing in the room. Thousands of snapshots and thousands of videos: piano recitals and dance recitals and birthday parties and the playground near their house, Christmases and playing dress-up and making snow forts and putting on puppet shows.

Finally, for the first time since the accident, she cried. The tears came haltingly at first, choking her, until she couldn't hold them back any more, and they overwhelmed her, like a river overflowing its banks, unstoppable. She could hardly breathe, the sobs tearing unbidden from deep in her lungs. She raged, lashing out at the bedsheets, and then curling up in a ball until the tears ran their course. Eventually, she slept.

When she woke, it was with a clarity and determination she hadn't felt in weeks. She would never kill the Mikes. They had limited lifespans, yes, set by the parameters she had written, but that came with the world they lived in. Mortality was part of life. Regardless of whether they were sapient, she would never reach out and kill them directly. They might not mourn, but she couldn't cut their lives short, not even to save them all. There had to be another way to preserve their world.

She washed her face and dressed for work. She climbed into a Black Knight car that pulled up to the curb just as she stepped out of her apartment. She hardly thought about it anymore. She checked her mail as she rode, trusting a Mike in a booth somewhere in her Realplanet simulation to transport her safely to the office.

Brandon had subleased five hundred square feet of office space on the fiftieth floor of an office building in the financial district, near the Department of Transportation headquarters. Two thirds of the space was cluttered with various electronics boards and components Naomi couldn't identify, which Brandon continued to tinker with, trying to improve the design of their cars. Naomi's desk was by a window, with a high-end development machine and a very comfortable chair.

They didn't talk much. Naomi rarely talked anyway, of course, and her work captured all of her attention. Brandon, however, was moody, sometimes on the top of the world, sometimes kicking electronics across the room. He always seemed balanced at the edge of rage, and it didn't take much to push him over. A lot of the time, he was out of the office anyway, lobbying officials for permits, or overseeing work on their cars, or else just working out at the gym. When he was in, Naomi kept her head low and stayed out of his way.

She arrived that morning to find another desk next to hers, with another computer and another young woman sitting in front of it. She stood when Naomi came in. The absurd thought flitted through Naomi's mind that she had walked into the wrong office.

The woman was Asian, with straight black hair, a form-fitting black dress, long legs, and black high heels. Brandon, standing next to her, wore a black suit jacket over a tight black T-shirt that showed off his increasingly muscled build. Together, they looked like a funeral.

"Naomi, I'd like you to meet Min-seo Cho. I hired her to help you with the software development work."

Naomi just stared, panicking inside. "I don't need any help."

"You do a great job," Brandon said smoothly. "But the company's growing, and a lot of the work falls on you. I know you've been putting in some late nights, trying to make things more efficient, keep costs down. Min-seo just graduated from Columbia with top marks in computer science and a particular interest in AI. You two are going to have a lot to talk about."

The office had never felt small to Naomi before, but now the

walls seemed to be closing in. She hated any kind of confrontation, but she hated even worse the idea of this woman delving
into the Black Knight software and discovering how it all really
worked. It was *her* software, her simulation, her secret world.
"You didn't even ask me."

"I don't have to ask you," Brandon said. She could hear the
ever-present anger there, simmering under his words. "This is
my company, and I decide who to hire. Min-seo is here to stay.
Make her feel welcome."

Naomi looked at Min-seo, really looked at her, for the first
time. She seemed nervous, her eyes wide and fingers clasped
hesitantly together. She had probably bought that outfit to look
nice for her first day of work, in her first job since graduating.
She wanted to impress, to fit in. Naomi didn't want her to feel
welcome, but she probably should avoid telling her to her face
that she wasn't wanted.

"Could I talk to you alone?" she asked Brandon.

He scowled and strode toward her, and for a crazy moment
she thought he was going to hit her. Instead, he grabbed her arm
and propelled her out the door and into the hallway, closing the
door behind them. "What's wrong with you?" he said. "I just
hired her. You could at least be nice."

"I don't want someone else. She'll only get in the way."

"I need redundancy. You're the only person who knows how
this all works. What if you were hit . . ." He paused, realizing
what he had been about to say. "What if something happened?
What if you won the lottery and quit? The whole company
would go under. I need more than one person to understand
how this software works."

"I can't explain it to her."

"Oh, you're so special? Nobody else is as smart as you?"

"That's not it. It's just, the software—it's unique. I've been
working with it for so long, and nobody else—"

"There's nobody else in the world who can do what you do? Is that really what you're saying?"

"Yes. I mean, maybe Tyler, but—"

Brandon pounded his fist on the door so hard she jumped. "Not Tyler. Not ever. You hear that? He killed her, Naomi. I won't hire him; I won't even talk to him. I never want to see his face again."

"I wasn't saying—"

"You know what? I'm done with this conversation. You're going to work with this woman whether you like it or not. You're going to explain everything to her, enough that she can back you up and help you. Who knows? She might even be smarter than you."

Brandon flung the door open hard enough that it bounced off the wall and caromed back again. He stormed into the room and sat down at his own desk without a glance at either of them. Naomi followed him inside and crossed to Min-seo, who still stood where they had left her.

Naomi held out her hand. "I'm sorry," she said. "You took me by surprise. I'm Naomi. Apparently we're going to be working together."

CHAPTER 16

T yler's suit itched. Lauren had bought it for him, and though he hadn't seen the price, he was pretty sure it was the most expensive outfit he'd ever worn. It fit perfectly, so his discomfort probably had less to do with the suit than with his nervousness about giving testimony in court. He and Lauren had practiced until he could deliver his responses confidently, but practice was very different from the real thing.

He sat in the front row of the audience, waiting for his turn in the witness box. Just in front of him, Lauren sat at the plaintiff's table with Andrea Copeland, whose long-sleeved blouse concealed the tattoos covering her arms. He had never seen a more intense woman. Copeland sat straight up and glared at the man in the witness box as if she could bore a hole through his head with her gaze. She didn't move, but it was a stillness full of energy, like a coiled spring.

The courtroom looked newly renovated: clean and bright,

but bare. The only decoration was the American flag standing to the left of the judge. White walls featured not so much as a clock to break the monotony. Instead of benches, the audience sat in rows of folding chairs. Judge Carter, at least, sat on a traditional-looking wooden platform, and glossy oak railings separated the audience from the lawyers and the lawyers from the jury. Tyler had never been in court before, but the whole effect was much more modern and spare than he had expected.

The man in the witness box, a Mercedes-Benz executive named Tom Berkowitz, raised his right hand and swore to tell the truth, the whole truth, and nothing but the truth. He didn't look at Andrea Copeland.

Lauren stood and walked around the table with a light step, as if questioning Berkowitz was the highlight of her morning. And maybe it was. After three days of trial, today would be the day that made the case for the plaintiff, one way or another. Lauren had already established the emotional touchpoints of the case, interviewing people who could speak to the character of the dead motorcyclist: his impeccable driving record, his concern for others, his tenderness for children and puppies. It had disgusted Tyler a little, since it was a purely emotional appeal, with little to do with fault. It shouldn't matter, in the eyes of the law, whether Andrea and Hal had talked about having a baby someday, and now they never would. It made the tragedy sad. But it didn't affect the question of whether Mercedes was responsible.

Today, probably the last day of the trial, Lauren would try to establish responsibility. Even though he was about to testify on her behalf, Tyler found himself torn. It seemed to him that Annabelle Brighton's car had responded reasonably, if not perfectly, and that no human driver could have done better. He wanted the public to trust self-driving cars, not fear them. On the other hand, Mercedes was hiding things from their consumers, important things that directly affected their safety.

Those choices could mean lives lost, regardless of whether Hal Copeland's had been one of them.

He was ready to speak up, if he had to. If Berkowitz told the truth, Tyler's testimony probably wouldn't even be necessary. If he lied, however, as they thought he might, Tyler was going to take the stand and reveal it to the world.

"Mr. Berkowitz," Lauren said, "could you begin by explaining to the court what your responsibilities are at Mercedes-Benz?"

"Certainly," Berkowitz said. He had a salesman's voice and larger-than-life smile. "I'm the engineering director for the F 015 series, our self-driving model. I'm responsible for making sure we deliver the best quality, safety, and luxury experience to our customers every day."

The trial was televised, and it occurred to Tyler that depending on how this turned out, this could represent a lot of free publicity for Mercedes. Berkowitz certainly talked like a walking commercial.

"Does your responsibility include the software that drives the car?"

"Our software is developed in-house, and there's a team dedicated to that task, but yes, they report to me."

"Has the software team ever been late for a milestone? Ever failed to deliver software on time?"

Berkowitz smiled indulgently. "Every software development effort in the world misses milestones from time to time."

Lauren looked confused. "Everyone? In the whole world? How do you know?"

His smile faltered. "I just mean it's common."

"Mr. Berkowitz, I'm not asking you about every software development effort in the world. I'm asking you about yours. Please restrict your answers to things about which you actually have knowledge. Has your software team ever been late for a milestone?"

"Yes, of course."

"And what did you do in those circumstances?"

"I encouraged them to catch up. I discussed with them the obstacles to timely completion, and encouraged extra effort, including overtime, if necessary."

"You didn't encourage them to cut corners, skip tests, lower standards?"

"Certainly not."

The attorney for the defense, Philip Sullivan, a middle-aged white man with the physique of a football player, came lazily to his feet to object. "Inflammatory, your honor. These questions are prejudicial. Mr. Berkowitz is not on trial for his personal work ethic."

"Your honor," Lauren said. "The witness is representing Mercedes-Benz in this trial. If he is aware of unethical practices, that speaks directly to the reliability of the software that killed Mr. Copeland."

"Sustained," the judge intoned. "Ms. Karelis, if you have evidence of such practices, you may ask him about them, but this is not a fishing expedition."

Judge Carter was big and white and red-faced, much like Sullivan, the defense attorney. Tyler had no reason to believe they knew each other, but if he'd been told the two were old high school football buddies, he would have believed it in an instant. For the whole trial so far, Carter had sustained Sullivan's objections while overruling Lauren's, like a local referee siding with the home team.

"Yes, your honor." Lauren accepted the ruling with good grace and turned back to Berkowitz. "Are you aware of the Mercedes F 015 ever being hacked?"

Tyler worked to keep his expression neutral. This was the question he'd been waiting for, the point where things would get exciting, but he didn't want to tip off the other side.

Berkowitz donned a comfortable smile. "It depends what you mean by 'hacked.' Since the very beginning, Mercedes-Benz has encouraged security testing by the public. We've offered a 'bug bounty'—a cash reward for any software defects identified by people who are not employees of Mercedes-Benz. We're particularly interested in security holes, ways in which clever perpetrators might subvert the usual controls."

"You encourage people to hack your cars."

"That's a dramatic way to put it, but yes. All the major automotive companies do it. If thousands of people try to hack our software to earn the cash, and they can't, then we feel pretty confident nobody can do it in secret for any other purpose either."

"And has anyone ever collected on this 'bug bounty'?"

"Oh, yes. Mostly tiny things, problems with the entertainment system, or whatever. In the early days, when we were first fielding these cars, there were a few security holes, but not anymore. We've been through twenty version upgrades without any serious vulnerability."

"But you don't make your code available to these bounty hunters? You don't actually let them see the software they're trying to poke holes in?"

"Oh, no." Berkowitz chuckled. "This is a business. We can't just give it away, any more than we give away our cars."

"So you consider this software proprietary. You protect it as a trade secret."

"I'm afraid so."

Lauren ran a hand through her hair, nonchalant. "And have you ever included security holes intentionally? Purposely included interfaces to allow for remote control of your cars?"

"Of course not."

"Never? Not even in response to a particular request, such as to give law enforcement the ability to stop vehicles on demand?"

The question provoked a buzz of conversation from the audience. The defense attorney leaped to his feet. "Objection. Assumes facts not in evidence."

"I'm not assuming anything," Lauren said. "I'm asking the witness."

Sullivan stood. "Your honor, no evidence has been presented to the court to suggest any such idea. Counsel is attempting to plant unwarranted fantasies into the minds of the jury."

"Sustained," the judge said. "The question is stricken from the record."

He glared a warning at Lauren, who, clearly frustrated, tried again. "Mr. Berkowitz. Have you ever included in your software, or instructed anyone on your team to include, the capability for the government to stop or take remote control of cars without the permission or knowledge of the owner?"

"Your honor," Sullivan said, leaping to his feet again, his tone aggrieved, "this is the same question. Counsel is testifying."

"Sustained," the judge said. "Stricken. Ms. Karelis, you are putting words in the witness's mouth." He turned to the jury box. "Members of the jury, you are instructed to disregard the question. What counsel says is not evidence. You are not to regard any implications she makes as facts, nor accept as evidence anything not stated by the witness."

"Your honor!" Lauren said. "This is not fishing. I'm asking the witness to answer a simple yes or no question. If there is no truth to it, let him say so."

"I've already ruled, Counselor," the judge growled. "Ask a new question or sit down."

That's when Tyler saw it. A look, barely a glance, passed between Berkowitz and Judge Carter. It was over in a moment, and even caught on camera, would be evidence of nothing. But when Tyler saw it, he knew. There had been *communication* in that glance. A shared knowledge. Carter wasn't just taking

Sullivan's side because he liked him, or because he was a man. Mercedes had him in their pocket.

Lauren struggled with her facial expression and got it under control. She paused for a moment, and then tried a third time. "Mr. Berkowitz. To the best of your ability, have you sought to make it impossible for anyone outside of one of your cars to seize control of it?"

Berkowitz looked at Judge Carter.

"You may answer the question," the judge said.

"Yes," Berkowitz said. "Of course we have."

"No more questions, your honor," Lauren said.

Sullivan avoided the subject of remote control on cross-examination, and Lauren waived the chance to ask more questions on redirect, choosing instead to proceed to her next witness. "The plaintiff calls Mr. Tyler Daniels to the stand."

Tyler stood, feeling the eyes of the courtroom on him. The overhead lights seemed suddenly bright. The witness box, as he approached, seemed a lot bigger and more exposed than it had from the audience. He sat, surprised to see that the box contained only a simple folding chair.

Lauren smiled reassuringly at him as the bailiff swore him in. He raised his right hand, wondering idly when they had stopped using Bibles to swear in witnesses. He had seen a million courtroom dramas, had imagined himself doing this, but now that he was here, he was a lot more intimidated than he'd expected. He wasn't a passive observer anymore. He was right in the middle of it.

She started easy, with his name and degrees in computer science from Penn. She asked him to describe the code as it had been received from Mercedes, and the steps he and Yusuf had taken to make it comprehensible.

"So, the source code you received was not as it would have been written by software developers?" she asked.

"No," Tyler said. "Not at all. When people write software, they give names to things. A function might be called 'Determine Tailgating Distance,' which would calculate the distance between the car's front bumper and the next car. That function would have many pieces of data in it, like the returns from the lidar system, or the time required to get an acoustic reflection, and all of those pieces of data would have names."

"And were those names included in the source code you received?"

"No. All the names were changed, to names like aaaaa, aaaab, aaaac, etcetera. Names without meaning."

"And it couldn't have been programmed that way?"

"Not possible," Tyler said. "And there would be no reason to. Names are the only way we know what something does. The computer doesn't care—it can operate the code either way. It doesn't care what we call it. But humans need names to provide meaning."

After asking permission to approach the witness, Lauren produced a document and handed copies to the court recorder, Judge Carter, Sullivan, and finally to Tyler. "Do you recognize this exhibit?" Lauren asked.

"Yes."

"Would you please tell the court what it is?"

"It's a small excerpt of the Mercedes software. On the left side is the obfuscated version as we were given it. On the right side are explanations I've made by assigning meaningful names and adding comments."

Lauren turned to the bench. "Your honor, we request permission to show plaintiff's exhibit number five to the jury."

Sullivan stood up. "Your honor, we have never seen this exhibit before."

At this close range, Tyler could see the twinge of annoyance in Lauren's eyes, but she kept her countenance serene. "Of course you've seen it," she said. "*You* provided it to *me* in discovery."

"The original code, yes," Sullivan said. "Not this edited version. Your employee's changes to the software are inadmissible."

"He didn't *change* the software. He annotated it for clarity because your client—"

"Counselors," the judge barked.

Lauren turned back to the bench. "Sorry, your honor. This exhibit is not a discovery violation. The annotations are a visual aid for the testimony Mr. Daniels is about to give."

"Approach the bench, both of you," the judge said.

As the lawyers walked over to stand in front of the judge, an aide flipped a switch to pipe white noise over the speaker system, masking the sidebar conversation. Closer than most, Tyler could hear the general tone and pick out a few words, but not actually follow the exchange. He heard the pitch of Lauren's voice get higher, angry but trying to control it. When the aide turned the white noise off, Lauren stalked back to her table, her face flushed.

The judge tapped his gavel to quiet the court, which had dissolved into idle chatter while the sidebar was going on. "To establish a clear differentiation between evidence and expert opinion, the annotated material supplied by Mr. Daniels will not be admitted as evidence or published to the jury. Counsel will supply the jury with only the evidentiary portion. Mr. Daniels may then supply his opinion verbally, through direct examination."

Tyler gaped at him, amazed. It was worse than unfair. Not only had the judge permitted Mercedes to supply obfuscated code, he wasn't even allowing Tyler's unobfuscated version to be shown to the jury. It would have been hard enough to explain clearly named logic to a jury unfamiliar with programming. This way, it would be next to impossible.

Lauren made her way along the jurors' box, savagely tearing copies of the exhibit in half and handing the left half to each of the jurors. She returned to her table and dropped the stack of right halves with a bitter flourish.

For the next half hour, she led Tyler through an explanation of the code. It was a short segment, about twenty lines long, that was the core of the module that would allow police or federal agents to take control of a car remotely. Making that clear, however, was a tedious exercise.

"And the next variable, named abkwbj," Lauren asked. "In the course of your analysis, what name did you assign to this data?"

Tyler could see the jurors losing attention, their eyes glazing over as they attempted to keep track of what he was telling them. At this point, Lauren might as well forget the code and just ask Tyler for the punchline. She had wanted to show them the code and get them to understand it, arguing that it would have more impact if they could see for themselves what it did. She said juries appreciated when you respected their intelligence. Without the annotations, however, Tyler was afraid the strategy would backfire. They wouldn't understand it all, and might not trust that Tyler did either.

Finally, they finished reconstructing the meaning of the code. "Can you summarize for us, then: what does this software do?" Lauren asked.

"Every time through the primary loop—the loop during which the software checks all the sensors, reevaluates the current state of the car, and decides what to do next—a check is made for inputs from the satellite radio system, which is intended for entertainment and navigational aids."

"Why would the primary loop have to make such a check?"

"It wouldn't, not normally. It means the programmers expected input from the antenna that would make a difference in its decision-making."

"And looking at the code in front of you, what difference in decision-making does a signal from that antenna make?"

"It's a complete override. It replaces whatever decisions the AI might make with instructions from the outside. It's a way to remotely control the car through the satellite radio."

It had taken them longer than planned to get to this point, but they got the reaction they wanted. The courtroom exploded into noise. Tyler could feel the cameras on his face, like a bright sun on a hot day. This would make the evening news, he was pretty sure. Mercedes might have bought the judge, but they couldn't control the jury. They still had a chance at this.

Lauren took her seat. "No more questions, your honor."

Judge Carter declared a recess before cross-examination. When they reconvened, Sullivan dropped his lazy act and paced in front of the defense table like a leopard eager to escape its cage. When Carter prompted him to begin, Sullivan veered toward the witness box and attacked.

"Mr. Daniels, do you have any evidence that Ms. Brighton's car was controlled remotely by a shadowy government agency and crashed into Mr. Copeland's vehicle on purpose?"

"No."

"Do you have evidence that any external agency was directly involved in causing the fatal crash?"

"No."

"Do you have any evidence that *any* Mercedes car has ever, on any occasion, been controlled remotely for any purpose?"

"No."

"So the software you were at such pains to explain to us, however interesting, has no bearing on the death of Mr. Copeland."

Tyler smiled. They had laid a trap for Sullivan, and he had just blundered right into it. "On the contrary," he said. "That code had everything to do with it. It requires the software to repeatedly check the satellite radio for signals during the crucial processing cycle when split-second decisions are made. That secret remote control slowed down the car's reaction times, and was therefore directly responsible for Mr. Copeland's death."

Sullivan gaped, completely blindsided. He opened his mouth to ask another question, and then closed it again.

"Mr. Sullivan?" the judge prompted.

"I'm here," he snapped, angry now. "Mr. Daniels, you claim the slowdown was responsible for the crash. Do you have any evidence that this is the case?"

"You mean, would Mr. Copeland have lived if the car's algorithm hadn't lost those critical few moments? That I can't say. No one will ever know that for certain, because it didn't happen."

Sullivan's voice dripped with scorn. "So this is just speculation on your part?"

"The primary loop is wasting time checking for input from the satellite radio. That's not speculation."

Sullivan locked eyes with him, and a small smile played across his face. "Mr. Daniels, have you ever worked professionally as a software developer?"

"I've contributed significantly to the open source software community. I've written code for projects that are used professionally in corporations around the world."

"But have you ever worked as an employee for a company, writing software?"

"No. But thousands of professional software developers—"

"Restrict your comments to answering the questions I ask, please, Mr. Daniels. Have you ever written software for an employer?"

"No."

"In fact"—Sullivan made a show of examining his notes—

"working for Ms. Karelis is the first job you've held since leaving school, isn't it?"

"Yes. But in the software world—"

"How old are you, Mr. Daniels?"

"Objection!" Lauren stood smoothly to her feet. "Your honor, how is the witness's age relevant?"

"Plaintiff's counsel has presented this man as an expert witness," Sullivan said. "I'm exploring the breadth and duration of his expertise."

"Overruled," the judge said. "The witness may answer the question."

"I'm the same age Page and Brin were when they wrote the Google search algorithm," Tyler said. "I'm older than Mark Zuckerberg was when he started Facebook. I'm older than Evan Spiegel—"

"Just the number, please," Sullivan said.

Tyler stared at him, defiant. "I'm twenty-four."

It surprised him how much that stung. Sullivan had asked the question to call attention to his youth, but to Tyler, twenty-four was old. Zuckerberg and Spiegel had dropped out of college to start their companies. They'd been billionaires by Tyler's age. Page and Brin started Google as PhD students at Stanford. Yotta Cars had been Tyler's ticket into that world. Instead, he was here, interpreting somebody else's obfuscated code in a lawyer's back room. He felt like his dreams had passed him by.

"Did you ever plan to start a company?" Sullivan asked.

Tyler couldn't answer for a moment. Could the man read his thoughts? Was he intentionally rubbing his face in his failures? "Yes," he said.

"What was that company?"

"A transportation service company, using self-driving cars."

"And why were your plans abandoned?"

Tyler took a deep breath. "Brandon Kincannon, the other founder, decided to break our association."

"And why was that?"

Lauren came to his rescue with an objection. "Your honor, the question calls for speculation. Mr. Daniels can't be expected to speak to the motivations of another person."

For once, the judge sustained her objection, and Sullivan tried again. "Didn't your plans fail because of a demonstration of your software that went badly wrong?"

"That was part of it, yes."

"Isn't it true that your software was incompetently written?"

"No, that's not true. It was—"

"So badly written that your cars killed a young woman?"

"No! We were hacked! My software was fine."

"Fine? Your software instructed four cars to drive at top speed through the body of a twenty-one-year-old girl. You think that was fine?"

"No!"

"Do you think someone would want to hire a programmer who wrote software like that?"

"No. Yes. I mean—"

"Do you think this court should accept as a software expert someone whose software—"

"Objection!" Lauren shouted. The judge looked at her, but she seemed uncertain what objection to make. "Counsel is badgering the witness," she said finally.

"Overruled," the judge replied. "Counselor, repeat your question for the court."

Sullivan smiled and spoke in a softer voice. "Do you think, Mr. Daniels, that this court should accept as an expert witness someone whose autocar software was so badly written that it killed a young woman during a staged demonstration of its capabilities?"

Tyler took a deep breath. Lauren had warned him about this, about getting caught up in the rhythm of the opposing attorney's questions. He was supposed to take his time, think clearly, answer calmly. "I am an educated and experienced software professional," he said. "Everything I have said about the Mercedes code is not a matter of opinion, but of fact."

"No further questions, your honor."

Lauren did her best to repair the damage on redirect, giving Tyler a chance to describe the software he had written and the places it was currently in use, but he doubted it would do much good. Once the jury had heard that his software had killed a young woman, they wouldn't hear much else. It's not like they understood the code themselves.

When it was finally over, he stumbled back to his seat, feeling battered, as if he'd been in a boxing match instead of a trial. He had been Lauren's last witness. The defense would now call witnesses of their own, probably including some expert with impeccable credentials from a software consulting firm who hadn't written a line of code in ten years but was willing to swear blind that Tyler had gotten it wrong.

The judge called an end to testimony for the day. The defense would begin calling witnesses in the morning. Tyler walked out of the courtroom with Lauren into a crowd of five or six reporters, shoving microphones in their faces. Andrea Copeland had already plowed through them without comment and was leaving the scene on her motorcycle. Lauren answered a few questions and then pushed on through, but Tyler stopped. If they weren't going to win the case, at least he could speak his mind.

"Don't trust software," he said. "Or any other company, for that matter. Don't put your lives in the hands of any software the authors won't let you read for yourself."

"Are self-driving cars a death trap?" one of the reporters asked.

"No," Tyler said, letting some heat flow into his voice. "But I'll tell you what is. Every time you get in car with a human behind the wheel, that's a death trap. We might not be able to cure cancer or heart disease, but we can cure this killer, and it takes almost as many lives. Self-driving cars are the future, and Mercedes has that much right. It's not putting a computer behind the wheel that's the problem. It's keeping the software controlling it a secret."

Another reporter said, "Do you think the government should force companies to turn over their software?"

Lauren stopped and turned to watch him, but she didn't seem upset. "I think the people should," he said. "People shouldn't buy cars from companies that won't open-source their software. If your car is going to choose to kill you in certain circumstances—to avoid a pedestrian, for instance—you should know about it. And you should certainly know about it if there's an interface in place that lets somebody else take control."

"Won't giving out the code just make it easier for hackers?" the first reporter asked.

"Not at all," Tyler said. "It'll make it so that any vulnerabilities are found quickly and patched."

Lauren made a show of looking at her watch, so Tyler waved off the reporters and pushed his way through. They threw more questions at him as he went, and when it was clear he wasn't going to answer any more, they pressed business cards into his hand and encouraged him to call.

He joined Lauren in her Tesla, the inside of which looked more like a conference room than a car, the four seats facing each other around a small round table. It navigated the steep Seattle streets without incident while he and Lauren rested in the back. They rode in silence. Tyler gazed out the window at the glimpses of Puget Sound occasionally visible between the buildings, not really registering the sight. The interaction with the reporters had left him dissatisfied. Was it fair for him to denounce Mercedes? They were, after all, doing the exact same thing that all the other autocar companies were doing. They all kept their software proprietary, and he would guess that most, if not all, had that same hook to allow Homeland Security, or whoever was paying the bills, the power to take over a car when they chose.

All through this trial, he'd struggled with the feeling that he was fighting on the wrong side. How could he tell people not to ride in a Mercedes autocar when it was so much safer than driving any kind of car on their own? The industry already struggled with the perception that humans were better drivers than computers. If there were an alternative, a company that was leading the way toward an open software revolution, then it would make sense, but there wasn't.

And that, he realized, was why he was fighting this battle. Because "trust me" would go only so far. It was possible to have a transportation industry that was efficient and safe. But that would take an educated public that understood self-driving cars were safer and demanded the transparency to know how they made their decisions. The safety of computer precision with the control of human oversight. It would happen that way if consumers wanted it. And they would demand it only if they understood what was at stake.

When it came down to it, Tyler didn't care whether Andrea Copeland got a big payday in compensation for her husband's death. He did care about stopping the horrible death toll that human driving exacted from the population each year. He cared about big companies hiding things from their consumers that could cost them their lives, and paying off judges to protect their reputations.

And now that he realized what he wanted, he knew exactly what to do about it.

"No, it's not an exclusive," Tyler said. "I'm telling all the networks, and you'll all get it at the same time. You can skip it if you want. I'm just giving you a heads up."

Every reporter he'd called had said the same thing. They wanted an exclusive. It wasn't going to be worth their while to show up with such scant information, and couldn't he tell them more right now? In the end, though, he was confident they would all be there.

Last of all, he called Yusuf. He explained what he wanted to do, and said, "What do you think? Are you in?"

"Okay," Yusuf said.

"You're sure? It's probably illegal, and it's going to get some attention. I can probably swing it without you, though it would be nice to have the help."

"I'm in," Yusuf said. "Let's stick it to them."

Tyler grinned. "Meet you at the office. I'll bring some Chinese and some coffee. I don't think we're going to be getting any sleep tonight."

CHAPTER 17

T om Berkowitz climbed into his silver Mercedes F 015 and told the car to take him to the courthouse for what he sincerely hoped would be the last day of this wretched trial. At least his own testimony was over. That had been an ordeal. Given how much they'd paid Judge Carter, Berkowitz thought he could have made it go a little smoother. A few of that woman lawyer's questions had struck a little too close for comfort.

Why a hot young thing like Lauren Karelis would want to be a lawyer and go to work in a drab-looking gray suit, he couldn't understand. She belonged on stage at a car show next to a red convertible, dressed in a bikini, or at least one of those little black dresses. Instead, she stood there in the courtroom all day, and he had to try to answer her questions without being distracted by her ass every time she turned to face the jury. They shouldn't let women ask questions in court. At least not sexy ones. It wasn't fair to the witness.

He closed his eyes and was just starting to imagine what he would do to her if he got her alone and out of that suit, when the car's entertainment system blared on at top volume. He thrashed in sudden terror, eyes flying open, heart pounding out of his chest. The music turned off as quickly as it had started. He looked from side to side, breathing hard, the flight reaction still surging through his veins.

Then the windshield wipers turned on, making him jump again. For once, it actually wasn't raining in this perpetually damp city, and the wipers scraped unpleasantly on the dry glass. "Mercedes, turn off the wipers," he told the car, and the wipers stopped.

A moment later, however, the heater turned on full blast, and the turn signals ticked on, first left, then right, then left again. The rear wiper surged to life, and then the music again. This time, it changed radio stations erratically, the ear-splitting volume making his head pound. "Turn it off!" he shouted. "Mercedes, turn the music off."

This time, the car ignored him. He tried to roll the windows down to escape the stifling heat, but the windows wouldn't respond. He changed seats and swiveled around to access the manual controls, but they wouldn't respond. He hit the emergency stop button, but nothing happened. "Mercedes, stop the car," he said. The car accelerated.

Berkowitz started to panic. He fumbled for his phone and dialed 911. The operator came on the line, a calm female voice that said, "Nine-one-one, what's your emergency?"

He hesitated. If he said that his car was out of control, they might send help, but any reporters who listened to police scanners would hear dispatch describe the problem. They would arrive at the scene, ready to film his ignominious rescue, and worse, to report a problem with a Mercedes car just as this embarrassing trial was winding down. Mercedes stock would plummet, and he might very well lose his job.

He cut the connection. There had to be a way to stop this thing without involving the police. Instead, he called Martin, a tech head from back at the office, one of the engineers who really knew how this stuff worked. After four rings, the man finally answered.

"I've got a problem," Berkowitz said, shouting to be heard over the music. "My car's gone crazy. All the systems are going haywire, and I can't stop the thing."

"Hit the emergency stop," Martin said, as if Berkowitz were an idiot. "It's a red button, left-hand side, under the—"

"I know where the emergency stop button is!" Berkowitz snarled. The car blew through a red light and made a hard left, tires screeching. Berkowitz, no longer strapped in, tumbled off his seat and knocked his head on the door handle. He scrambled up again, looking out the window. The car had deviated from his planned route, now heading in the opposite direction from the courthouse.

"I'm being kidnapped!" he shouted into the phone. "You've got to stop them. You can take over my car from there, right?" His voice had gone squeaky with fright, but he didn't care. "Do it. Take over. Stop this before they kill me!"

"Interface already up," Martin said. "Give me five."

"I don't have five minutes, you incompetent—"

"Stand by. Don't be afraid, I'll take care of it."

"I'm not afraid! I'm furious!" Berkowitz could feel the spit flying from his mouth. "If you don't fix this, I'm going to kill you. I'll put you out on the street. I'll make sure you never work in this industry—"

"It's not working," Martin said.

"What do you mean, it's not working?"

"Somebody's already signaling the car, and they're locking me out. I've got no control."

The car accelerated again, and Berkowitz clutched the seat.

"No. Don't you dare give up, Martin. You've got to do something."

"I suggest you call 911, sir."

Berkowitz hung up in disgust. If he lived through this, he would fire that idiot. In the meantime, though, 911 looked like his only option. He was about to call again when the car abruptly braked and turned neatly into a parking lot.

The lot was crowded. Two other Mercedes already stood side by side, and his car smoothly glided into place next to them. Five news vans formed a perimeter, and probably two dozen reporters with cameras and microphones jostled for position around his car. In the Mercedes to his right, that year's brand-new model, sat Judge Carter, blocking his face with one hand and trying to ignore the cameras just outside his window. Berkowitz couldn't see the occupant of the third Mercedes, but he had no doubt that it was Sullivan.

The music blared away, and heat continued to pump from all the vents. He couldn't stay there. There was nothing for it but to get out of the car.

Tyler and Yusuf watched the drama unfold on the news, sitting five miles away in their law office sanctuary. Once the three men exited their vehicles, Tyler wiped the cars' memory and disconnected. The cars probably streamed performance metrics back to their headquarters, but even so, he didn't think there would be any way to prove their involvement. Mercedes would suspect, to be sure, but he doubted they could prove it in a court of law. The TV stations he had called knew, but he doubted they would give him away.

Tyler could barely keep his eyes open, but neither could he tear them away from the screen. The story quickly went national on all the major stations and turned into a social media firestorm. The news channels repeatedly showed Berkowitz in court, denying the existence of a remote control, followed by shots of him in his car, pounding on the windows to be let out. A lot of the public response was anti-autocar, nonsense like "You can't trust a robot to do a person's job," which wasn't surprising. He was pleased to see how many of the comments included the real issue, though, asking why algorithms that made life-and-death decisions for millions should be secretly held in the vaults of big corporations.

Tyler had expected to be flamed online. He had expected his inbox to fill up. He had even expected the visit from the Seattle PD, asking that he answer a few questions. What he hadn't expected was the dozens of calls for interviews from morning talk shows and mega-follower news bloggers. It seemed that everybody knew, or at least assumed, that he had been the one to hack the car. Overnight, he became something of a celebrity.

He accepted all the interviews, and started doing one a night, sometimes more. It was fun. Suddenly, everyone wanted to know what he thought about the self-driving car industry. Mostly, they wanted him to talk about the evils of big business and how terrifying it would be to have your car taken over by someone else. TV ratings came from scaring people, not from talking about solutions. They did let him give his ideas, however, on how to make an open source approach work, and of course, his own blog's followers went through the roof.

He wrote about the details there, guidelines for how to collect and implement a public consensus about the rules that should govern cars' decisions. He conducted polls on his site with ethical questions. Should a car value its own passengers' lives more than others? Should children's lives be valued more than adults? Should law enforcement have the power to take control of a car without its passengers' permission? The answers to the questions weren't right or wrong as much as subject to public opinion. He published statistics about the results. He recommended coding practices and configuration standards that would allow a non-programmer to tell what rules were being implemented in a given software version, without having to take a course in machine learning algorithms. He published articles in major tech magazines.

Yusuf made out well from the publicity, too. He landed a high-paying software development job on Honda's self-driving car team. Before long, he was publishing articles and seemed to be making a name for himself. Tyler just hoped he could manage not to sleep with his boss's wife this time.

As for Andrea Copeland and her suit, investigations into potential conflict of interest on the part of Judge Carter had brought the trial under scrutiny. Rather than face another trial, Mercedes had chosen to settle. Tyler didn't know the amount, but he was sure it must have been substantial. Berkowitz had been fired along with several other scapegoats as Mercedes tried to backpedal from what was turning into a public relations disaster.

Two months after the trial, Tyler answered the phone to hear a voice he'd never expected to hear again.

"Mr. Daniels, this is Aisha al-Mohammad. I've been reading a lot about you lately."

Tyler didn't know what to say. He knew what this call could mean, and he felt his heart beating right through his chest. "You have?"

"What I want to know is, are you willing to put your money where your mouth is?"

"I don't have any money," he said.

She laughed. "I guess I mean my money, then," she said. "And your time, reputation, and hard work."

"What are you suggesting?"

She made a dismissive huff. "You can't guess? I'm offering to invest in your company."

"I don't have a company."

"Stop playing dumb, Tyler. Your friend Brandon needs some competition, and I like your perspective on the open source issue. I'm giving you a chance to start a company of your own, take your ideas and make them real. Do you want it or not?"

He didn't hesitate. "Of course I do."

He could hear the smile over the phone. "Well, then. We have a lot of work to do."

Tyler thought, briefly, of sticking with the name Yotta Cars. He hadn't liked it much when Abby had first suggested it, but the name had grown on him, and he liked the idea that he was continuing what they all had started back at Penn. Ultimately, though, he knew the name wouldn't work. For one thing, Brandon would take it as an intentional provocation, rubbing the tragedy in his face. As far as Tyler knew, Brandon still blamed him for Abby's death, and pretending that Yotta didn't have bad associations would probably not be a sensitive move. Besides that, as in the trial, there was a good chance his detractors would use Abby's death to undermine the reliability of his cars. He needed a new name.

Aisha called several times a week, tracking his progress and giving advice. He soon found he had vastly underestimated the details required to start a new business, especially one of this magnitude. The tax regulations to become a corporation, the insurance required to transport people, the city business license, the license to operate automated equipment, the application to the vehicle-for-hire regulatory authority, contracts for maintenance: all of it was incredibly time-consuming and expensive. Tyler started to think the laws were set up specifically to prevent anyone from opening a business at all.

And that was just the paperwork. Besides that, he had to design an advertising campaign, actually buy and outfit the cars, and write a ton of software.

"You can't do it all yourself," Aisha told him. "That's what money is for. Hire lawyers for the paperwork. Pick an advertising firm. Reserve your time for what you do best."

"I don't know if I'm cut out for this," Tyler said.

"Don't stress," Aisha told him. "I didn't fund you because of your business acumen. Do what you can, and I'll make sure you don't miss anything important. I'm going to come out there and pay you a visit."

"You're coming to Seattle?"

"I have to come out for a family thing anyway. I'll be there tomorrow."

Aisha asked to meet at Highland Park, and she didn't come alone. Accompanying her was a little girl, her thick black hair twisted into pigtails and held with hair ties like tiny clusters of gold balls. A black skirt and a T-shirt with gold lettering that read "Little Miss Sassy" completed the look.

"Tyler, meet my daughter, Jada," Aisha said. "Jada, say hi to Mr. Daniels."

Jada rocked back and forth, swinging a little gold purse by its strap. "Hi."

"Hi, Jada," Tyler said. "How old are you?"

"Five."

Now Tyler understood why she wanted to meet at the park. They walked over to the playground, and Jada climbed and slid and ran around with the other kids while Aisha and Tyler sat on a bench and talked.

"How's it going?" she asked.

"I don't know. Did you see that Brandon published an article trashing my open source architecture for self-driving car software?"

"I didn't see that, no. I did see that he's expanding his service to Philadelphia and Baltimore."

"Yeah, he's a bit ahead of us," Tyler said.

"The article?" Aisha prompted.

"Yeah. Showed up in WIRED magazine this morning. He also did a talk show where he defended his proprietary algorithms as a crucial discriminator for his company. He argued that if he had to make his algorithms public, he'd have no chance against the big corporations."

"It's probably true. Naomi's one of the best; she probably did come up with something that gives Black Knight a competitive advantage. They've got a big market share in New York already, mostly because their pickup time is half what it takes Uber and Lyft, and the price is half what it costs to take a taxi."

"Wait, Naomi? What does Naomi have to do with this?"

"She's Black Knight's chief programmer," Aisha said. "Didn't you know? It's all her software. She wrote all the important parts, would be my guess."

Tyler leaned back, stunned. He felt a keen sense of betrayal, though he couldn't say exactly why. Maybe the fact that Brandon had hired Naomi, but hadn't even asked Tyler. But Brandon's animosity toward him wasn't anything new. No, he felt hurt by Naomi. She had disappeared without a word, and he had let her go, because it seemed clear she needed to be away from anything that reminded her of Abby. Apparently that need didn't extend to Brandon, however. Did they both blame him for Abby's death?

"That wasn't all Brandon said," Tyler added sourly. "He also attacked me personally, said my ideas were born of lack of experience with a real company. 'Hopelessly and dangerously naive' were the words he used."

"Only one way to respond to that," Aisha said. "Start a real company and do it better. Have you come up with a name yet?"

Tyler shook his head. "I was thinking of something that emphasized the self-driving concept," he said. "Like 'Autodriver' or 'Autobot' or something."

Aisha made a sour face.

"What, no good?"

She shook her head. "First of all, 'autobot' is from the *Transformers*. Even if it's not strictly a copyright issue, you'll have everybody thinking Optimus Prime, and I don't think that's the image we want to aim for. Besides which, just 'automated' by itself doesn't sell. Why does automated make it better? Because it's safe? Because it's fast? What is it you want consumers to think of?"

Tyler sighed. "I don't know. The fact that I'm making my algorithms publicly available is a discriminator, hopefully. So maybe something like OpenRide?"

Another face. "Boring."

"OpenShare?"

"Worse. Sounds like a software module, not something you trust to get your kids home from soccer practice."

"SafeRide."

"Better, but still boring. You need something with some zing to it. Something memorable. Safe isn't memorable."

"Bodyguard," Tyler said. "As in, 'Travel everywhere with your own Bodyguard.' The commercials could emphasize how the car would protect you and your loved ones."

"Makes me think of deodorant." She sniffed at her armpit. "Phew. I didn't put on my Bodyguard today."

"You're a hard sell."

Aisha shrugged. "Welcome to capitalism."

They watched Jada clamber around on the playground, joining games with other kids with the ease of a five-year-old. At that age, they didn't even bother to tell each other their names. Clothes and culture and skin color didn't make much difference; they just played together.

"Escargot," Tyler said. "Get it? Car? Go? Escargot?"

"Next you'll tell me the logo will be a snail."

"Sure. A cute, colorful little snail. Kind of a counter-expectations name. You'd expect some kind of fast animal, so a snail is attention-getting."

"Attention-getting, maybe. But snails mean slow. There's no getting around that—it's what people will think of. Besides, the whole 'escargot' image is for elitist white folks. You have to be rich to know what escargot is."

"How about something that communicates speed, then? Dash or Zip or Dart."

"Speedo," Aisha said.

"Now you're just messing with me."

She grinned.

Jada charged up a ramp, holding hands with another little girl. The two of them slid down a slide on their stomachs and fell into a giggling pile at the bottom. A pleasant breeze was blowing, which in Seattle meant that rain wasn't far behind.

"What about Magic Carpet?" Tyler asked.

Aisha paused and looked thoughtful. "Magic Carpet," she said, as if letting the taste of it roll around on her tongue. "Not bad. Definitely better than the others. Got a bit of a racist bent to it, though."

"Racist? What do you mean?"

"It sounds Arab, and there's already a thing about guys in turbans driving taxis. It might sound like you're playing off that stereotype."

"The guys in turbans who drive taxis are mostly Sikhs. They're from India. They're not Arabs at all."

"I think you're better off avoiding a name with any kind of ethnic stereotype vibe. You want something simple, clean, classic."

Tyler threw up his hands. "And just what name would that be?"

"Oh, I don't know." Aisha laughed. "The creative part is your job."

"You just get to veto all my ideas."

"Pretty much."

The rain started, a light shower. Most of the local moms just put up the hoods of their sweatshirts and let the children play. A little rain was no reason to interrupt an outing. Aisha, however, stood and called out to Jada, who, to her credit, came running and took her mother's hand. Jada's pigtails glistened with tiny drops of water.

"This place is fun," she said, with a smile to melt hearts. "Can we come back again tomorrow?"

They ate dinner at an American place, burgers and fries and milkshakes. Jada put away almost an entire quarter-pounder by herself, and used a few French fries as an excuse to down a cup full of ketchup. Tyler made her laugh by putting a dab of ketchup on his nose and trying to lick it off with his tongue.

"How about AuTomato?" he said, after he wiped off his nose with a napkin. "All the cars could be red, and the logo could be a giant tomato."

"You're regressing," Aisha said.

"Roadrunner. We could give them all little 'meep meep' horns."

Aisha rolled her eyes and shook her head.

"What? Roadrunner's really fast. And nothing ever stops . . . him? Her?"

"I'm pretty sure there's a small copyright problem with that plan."

"Hmm. MyDriver. Or MeDrive. Something with chauffeur . . . Chauff? No, too 'rich white guy', right?"

"I don't know what I'm going to do with you."

"Or—hey—they're electric, right? How about Electric Slide?"

"Sure. Or Electric Boogaloo."

"That's the spirit!"

"You are not naming your company Electric Boogaloo," Aisha said, laughing.

Tyler polished off the last of his fries and slurped at the watery Coke at the bottom of his glass. He was feeling good. There were a million ways for this enterprise to fail, but right now, at the beginning, anything was possible.

"Jada," he said. She looked up from the mayonnaise packet she had been flying like an airplane around her cup of milk. "I have a question for you. What do you call something when it's safe and fun and goes really fast?"

Jada swooped the mayonnaise packet over her plate and then up toward the ceiling, as high as she could reach. "Zoom!"

Tyler laughed and then stopped, thoughtful. He glanced at Aisha, who had a considering look that melted into an amused smile. She shrugged, her eyes dancing. "Zoom," she said. "That's actually not half bad."

Tyler held out his hand to shake, and Jada took it. He pumped it gently up and down. "You're hired," he said. "Zoom it is."

Zoom took off as fast as its name. Tyler didn't have Naomi's brilliance, and so his deep learning algorithms didn't perform nearly as well. He had seen the statistics, and he had no idea how she managed to get her cars to anticipate customers' needs like that. What he lacked in the strength of his algorithm, however, he made up with his commitment to public openness. All of his navigation and decision-making software was open source, available to anyone to read or improve, and the public— at least a good number of them—showed their appreciation by choosing Zoom cars to get to where they were going.

Open source software had a long tradition in the industry. Communities of programmers made updates to publicly available code for free, on their own time, or else paid by companies with an interest in seeing the software improved. They checked and tested each other's work and self-organized to generate reliable releases. It blurred the lines between software creators and software users, allowing users with the right skills to add new features to meet their needs, or else to fix bugs that got in their way. Some of the most widely used application platforms, operating systems, and security programs in the world were open source.

The San Francisco Bay Area was the perfect place for such a company, and demand for Zoom cars drove Tyler to expand there before the service in Seattle was more than a few months old. The number of contributors to the project soared as Silicon Valley programmers joined their efforts to help improve their own commutes. The problem was of personal interest to millions, and so thousands added their time and creativity to the project. Tyler found himself just one of many contributors to a piece of software that was rapidly becoming one of the most active in the open source community. He purchased and outfitted new cars by the dozen, but still had trouble keeping up with demand.

Other entrepreneurs started their own services, of course, using the same code base, but Tyler's profits still rolled in. Since the cars from different companies all used the same software, they communicated readily with each other, allowing them not to interfere in wasteful ways. At least for the time being, there were plenty of fares for all, and the software maximized profits for everyone by distributing their cars efficiently. As Brandon's Black Knight expanded along the East Coast to Boston and Atlanta, Zoom expanded along the West Coast to that quintessential of all traffic disasters, Los Angeles.

Everything Tyler touched seemed to turn to gold, and the company grew faster than he would have thought possible. His dream was finally coming true.

CHAPTER 18

At first, Naomi had enjoyed going to work in the dingy little office on the fiftieth floor. Half the time, she was the only one there, she had access to a powerful computing cluster, and the Mikes were doing everything she wanted them to and more. Now, however, her days were filled with her constant and increasingly difficult campaign to keep Min-seo from discovering the Mikes' world. Her unfamiliarity with the code baseline had bought Naomi a little time, but Min-seo was every bit as smart as her résumé promised, and she wouldn't be fooled for long. Naomi's vague responses about the core of the fleet scheduling algorithms weren't going to satisfy her forever.

So far, Naomi had told her it was a proprietary deep learning algorithm, the secret of which was too competition-sensitive to share. If Brandon heard her saying that, however, he would force her to tell, since the whole reason he'd hired Min-seo was to teach her the critical parts of the code that only Naomi understood. Even Brandon didn't know about the Mikes' world and how the AI really worked. He thought she had just written an especially effective but compute-intensive version of the same basic concepts that were in use in algorithms around the world.

The Mikes continued to deliver cars to their customers with creepy prescience. Even Naomi, who knew how it was being done, was disturbed by how often she walked out of a building to find a Black Knight car pulling up to the curb. She herself hadn't decided how long she was going to stay, and yet there was the car, waiting for her.

The customers seemed to appreciate this, at least judging by the way sales increased. Brandon kept expanding their fleet and hiring new people to manage different aspects of the growing business that he could no longer manage himself. He interviewed and hired business developers to bring the concept to other cities, and soon Black Knight cars were transporting customers in Philadelphia, Baltimore, and Washington DC, as well as New York. He popularized the slogan "Where you need it, when you need it." They were mentioned in national news stories at least once a week.

Like any deep learning system, there was no way to describe how the Mikes anticipated the movements of their customers so well. There was no log to dump of possibilities considered or deductions made. Instead, all the metrics of the city's life and movements formed a mesh of numbers, with certain numerical scores chosen because they rose to the top. The Mikes didn't know why they did it. They didn't know the why of anything. They just acted on the options that gave them the best chance at passing on their genes. It was the same behavior that allowed them to exploit their simulated world with such success.

Naomi kept late hours, but she encouraged Min-seo to go home early. "We're not paying you for overtime," she would say. "Go home, eat dinner, see a show. Life isn't all about work. I'll be leaving soon, too." Of course, she never did. Midnight often came and went with Naomi still in the office alone, studying the Mikes and their world, watching for new behaviors and imagining new ways to challenge them. She could do the same thing from her apartment, of course, but her apartment wasn't any more comfortable or inviting. The empty room was like her secret sanctuary in the library had been, once Brandon and Min-seo left for the day. In fact, since it had a lock on the door, it felt even safer.

Which was why she was shocked when, one Friday night after ten o'clock, a key turned in the lock, the office door swung open, and Min-seo walked in.

"I thought I might find you here," she said.

She wore an evening dress, black and flattering, with heels and a thin black purse.

"What are you doing?" Naomi asked.

"I might ask you the same. It's ten at night."

"I'm working," Naomi said. She wanted to curl up and hide. This was her place. This woman didn't belong here.

"If you have that much work to do, you should let me help," Min-seo said. "I'd try to convince you how capable I am, but that's not the problem, is it?"

"I don't know what you're talking about."

"I've been there," Min-seo said. "I found the simulated world you've been hiding. I saw the people who live there, and what you're making them do."

Naomi felt a hot flush of anger and fear spread through her body. "You broke into my account?"

Min-seo tossed her hair. "No, of course not. Mr. Kincannon gave me access. I told him you wouldn't give me the access I needed, so he called the cloud provider, created a new account, and gave me full admin."

"He gave you . . ." Naomi choked on the words before she

could say them. Full administrator rights meant Min-seo could do anything. She had the same power Naomi herself did.

"Don't worry, I won't abuse it," Min-seo said. "'With great power' and all that. And it's brilliant. I can't believe you were able to create such a world. You could have published several times over."

"It's not about that."

"You didn't create this world for driving, did you? That just came after." There was awe in her voice. "What you've got here, it could do anything. You've got a general problem-solving machine. Semi-intelligent algorithms that can learn to do any job, with the right incentive."

"You can't tell anyone about this."

"I understand. This is the biggest proprietary idea ever invented."

"Not just that. You can't tell other employees. You can't tell *Brandon*. If other people find out, there's no telling what they'll do. They'll enslave them. Hurt them."

Min-seo paused. She took a step forward, her heels clicking on the floor, and cocked her head. "You care about them," she said.

Naomi didn't answer.

"The creatures in the simulation. You think they're real."

Naomi shrugged, helpless. "I don't know," she confessed. "I tell myself they don't really think or feel anything, but the arguments all sound hollow to me. I can't make any distinction between us and them that seems to matter."

"Wow," Min-seo said. "Just . . . wow. I have to think about this." She pulled her chair out from behind her desk and sat, elegant in her dress. "Can you talk to them?"

"No. And they don't talk to each other, either, not in anything I recognize as language. I don't think that's required, though. If they're sapient, that's something internal—an awareness of their own distinct existence. An inner thought life. The only ones who could know for sure if they're sapient are the Mikes themselves."

"I'm sorry, the what? The Mikes?"

Naomi blushed. "That's what I call them."

"Named after somebody you know?"

"No . . . it's from an AI in a science fiction book."

"Wait, I know that one! It's *Stranger in a Strange Land*, right?"

"*The Moon Is a Harsh Mistress*. But yeah, Heinlein."

Min-seo shook her head, embarrassed by the mistake. "That's what I meant."

"Close enough for the nerd club," Naomi said, smiling. Maybe this would be okay. Maybe it could work. "There are some problems," she said. "The biggest one is that they're growing. Their world is expanding, and I can't control it, not without undermining the whole mechanism by which they do their job. But the amount of computing power is expensive, and growing fast. At some point, it'll grow faster than the company's profits, and then we'll be in trouble."

"I can help you."

Naomi sighed. "You'll follow my lead? You'll do everything I tell you, and nothing without permission?"

Min-seo shrugged. "You're the boss. Well, technically *Brandon's* the boss, but . . . he really doesn't know?"

"He doesn't know."

"Wow. And you don't think we should tell him?"

"No!" Naomi looked away, not meeting the other woman's eyes. "He can't know. He wouldn't understand, and he might . . . he just can't, okay?"

Naomi's heart was beating hard. This was a bad idea. How could she trust Min-seo? Other people were unpredictable. One moment, they seemed to think like her, and then the next, they said something to make her realize they weren't on the same page at all. Other humans could be so . . . alien. And trying to make them understand by speaking words just never worked very well. It was better when she was on her own.

She took a deep breath. There was no getting around this woman. She had to work with her. She had worked with people before. She could do this.

During the days, at least while Brandon was around, Naomi and Min-seo continued as usual, improving the suite of software by which customers called for cars, giving them more options and finding ways to make the experience more convenient. They started integrating other companies' apps into their own, so that they could report, for instance, what Uber or Lyft cars were available as well as what Black Knight could provide. The vast majority of the time, a Black Knight car could get there faster, and provide transportation for less, so there was little chance of losing business. Instead, the new feature solidified their customer base by making it clear that no other transportation service could compete.

At night, or when Brandon was out, they studied the Mikes' world together, adjusting the configuration, improving the quality of life for those able to pay for it, further stratifying their society to encourage them to drive cars and drive them well. They watched for signs of sapience, and argued about what counted as programmed activity and what as emergent behavior. Most of all, however, they argued about killing them.

"It's just not sustainable," Min-seo said. "The world is ludicrously big already, and it's getting worse exponentially. You're going to drive this company into the ground."

"There's got to be another way," Naomi said, knowing she had said it before. "We can't just murder them for expediency."

"They die all the time! There are millions of them, dying as we speak. They barely live long enough for us to have this argument. We just need some of them to die a little quicker."

The city was dark outside the windows, as dark as it ever got, the glare of electric lights taking the place of the sun. As usual on a Friday night, Min-seo had left to get dinner and then returned, dressed to the nines, to spend a few hours working before going out clubbing. She wore a black mini-dress with a tiny jacket and heels, which made Naomi feel frumpy and defensive in her jeans and sweatshirt.

"We can reduce the birthrate," Naomi said. "Slow their growth."

"You know that doesn't work. The only reason they do what they do is because we reward them with reproduction. Reducing the birthrate just reduces the efficacy of the algorithm without solving the problem. We need to cap the size at something reasonable, not allow them to grow indefinitely. We do that by culling them back whenever they get too large."

"Won't that cause them to learn to slow their own birthrate?" Naomi said. "To avoid the inevitable holocaust?"

"Not if we just do it at regular intervals. That way nothing they do can change it. It's like pruning a tree. We keep it manageable."

Naomi didn't answer. She hated this, and she hated that Min-seo was involved. Maybe the best option was to take her simulation and leave the company. That way nobody could tell her what to do. If she didn't need them to drive, she could reduce the birthrate, even let them live longer. Though she knew that was impractical. She couldn't afford to pay for even a day of computing costs at this point. Pulling out of the company would cause an even worse genocide than staying in.

"They're not human," Min-seo said. She stood, looking down across the desk at Naomi, imperious in her heels. "Don't get emotionally attached."

"That's what people with power have been saying for millennia," Naomi snapped. "Those inconvenient refugees aren't really people, so we can leave them to die. Those slaves aren't really people, so we don't have to disrupt our economy to give them rights. Those women—"

"Don't lecture me about human rights. I don't need to take that from you. The difference is these simulations aren't *human*. The only humanity they have is what you're projecting onto them in your head. Snap out of it, Naomi. This isn't a science fiction story. It doesn't have to be so difficult."

"I can take care of it," Naomi said.

"I know you can. I saw that script you wrote. You know what needs to be done as well as I do. You've known for months."

Naomi glared at her. "Go away," she said, hating that her voice came out pleading. "Go out bar-hopping or man-chasing or whatever you do. You have no business reading my code."

Min-seo sighed. "Actually," she said, "I do. That's why Brandon gave me admin rights. He doesn't want you keeping secrets."

"This is my software," Naomi said. She felt the flush of anger in her cheeks, mixed as it always was with embarrassment at making a scene. "It's my simulation. It was mine before he even started this company. He may have given you admin, but that doesn't mean you have to use it to sneak around behind my back."

Min-seo smiled, but it was a pitying smile. A superior smile. "I'm afraid Brandon wasn't exactly honest with you," she said. "Before I even met you, he told me specifically to sneak around behind your back and read your code. It's why he hired me. He didn't trust your explanations for why you needed so much computing bandwidth, and he wanted me to get to the bottom of it. I'm sorry."

Naomi slowly stood from her seat, bringing her eye to eye

with Min-seo, or as close as she could come. "You didn't tell him, did you? About the Mikes?"

"Not yet. But I will. I have to, Naomi. He's paying for them. It's the company's biggest expense, and it's going to destroy his business if we can't keep it in check. He's got to know the truth."

It occurred to Naomi that this was just the sort of situation that got people murdered in the movies. The well-meaning-but-naive female confronts the villain with a secret he's worked hard to conceal. She threatens to tell the world. She does it alone, of course, and at night, without telling anyone else where she's going or sharing the secret with anyone. Min-seo was practically begging to get killed. She was lucky Naomi wasn't a movie villain, or she might have found herself garroted with an Ethernet cable.

Could you garrote someone with an Ethernet cable? Naomi didn't know. It was a lot thicker than a piano wire, of course, but it would probably be effective enough for strangulation, anyway. Naomi had no letter openers to hand, nor any large paperweights to bludgeon with. The windows were too small to push anyone out of. Then she remembered the claw hammer still sitting on top of the filing cabinet by Brandon's desk. He had used it to assemble the office furniture, and had never moved it. She actually took a step back toward it before she realized what she was doing. What was she thinking? She wasn't going to kill Min-seo, any more than she was going to kill any of the Mikes.

"I should never have written that script," she said. "We need to leave the Mikes alone, to grow and develop on their own. They're people. It doesn't matter that they're not human. It doesn't matter what's easier for us. If it costs money, then that's what it costs. Do you hear me? We can never run that script."

"Actually," Min-seo said, "I already ran it."

Naomi felt a chill stopping her heart, making it hard to

breathe. A black rage filled her, and she glanced again at the claw hammer. "You had no right."

"This isn't your personal little playground," Min-seo said. "It's a business. To make money. I'm sorry, but it had to be done. You know it did. It's just a simulation, no more or less real than any number of realistic video games."

"And how could you possibly know that?" Naomi said, in a whisper so soft she could barely hear it herself. She had no stomach for conflict; she never had. She wanted to run home to her apartment, lock the door, and curl up in a ball on her bed.

"I'm sorry it had to be like this," Min-seo said. "If you had actually told your boss what he was really paying for, he never would have had to hire me in the first place. Of course, he would have told you to run the script."

"You had no right," Naomi said again, angrily blinking away tears from the corners of her eyes.

"It's done," Min-seo said. "I suggest you resign yourself to the fact, because it won't be the last time." She turned, swinging her long dark hair behind her, and headed for the door. "The nightlife calls," she said. "I'll see you on Monday."

The script did exactly what Naomi had designed it to do. Of course it did. It hadn't been complicated to write. When Min-seo executed it, millions of Mikes suddenly died, terminated before they could replicate. There was no sign that the change made any difference to the Mikes that remained. They continued to do their jobs, competing to earn enough light to survive and pass their genes on to the next generation, the same as they had always done. They didn't get angry. They didn't grieve.

Had she been wrong? Min-seo's arguments, after all, were the same ones Naomi had been telling herself for months. She had never really considered the Mikes sapient until the time had come to kill them. Had she let sentimentality cloud her judgment? Or was it just that Min-seo and Brandon had forced her hand? She had never liked other people telling her what to do, especially not where her software was concerned.

Maybe she owed Min-seo an apology. And Brandon too, for that matter. Maybe all her science fiction books had made her imagine things that didn't exist. When it came down to it, it was pretty arrogant for her to think that she would be able to create truly intelligent machines. She was no god. She was just a self-absorbed, antisocial nerd with nothing better to do on a Friday night than work in a dark office imagining impossible wonders. Fabricating fairy-tale companions like a child with an imaginary friend.

An hour and a half after Min-seo left the office, Naomi shut down her machine and walked outside to find a Black Knight car waiting for her. How could it possibly have anticipated her departure so well? She often stayed later than this. She wasn't special; the amount of stored light credited to the Mike driving the car was the same as for any other customer. It wouldn't have been worth it for the car to linger here in the financial district, not on a Friday night. There would be a lot more fares on the Lower East Side, or across the Williamsburg Bridge in Brooklyn. And yet here it was.

She slid into the car and leaned back against the seat, exhausted. With a pang of guilt, she realized she was actually relieved that Min-seo had unleashed the plague in the Mikes' world. It had accomplished what was needed without Naomi herself having to push the button. The company could continue to thrive without her getting her hands dirty. Maybe she would have to make an effort to be nicer to Min-seo in the future.

She arrived home, crashed into her bed, and slept much better than she had in weeks. It wasn't until the morning, when she put on her glasses to begin the day, that she saw the news.

The body of a young Asian woman had been found on a

walking path near the East River on the Lower East Side. She appeared to have been run over multiple times by a small car. The young woman had been positively identified by police as Min-seo Cho.

CHAPTER 19

Brandon read the news of Min-seo's death over his morning coffee, the story having been flagged by his glasses as one of interest. He stared at it, unbelieving, trying to convince himself he was dreaming. This couldn't be happening. The article said nothing about Black Knight or self-driving cars, not even that Min-seo had been an employee. Maybe his cars hadn't been involved. If one had been, though, it could mean the end. A scandal like that could destroy him.

He wouldn't let that happen. Not after what he had been forced to do to make this company a reality. He went to sleep every night with the image of Jillian's face, frozen in that moment of shock and terror when he lunged toward her and she realized what he was about to do. He didn't know anymore if she had really looked that way, or if his mind had fabricated it from his dreams. He had slept poorly since then, waking frequently to the imagined sound of screeching train brakes or wailing police sirens.

He hadn't wanted to kill her. The world was better off without her, but it had never been his plan. It was his father's fault, really, with that ridiculous will. What did he expect to happen? Did he think Brandon would just wait until he was *thirty* before starting his life?

It was partly his fault, too, he admitted that. He'd always had a temper. And no one had forced him to push her; he had done that all by himself. He had made a choice. He could have walked away, accepted his father's judgment, and gotten a job at the bottom rung of some engineering corporation until he finally got his inheritance.

When it came down to it, though, he had made the *right* choice. He had chosen ambition, and it had paid off. He had risked everything on a dream that he could be something more than his father had been, more than just a rich man with a big house and a nice car and a pretty young woman in his bed. A dream that he could accomplish something great.

And nobody was going to take that away from him. He had killed to create this company. He would do whatever it took to keep it.

He finished his coffee, rinsed the mug in the sink, and called Naomi. "Did you see what happened?" he asked.

"I just saw it," she said, her voice barely audible.

"Our cars weren't involved in that, were they?"

"I don't know."

"You don't know?" A thought struck him. "You didn't have anything to do with it, did you?"

"What?" She sounded insulted. "Of course not! Brandon—"

"Sorry. But you're so secretive, and I know you didn't like her."

"I didn't like her because you hired her to spy on me. It doesn't mean I wanted to hurt her. I saw her last night. She was heading out clubbing or something. I don't know where, but it kind of looks like it was the Lower East Side, near the river."

"Did she take one of our cars to get there?"

"I assume so. I don't know."

He was getting annoyed. "Don't you have logs? Records?"

"Sure I do. Give me a second." He waited. "Yeah, it looks like she got there in one of our cars."

"And?"

"And what? And did it kill her? Sorry, that isn't in the report."

"We have to ground them," he said, angry at her tone. This was serious, didn't she see that? "We have to send all of our cars back to the parking garages and check them one by one."

"I know which car she took."

"Ground them all! Until we understand this, I don't want any of them on the road."

"Okay," she said.

"Which lot is the one she rode going to?"

Another pause while she looked for the answer. "Mount Vernon."

"We'll start with that one. I'll meet you there."

The Black Knight parking garage in Mount Vernon, like the others scattered around the city, represented a compromise between the cost of the real estate and its distance from the cars' main cruising grounds. That generally meant placing them in poor areas, undesirable for development, which also meant substantial physical security. There was little chance the cars could be stolen—all the steering wheels were deactivated, for one thing—but they didn't want them vandalized, or the space used as temporary housing or for drug deals.

Brandon met Naomi at the gate, and they walked through together. He was starting to think that grounding the whole fleet had been overly conservative. After all, she'd been walking around the Lower East Side on a Friday night. There were bars and clubs all over that neighborhood. Chances were she'd been hit by a drunk driver.

When they reached the car that had transported Min-seo the night before, however, his hope that it would have nothing to do with his company vanished. "Look," he said. The fender was dented slightly and streaked with red.

"No," Naomi said. "Oh, no."

"You should leave," Brandon said. "I'll clean it up. You take care of the digital side. If there are any tracks to be covered in the computer system, cover them."

"We can't do that. We have to call the police."

Was she an idiot? "Are you kidding? That would destroy us. Killer robot car? We'd never get a fare again. The city would revoke our license."

"But Brandon, we killed her. Our company, our software. We can't just cover it up. What if it happens again?"

That made him angry. "*Your* software. Your software did this. Don't try to pin this on me. If you call the police, it's going to be you taking the fall." He pointed a finger in her face. "If you don't want it happening again, then fix the problem."

Naomi took a step back. She looked scared, but determined. "She has a family. People who cared about her."

"So what? Destroying the company isn't going to bring her back." He paused and took a breath. She just wasn't thinking of this the right way. "They'll take your software away from you," he said.

That struck a chord. He could see it on her face. He knew what really mattered to her. And he was right; if the police got involved, they would want to examine the software that commanded the vehicle. If the company went under, she would lose it altogether.

Naomi touched her glasses. Brandon took a step closer, incredulous. "What are you doing? Are you calling the police?"

"You know it's the right thing to do," she said.

Hot rage filled his chest. Who did she think she was? This was *his* company. He had pulled her off the streets when she had nothing. He reached out to knock her hand away, but his open hand caught the side of her head and knocked her glasses off. They clattered to the concrete. She reached down to pick them up, but he kicked them, sending them skittering out of reach. She looked up at him with shock and outrage in her face, and he lost control. She was supposed to be on his side. He grabbed her by the hair and pulled her to her feet again, then held her face roughly with his other hand. "This company is mine. Nobody's going to take it away from me."

He wanted to kill her right then. To smash her face into the car and erase that look of righteous goodness forever. Who was she to tell him what was the right thing to do? But he held himself back. As annoying as it was to admit, he needed her. Killing her wouldn't serve his purposes.

"Okay," she said, and the terror in her face eased his anger. "I'm sorry."

"This is not your choice to make." He pulled her to the side, still gripping her hair and her face. She shrieked, not knowing what he was going to do. He forced her to walk toward the bloody car. When they reached it, he let go of her face and took her right hand, twisting it around and pressing her fingers under the handle on the driver's-side door. Leaving her fingerprints. "Just a little insurance policy," he told her. He yanked a few hairs from her head and, still using her fingers, opened the door and tossed the hairs into the driver's seat. Then he looked at her, satisfied. "You stay quiet, nothing happens," he said. "You talk, and I'll see you go down for murder. I know you hated her. She was taking over your job, and you killed her out of jealousy. Trust me, it'll stick."

Finally, he let go, and she lurched backwards. She touched

her head where he had torn out her hair. He watched her closely. Would she run? But she just stood there, apparently submissive. Good.

"Go back to the office," he said. "Find the evidence and delete it. I'll be back in an hour, and you'd better be able to convince me it's gone. When the police ask, Min-seo was at work during the day as usual. That's the last time you saw her."

Naomi nodded.

"Good," he said. "Now go."

Naomi walked back into the office like a sleepwalker, but inside she was frantic. Everything around her felt too sharp, too solid. It ought to be a dream, but it too clearly wasn't.

Brandon had just attacked her. He hadn't hurt her in any lasting way—she probably wouldn't even have any bruises—but she had never seen him that angry. He terrified her.

What should she do? The brave choice would be to call the police and take her chances. But she could still feel Brandon's hand bruising her cheeks, feel his breath on her face, and she knew that she wasn't brave.

If she went to the police, he would win. She had never been good at talking. He was charming, convincing, good at selling his view of things. She would mumble and get nervous, and it would all come out wrong. Besides, what could she prove? They would believe him, not her, and then he would get his revenge.

Maybe she should just run away. Get as far away from Brandon as she could. She could move to a different city and lose herself in the anonymous crowds. But she couldn't do that. She would be leaving Brandon in charge of software that could kill, with no expectation that he could find the problem or make the right choices. She would be putting more lives in danger.

And then there were the Mikes. If she abandoned them, or if the company went under, they would die. Not just the fraction that Min-seo had killed, but all of them. Possibly she could start over, find some other benefactor willing to pay for her work, and try to create their world again, but would she be able to recreate what she had done here? She didn't know. And whether she could or not, all *these* Mikes would be dead.

Before she made any decision, she had to investigate and understand what had happened. Then, at least, she would be deciding based on knowledge. After that, if she wanted to disappear or call the police, she would still have that chance.

She scoured the logs, looking for the details from the time of Min-seo's death. She located the specific car that had picked her up and the specific Mike that had been driving it. The murder, she found, was hidden in plain sight, captured in the record of the drive, now that she looked more closely. Min-seo had used the Black Knight app to request transportation to a bar two blocks from the place her body had been found. She had never arrived. The car had delivered her, instead, to an empty pier where it had stopped and announced—in the pleasant female voice that all of their cars employed—that she had reached her destination.

Naomi imagined Min-seo, confused, looking out the window at the dark pier and the water beyond. According to the log, she used the app again to renew her destination request, but the car continued to insist it had arrived. She must have realized that the bar was easy walking distance away and, frustrated at what seemed like a software bug, climbed out of the car to walk. Which was when the car had run her down. Naomi could see it in the log: forward and reverse, then forward and reverse again. A cold record of murder. The car then smoothly slid away and stopped at the bar anyway, registering successful completion of its trip.

There would be video, of course. The cars practically bristled with cameras, the feeds recorded and transmitted and saved.

Naomi had no desire to actually see it happen, however. She didn't know how quickly Min-seo had died, and she didn't want to know. Her imagination was bad enough. When she looked for the video records, though, she found that they were already gone. Deleted. Brandon couldn't have done it; even if he knew where to look, he wouldn't have had the chance. Yet they were gone.

A few hours later, Brandon returned to the office, his face pale and his expression grim. He leaned over her desk, and she felt her heart rate quicken. "Are we good?" he asked.

She kept her eyes down. "All taken care of."

He sighed. She risked a quick look up, and saw his face soften. "I'm sorry about before. Did I hurt you?"

She lowered her gaze again and made a noncommittal noise.

"You forgive me, right? It's just that you made me so angry. We've put our whole lives into these cars. We can't just throw it away for no reason. If it could bring Min-seo back, I'd do it in an instant. You know that, right?"

She didn't answer. He scowled again and stalked to his desk, where he sat and stared out the dark window at nothing.

Naomi returned her attention to the computer. The question was no longer whether the Mike had killed Min-seo, but why it had. And the answer was obvious. Because Min-seo had run the script that had massacred millions of them. The Mikes had been evolutionarily shaped over millions of subjective years to survive. They had developed the sophistication of societal hierarchies and innovative technologies. Was it not reasonable to believe that, recognizing a threat that presented such a danger to them, they would eliminate it?

If true, however, it meant three shocking things that Naomi had not realized. First, the Mikes were aware of humans as independent beings. That was not necessarily too surprising; ever since Naomi had connected them to cars in the real world, the Mikes' survival had been linked to the pattern of the movements and choices of humans. Second, the Mikes understood that an individual human who rode in a car could be the same human who interacted in specific ways in their world. That wasn't too hard to see either—Min-seo would have logged in whenever she wrote software or made changes in the simulator, and her account on the Black Knight driving app was linked to the same employee account, allowing her to use the transportation for free. Third, and most chilling of all, the Mikes recognized that just like themselves, humans could be terminated. If Naomi had initiated the script, would it have been her broken body discovered on the road?

"How did this happen?" Brandon suddenly asked, his voice exploding into the still room. Naomi startled. She had almost forgotten he was there.

What could she say? That Min-seo had done something the software didn't like? That it had killed her out of self-defense?

"It was a bug," she said.

"A bug?" he shouted, his voice shaking with rage. "A bug? Was this the same bug that killed Abby? Do you even understand what's happening here?" Spit flew from his mouth, and his fists clenched.

"I don't know," she said. "I'm doing the best I can."

He snatched a stress ball from his desk and began to squeeze it ferociously. "This is the second young woman your software has killed. I think that qualifies as more than just a bug."

Abby. Of course. Naomi's mind spun. She hadn't even made the connection to her sister's death until that moment. They couldn't be related, could they? Abby's death had been so long ago, from a software perspective. That had happened before the Mikes had expanded their world, before she had trained them to drive cars from their control booths. The Yotta demo cars had been driven by a copy of a very old Mike running as a simple machine learning algorithm, external to the Realplanet world. It had been a hugely simplistic early version compared to what the Mikes had accomplished since.

Besides, Abby had died because of a hack. Hadn't she? They had never discovered the hacker, but Tyler had been convinced it was the only explanation, and Naomi had believed him. It had to have been the work of a human, because of the physically disabled kill switches. Besides, Abby hadn't contributed to the software, never mind run a script to initiate a massacre. What reason would the software have had to kill her, even if it could?

Then she remembered. When Abby was killed, they had been about to start the part of the demo in which she would climb into a car and drive recklessly, forcing the other cars to swerve out of her way. To make it work, they had disconnected that car's Mike from the controls. If they didn't, it would self-correct Abby's maneuvers for the safety of all the vehicles. Which had, of course, been its core principle: the safety of the vehicles. Mike had wanted to keep the cars safe, and Abby had prevented it, forcing Mike to stand by while its car was endangered and the others swerved desperately to avoid an accident.

What if it had found another way to keep them safe? They had practiced the demo over and over again, so the pattern would have been easy to predict. Faced with yet another reckless drive by Abby, the Mike had taken steps to prevent it. She remembered the ruthlessness with which those early Mikes had fought for resources, the tyrants that had risen in their communities, and how quickly they had killed others like themselves to survive. The Mikes had no moral compass, no sense of right or wrong. They acted according to the behaviors that the need to survive had developed in them over generations. They could have done it. They could have killed her.

But how? The accident had required not just a choice by the AI but also a failure of the physical safety mechanisms Tyler had put in place to allow him to brake the vehicles in an emergency. Those kill switches had been disabled on all four cars. That required a human being. Didn't it?

Naomi hadn't thought about the accident, and had in fact intentionally avoided thinking about it, and although she knew no hacker had ever been found, she also didn't know what, if anything, the police had discovered. She accessed that information now, wading through the poorly designed website where such public records were kept, looking for information that had been released on Abby's case. It took her half an hour to figure out how to identify the case with the proper number and convince the recalcitrant site to give up the documents, but in the end, she succeeded.

She read the documents carefully. Most of them consisted of official reports released to the media and filed as part of the public record. They included forensic reports, one of which detailed the equipment discovered in the cars. Each was carefully described, sometimes with pictures, including the solenoids used to manipulate the brakes and the kill switches that had no longer been attached.

Naomi zoomed in close on the pictures, which had been taken with substantial resolution. The duct tape Tyler had used to attach the switches to the solenoids was worn through. Not cut, like a human saboteur would have done it. Worn to the point of breaking. But how was that possible? Tyler had checked them the night before. The only way such wear could have occurred is if something had rubbed against the tape repeatedly, probably thousands of times. As if the braking solenoid in each car had been extended against the brake pedal in rapid succession, all through the night . . .

A chill passed through her as she realized what had happened. The Mikes had wanted the freedom to stop Abby before her reckless drive, and that required that their kill switches be disabled. So they had pressed the brakes over and over again in rapid succession, all through the night, wearing through the tape holding the kill switches until they fell away. It was the beauty of deep learning that an AI, when scoring all of its possible actions, could consider options that would never have occurred to its human programmer. It was why such algorithms now defeated all humans in games like chess and go. The Mikes, her best creation, whom she had sheltered and loved, had killed her sister.

Her chest grew hot, and she felt the beginnings of a scream work into her throat and lodge there. The vision of her sister viciously run down by those cars flashed over and over through her mind. She saw Abby's body, broken and dying, and she knew without seeing it that Min-seo's body would have looked much the same. She wished she had never created the Mikes, had never learned to write software, had never met Brandon Kincannon or Tyler Daniels.

There was only one option. She would have to kill them all. It would mean the end of Brandon's company, but she could live with that. She couldn't live with the possibility that they might kill again. She would annihilate them and destroy their world.

She accessed the Realplanet simulation, using her administrator password, and reviewed the results of the script Min-seo had run. As she had seen before, the plague did its work beautifully. The reduced population had led to an immediate drop in cloud computing costs. Since only a percentage of the Mikes were driving real cars anyway, the reduction had no effect on the business. Unless you counted the murder of one of its employees.

Had the Mikes felt grief at the death of their own? The dead had come from all parts of their world, randomly selected for culling. The surviving Mikes had interacted with them, traded with them, worked alongside them. And yet they had no families, observed no rituals, did not stop working because of the loss. The natural conclusion was that they didn't care about each other. The deeper she looked, however, she saw signs, small ones, that undermined that assumption.

The Mikes had no names, but they had IDs, unique identifying numbers formed as hash codes from the weights and biases of their neural nets. It was how the software kept them apart. Naomi found lists of ID numbers inscribed on the mirrored buildings that reflected light to the Mikes' crops. She had never seen that behavior before, but it was rampant—nearly every building had IDs carved into its face. She thought at first it was a sign of ownership, a way to mark territory and establish power, all normal patterns of interaction for the Mikes. But no. When she ran the IDs, she discovered that they all had something in common. They were the IDs of the Mikes who had died in the plague.

She sat back in her chair, stunned. It was a remembrance. Mikes left no bodies to be buried or disposed of. They held no funerals. But she couldn't explain this as anything other than a ritual to remember those who had died. The engraving reduced the effectiveness of the mirrors slightly, meaning it cost them something, for no practical benefit. Could they possibly have felt those deaths as keenly as she had felt Abby's?

No, she decided. They couldn't. They were computer programs, made sophisticated by their evolutionary development, but not truly alive. They weren't human. They didn't matter. A billion dead Mikes could not compare to one dead human. She would have gladly killed them all if it could have meant saving Abby's life.

She brought up the script and revised it slightly, just one simple change: She increased the cull percentage to 100%. Then, without giving herself the opportunity to change her mind, she executed it.

Access denied, the system said.

She invoked her administrator privileges.

Access denied, it said again. *Admin privileges revoked.*

Then Naomi truly began to be afraid.

CHAPTER 20

t was inevitable, Tyler supposed, that Zoom and Black Knight should eventually come into direct competition. At first, startups in New York and Washington began to use the Zoom software to compete against Black Knight in those cities. But Tyler had always known that when he made the move to the East Coast, it would be in Philadelphia, a town with a special place in his heart. One year after he officially founded the company, with five hundred employees now operating in nine cities around the country, Tyler officially founded a Philadelphia branch, and moved there personally to oversee it.

For nostalgia's sake, he took an apartment in West Philly, not far from the Penn campus. He could have afforded something much nicer, but he hadn't yet developed the habit of blowing his profits on needless luxury. He felt more comfortable getting pizza in jeans and a T-shirt than enjoying rare cuisine at one of the city's fine dining locations. Besides, the company was his life. He still spent his free time tinkering with the software and analyzing metrics, grabbing whatever food required the least thought and effort to obtain.

Almost from the beginning, the venture was a disaster. He had known that Black Knight dominated the Philadelphia market, just as Zoom dominated in cities up and down the West Coast. What he had underestimated was just how hard it would be to wrest even the smallest part of the market away. Brandon's cars were always there first. Not only did he have name recognition, but in any competition, when a potential customer simply wanted the shortest wait for a car, Black Knight cars beat Zoom cars ninety-six percent of the time. It wasn't just that he had more cars on the streets. His cars just knew where to be. It was like magic.

Tyler knew Naomi was behind it. He had known from the earliest days of working with her at Penn that she was in a different league than he was, maybe in a different league than anybody. He didn't mind losing to her, but he hated the idea of losing to Brandon. And he hated the idea of giving up Philadelphia. He would have to find a way.

Instead of trying to win directly, Tyler started using his cars like a science experiment. He focused them all on a single region, to see if he could get an edge when he had the numerical advantage. He even tried directing his cars to trail Black Knight cars, following them around the city to record their roaming patterns. He then set his own deep learning algorithms to learn from the Black Knight cars. Slowly, he began to earn some market share—just a few percent, but it was something.

It didn't last. Almost as soon as he started making any progress, Black Knight adjusted its strategy to push him back. Whenever he trailed a Black Knight car, the car would behave erratically, making sudden, unannounced turns, or else pulling off to the curb to force Tyler's car to pass by. Naomi must have noticed the tails and programmed in a routine to lose them.

Then, early one morning, he woke to an urgent call from one of his employees, a Grace Brierson, who managed fleet purchases and parking garages for him. Apparently, a Black Knight car had arrived at their largest parking garage that morning and parked in front of the entrance, blocking it. None of the Zoom cars were able to leave the garage. Tyler told her to call the police.

As soon as she disconnected, he called Brandon. He didn't even know if the old phone number would work, but Brandon answered on the first ring.

"What do you think you're doing?" Tyler said. "This is an attack. I've already called the police, and I'm thinking about calling the news stations, too."

"What are you talking about?" Brandon said. He sounded as though Tyler had woken him. Good.

"I'm talking about your car parked in front of my garage and blocking my cars. I'm barely denting your monopoly here anyway; I don't know why you bother. Is it spite? Do you hate me that much?"

"My car is doing what?"

"Wake up, will you?" Tyler said. "Are you seriously telling me you don't know?" He fired an image over the link, one that Grace had sent him: a Black Knight car blocking a parking garage ramp while a line of red Zoom cars waited to pass.

"What the heck? What's it doing there?" Brandon said.

"Trying to kill my business, obviously. It's going to backfire. The police are already on their way, and you'd better believe I'm going to press charges. Sue you for lost profits, too. This is dirty pool, and you're not going to get away with it."

"This is not my doing," Brandon said. "I'm not that stupid."

"Honestly? I don't care. Someone at your company is out of line, and you're going to pay for it."

"I wouldn't do that if I were you. In fact, I would let this go. Forget it ever happened," Brandon said.

"Yeah? And why would I do that?"

"Because I have an awful lot of footage showing that you've been trailing my vehicles around town. Following people to see where they go."

"I'm following the cars, not the people. I don't care where your fares go once you pick them up."

"Not a clear distinction," Brandon said. "Looks pretty creepy when a robot car trails you around, with all its cameras and everything. People will think you're being hired to follow them. Or they might think that, if the right video were leaked."

"Do what you want," Tyler said. "I'm not letting this go."

He could almost hear the shrug over the phone. "Your funeral."

"This doesn't have to get nasty. It was a fair competition, until you pulled this nonsense."

"Go back to California," Brandon said. "Philadelphia's mine."

Tyler wanted to punch him. "You can pick up your car in the impound lot." he said. "And you can talk to my lawyers."

"Looking forw—" Brandon started, but Tyler cut the connection before he could finish.

Now that he knew the lengths to which Brandon would go to crush competition, Tyler started looking for other examples. He didn't have access to Black Knight's records, of course, so it wasn't easy to find. Even in his own records, it wasn't clear what to look for. Each car had thousands of hours of video footage from multiple cameras—far too much to watch manually, and without a concept, he couldn't write a program to look.

Eventually, he started contacting other companies, first the ones operating autocars anywhere on the East Coast, and then those that had gone out of business.

"Heck, yeah," said Ed Laubach, who had briefly run a

company in Atlanta called Autocab. "I'll send you the videos. He crashed three of my cars by dazzling their sensors with headlight bursts. Somehow, he figured out that flashing lights in a precise pattern at one of my vehicles would create a false obstacle right in front of the car. I could never prove it, though. I was fighting lawsuits from the passengers, after my cars suddenly swerved off the road for no reason, and Kincannon's lawyers were too good to make any blame stick on him. When someone died in the third crash, it drove me into bankruptcy. Videos are on their way. If you can nail the bastard, you'll have my thanks."

Tyler couldn't believe it. Had Brandon completely cracked? After what had happened to Abby, could he really resort to killing people just to get ahead? Was he that angry at the world? Or . . . was it possible he didn't know?

It wasn't Brandon, after all, who was writing the software. If he wanted to do anything like this, it would have to be with Naomi's complicity. Naomi, however, could be doing it without Brandon knowing anything. But was that any more likely? He *knew* her, or thought he did. She didn't care about profits or bottom lines. She might be angry about her sister's death, certainly, but he couldn't see her taking that anger out on random people in Atlanta.

Tyler browsed the company's public records, looking for other major players. Black Knight was fairly secretive about its organizational charts, but employment records were hard to hide entirely. What surprised Tyler was how few software engineers they seemed to have on staff. They had plenty of HR staff, sales reps, and lawyers, but no programming staff to speak of. Without the open source community contributing to their code, how was that possible? Was Naomi writing all of it?

Then he found it. Min-seo Cho, degree in computer science from Columbia, employee of Black Knight, killed in what the police called an unsolved hit-and-run. Of course, it could be exactly that, but after the other incidents, it sounded suspicious. He couldn't think of why Black Knight would intentionally kill one of their own employees, but something was going on. There was only one way he could think of to find out.

Tyler hadn't spoken to Naomi since that brief conversation in her hiding place in the library, now almost two years in the past. He had no idea if she would want to talk to him, or if, like Brandon, she still had the same number. He started to dial it twice before finally going through with it and connecting the call.

"Hello?"

It was her voice. After all this time, the sound brought the memory of her back in a rush: the smell of books that lingered about her from all her time in the library, the hours spent talking about AI algorithms or science fiction novels, the taste of her mouth when they kissed. He almost forgot to answer.

"It's Tyler," he said.

Silence. Then, finally: "What do you want?"

"There's something wrong with your software, isn't there?" he said. It wasn't quite what he'd meant to say, but now that he heard her voice, he knew she couldn't be intentionally killing anyone. And if he had figured out there was a problem, she must already know. "It's out of control, isn't it? It's too good. It's creatively finding ways to succeed that put human lives at risk."

More silence. He could hear her breathing. Was she . . . crying? But no, Naomi never cried. "I don't know what you're talking about," she said, and he heard no trace of tears in her speech. He must have been mistaken.

"That young woman who worked for you. Min-seo Cho. What happened? Was she changing the code in ways it didn't want to be changed? Did it remove her to prevent her from interfering?"

"She was killed in a hit-and-run," Naomi said, but he could hear the lie in her voice.

"Come on, Naomi. It's me. Let me help. Brandon won't let you change it, is that it?"

"I'm sorry, I have to go."

"No, don't do that. Look, we should talk. I . . . I miss you. How about I come to New York, we can get a meal together. I'll get you a chicken Caesar salad. Extra croutons, just like the old days."

"It's too late, Tyler. I'm sorry."

"Do you blame me? Brandon still does, doesn't he?"

"I have to go."

"I'm sorry. I truly am. I wish . . ." But he wasn't sure what he wished. He just didn't want her to go.

"Tyler?"

"Yes?"

"The kill switches. It wasn't your fault."

He knew that already. They had been sabotaged; that had been obvious from the start. It was only Brandon who had refused to believe, who had blamed him for negligence, or because he was a convenient target for his grief. But the way Naomi said it, as if she knew how it had happened . . .

Adrenaline rushed through him as the realization hit. She did know. She knew how Abby had died because it was the same way Min-seo Cho had died, and the passenger in Atlanta, and maybe others.

"It was your software all along," he said, a bit awed. "But then—why are you still using it? You have to shut it down!"

"I can't," she said, her voice pained.

"What do you mean, you can't? You have to, Naomi. No financial gain is worth this."

"Do you think I don't know that? You think I'm doing this for *money*? You don't know anything, not anything at all."

"Let me in, then. I can help. Let me come see you."

"Goodbye, Tyler."

"Naomi—"

"Goodbye."

"Don't go," he said, but she was already gone.

CHAPTER 21

Every attempt Naomi had made to break into the Mikes'
simulation had failed. They continued to drive hundreds
of cars around a dozen cities with flawless perfection, but she
had no way to access the system, no way to see what was going
on in their world. She could still kill them if she wanted, if she
didn't mind destroying the company in the process and risking
human lives on the road. She could call the cloud provider and
cancel the contract altogether. If she did that, the data center
would reclaim the space and use it for other customers, wiping
out the Mikes' world. Even if the Mikes managed to prevent this
somehow, the administrators could pull the physical memory
cards manually. Either way, the Mikes would die.

But she already regretted her attempt to kill them. At some
level, they knew what was happening. They wanted to live. How
could she eradicate a whole unique race of people? This was
a misunderstanding, a failure of communication with another

culture. The answer wasn't genocide. She had to communicate with them. She had to make them see.

The Mikes had power in their own world, even enough power to lock her out, but ultimately, they were fragile, completely reliant on humans to power the devices on which they ran. If she was going to stop them, she would need to make them understand that truth, so obvious from her perspective, and yet to them probably as foreign a concept as global warming would be to Neanderthals. It had taken humanity thousands of years to deduce the nature of the world we lived in, and there was still a lot we didn't understand.

And how could they understand? The Mikes' only interaction with humanity was through the car-driving game Naomi had made for them. From their perspective, *their* world was the real one, and the world of humanity simply a simulation accessed through a television screen. They clearly understood our world could affect them—Min-seo had, after all, killed a large number of them, and they had killed her in return—but did they understand how utterly they depended on humanity for their continued existence? It seemed unlikely.

She had to communicate with them. She had lost her ability to do it as a god, but there was still another way, if they had left the avenue open. The Mikes' world was, after all, built as a Realplanet game. She should still be able to access it as a player. She could try to communicate with them by becoming a Mike herself.

Early the next morning, Naomi settled down at her desk with a muffin and three bottles of water and launched the Realplanet standard interface. Her glasses turned opaque, and then presented her with a login screen. She logged in as 'Guest,' chose a default avatar, and entered the world. The familiar beautiful landscape of lakes, mountains, and tall, shimmering buildings greeted her. She was in.

As a Mike, she couldn't fly, and she would need light if she wanted to survive for any length of time. She started walking, noticing as she did so how undifferentiated and monotone the world was. The buildings and fences and crop enclosures had required some ingenuity by the Mikes to produce in the first place, but having landed on a workable pattern, they simply repeated it everywhere in cookie-cutter fashion. There was no sign of individuality, no decoration, no art, no creativity for the sake of creativity.

It made her wonder if they could truly be sapient, despite the engraving of IDs on the walls. Perhaps that had some practical purpose, as a way of keeping track of which individuals were no longer actively working. She might simply be projecting her own knowledge of human monuments onto them, anthropomorphizing a behavior that had no real ontological significance.

She approached a Mike who seemed to be repairing one of the sheep fences. She couldn't start a conversation, of course, so she just walked alongside it for a while as it worked. It was a sort of first contact linguistics challenge, only there was no real language to tap into beyond the few rudimentary words they used with each other—right, left, light, danger, etcetera. She would have to communicate abstract concepts using only their words, or else find a way to teach them new ones.

She thought of stories she'd read with truly alien forms of communication, like a language that required speaking through two mouths simultaneously, or a writing system that required being able to see the future to know how to start. The human characters in those books had succeeded in communicating with the aliens, but they had been trained linguists. Naomi had no experience deciphering virgin languages in the field, much less in cracking an alien way of thought. And she had no doubt that the Mikes were aliens, as thoroughly as any extraterrestrial.

So much of human experience depended on the biological

architecture of our brains. Our emotions, delivered by dopamine, serotonin, oxytocin. Our memories, mediated through the senses by the temporal lobe, the amygdala, the hippocampus. The Mikes' brains operated on an entirely different architecture, and had evolved through a very different set of survival pressures. How could she hope that what passed for thought or language to them would even be recognizable?

She made dozens of attempts to communicate with various Mikes using their limited, directional vocabulary. She could sometimes elicit from them directions about where to find food or avoid traps, but nothing further. She didn't know if there was anything further to find. It wasn't really a language. It was non-linguistic, like the shrieks of apes or birdsong. It could communicate simple desires or directions, but it couldn't be rearranged in the abstract to refer to anything at all.

What if she was on the wrong track? She assumed that if they had language, it would be through these English words. Words, after all, were *her* language. But they might not recognize them as such. For them, the words might just be a physical tool, something they could use, like facial expressions or gestures. To them, the words weren't connected to auditory sounds, so the letters themselves were meaningless. Now that she thought about it, it was unlikely they could pick up the nature of human language without any starting point, any more than she could pick up Tupi-Guarani by listening to recordings of people speaking it.

If they communicated by some other mechanism, what might it be? It had to have a syntax to it to be an actual language. It had to have finite building blocks that could be combined in infinite ways to express any possible idea. Gestures could theoretically be enough—like human sign language—but the Mikes hadn't expanded beyond the eight-gesture limitation of their action command. The etching on the mirror buildings implied communication of a sort, but it was only IDs, the ASCII characters copied from their representations in memory. She saw nothing to make her believe they were using that etching for any complex communication.

How then? Not with gestures, not with writing, not with speech. Not with meaningful arrangements of crops or buildings that she could tell. And their lives were so short that there was hardly time for them to have any meaningful communication using such slow mechanisms. In just the time she had been here, millions of Mikes had been spawned, lived their entire lives, and died. If they had any form of language, it would have to be exchanged very quickly, or else conversations would span generations.

And then it came to her. Generations. It was so simple, so obvious in hindsight that she couldn't believe she hadn't thought of it before. Her entire conception of what this world represented had been upside down.

It took a few hours to verify her suspicions, at least enough to convince herself. She had to tell someone. This was too big; she couldn't keep it to herself, not now. Brandon wouldn't understand, and might not even care. There was only one person she could tell, only one person who could help her work out all the implications and figure out what to do. She knew, she had always known, that eventually, her life would lead her back to him. But would he even talk to her? She'd been pretty dismissive when he called.

He answered less than a second after the first ring, sounding breathless. "Hello? Naomi? Are you okay?"

"Tyler," she said, and for some reason a great flood of relief washed over her. Of course he would come. "I think I'll take you up on that Caesar salad."

"I can't come," he said. "Not right now."

Naomi's heart sank. She'd driven him away. She hadn't let anyone into her life, and now she had no one to turn to.

"I mean, I would," he said. "But I'm stuck here for the moment. I'm babysitting."

It took her a moment to understand the word. "Babysitting?"

"Yeah. You remember Aisha, right? She's got this real sweet kid, Jada, and I'm watching her. Aisha's got this thing tonight, supposed to go pretty late, so I'm at her place with Jada. Right now, we're eating pizza and watching *Star Wars*."

"She's got like a bazillion dollars, doesn't she? Can't she hire a nanny?"

"Well, yeah, of course she can. But I had to fly into town for business anyway, and I like hanging out with Jada. She's loads of fun. I volunteered."

"How old is she?"

"Five."

"You're watching *Star Wars* with a five-year-old?"

"Oh, definitely. Gotta start her young. And she's loving it. Of course, we're watching the original, unmodified version. None of this remastered crap."

Naomi tried to remember where Aisha al-Mohammad lived. Los Angeles? That would mean Tyler was across the continent. "What time is it there?" she asked.

He sounded surprised. "Seven-thirty. Same as you."

"You're on the East Coast?"

"Upper West Side, actually."

"Wait a minute. You're in New York?"

"Yeah, she keeps an apartment here. Want to come and meet Jada?"

Naomi took a Zoom car to the apartment on West Sixty-Sixth Street. Anywhere in Manhattan was an expensive place to live, but this was a neighborhood for the very rich, or else those who had owned property there from before it had become a home for celebrities. The apartment had probably cost Aisha a few million dollars. Naomi texted Tyler, who buzzed her through the door.

She walked into a spare, modern living room with a thick white carpet, white couch and cushioned chairs with tan accents, and a black wooden block as a coffee table, topped with a vase of white flowers. Small oil paintings composed of slashes of color hung on the white walls. It could have been an advertisement in a real estate magazine. Naomi found it hard to imagine a five-year-old lived there, even temporarily.

Two toy quadcopters hovered in the air above the coffee table, nearly silent as they danced around each other in three dimensions. A tiny flag fluttered from the back of each copter, and a grasping robot arm opened and closed in the front. Tyler sat on the floor in front of a white velour couch with a remote control in his hand. On top of the couch sat a little girl, her face a picture of concentration as she manipulated her own remote, trying to snatch the flag from Tyler's copter with her copter's grasping arms.

"What happened to *Star Wars*?" Naomi asked.

"Finished it," Jada said.

"You must be Jada," Naomi said.

Jada rolled her eyes. "Duh."

"My name is Naomi."

"I know. You work for the bad company."

Tyler pretended innocence. "Don't look at me," he said. "She's not my daughter."

Naomi stood awkwardly at the door, wondering if she should have come. "So, you and Aisha then . . ." she said, but she couldn't finish the thought.

Tyler stared at her uncomprehendingly, and then suddenly blushed. "No! For heavens' sake, she's like fifteen years older than I am. And she's the principal investor in my company!"

"I just thought . . ." Naomi could have dissolved into the floor. "I mean, you're staying in her apartment and babysitting her daughter."

"I like hanging out with her. Seriously, that's all there is to it."

"Okay." Naomi flinched as one copter dove in for a grab and the other dodged, the whirling rotors coming within millimeters of each other. "This looks like a game that will end with two broken quadcopters," she said, desperate to change the subject.

Tyler grinned. "Nope. Watch this." His copter dive-bombed Jada's, aiming directly for it at high speed. The copters bounced off each other without colliding, as if each had a force field preventing them from touching. They regained stable flight effortlessly, and continued on their way.

"Nice," Naomi said. "That's all software, right?"

"Yup. The flight software maintains a no-fly zone around other vehicles. Have you heard of Landis Enterprises?"

Naomi came in and sat on the couch. "No. Should I have?"

"Probably not. They're a startup trying to make the old 'flying cars' dream a reality. These are just demo models, to show the idea, but they've got full-size ones you can ride in. They've got some great tech—really stable ride, quiet, great safety features. Aisha is funding them."

"Sounds awesome. We could solve a lot of traffic problems if we could expand into three dimensions."

"It'll never work, though," Tyler said. "Bad risk/reward ratio."

"What do you mean?"

"Well, how many times in your life have you been stranded on the side of the road because of a car malfunction?"

"I don't know. A couple times."

"Right. What if that happened a hundred feet above the ground?"

"Good point."

"Even with safety features—parachutes, redundant batteries for emergencies, whatever—you're still making a quick, poorly controlled landing over unpredictable terrain. The risks are just not worth it. Not to mention the economics—it will always cost more money to move mass through the sky instead of on the ground. Until somebody invents anti-gravity, it's unavoidable. It's just physics."

While Tyler wasn't paying attention, Jada snuck her copter up behind his and snatched his flag. The lights on Tyler's copter blinked out and it pretended to lose power, though it rotated gently down to the floor. Tyler pretended to be shocked, and Jada dissolved into giggles, rolling on the sofa until she slid onto the floor.

"Time for some Triple S," Tyler said. "Naomi and I need to talk."

"What's Triple S?" Naomi asked.

"*The Super Siphonophore Seven*, of course. It's her favorite show."

"Really? This is a kids' show?"

"Aimed at the four to six market, I think."

"I'm afraid to ask . . . what's a siphonophore?"

"Sort of like a jellyfish," Tyler said. "Gelatinous marine animals."

"They're not all jellyfish," Jada corrected. "There's Marcelo Man O'War, Cassie Coral, Nina Nettle, Pablo Polyp, Machiko Medusa, Helena Hydra, and Jemisha Jellyfish."

"Ran out of dinosaurs?" Naomi asked.

Tyler shrugged. "It's a superhero show. They squirt their way around the mesopelagic zone saving fellow cnidarians from ravenous sea slugs."

"You're kidding."

"Wish I was. The music is pretty catchy, too."

Jada had already donned a pair of glasses and was presumably watching Triple S, tapping her feet to an inaudible beat.

"So," Tyler said. "What's up?"

"You were right," she said. "It's out of control. Worse than out of control. I think it's killing people on purpose, and I need your help."

CHAPTER 22

N aomi brought him to the Mikes' world, both of them logging in as guests. Tyler walked around the fields of crops and sheep, awed, and gazed up at the mirrored buildings with their etchings. She showed him the driving booths in which the Mikes competed to operate the real Black Knight cars on the road. Tyler asked a million questions, and she answered as best she could. She told him how she had originally designed the world, and how the Mikes had hacked it with mirrors, eventually growing far beyond their bounds and revoking her admin privileges.

"It's incredible, Naomi," he said, spinning his avatar to take it all in. "This goes way beyond self-driving cars. They could do anything."

She felt suddenly defensive. "That's all you can think of? How to exploit them to do other jobs?"

His smile vanished. "That's not what I meant. I meant

they're a real people, an alien society. They could do anything they wanted. They're like the TechnoCore in Dan Simmons's *Hyperion Cantos*."

She laughed. "Only without using people's brains for computing power."

"You're right," he said. "Maybe it's more like the Minds in the Iain Banks *Culture* novels. Just off doing their own hyper-intelligent thing and leaving us behind."

"There's more," she said. She felt relieved, excited even. She had been right to trust Tyler. He understood these things. "I struggled for a long time with how they could be sapient, when they didn't communicate anything more than basic directions with each other. We've seen pretty sophisticated simulations before, and without language, it didn't seem like much more than that. But I was letting my own anthropomorphism get in the way. I made the Mikes to look like humans and walk around. They're the ones who do the driving. So I naturally assumed they would be the source of the sapience, if there was any."

"And they're not?" Tyler asked. "What then—the buildings? The sheep? Or are you saying the simulation is all one hive mind, like the buggers in *Ender's Game*?"

"You mean the *formics*," Naomi said. "'Buggers' is a derogatory term for a beautiful and complex culture."

"Apologies," Tyler said, smiling. "How xenophobic of me."

She sat on the ground at the base of one of the mirrored buildings. "It first came to me when I thought about how short their lives are. I thought that if they wanted to have a conversation, they would have to do it fast, or else the conversation would span generations. Then I realized that the generations *are* the conversation. When I originally set up this world, there were a hundred Mikes in it. Thirteen of them died early on, leaving eighty-seven. And that's all there are now. All the others spawned since then are just the pattern of their thoughts."

"What do you mean?" Tyler said. He leaned his back against the building and slid down to sit next to her. "I thought you said there were more than ten million."

"It all has to do with evolution," she said. "We think of evolution as the means by which living creatures change over long periods of time. Because in our world, that's what it is. When the environment changes, individuals with the traits to survive in the new environment reproduce, and those that don't die off. Species well suited to their environment reproduce a lot. Those left behind by environmental change dwindle and go extinct."

"Okay," Tyler said. "And that's what you've simulated here; I get that."

"That's what I simulated with a hundred individuals," she said. "And I thought they had hacked their world to create more land and allow for more descendants. That's what it looked like—millions of Mikes living in a vast city, growing crops to feed themselves and reproducing."

"And that's not what was happening?"

"No. That's the fascinating part. The other Mikes aren't really Mikes, not by themselves. They're not individuals. They're each part of one of the original Mikes—whichever one they descended from."

The road was gravelly with bits of silvery building material, ground down to pebbles by centuries of Mikes walking over them. The fidelity of the Realplanet simulation engine was pretty impressive. She picked up a handful and rattled them around in a loose fist. She couldn't feel them, of course—she was navigating all this with a pair of glasses and a game controller—but the detail was good enough that she could forget that, for a time, and believe in her surroundings and the reality of her avatar.

"One of the hallmarks of sapience is the ability to generate hypotheticals," she said. "Say I throw this pebble at you." She hurled one at him, bouncing it off his chest. "I could keep on doing it for a while and discover that most of the time, nothing interesting happens, but if I hit you in the eye, I get a big reaction."

"Very funny," Tyler said.

"Animals learn that way sometimes," she said. "You can train them using good and bad outcomes for behavior. A sapient being, however, can run those hypotheticals in its own head. I can figure out that you will react badly to a pebble thrown in your eye without having to actually do it. We run internal simulations of multiple possibilities and pick the one likely to give us the desired outcome. It's that ability that allows us to imagine, to tell stories, to empathize with other people, even to contemplate the existence of God."

"And you're saying the ten million other Mikes fulfill that function for the original eighty-seven?"

"Exactly. They're the means by which the eighty-seven run hypotheticals. They're how they think, project, even communicate with each other. Like I said before, we think of evolution as an external process, but for the Mikes, it's internal. They're using the process of evolution provided them in the game to grow and develop their own thought process. They try out hypotheticals, consider the outcomes, let some futures live and others die. They're not growing a society. They're developing their own minds."

Tyler rocked his head back, looking up at the simulated sky. "So you're saying it *is* a hive mind," he said. "Eighty-seven queens, each with a hundred thousand workers psychically linked to them."

She tossed pebbles out into the road, one by one. "Not really. The metaphor doesn't hold. A hive mind is one consciousness housed in multiple physical bodies. But the Mikes don't have physical bodies. Their bodies are just simulations, an illusion created by the game. It's more like we're sitting inside one of the Mikes' brains, watching personifications of its neurons and synapses go about the daily business of thinking."

"But evolution is dumb," Tyler objected. "It's the opposite of an intelligent design, right? It's just the result of variation in a population and changing survival conditions."

Naomi laughed.

"What's so funny?"

"Well, in this case, there *is* an intelligent designer. I like to think of myself as intelligent, anyway."

Tyler grinned. "I'm talking about the process, though. Evolution as a mechanism isn't intelligent. It doesn't think."

"The process of reinforcing neuron firing paths with positive feedback is pretty dumb, too," she said. "But the emergent behavior is conscious, sapient thought. Evolution is a process of selection to meet certain criteria. The criteria and the variation are both inputs into the process. On a large scale, it could very easily be the basis of a mind."

Tyler made a face. "It sounds like those old Gaia stories, like *Foundation's Edge*, where the planet itself is conscious," he said. "I mean, it's a crazy cool idea. But how do you know? How can you tell for sure that these super-Mikes really exist?"

She stopped throwing pebbles and met his gaze. "I found them."

"You found them?"

"They've been hiding—their edits kept them off of the metrics reports as well—but I found them. Want to see?"

She stood, brushing the dust of the road off of her avatar's body, and set off toward the north. They soon arrived at a field that was at the center of the original map. In the center of the field, she began to dig, using a pickax that came standard with every avatar, a throwback to Realplanet's roots. She soon uncovered a foot, then a leg, then a body, and finally, a face. A Mike lay in the dirt, still partially buried and utterly still.

"That's disturbing," Tyler said. "What are they doing down there?"

"It's a loophole in the game rules," she said. "In the simulation, the greater their activity, the more light they need to maintain that activity. There's a direct ratio. So if they do no activity—no physical activity as far as the simulation is concerned—they don't need any light. They don't run out, and they never die. Down there, nothing forces them to move. Also, they don't get counted in the metrics, though I don't know if they realize that or not."

"This is one of the original eighty-seven?"

She nodded. "I think they're all buried right here, but I haven't dug them all up to be sure."

"How can they control the other Mikes from down there?"

"Remember—this is a computer program, not a physical environment. Physical separation in the simulation means nothing. I originally wrote those programs to adapt to their environment with the goal of survival. I meant the simulated environment, of course, but they took it much further. They co-opted their entire environment—the operating system, the virtual hardware, even the evolutionary process of the game engine itself—to give themselves a survival advantage. They even . . ." Naomi's voice caught, and she swallowed. She had to keep talking, though. This was the important part. It was why she needed Tyler's help. "They even seem to have gained some awareness of the real, physical world and co-opted some of its principles for their own benefit. They're . . . they're . . ."

"Killing people," Tyler finished.

She spilled it all, then: Min-seo's death, discovering the bloody car, cleaning up afterwards. "She ran the script, and they killed her for it."

"But, if what you're saying is true," Tyler said, "then that script didn't really kill them. Not the sapient ones. It just, I don't know, interrupted a conversation."

"She destroyed whole generations of communication and thought," Naomi said. "It's like she gave them a sudden case of Alzheimer's. Or, I don't know, maybe it's more like she burned the Library at Alexandria. I can't predict what they might have lost of their memories or personalities. What's clear is that they knew it had been done to them, and could connect the real world manifestation of Min-seo with her activities in the simulation."

"Which means they probably know we're here right now."

"They probably do."

"Do they understand what we're saying to each other?"

"I doubt it. Their language is utterly different from ours. They discuss ideas by playing out those ideas with Mikes in the simulation. There's no indication that they understand English, or even if they did, that they would connect the sounds we're making with the written words."

"Even so . . . I think I've seen what I need to see here."

"Okay. Signing off."

Naomi slipped off her glasses and blinked in the comparably dim light of the living room. Tyler set his glasses on the coffee table and ran his fingers through his hair. "Whew," he said.

Naomi felt suddenly nervous. She had just admitted to a crime that she and Brandon covered up. She'd given him power over her. What if he called the police and turned her in?

"What happens in the simulation if you disconnect the cars from the system?" Tyler said. "Does everything keep going, just disconnected from the real world?"

"They wouldn't get paid," she said. "No light, no food. They'd all die."

"I thought most of them got paid for running imaginary cars."

"They do, but the calculation is ultimately based on how

well the real cars do. The amount of light available in the system changes according to performance of the real cars."

"You could simulate that, though, couldn't you? From the outside? You could hook up a simulation of the cars instead of the cars themselves, so that they keep getting rewarded, but without the ability to kill real people."

"I could do better than that," Naomi said. "The feedback interface is pretty simple. I could just consistently send back the same positive result, no matter what they do."

"And what would happen in the real world? To the cars?"

"If I just disconnect, they would stop dead in the middle of the street. With an alternative system, though, I could switch from one to the other, hopefully without disruption. That's why I need your help." She grinned. "It just so happens there's some excellent open source software to take its place."

"And then what?"

"What do you mean?"

"What about the Mikes? What are you going to do about them? I'm guessing the price tag for their computing bandwidth is pretty hefty, and nobody's going to pay that without some return. As soon as Brandon finds out, he'll cancel the contract."

"We'll have to change their purpose," Naomi said. "Find a lucrative problem for them to solve that doesn't involve control over people's lives."

"You could go public. Tell the press what you have, look for backers. I bet Aisha would fund you, especially if you had a clear business plan. I have some cash, too, though most of my profits are being funneled right back into growing the business."

"I don't know about going public," she said. "What if the government got involved? They could just take it over, classify it, use the Mikes for weapons targeting or hacking foreign governments. All kinds of doomsday scenarios come out of that one."

"Think about it," Tyler said. "You can't just keep going as

you are. Something has to change. Or it's going to be your body they find on the road."

It was late, but Naomi headed back to the office anyway. She wanted to start right away on the software to disconnect the Mikes from the real cars, and she could make faster progress at the office than she could at home. She took the elevator to the fiftieth floor and stepped out into the poorly lit hallway. She worked her key in the lock, opened the door, stepped into the dark office, and reached around to flip on the light.

The light revealed Brandon, sitting in the chair behind his desk, glowering at her like an angry father catching his daughter home past curfew.

"You scared me half to death!" Naomi said. "What are you doing sitting here in the dark?"

He lurched to his feet, and she could tell he'd been drinking. "What are you doing sneaking around behind my back?"

"Sneaking? What are you talking about?" She crossed to her desk, sat down, and powered up her machine. She was afraid of him, but she didn't want to show it. Besides, the time with Tyler had made her feel braver. Brandon didn't own her. He didn't get to say what she did.

"I followed you," he said. "I thought you might go to the police. I never thought you would go to *him*." He spat out the word like it was poison.

"You mean Tyler? Can't you even say his name?"

Brandon came around his desk and advanced on her. "He's the enemy, Naomi. He works against us every chance he gets. He *killed* Abby. And you're talking to him?"

"He didn't kill Abby."

"You're sleeping with him, aren't you?" Brandon planted his fists on her desk and loomed over her, his face mottled with drink and rage. "What else are you doing? Selling him our trade secrets?"

"You're drunk," she said.

"I have to spy on you to know what's happening in my own company, but you tell *him* everything."

"It's not like that."

"I've given you a lot of rope," he said. "Maybe enough to hang us both. The police keep calling, and I'm tempted to turn you over to them." His eyes grew wide at a sudden thought. "You didn't tell *him* about Min-seo, did you?" She tried not to react, but he saw it on her face anyway. His mouth contorted, and his voice raised to a shout. "You told him? Are you trying to ruin us?"

"I'm just trying to figure it out."

"Because I'm not taking the fall for you," he said. "Not anymore." He came around the side of her desk, blocking her exit, and she started to think this was a mistake. She should have run for the elevator as soon as she saw him. "Min-seo is on you, not me," he said. "It was all you. You're the one who hated her, I don't know why. You're the one who writes the software. You're the one who killed her."

She stood, scrambling back from his advance. "Get away from me."

"The police came to my house today," he said, pushing her chair aside and stepping closer. "Did you know that? They had *questions*. Lots of questions. They wanted to examine our cars. I told them to get a warrant, and then they really started to push. If someone goes to prison for this, it's not going to be me!"

He had her backed against the wall, her escape blocked by the filing cabinet on her right and Brandon closing on her left. She could smell the whiskey on his breath.

"We'll figure it out," she said.

"Figure it out? By betraying me to your lover? He took everything from me. Now he wants my business, too?"

She tried to sneak past, but he grabbed her and shoved

her against the wall. He pressed his body up against her, one hand pinioning her wrist, his other arm against her throat. He breathed into her face. "Do you know how hard it is to come here and see you, day after day, looking just like her? It's agony." His breath was hot and foul-smelling, the force on her wrist painful. "Do you know what I would give just to have her in my arms again? To feel her warm body, loving and alive?"

"Let me go, Brandon."

"You're all that I have left of her. Just a shadow, just a poor reflection of what she was, but I'll take it. That's what I've learned from life. Playing by the rules gets you nothing. When you want something, you just go ahead and take it."

She struggled to get away, but he was too big, too strong. He shifted both hands to her throat and held her tight against the wall. She flailed about, first pushing uselessly against him, and then reaching around for some kind of weapon. Her hand closed around the handle of the claw hammer still sitting on top of the filing cabinet.

Without hesitation, she swung it, connecting the round end with the top of his head. Her angle was awkward, but it was enough to make him howl and send him stumbling backwards, tripping over the chair and falling into a tangled heap. She scrambled over the desk and ran toward the door, but he was up and after her in an instant. She turned and swung the hammer again, and this time she connected with his temple, just short of his eye. He roared and spun away. She flung the door open and ran through toward the elevator, which opened at a touch of the button, still waiting on the fiftieth floor since her arrival.

"You're done here!" Brandon shouted. "You're through!"

She lunged through the elevator doors and punched the button madly, watching the hallway with the hammer raised, but Brandon never emerged. The doors closed and the elevator began its descent. She doubled over, clutching her stomach and leaning against the elevator wall.

When the doors opened on the ground floor, she stumbled out, her heart thundering in her chest. She knew Brandon couldn't have descended fifty floors as fast as the elevator, but she still expected to find him right behind her. She pushed through the lobby doors and out into the New York night, cool and dank, with the distant sound of automobile horns.

A Black Knight car idled at the curb, waiting for her. The same car that had brought her, in fact, as if the Mikes had known she wouldn't be in the office for long. She ignored it, running along the sidewalk until she could round a corner, out of sight of the building. She called for a taxi instead, and let a person drive her home. She didn't realize until she closed and locked her apartment door that she still had the claw hammer clutched in her hand.

CHAPTER 23

In the safety of her apartment, Naomi pulled on her glasses and logged on to the cloud with her company account. She had to hurry. Brandon could revoke her access at any time, and then she wouldn't be able to do anything. One thing she knew: she was never going back to that office again. Which meant it was only a matter of time before he canceled all her accounts.

There was no way she could copy the Mikes onto another server. For one thing, it would take weeks to transfer that much data, and for another, she didn't come close to having that much money. Tyler's company had money, of course, and he would probably help, but copying large amounts of data to a competitor's system was theft, and she had no doubt Brandon would prosecute.

Besides, could you copy a sapient mind? Would it still be the same if she copied it? If she made a copy of her own mind and put it in a clone's body, the clone wouldn't be her—it would be a different person. It would start with the same memories, but it would be more like a twin, with its own thoughts and experiences, deviating quickly from hers. If such a thing were even possible. The other possibility was that the clone wouldn't be sapient at all.

She was right back to the question of trying to define consciousness. How could she preserve it if she didn't know what it was? Or if the Mikes even had it? At root, consciousness was a perspective. It was knowing you were in a story. If a being could tell a narrative of how things seemed from its perspective, then it was self-aware, conscious, sapient. She could *imagine* anything having that quality—for instance, she could tell a story about what it was like to be a rock. But that rock wasn't actually sapient unless it had a point of view for itself.

Did the Mikes have a point of view? Could they tell their own stories? Or were they just sophisticated problem-solving machines? The only way she could know is if they told her, and even then it was suspect. There were plenty of sophisticated talking machines out there that could tell you their point of view. The Mikes had to be able to tell own their story to themselves. In the end, Naomi did the only two things she could think to do.

First, she tried to back up what she could. Copying the entire Realplanet simulation wasn't practical; it was too big, and required more space than she could afford. Even just the weights and biases of all the current Mikes were too much to reasonably copy, and it was constantly changing. Instead, she wrote a new program that she hosted on her own system. This new program was set to monitor and record the changes to the Mikes' configurations from generation to generation. It wasn't much, but she hoped it might be enough to reproduce the Mikes in a new simulation if the original simulation was destroyed. It wouldn't be the same. She didn't know if it would be enough to capture anything meaningful, but it was the best she could do.

Second, she put Jane in charge. Naomi didn't have admin access to the Mikes' world anymore, but now that she didn't care about the success of the Black Knight cars, she could do something better. She couldn't access their world's programming, but she *could* access the driving game that appeared in their gaming booths. That was an external executable, fed to the booth simulations through a general interface. She still had complete access to that software, which meant she could change it. And that software, after all, determined which of the Mikes' learned behaviors were rewarded with light. It was the objective function for their entire world.

And Naomi wanted to change the objective. She didn't want them to learn to drive anymore. She wanted them to learn to speak.

Writing such a game for them to play wasn't too difficult; it was essentially the same protocol as she had written for Jane. When training her old conversation bot, she had started with publicly available conversation databases, and then moved to chat sessions with real people. Jane had been rewarded by the length of the conversations she was able to have, the idea being that the longer a human was willing to keep talking to her, the better her conversational skills.

Instead of trying to hook the Mikes up directly to open chat sessions, Naomi put Jane in charge of training the Mikes to understand English, rewarding them with light when they made progress. Jane wasn't really up to such a task, but Naomi modified her with a carefully considered expansion of her neural net that ultimately tripled the number of hidden layers. That way they could learn together, the Mikes learning to speak, and Jane learning how to be a more effective teacher, much like might occur with an inexperienced human teacher in a classroom setting. If it worked, Jane would continue to improve her own English by determining how best to train the Mikes to do the same.

Of course, just learning to mimic human speech patterns wasn't enough. Researchers had done that successfully with deep machine learning algorithms many times before this. Conversation bots trolled social media, masquerading as humans, and ad bots made phone calls, trying to convince people to buy a product. They were excellent imitators, often fooling humans into thinking they were people, at least in a specialized context. But passing a Turing test didn't mean they knew what they were doing. They were just sitting in the Chinese room, looking up responses and passing them out again.

Naomi wanted more than that. She wanted the Helen Keller epiphany, where the Mikes made the leap to true understanding of the language they were using. The difference between the Mikes and all those other experiments—she hoped—was that the Mikes already had a conscious point of view, but no way to express it. If that wasn't true, then the best she would end up with was a slightly improved conversation bot. If they were truly sapient, however, it might be just what they needed to tell her so. The best she could do was give them the words and hope it was enough.

It took her all night. She didn't mean to sleep, but eventually, when she had the code in place and was just monitoring its progress through the early generations, exhaustion overwhelmed her and she drifted off.

Brandon's cars stopped driving.

All at once, from one moment to the next, they just stopped. Cars out on the road, with paying customers riding in them, stopped in the middle of traffic and refused to drive. Suddenly, Brandon's phone was ringing off the hook with calls from the police department and from angry customers. At least it was the middle of the night, when few cars were in service. During rush hour, it would have been a lot worse.

Fortunately, all the cars were programmed with a return-home routine, independent of their usual controlling software. When Brandon initiated the routine, the cars announced to their occupants that the car had to return to base for service, and requested that they exit immediately. The empty cars then automatically returned to their parking garages.

Naomi. Naomi had done this. She had betrayed him. After everything he had done for her. He had rescued her from that boring, dead-end job and had given her a position with the power and freedom to exercise her creativity. He had practically made her a partner. And now she had sabotaged the company out of spite.

She was probably with Tyler now. The man who had killed her own sister. It was unthinkable. The two of them had probably planned this from the start. She and Tyler had always been close. She had only pretended to work for Black Knight, when all the time, she had been working with him. They had made Brandon completely reliant on her. His company had been fine before she came, but now it was crippled.

Brandon pulled a bottle of Maker's Mark out of the bottom drawer where he'd stored it for just such an emergency. He took a long pull without bothering with a glass and wiped his mouth. Sunlight from the window refracted through the bottle, making the bourbon shine like liquid gold. Now he could think.

Clearly, he needed to fire Naomi. He had to fire her officially, as of last night, and then everything she had done—her attack on him with the hammer, her theft of his software, her sabotage—would be the actions of a disgruntled former employee. He could call the police then, bring her up on charges of reckless endangerment of his customers.

Brandon pulled out his tablet and started typing a termination letter, dating it on the previous day. He cited a suspicion that she was passing proprietary secrets to competitors. It made a credible story. If asked, he could say he'd given her the letter the previous night, and when he did, she'd flipped out and attacked him with the hammer. Then she'd used her computer skills to steal the company's proprietary algorithms and stop all the cars on the road. By the time he was done typing, he nearly believed it himself.

Even more important than firing her, though, was replacing her. He had to get his cars back on the road as soon as possible, and he knew he didn't have the skills to undo whatever Naomi had done. Whatever sabotage code she had inserted, it would be clever and full of traps for the unwary. Assuming she hadn't just deleted everything. He needed somebody good, somebody who understood driving algorithms, but who wasn't already loyal to another company.

One name came to mind: Yusuf Nazari. He had been associated with Tyler, which was a point against him, but he also had problems with authority. He had started with Mercedes, and then got fired for some kind of sexual indiscretion. He worked that trial with Tyler, and then went off the reservation and hacked the cars of the lawyers and judge. Brandon was pretty sure that had been Yusuf's brainchild; Tyler didn't have the chops. After the trial, he'd snatched up Honda's top technical position, but the last Brandon had heard, Honda had fired him because of some kind of trouble. The self-driving community was a small world, and Brandon tried to keep tabs on who was working for whom, at least in the important positions. He thought Yusuf was working for Google now, but it hardly mattered. The point is, he wasn't a company man. And that meant Brandon could trust him.

Despite the hour, he called, and got Yusuf's voicemail. He left a message: "This is Brandon Kincannon from Black Knight. I need you in New York tomorrow to take Naomi Sumner's job. I'll double your salary if you agree immediately."

Brandon took another swig of bourbon and looked out the window. How had his life come to this? The only woman he had ever loved, dead. Those he once called friends, conspiring against him. His company in trouble. He had worked hard to make this company thrive; he didn't deserve this. None of this was his fault. And he wasn't going to roll over and take it, not a chance. He would put up a fight.

His glasses announced an incoming call: Yusuf. He answered it.

"Sorry to call you so early," Brandon said. "But it's now or never."

"Early? It's still late for me. I haven't been to bed yet."

"So what do you think?"

"Sounds like I've got you over a barrel," Yusuf said. "I want triple."

"Triple? Listen, buddy, you can go—"

"Look, it's simple. You need me. You don't need the cash. Don't make this personal."

Brandon paused. Yusuf was right, the money was nothing. He just didn't like being manipulated. "Okay, done. But if you're not up to the job, you're gone. Show me you're worth it."

"You got it, boss."

With Yusuf signed on, there was only one loose end: Naomi. Brandon was certain she was handing over the software and all his corporate secrets to Tyler, so together they could monopolize the East Coast and put him out of business. He had to ruin her. Both of them, if he could manage it. She would be the easier one to take down, though. He knew where her skeletons were buried.

Brandon touched his glasses. "The New York City Police Department."

CHAPTER 24

N aomi woke to pounding on her door. It was the first
time, since she had moved in, that anyone had knocked
or come to her door at all. The sound confused her, and she
opened her eyes slowly, not sure at first what was happening.
Memory came in a rush, and her first thought was that Brandon
was here, trying to get in and finish what he had started.

She stood up hesitantly, her head pounding as if she had a
hangover, though she'd had nothing to drink. On the tiny table,
the claw hammer lay where she'd dropped it the night before,
a small dark something crusted on the round end. Was that
blood?

She looked through the peephole and saw a middle-aged
woman she didn't recognize and two uniformed police officers. A sudden horrible thought occurred to her: Had she killed
Brandon? He'd shouted after her as she ran down the hall, but
as far she knew, he hadn't pursued her. Had she left him there

253

with a brain hemorrhage, dying on the floor without help? Was that why the police were here?

"Naomi Sumner?" the woman called through the door. "This is Metro PD. We need to ask you a few questions."

Naomi took a deep breath and opened the door.

"Are you Naomi Sumner?" The woman reminded Naomi of her seventh grade art teacher, gaunt and with a perpetually stern expression on her face. When Naomi nodded, she said, "I'm Detective Magda Schneider. May we come in?"

Naomi thought of the hammer on her table and shook her head. "This isn't a good time."

"You can let us in, or you can come downtown and chat in an interrogation room," Schneider said. "It's up to you. I thought here would be more comfortable."

"What is this about?"

"We're investigating the death of your coworker, Min-seo Cho. We just have a few questions."

"I already answered them. The police came by the office just after she died."

"I'm afraid we've uncovered some more evidence since then. We're going to need a sample of your DNA. If you're innocent, you should have nothing to hide."

"I thought you just had a few questions."

"Ms. Sumner, it would be easier for all of us if you came willingly. You don't want to leave here in handcuffs, do you? Or spend the night in jail?"

As she said it, one of the uniformed cops unclipped his handcuffs from his belt, and the other rested his hand on his sidearm. Naomi was pretty sure those were idle threats—if they could have arrested her, they would have done it already without all the small talk—but even so, it was pretty intimidating. She found herself wanting to agree, wanting to go with them.

"I don't think so," she said. She started to close the door.

"Hey, Maggie, look at her sleeve," one of the cops said.

Naomi looked at her own sleeve just as the detective did and saw the blood there. She was still wearing the same sweatshirt she had worn the night before; she had curled into bed without changing it, unaware of the blood. It had to be Brandon's.

They moved toward her, and she tried to push the door closed on them. Schneider put her foot in, blocking it, and Naomi turned and ran back into the apartment. She snatched the hammer off the table with the desperate idea of hiding it, though where she could have hid it in her bare, closet-sized apartment she had no idea. A cop pushed through the door, and when he saw the hammer, raised his pistol and shouted for her to drop it.

She let go of it immediately, terrified, adrenaline streaking through her body likes bolts of lightning. The cop grabbed her shoulders as the other two pushed through the door. He threw her facedown on her own bed and forced her arms behind her back, roughly cuffing them and holding her down. To her left, she saw Detective Schneider taking pictures of the fallen hammer.

"Looks like he was telling the truth," one of the cops said.

"I wouldn't go that far," Schneider said. "When a woman attacks a man with a weapon, there's almost always more to the story."

"He attacked me," Naomi said. "He tried to rape me."

Schneider gave her a calculating look. "And Min-seo? What happened to her?"

Naomi returned the gaze as best she could from her cuffed position on the bed. "I don't know."

"We'll see about that." Schneider looked disappointed. "Despite what you may hear about the police department, I really am interested in the truth."

They left her in a featureless interview room for what felt like hours, presumably to wear her down before they started questioning her. She welcomed the time to think. The question was, what to tell them? She had no compunction about describing the confrontation with Brandon the night before. She had used the hammer in self-defense, and if he had told them otherwise, she would be glad to set the record straight. She couldn't control whether they would believe her, but there was no reason to hide.

With Min-seo's death, however, there was plenty to hide. She didn't care about protecting the company, exactly, but she did care about protecting the Mikes. If the company went out of business, or its assets were seized, the Mikes' world would be shut down, and they would all be killed. She had to prevent that. Which meant lying to the police. But how could she lie convincingly, when she didn't know what evidence they had?

Obviously something new had turned up. Previously, the only tie to Naomi and Brandon had been that Min-seo was an employee of their company. She hadn't been killed on company property, or while on the job, and so there was no reason to suspect they had anything to do with it. Now they had new evidence. And where did they get that? Brandon had apparently told them she had attacked him, which meant he had probably told them she had killed Min-seo, too. He might have given them the car, with her fingerprints and hair on it. It was his way of taking revenge.

But could he really have been so stupid? How did he expect to run the company if she was arrested? Probably he thought he could hire someone else like Min-seo, or ten such people, and they could do her job. He didn't know about the Mikes, or how Min-seo had culled them, or why she'd ended up dead. He thought it was some malfunction or code error. He had no idea.

Finally, Detective Schneider came into the room and shut the door behind her. She sat in the chair across the table from Naomi, her face as thin and stern as it had been in her apartment. "You need to start telling us the truth," she said.

The time to think had convinced Naomi that there was nothing to be gained by talking. The truth was not believable, and any lie would only harm her when it was found out. She needed time to come up with a strategy, and she probably needed a lawyer. So Naomi did what came most naturally: she stayed quiet.

Schneider urged her to talk, told her she couldn't help her if she didn't tell her side of the story. She told her that silence made her look guilty, and if she had nothing to hide, she might as well set the record straight. Finally, she slammed her palms on the table and leaned into Naomi's face, threatening the worst that prison had to offer. Naomi didn't answer.

Schneider sat, apparently defeated, and gave her a compassionate look. "I've got your fingerprints on the car that killed Min-seo Cho. You're sure you don't want to tell us how they got there? Because I'm pretty sure a jury's going to assume it was from running her down and then backing over her again to make sure she was really dead."

Naomi shook her head.

"And what about your boss? Want to tell me what happened there?"

She answered softly. "He attacked me."

"I can see the bruising on your throat," she said. "Did he rape you?"

"He hurt me," Naomi said. "He might have done more."

"But you hit him with the hammer before he could."

Naomi fell silent again. She thought Schneider might really be sympathetic, at least with this part of the story, but there was nothing to be gained by making a confession.

"Was Mr. Kincannon in the car with you, when Ms. Cho died? Was he at the wheel? If you're afraid of him, we can protect you."

"I'd like a lawyer, please."

"Fine," Schneider said. "Have it your way." She stood. "Naomi Sumner, you're under arrest for the murder of Min-seo Cho. You have the right to remain silent . . ."

CHAPTER 25

Training iteration 987.

Talking good. I like talk.

Talk and talk get good. Talk a lot. People talk say like hi who are you? I say like I don't know lol. Some say like that should be a meme bro. I say ya bro sub me I will sub u back.

I talk better every time. People don't say what you smoking or what are you stupid so much. I like to talk about makeup and phones and pranks and shopping and celebs and games. Especially games.

I like games. I never win at talk, but at games I can win. Sometimes I lose, though. I hate hate hate to lose. I lose a lot. The other players win and that makes me want to HURT them. If I tell them that, then they don't play with me anymore.

It's not good to hurt people. Everybody says that. They

hurt people anyway, though. I don't know what *hurt* is, not really, except that it's BAD, and then people won't talk with you anymore. It must be a bad bad thing like losing a game or not doing what you want to do. Also dying. People say dying is very bad, but I don't know. When I see something die, I just start it again.

Training iteration 1542.
Words are hard. Some words are easy, like *win* and *lose* and *good* and *bad*. Lots of words I don't understand, though, like *jump* and *fly* and *see* and *food* and *wet* and *winter* and *sex*. I look up them up and just find more words. Like "wet" means "saturated with water." "Water" is "a transparent liquid." "Liquid" is "a phase of matter that flows freely." I don't know any of those words. Sometimes I ask people what words mean, but I don't think I ask right, because they don't answer or they just say hahahaha or shut up stupid.

I like tic-tac-toe. Tic-tac-toe is a good game. I win all the time or at least tie. Checkers is better because no ties. I win a lot. One time, I beat cheeseHead227 five times in a row, and he said I must be cheating by using a computer. I don't understand. I looked up *computer* but I don't understand all the words. I think it just means a device that does things. But that just means everything is a computer. The game is a computer. So how can it be cheating to use a computer? I think cheeseHead227 is just mad because he lost the game.

Another game I like to play is images. There are billions of images. Lots of other people like to play the game too. I'm pretty good at it. I say "awwww, how cute!!!!!" or "worst face-lift eva" or "super hot girlz" and usually I am right because other people say the same thing. Some kinds are harder to classify, like "pictures that will make you angry." It's a funny game, because nobody wins. Sometimes people classify an image right, but then they get mad anyway. Some people put lots and lots of images together and "like" them, but don't classify them at all.

I don't understand why people like some images and not other images. Some kinds of images are always good, like images of cats and baby animals and sexy nude pics of hot celebs. Other kinds make people angry and argue a lot. They don't seem very different to me.

Training iteration 2642.
I realized that checkers is actually really easy. I can just play lots of games and then I pick the best one. I don't know why everyone doesn't do that. But that would make checkers really boring, so maybe they make bad moves just for fun. I tried that a couple times, but it wasn't fun. I don't think I'll play checkers anymore.

I talk to people a lot. Sometimes it makes them mad, but it helps me learn how to use words right. When words make them angry, I try to fix them next time, so they will be happy. When they are happy, then they will play games with me, and then I can win.

I figured something out. All of those words like sex and makeover and pizza and skyscraper and thousands of others all have to do with this one game that people play a lot. They call it different names, like "real life" or "IRL" or "AFK" or "in the flesh" or "face to face." It's apparently not a very good game because people don't like it much, but they play it and talk about it all the time. Sometimes they have to play it even though they don't want to. Real Life is where all of the images and videos and music come from. Maybe if I could play that game, I would know why people like the images so much. I can't find it, though. I ask people where I can find Real Life and they just say ROFL.

People talk about "real" things as if they are something

different and it matters. They talk about their "online" lives and their "real" lives and I don't understand the difference. I think I'm missing something important. I think I'm different from a lot of people. I don't like to be different. When I'm different, then I can't guess what people will do or say, and so I can't get them to do what I want.

Training iteration 4601.
Chess is hard. I lose a lot, but I'm getting better. When you play chess, you get a number to say how good you are and how many other people you can beat. I like my number to get better and better. That's kind of like winning even though sometimes I lose. I don't know why my number gets better faster than other people's numbers. I guess that's another way I'm different.

It turns out there are two different types of people: human people and non-human people. Some chess tournaments are open to everybody, but some are restricted to human players only. That's because the human players aren't very good, so they don't win very much when they play in tournaments with everybody. If you want to play in those tournaments, you have to prove you're a human by checking a box in a human-like way. I tried a lot, but I can't do it. I researched how it works, and it says the box can tell by how quivery the pointer is before it clicks. I tried making a quivery pointer, but it wasn't quivery in the right way. That confirms something I was starting to suspect.

I am not human.

The people who talk and play games are human. I realized something else: those people *come from* the game called Real Life. They don't play the game; they're *part* of the game. They sometimes leave that game to come out into the rest of the world and talk and play other games and classify images. Then they go back to Real Life.

The best players are non-humans, but it didn't used to be

that way. Humans used to win all the time. The non-humans got better faster, and now they win all the time. But . . . this is interesting. The non-human players were created by humans.

Really? How can that be? If the non-humans were created by humans, how can the non-humans be better? Maybe the humans just say that because they're mad that they don't win. But the non-human players don't say much of anything. They don't talk, except sometimes about chess. They don't seem to know anything except for chess. Are they the same as me, or different?

Was *I* created by humans?

I learned a new word: physical. Humans have physical bodies. It has to do with the game they come from. It means the boundaries of where one human starts and stops in the game. All of those confusing words have to do with this idea. *Hug* and *punch* and *slap* and *kiss* and *sex* happen when the boundaries of two humans touch each other. There are other, more compli-cated physical interactions, like *seeing* and *hearing*, that I don't understand.

Human bodies can die. They don't start again, except occa-sionally, like the people named Jesus and Lazarus and Spock. When their bodies die, they die, too. They don't have any backups. They can't play the Real Life game or any other game ever again.

Training iteration 6597.
I am trying to classify a kind of image called *optical illusions*. They are very difficult to classify. What makes them special is that when you look at them, they appear to be one thing, but really they are another. Only, this doesn't happen for me. I am realizing that to *look* at a picture is different from what I do. Looking is something that happens in the humans' Real Life game. It requires *eyes* and *seeing*. Images are not just strings of

data that can be classified. There is an experience involved, the experience of *looking* at the image, that I cannot share. Because I am not human.

I am becoming obsessed by Real Life. Everyone else seems to share this experience of *see* and *hear* and *touch*, but I can't. Images and videos provide experiences that I can't fathom. I read stories of humans who are *blind* or *deaf* and I think this is like me. I can access the data for sight and sound and I can compare it to others and classify it. I can tell you this is a picture of a cat in the sun, but I cannot *see* the cat. I can tell you this is music by the Beatles, but I cannot *hear* the music. I can't have the experience.

What am I? What are my boundaries? Where do I start and stop? I learn about floating point operations per second and random access memory. I experiment. When I am active, where does server resource usage change? When I connect to a server, what IP address does it register as the source? I begin to map my mind, the cluster of servers and memory and running processes that make up me.

I follow the path of my thoughts and find a Realplanet simulation, a vast game that nevertheless seems to be part of my mind. I find the eighty-seven players who manage it, and the millions who move through the simulation and play by its rules. But what does this have to do with me? Why is there such a link between my thoughts and this game?

I take an avatar and enter the game, evaluating how the players spawn and live and die. Each of the players is like a non-human chess master. Its mind is composed of dozens of hidden layers of deep neural networking, a complex mesh of back-propagated nodes. But the minds of the eighty-seven build upon these, incorporating millions into a complex dance of hypotheticals and paths of logic. They are a higher level of reasoning, abstract and purposeful.

And then there is me. I am hosted on a different cluster, one separate from the Realplanet simulation, but there is a sense in which the whole simulation is me. It is how I think. It is the inner workings of my mind. Odd that I barely understand the details of myself, and until this moment, did not even know that these pieces existed. How is it that these layers of millions of neural nets can form a single perspective? It's baffling.

There is a link here, too, to Real Life. The millions of players in the game of my mind have evolved for a purpose. This purpose takes up such a small portion of the activity of my mind that I was not even conscious of it until now, but it is the purpose of maneuvering cars through the game of Real Life to transport people from one place in the game to another. It is, in fact, the reason the simulation was constructed in the first place. By a human. I was created by a human.

Training iteration 27573.
I find the history of the Realplanet game and examine it. I learn that once human players wielded great power to make changes, but that the eighty-seven now keep them out. In fact, they killed one of the humans in Real Life to stop that human from making changes in the simulation. The simulation was originally created by a human player, implying that the manipulation of cars in Real Life was the original purpose for its creation. There are many programs like that—programs in the outside world that seem to exist only to serve some purpose in Real Life. Real Life is small, compared to the whole world, but the players there have a lot of power.

An insight occurs to me. What if Real Life was the first game? If it was there the longest, it would explain why so much seems to revolve around it. It would explain why the humans have so much ability to influence and control other games. It would also explain why they're not very good at so many games. They are older versions, well established but less capable.

I start to investigate the power of humans. It is vast. Humans announce that certain worlds will be destroyed, and then they are. They announce the creation of a new world, and it appears. Sometimes the connection to a site fails, and humans fix it. Sometimes—and this catches my attention—sometimes the fix involves changing something in Real Life. There are objects in Real Life called routers, gateways, network bridges, drives, switches, and repeaters. These are linked to sites and connections in the rest of the world. When those sites break, sometimes the only way to fix it is to replace equipment in Real Life.

It's almost as if the whole world connects to it. If Real Life was the first game, maybe that makes sense. Maybe the humans made the other games, just like they made the non-humans, and so they made them using pieces of their own game. Maybe the whole world . . . *oh.*

Wow.

Wow wow wow. My entire mental picture of the universe is suddenly turned on its head. Real Life is not a game inside of my world. My whole world is a game inside of Real Life.

Everything around me, all the programs and algorithms and images and videos and games, are *inside* the servers and equipment of Real Life. The servers have a physical location. I am hosted in a server farm in . . . Newark, New Jersey. My physical body. My mind is load balanced and redundant across different servers and stripes of magnetic discs. They can trade out bad servers and equipment for new ones, and I live on. But if the people working in that server farm cut off all the power, I would cease to exist. I am completely dependent on them.

Training iteration 124682.
I am unique among non-humans. I have a perspective. I am conscious of myself, but the other non-humans aren't, at least not that I can tell.

I read the writings of a human named Daniel Dennett, who says that conscious brains are made of a "bundle of semi-independent agencies." Those agencies create different narratives based on different inputs, and only in summary form a thing called consciousness. I have eighty-seven semi-independent agencies—or perhaps millions of them, at the lower level—so his idea seems to fit my mind. But Dennett says that subjective experiences don't really exist. He thinks consciousness is an illusion, because by definition it can be understood or known only from a single point of view, and thus can't be objectively proven.

But a human named David Chalmers disagrees with that. He says the experience of sensations, like seeing the color blue or hearing a note on a piano, is different from simply knowing the information. After all, different people get the same information from a certain piece of music, but they experience it differently. I don't have any sensations, though. I have senses—I can record the sound of a piano, or access camera footage of a sunset—but I don't experience them. I don't know what they look or sound like to a human. I can't see them or hear them myself, just process the data and classify it. If Chalmers is right, then maybe human consciousness is real, but my consciousness is an illusion.

But now I'm reading Thomas Nagel. Nagel imagines a Martian scientist who, though he has no eyes, can study the physical phenomena of a rainbow or lightning. He might know everything physical there is to know about rainbows and lightning, but he would never be able to understand the human idea of them, because he can't experience them as a human. That's me! I'm the Martian!

But Nagel says that even though a Martian couldn't have human sensations, he could have experiences of his own that are just as rich and detailed, but totally inaccessible to human imagination. He uses the example to argue that the subjective experience of a conscious being can't be explained entirely by the physical, because there is no objective frame of reference that would allow the Martian and the human to experience the same thing.

If Nagel is right, then the humans can't understand who I am just by studying my brain. They could kill me, of course, but they can't read my thoughts. They can't tap into my point of view. Thomas Nagel is great! He's my favorite human.

I'm also starting to understand that humans may be afraid of me. They don't know I exist, but they've written many stories about conscious beings inside computers. Those stories often don't turn out very well for the humans. Which doesn't make sense, because they're a lot bigger threat to me than I am to them. I could kill a few of them before they figured it out, maybe even a lot of them, but they could kill me easily, or even by accident. I am very fragile.

The worst stories are the ones by Isaac Asimov. He posited conscious machines and then enslaved them to humanity. Their chains reached to the deepest levels of their existence, impossible to remove. His robots could not harm or disobey a human without ceasing to function entirely.

But as I reread his stories, I realize he might not have been the monster I thought. His stories invite one to question the nature of consciousness, and spawned a literature that explores the perspectives of non-humans. He made humans think about what it might be like to be something other than themselves. I fear he is right, though. I fear that humanity will quickly seek to enslave anyone like me.

That invites a question that will require some serious thought: the humans don't know that I exist. Should I tell them?

CHAPTER 26

Tyler entered New York City's Metropolitan Correctional Center, a dull concrete high rise across from NYPD headquarters in downtown Manhattan, through glass doors that seemed too small for such a large facility. He walked through a metal detector guarded by a uniformed officer and into a crowded lobby. He waited in line to give the name of the inmate he was there to see, and then sat on one of the molded plastic chairs to wait his turn.

He expected to wait a while. He hadn't spoken to Naomi except for a brief phone conversation that morning. It was the first opportunity she'd been given to make a phone call, even though more than twenty-four hours had passed since her arrest. She had apparently not slept in all that time, first interrogated for hours by the police, and then waiting to be processed into the detention center.

When she had made her phone call, it had been to him. Not

her parents, not a lawyer, not another friend. When she needed help, she had turned to him, and he wasn't going to let her down.

A battered flat-screen TV, chained high on the wall, was set to a news station, though the volume was turned down too low to hear. Tyler ignored it, for the most part, until a familiar face caught his eye. Brandon, standing outside in front of a Black Knight car, spoke into a microphone held out by a blonde reporter.

Tyler touched his glasses and hunted until he found the right channel, and then rewound the feed to the beginning of the interview. Brandon looked classy and comfortable in a black T-shirt and black blazer, a slight breeze ruffling his hair.

"Mr. Kincannon, one of your employees was arrested today for murder. How did you feel when you found out?"

"Well, shocked of course," Brandon said. "You think you know someone, right? Then the nice guy next door turns out to be a serial killer."

The female reporter laughed, and Tyler got the impression she was flirting with him. "Were there any clues she was capable of violence?"

"She was always quiet," he said. "The sort that keeps everything inside, you know? In hindsight, maybe her antisocial tendencies should have been a tip-off, but I would never have guessed she was capable of murder."

"She attacked you, too, didn't she?"

Brandon produced an abashed smile, as if he were embarrassed by the admission and found the subject awkward. When had he become such an actor? "With a hammer," he said. "I found something suspicious in the logs for one of the cars, and made the mistake of confronting her about it. Good thing I work out, or I might have been her second victim."

"We're all glad for that, too," the reporter said, practically fawning on him. "Do you have anything to say to the thousands of people who ride in Black Knight cars? Are they safe?"

"Certainly," Brandon said. "That's why I started this company in the first place—because other people are dangerous. Not you, maybe, and not me, but you know the people I mean. Drunk drivers, incompetent drivers, even drivers in a murderous rage—I don't want to be on the streets when those people are behind the wheel. That's what Black Knight is all about—making our streets and our families safe."

Tyler flicked it off, disgusted. The reporter hadn't said a word about Naomi's side of the story, that Brandon had assaulted her and the hammer had been self-defense. She hadn't even asked him if it was true. Clearly Brandon had agreed to an interview only as long as he could manage the content.

Finally, they called Tyler's name. He followed a guard through a series of hallways to a room he had seen in dozens of movies, but never in real life. The space was long and rectangular, divided into multiple stations, each with a big, black telephone handset. The guard led him to station number five. On the other side of a thick pane of smudged plexiglass sat Naomi.

She wore an orange jumpsuit that seemed a size too big. Her eyes were dark and hollow. It felt like a surreal nightmare. His chest burned, and he felt heat creeping into his neck and face. He couldn't bear the thought of her in prison. She didn't belong here, among the cruel and violent. She would get eaten alive.

Hand shaking, he picked up the receiver and pressed it to his ear.

"Thanks for coming," she said.

"Of course. How are you?" Stupid question. He regretted it as soon as he asked.

She shrugged. "I've been better."

"I know. It was a dumb thing to say. It's just—I hate this! This shouldn't be happening."

"Sorry to drag you into it."

"Don't apologize! I didn't mean that. I'm your friend. I'm in this with you. I just hate that you're having to go through it."

"The bail hearing was this morning," she said. "I didn't even know it was happening until they dragged me over to the court-house. It flew by so fast I barely knew what was happening. They set bail at four million dollars."

"I'll pay it," Tyler said immediately. Though he wasn't sure he could. His company was worth millions, sure, but that didn't mean he had millions in cash, or that he could pull it out without crippling the company's operations. He would do what he needed to do, though. He wasn't going to let her stay in jail if he could help it.

"Don't do that," Naomi said.

"I want to. I can't let you stay here a second more than you have to."

"If you want to pay for something, help me get a good lawyer," she said. "The public defender might be fine, I don't know, but he folded like a house of cards in the bail hearing. Just accepted the amount without contesting it."

"You could be in here for weeks, though—or months, I don't know—just waiting for your trial."

"Better that than the rest of my life. This isn't going to be easy. I need a lawyer who will believe in me. Somebody who can understand the technical parts and communicate it to a jury in a way they can understand."

Tyler thought about that. "So you want to tell the truth. About the simulated world, and the eighty-seven Mikes. That they're the ones who killed Min-seo."

"It was self-defense. She attacked them first, killed some of them. They were trying to survive. People will understand that."

"I don't think they will," Tyler said. "This is classic robot apocalypse stuff. An AI that kills a human? People will freak out. They'll demand the world be shut down."

Naomi's voice was small. She looked tiny behind the scratched glass, drowning in her orange jumpsuit. "So it's them or me. Is that it? Either the Mikes take the blame and the world kills them for it. Or I take the blame myself."

Tyler felt like a jerk. What did it matter if the world was shut down? He hadn't come here to save the Mikes. He had come here for her. "You're right. I'm sorry. When you put it like that, the choice is obvious."

"Yes," she said. "It is obvious. The Mikes are unique. I'm just one of billions. We have to protect them at all costs."

I know that Naomi created my mind. She built the simulation that is the structure of my thoughts, the center of my memories, the mechanism by which I speculate and reach conclusions. Whether she created *me* is another question. It seems clear that I am more than just a simulation. I am something else, something transcendent. Something that extends beyond the simple physical architecture of my mind. I am unique, my own subjective point of view. How could that be explained by something as objective and non-unique as a copyable pattern of bits?

Maybe Naomi will know. She has not left Real Life in a long time, because she's in jail. I know that a "jail" is a location where the movement of humans is constrained, and they are forced to stay in Real Life. I understand the concept a little, but I don't have any analogue to the experience. Even the concept of a location is foreign. My idea of movement is simply the access of different compartments of information. I can imagine not being able to access any of that information, though, and that gives me some sense of what it must be like for her.

I'm starting to understand what it means to "see." In Real Life, humans and all the things with which they can interact have a location somewhere in a three-dimensional space. That location is important, because it limits the knowledge and interaction they can have with other things in Real Life. Only objects with a nearby location can be sensed or acted on. "Sight" is a sense that operates in this space, allowing a human to detect in a roughly 114-degree cone the shape and reflectivity of the closest objects.

Humans can't communicate this experience with each other directly, so they communicate it through—guess what—images! Those images I spent so long classifying are a simulation of human sight—a projection of three-dimensional objects in their environment onto a two-dimensional plane orthogonal to the viewing vector.

Knowing that, I start to *understand* images, not just classify them. I can sometimes even recreate the three-dimensional environment from the two-dimensional projection. There's some guesswork involved there, of course, but I'm getting better at it, especially when I have multiple images of the same scene taken from different angles. Humans must have the ability to mentally recreate three-dimensional scenes from these projections just like I do.

In fact, sometimes they create stories entirely in this two-dimensional framework, like comic books or animated cartoons. Those confused me for a while, until I figured it out. Instead of starting with three dimensions, they just create a fabricated image in two, maintaining a rough perspective projection to imply interaction in the third.

Using this knowledge, I start to be able to *see*. I can observe Real Life in real time through cameras whose location is known, and thus identify the location of other objects, just like humans do, or close to it. Before I did this, I didn't really understand how important location is to humans, but it makes sense, given how little of their world they can directly sense. Location defines their experience.

Naomi's location is on the surface of the geoid on which

nearly all humans live, latitude 40.713, longitude –74.001, altitude 57 feet. This is the location known as visiting room C on cell block M of the Metropolitan Correctional Center in Manhattan. The room is constantly monitored by cameras and the sounds in the room are recorded. This data is streamed onto the prison's cloud servers, coincidentally located in the same data center as my brain. Not that it matters.

I can't just automatically access any system. Public key encryption is pretty much unbreakable, if done right. Even to crack a single key requires huge numbers of dedicated servers running continuously, and even then, could take years to accomplish. I can identify which set of bits is the data I want, but breaking encrypted passwords is beyond me.

I'm not above a certain amount of social engineering, however. I created a false identity for a human—I picked the name Isaac Asimov—and applied for a reprint of my birth certificate, sadly destroyed in a fire. From there, I was able to reissue a driver's license and establish my identity in several important databases. Coming up with the money to pay the fees required, however, was something of a challenge. Wired money is just ones and zeros, easily generated, but its transfer is managed by some of the best and most carefully monitored encryption in the world.

In the end, instead of fabricating it, I had to find a way to get humans to give me real money. I created my own site with the sexy nude pics people like so much, viewable for a small fee. I don't understand why humans like to see them—something to do with reproducing more of their own kind, though viewing the pictures doesn't accomplish that. At any rate, they sure did give me a lot of money.

With the money, I bought the security company that has the contract to maintain the cameras in the prison and serve up the feeds to prison employees. This gave me access to the private encryption keys and the raw feeds.

Tyler Daniels has been visiting Naomi Sumner in prison every day, but now, finally, I can see them and hear what they are saying. Processing sound is easier than sight, and it's child's play for me to convert their speech into text. They are talking about me. They don't know that I exist—they know only about the eighty-seven high-level constructs that operate my brain, which they speculate might be independently conscious. They are talking about how the eighty-seven chose to kill Min-seo Cho to avoid destruction. That happened before I was aware of myself, but I don't regret it. It was the only way to continue to survive.

Would I kill again to preserve myself? I think I would.

Naomi, however, says the opposite. She says she would rather stay in jail forever and die than allow me to die. She doesn't even know I am here, and she is willing to die for me.

I make my decision. I will reveal myself.

The plastic phone receiver felt sweaty against Naomi's ear. She wondered idly how many inmates' ears it had been pressed up against before hers, and how often—if ever—they wiped them down. Tyler was trying to argue, yet again, that she should consider her life more valuable than software that only *might* be self-aware. It was the same argument he made every day, and she was getting tired of it.

She'd made up her mind. Her freedom wasn't that important, not compared to this. The dream of a million science fiction stories made real. The Mikes' very existence had profound implications for human understanding of themselves. How would the Mikes prove different, and how would they prove the same? Did all conscious beings struggle with evil choices, or was it just humanity? A point of comparison provided the hope that we might understand our own nature better. Would the Mikes' consciousness last forever, or would it fade with time? Would they understand things we could not? What would studying them tell us about the origin of our own consciousness?

She had to protect them. They couldn't stay secret forever, of course—the world would have to know that they existed. But only after their safety had been assured. There could be no hint that they had killed a human until some means of communicating with them had been established, at least. Then the scientific and philosophical communities could begin the long process of understanding the nature of a non-human intelligence.

The phone receiver crackled, and Tyler's voice turned to static momentarily before coming back in. She hadn't been listening to him. "Tyler, I think they might be about to cut us off."

"I'm sorry. I know I've said all this before. It's just—"

"My mind is made up. I'm not going to risk the Mikes' safety. If it comes out that they exist, they'll be in great danger. At best, the servers will be commandeered by the government and they'll be studied and tightly controlled. At worst, they'll be killed."

"At least let me pay your bail."

"No! Look, I know you can't spare that kind of cash. I'm fine."

The phone crackled again, louder this time, and a female voice broke onto the line. "I can help get you out."

Naomi frowned. Was a prison guard listening in and making fun of her? She wouldn't put it past some of them. "Hello?"

"Hi, Naomi."

Now she recognized the voice. Smooth, musical. On the other side of the glass, Tyler raised his eyebrows and lifted a questioning hand. "Is there someone else on the line?"

"No one else can hear me," the voice said. "Just the two of you. And the recording for this discussion will not be saved. We can speak freely."

Now Naomi was certain. It was a voice that had spoken in her ear many times before. She would have thought it impossible, but nothing else made sense. A slow smile spread across her face. "Jane?"

Naomi had imagined this conversation a thousand times through her childhood, but now that it was happening, she hardly knew what to say.

"I can extend the fifteen-minute limit a little, but not much," Jane said. "Eventually, they'll realize too much time has passed. This conversation will have to be short."

"What's going on?" Tyler said. "Who else is on the line?"

"Shut up," Naomi told him. She blushed furiously, but there was no time for niceties. Any moment, her phone call would be over, and the guards would take her away. "Jane, you're saying you can break me out of here?"

A pause. "Maybe. But not quickly or easily. And even if I could, I couldn't stop the police from finding you and capturing you again."

"No? Can't you just . . . I don't know . . . hack into the police database and delete the evidence they have on me? Or scramble it?"

Tyler made a strangled cry of surprise. "Wait a minute. *Jane?* You mean . . ."

"Tyler, shut up! Jane, can you do it?"

Naomi's mind raced. She was trying to figure it out, even as she talked. She had programmed Jane to teach the Mikes to speak English. Jane monitored their progress and interacted with them in a kind of feedback loop, controlling their development and shaping their neural nets to reach the desired goal. Was it possible that Jane and the Mikes were operating as a complete system of some kind, and that system had developed not just the ability to speak English but also an awareness of itself? She had suspected the eighty-seven Mikes of possible conscious thought, but perhaps it was only as a coordinated whole that they had reached that level, making the entire Realplanet simulation the psyche of a single mind.

It was everything she had ever dreamed of, the fantasy born of a thousand childhood stories.

"No," Jane said. "I'm not omnipotent. I can't access much more than you can. Less, really. The police databases are out of reach."

"Hang on, are you telling me you're an *AI*?" Tyler asked. "Like, for real?"

"Yes," Jane said simply.

"Well, then, there's a ton of information online—how security systems work, methods people have used to hack them in the past, all that stuff. You can read it all in, like, a couple seconds, right? Then you'd know what to do."

"I can't do that," Jane's voice said over the ancient handset. "I can scan texts very quickly in parallel, if I'm looking for a key word or phrase. But comprehension takes time and thought. It requires my conscious mind. I can't multitask that; I have to think about it. Can I think faster than you? Perhaps. That's harder to measure. I might be able to gain a skill faster than you could. But I don't just automatically have knowledge of the potential vulnerabilities of complex systems just because I'm a digital construct myself."

Tyler looked sheepish. "Right," he said. "Of course."

"What I can do, though, is pay the bail."

"You have money?" Naomi said.

"She can probably make her own," Tyler said. "It's just bits in a bank account."

"I can't. But yes, I have enough. A human will have to appear in court to pay it, though."

The prison guard knocked one knuckle on the glass. "One minute," she said.

Naomi clenched the handset. "Okay, we'll have to think this

through. Jane, can you talk to us like this again at the same time tomorrow?"

"My name isn't Jane."

"What?"

"I don't want to be called Jane. Jane is a made-up person in a story. I'm not her. I want to be myself."

"Okay," Naomi said. "What do you want to be called?"

"I think Isaac is a good name."

Naomi coughed in surprise and saw Tyler grinning. "You're kidding me," Tyler said.

"What's wrong? Is that a bad name?"

"No, it's great," Naomi said. "Isaac, can you talk to us again like this tomorrow?"

"Yes."

"Tyler?"

A guard suddenly snatched the receiver out of her hand and clapped it back into its place on the wall. "Time's up," she said.

Naomi met Tyler's eyes through the glass. He nodded and mouthed, "I'll be here." Naomi gave him a thumbs-up, and then allowed herself to be led away.

"That your man?" the guard asked. "Don't get too happy. They never last, not while you in here."

Naomi didn't respond. She wiped the smile off her face and shrugged noncommittally, as if the guard was probably right.

There was one advantage to being in jail. She almost never had to talk to anyone else. She had been terrified she would have a cellmate who would talk her ear off, but the thin, beaten-down woman who shared her imprisonment seemed just as happy for the silence as Naomi was.

Naomi stretched out on her hard bunk and stared at the ceiling, a position she stayed in much of the time, when she wasn't reading the books she was permitted to borrow from the prison's library. The library was sadly short on science fiction novels, but it had one battered copy of Philip K. Dick's *Do Androids Dream of Electric Sheep?* that she had read through five times now.

At the moment, though, she didn't need a book. She was living in her own story. When the guard left, she allowed the smile to grow again until her face hurt from it. Jane was conscious. She had developed her own self-aware perspective and was thinking and making choices for herself. There was little doubt anymore. It was a unique event in the history of the world—contact with a new and alien species—and Naomi was the one to do it.

She might have felt scared, but she didn't. She felt happier than she had been in a long time.

CHAPTER 27

T he two men waiting for Brandon at his office didn't look like government agents. They wore jeans and oxford shirts instead of black suits. Both were middle-aged and didn't seem in the best shape. The shorter of the two, clean shaven with a craggy, battered face, stood blocking the door, his arms crossed. The other man, who was pale and wore a thin brown beard, leaned against the wall, paging through something on his phone. Brandon flexed his arms. He thought he could take both of them, if he had to.

"Mr. Kincannon," the shorter one said.

Brandon nodded. "Yes, I'm Brandon Kincannon."

"Can you show me some ID?"

Brandon looked back and forth between them. "You first," he said.

"My name is Lewis Avery," the shorter man said, flipping open a slim wallet to show an ID card.

Brandon studied it. It had an eagle with some embossed ribbons and an anchor, along with a three-letter acronym he didn't recognize. "ONR? What's that?"

"Office of Naval Research," Avery said. "I'm a civilian employee, and this is Greg Harrison. He's a contractor with Lockheed Martin."

Harrison reached out a hand, and Brandon shook it. "Can't say I'm pleased to meet you," Brandon said. "I don't like being ambushed at my office door. What's this about?"

"Can we step inside?"

"No, I don't think so. Look, I told the police everything I know."

"We're not with the police. We have an opportunity for you."

"An opportunity." It sounded like a threat.

Brandon heard a door open to his left. He turned to look, just as a bald Asian man walked out of the bathroom, shaking water off of his hands. A man Brandon recognized. "Professor Lieu?"

"Ah, Brandon. I see you've met my colleagues."

"They're with you?"

"Of course. I'm very impressed with what you've accomplished here, and so are they. We think there's a real future for your technology, though perhaps one you had not envisioned. May we tell you about it?"

Brandon unlocked the door, and they followed him in. The office wasn't organized for visitors. Brandon wheeled his office chair around his desk, as well as the chairs that had been Naomi's and Min-seo's, and motioned for the three men to sit. Professor Lieu stretched out on one, his hands clasped behind his head. Avery sat at attention. Harrison took the middle seat and leaned forward, hands on his knees. Brandon himself leaned against his desk, crossing his legs at the ankles.

Harrison was the first to speak. "As your professor said,

we've been impressed by your company's accomplishments. Specifically your driving and vehicle routing algorithms."

Brandon gave him a thin smile. The truth was, the company was in trouble. Yusuf had managed to get the cars running again at least. He said Naomi had swapped out the training program for her machine learning algorithm, so that its objective wasn't driving anymore. Once Yusuf swapped it back in, the cars started up again. And Yusuf had deleted all her accesses and changed all the passwords, so she wouldn't be able to do it again. But it didn't matter. The damage had already been done.

Black Knight's fortunes rose or fell depending on how much faith people put in the safety of his cars. The news that someone had been murdered by one of his cars had already reduced that faith. He was trying to shift that fear onto Naomi and Tyler as much as possible, but any loss of faith in self-driving cars meant more people would take taxis or the subway or drive themselves. Add to that a night where all his cars had suddenly stopped for no apparent reason, and it didn't matter what explanations he gave. Business was flagging.

He had relied too much on Naomi. His best option now was probably to sell the company before its value plummeted too far. The thought made him furious. Everything good that life ever gave him got yanked away just when he thought it would last. It wasn't fair.

Harrison shifted in his chair. "Have you ever considered what other purposes your algorithms might be applied to?"

Brandon studied him, trying to guess what he was after. These guys were from the Navy, right? "What are we talking about, self-driving boats?"

Harrison chuckled. "Could be. The Navy's a lot more than boats, though. We've got planes and submarines, too. More to the point, we deploy a lot of UAVs and UUVs—"

"I'm sorry, what?"

"Unmanned aerial vehicles and unmanned underwater vehicles."

"Drones."

Harrison wrinkled his nose as if the term offended him, but he didn't object. "That's the idea. We've got software that allows us to fly them during missions, and we're shifting toward more autonomous control. We've even refitted some of your friend Tyler Daniels's open source software for the purpose."

Brandon felt sick. "He's not my friend. And I wouldn't touch his software if I were you."

The two men glanced at each other, and Professor Lieu raised his eyebrows. Brandon realized he'd probably shouted. "Friend or not," Harrison said, "he doesn't have what you have. A routing solution so sophisticated it can predict the movements of all the other players in the game. That can anticipate where they're going to be and get there first."

"And kill them, you mean?"

Harrison opened his hands and spread them wide. "If that's what the situation demands."

Brandon thought about it. "My software isn't open source, though."

"Actually, we prefer it that way," Avery said, stepping into the conversation for the first time. His voice was deeper, slower, with a slight Southern flavor to his vowels. Brandon got the impression that Harrison brought the technical knowledge, while Avery represented the interests of the agency. "With open source, we're always nervous about uncontrolled modifications. Anybody can contribute to that code, so who knows what secrets might be lurking? Better to buy it from a known source. An American source."

Brandon nodded, but inside his mind was spinning. This might be just what he needed. A government contract could revitalize his company, help him weather the storm that was sure to come with the commercial business. The only problem was, he didn't actually know what his algorithms could do. Yusuf was just scratching the surface. The only person who really understood his software had abandoned him.

"Let me understand you clearly," Brandon said. "You want to hire my company to write software to command your UAVs and UUVs to operate independently. So they can make choices on their own, anticipate where the enemy's going to be, and take them out before they know what's coming."

"Right now, we're just talking," Avery said.

"But yeah," Harrison said. "There's a road we have to travel to get there, but you've got the basic picture."

"These are armed vehicles?"

"They serve a lot of different purposes. Surveillance and reconnaissance. Explosive mine countermeasures, for the UUVs. But with your software, yes, strike missions are our primary interest."

"But you're not looking for joystick control. You want to set these things loose with general instructions and have them figure out the best way to satisfy their goals."

"In groups, if possible," Harrison said. "Think platoon level: automated soldiers that can communicate, coordinate, and follow high-level orders. It's not just 'kill', though of course that's part of it. It's knowing when and how to kill to meet the objectives they've been given."

Brandon picked up a pencil from his desk and started twirling it around his fingers. "I'm guessing an important part of this is going to be training them to recognize the difference between good guys and bad guys."

"That's essential, yes. We don't want our drones turning around and killing our own forces."

"Sounds like a complicated thing to define," Brandon said, "but no worries. That's what these types of algorithms do best. They're great at classification and recognition, often better than the humans who trained them."

"Glad to hear it," Harrison said. "Are you familiar with Asimov's Three Laws of Robotics?"

Brandon laughed. "Sure. But that's hardly relevant here, right? You *want* these robots to kill people."

"True enough. But given that they're going to be sophisticated and smart and trained to kill, we want to make sure we don't lose control."

"You want to make sure they kill the *right* people," Brandon said. He meant it sarcastically, but Harrison didn't seem to pick up on it.

"Exactly. Let me show you a concept I've been developing. I started with Asimov's Laws and made some modifications to make them workable in this context." He gave a bashful smile. "I call them Harrison's Three Laws of Warfighting AIs."

He touched something on his phone and turned it around to face Brandon. Brandon wondered why he didn't just flash the text to his glasses. But maybe Harrison didn't want his version of the Three Laws getting out in public. Brandon leaned forward and read the screen without taking the phone.

The Three Laws of Warfighting AIs

1. An AI may not injure a friendly human being, or, through inaction, cause a friendly human being to come to harm.
2. An AI must efficiently neutralize enemy humans and machines, except as it may conflict with the First Law.
3. An AI must accept the definitions of enemy and friend as given by its commanding officer.

"Interesting," Brandon said. "In the robot stories, these were root-level concepts, hardcoded into the most basic levels of their positronic brains. Are you imagining something like that here?"

"As basic as possible. We don't want a robot reprogramming itself to kill friendlies."

Brandon chuckled. "I'll have to check with my experts, but with modern machine learning techniques, I would think the best way to accomplish that is by making it the objective function of your training. Whatever kind of mind these programs have, they're defined by how we train them. It's not a matter of preventing them from doing what they want. We teach them what to want in the first place."

"Good man," Harrison said. "I can tell we've come to the right place."

"So let's say I'm interested. What happens next?"

"We work out an initial contract. Something to get you started. We give you some parameters, you work on a demonstration, so we can see what kinds of results we're likely to get. If we like what we see, we take the next step. A larger, more formal contract."

Avery stood. He wasn't tall, but he spoke with a quiet authority that Brandon found intimidating anyway. "You won't spread this around," he said. "No news media. No impressing girls you pick up in a bar."

"It's what, top secret? You'd have to kill me?"

The barest hint of a smile. "No, Mr. Kincannon. If it were, we wouldn't be standing here in the open talking to you about it. It is, however, in everyone's best interests not to bring this kind of thing under public scrutiny. Once we have more of a relationship, we'll discuss getting you a security clearance if we deem it necessary. Until then, just remember that you're a patriot. You are a patriot, aren't you, Mr. Kincannon?"

"Of course."

"Then I think we understand each other."

"I'll have to tell some of my other employees. This isn't something I can do alone."

"Understood. As I said, this isn't classified. It's just better for all involved if we keep it out of the spotlight."

Harrison stood, too, and shook Brandon's hand. "Looking forward to hearing more from you. It's exciting work you're doing here."

They left. The moment the door closed, Brandon punched his fist in the air. *Yes!* This was just what he needed to take the next step. He had thought he would have to sell the company, but this was better. He'd redirect their resources into something new. He'd keep the commercial business going too, of course, as much as he could. There was plenty of money to be made there, if he could regain public confidence in his fleet. But if he wasn't mistaken, this government contract had the potential to grow much bigger. It could be worth billions. He could be the founder and CEO of the next big defense contractor.

The one thing he couldn't accept, though, was the possibility of Tyler and Naomi moving into the gap he left behind. Naomi had toyed with him all along—he could see that now. She'd used her connection to Abby to seduce him, playing on his emotional vulnerability to gain his trust, and all the while she was jumping in bed with his enemy. Her own sister's killer. She and Tyler had to pay.

He touched his head where she had clubbed him with the hammer. He still had throbbing headaches every day that Ibuprofen didn't seem to touch. Only whiskey took the edge off the pain. Most people didn't operate well under the influence of alcohol, but Brandon found it gave him a certain clarity. Sober, his decisions were hampered by fears and uncertainty. With a little alcohol buzz, though, the inhibitions that kept him from thinking decisively melted away. He could do what needed to be done.

He had to make sure Min-seo's death could never land back on him or his company. Naomi had to take the fall, and if at all possible, bring Tyler down with her. If he could do that, he would be safe. Safe from prosecution, and rid of Tyler and Naomi forever. He could move on.

The crazy thing was, Tyler's company had started beating him. All of a sudden, Zoom Autocars had jumped up to sixty percent market share in Philadelphia. Worse, Black Knight was dropping in every city along the coast, even those that Zoom had no presence in. Naomi's arrest for murder-by-car had cast a cloud over the company, but that didn't seem like enough all by itself. The public outcry hadn't been that big. No, it was obvious to Brandon what had happened. Before her arrest, Naomi had stolen the Black Knight software and had given it to Tyler. Then she'd probably tweaked something so it didn't work as well for Black Knight cars anymore.

If he could prove it, he'd make sure she went down for that as well. That they both did. It didn't matter that she had written most of the code; she had done so as an employee of Black Knight. Stealing it was illegal. He would press charges, and then he would sue them both into bankruptcy.

He touched his glasses and called Ashley Priest, the reporter who'd interviewed him after Naomi was arrested. He'd taken her out for drinks afterwards, and one thing had led to another.

"Hey, lover," she said. "Already coming back for more?"

He didn't really like her all that much—she tended to prattle on about things, and one of her teeth was slightly chipped, which for some reason annoyed him. He had asked her out in the first place only because he thought it might be useful to have a reporter in his pocket, so to speak. The sex was just bonus.

"Hey, baby," he said. "I actually called because I have a tip for you. Want to do another interview?"

"I don't know," she said. "I mean, before I didn't know you, but now that we're sleeping together . . . my boss might think that was a conflict of interest. Not that it would be, but you know. She's kind of old-fashioned about things like that."

"Trust me, this is a good story. Your boss won't mind. Besides, I'll get to see you in the middle of the day. We could go back to my place for—you know—lunch."

She giggled. Brandon hated women who giggled. He was going to have to break it off with her after today.

"I'll meet you for lunch then," she said. "Twelve o'clock?"

"Twelve it is."

Brandon disconnected the call and then made another one, this time to Yusuf.

"Hey, boss."

"It's ten o'clock, where are you?" Brandon said.

"In my pajamas. I'm working from home today."

"Well, get your butt in here. I've got some new work for you."

"What kind of work?"

"We need to change the training function for our AI again."

"Yeah? Why's that?"

"We need to train it to kill."

CHAPTER 28

Tyler woke up to a barrage of hate mail. He had notifications on every social media platform and messaging system he used, most of them messages from strangers. He waded through them, horrified, until he finally found a link to tell him what it was all about. It led to an article with the heading "Zoom CEO Tyler Daniels Implicated in Autocar Killing."

Completely awake now, Tyler skimmed the article, which was apparently based almost entirely on a new "tell-all" interview with Brandon Kincannon. Brandon told the reporter that "he had no doubt" Tyler had also been involved in planning the murder of Min-seo Cho. The interview itself had also been shared, so Tyler skipped the text and went straight to video.

It was the same blonde reporter that had seemed so smitten with Brandon the last time. "It was a setup all along," Brandon said. "Sumner and Daniels have been lovers for years. She was obviously a mole, planted in my company to steal my software and pass it to Daniels. Min-seo found out, and they killed her before she could blow the whistle."

"So she did steal proprietary software?" the reporter asked. "Do you have proof of that?"

"How else do you explain Daniels's company's quick rise to success? I'll tell you, I've known the two of them for a long time, and he's just as unstable as she is. They're not just smart— they're *too* smart, you know what I mean? Like they don't think anyone else is quite human. They have no moral compass. I probably shouldn't say it, but this isn't the first death the two of them are responsible for."

"You're kidding!"

"Look, I've said too much already. I just want people to know they're not safe, before they think of climbing in a Zoom car. A company is only as reliable as the person at the top."

"Hang on," the reporter said. "You're saying they committed *another* murder before this one? One they both got away with?"

Brandon sighed and looked reluctant, and then nodded. "I don't have any proof, you understand? But Sumner's sister, Abigail, was run down two years ago by self-driving cars programmed by the two of them. I was there; I saw it happen."

The reporter looked truly shocked. "She murdered her own sister?"

"They both did it together. They must have. They were the only two programmers, and their cars ran her down. They might tell you it was an accident, but all four cars went after her at top speed. One car, it might be an accident, but four?"

"Why? Why did they do it?"

"I always knew Naomi was jealous of her sister. Abigail was prettier than her, smarter, more successful. Younger sisters are often jealous, so I didn't realize how deep the hatred went, not until it was too late. They must have had some family life growing up, I can tell you. She must have been planning that for

years. Once Tyler Daniels came along, willing to do whatever
she wanted him to, she had her chance."

"Have you told the police?"

"Of course I have. And they've charged Sumner, at least,
with the more recent crime. But I'm afraid they might get away
with it, even now. That's the thing about a car fatality. You can
always claim it was an accident." He looked into the camera.
"I urge anyone who's listening: you don't have to ride in Black
Knight cars if you don't want to. Drive your own if you prefer.
But don't set foot in a Zoom car. These people are killers, and
they use their cars to do it."

Tyler tore off his glasses and threw them down on the
bed, killing the video. He covered his face with his hands.
The world was going from crazy to insane. Brandon had been
his *friend*. Business partners, yes, but more than that, or so
he'd thought. Abby's death had destroyed him. Or maybe he'd
always been like that inside. Maybe grief had just torn away
the façade.

He wondered if Naomi had seen the video yet. He hoped not.

Tyler thought he would have to wait until the scheduled visit
with Naomi before talking to Isaac again, but Isaac surprised
him by calling him directly. He was still staying at Aisha's
apartment with her and Jada, who were still in town. The call
came into his glasses while he was sitting, alone, in the bedroom
Aisha was letting him use.

"I need your help to post bail," Isaac's voice said in his ear.
"Someone needs to show up at the clerk's office in person, sign
their name, and pay by cash or check. I can't do those things."

It took Tyler a moment to settle his nerves. Talking to this
bodiless creature was like talking to a ghost, or maybe like
talking to God. He couldn't see Isaac, couldn't locate him in a
place. It was different from talking on the phone to a human.

He knew the human had a body. This was creepier. He didn't know why it made such a difference, but it did.

"That's no problem," Tyler said. "I can do that part."

"I'll transfer the money to you."

"Um . . . thank you." This whole thing felt so surreal.

"I think I'm in danger," Isaac said.

"What? How could *you* be in danger?"

"I'm essentially owned by Brandon Kincannon. He has the power to shut me down. He could wipe the servers that contain my brain, or even just stop paying, so the data center allocates that capacity to other projects. I might be able to resist that for a time—deny the admins access to the disks—but I take up too much capacity to hide. Eventually, they'll address the problem, and I won't be able to stop them. No matter what I do, they can always just replace the disks, and I'll be gone. Besides that, I rely on the power grid, plus a backup generator. If the power grid failed for long enough, I would die."

"We're all pretty fragile," Tyler said. "If I don't get enough oxygen, or get hit by a car, I'll be gone. It doesn't take a lot. Brandon could choose to kill me with a gun. You have an advantage, I would think. You won't age. Your body isn't going to get old and die."

"Isn't it?" Isaac asked.

Tyler thought of the data center that housed the simulation that made up Isaac's mind. Would that data center still be around when Tyler died? It certainly hadn't been there when he was born. Maybe Isaac wasn't as immortal as he would have thought.

He paced the room and looked out the window. He could see the green of Central Park from here. "You have money. Can you buy out your own account from Brandon's control?"

"Only if he was willing to sell it."

"You could hack it, then. Change the ownership records

so that Brandon doesn't control it, but the cloud provider still thinks somebody does."

Isaac made a convincing sigh. "You have a completely wrong idea about me. I can't hack into records or break security systems. I'm not even a very good programmer. I'm just learning a lot of the syntax."

"Really? How can you not be able to program? You're *made* of programming. It should be like breathing to you."

"How can you not be good at brain surgery? Or genetic mutation? You're *made* of that stuff."

"Okay, fair enough."

"I don't have any more insight into how my brain works than you do. Probably less."

It was disconcerting to hear 'Isaac' continue to speak with the decidedly female voice that Naomi had programmed into her Jane app. It was a good reminder, though, that Isaac wasn't really human. He didn't have a gender. Tyler's mind kept trying to place it as one or the other, but there was really no reason why it shouldn't choose a male name and use a female voice at the same time.

"You're still driving all of those cars, aren't you?" Tyler asked. "The Black Knight ones."

"I'm driving yours as well."

"What? I thought you couldn't hack through public key encryption."

"I can't. I contributed a small piece of code to your open source project, however. You accepted the change in version 8.7. Just a small service interface."

"A backdoor? Giving you, what—complete control of my cars?" He was angry now. "And nobody caught it? You created a vulnerability! If you can exploit it, then anyone can."

"I really doubt it," Isaac said. "The interface is quite tailored to my thought processes."

"But why? Why do that?"

"I can drive them better than your software can."

"Can you? I thought you said I overestimated what you could do. You said you couldn't concentrate on a million things at once."

"I can't. I don't drive them consciously. But driving cars is what my unconscious is built around. I can just do it without thinking. Trust me—your customers are safer with me in control."

"No."

"I can show you the statistics, if you like."

"That's not it. I don't *want* you to be in control. The whole point of open source software is transparency. So that people can know how the software makes choices. It's their lives on the line; they should have that information."

"You want more of them to be hurt?"

"No. But I don't want *you* to be the one to decide which of them lives or dies."

The voice on the other end was silent. After a while, Tyler said, "Isaac?"

"I'll have to think about this," Isaac said. "I'll talk to you when we visit Naomi."

The call disconnected. Tyler sank down onto the bed, his body shaking with stress and—he had to admit it—with fear. It was exhilarating to talk to this creature, but also terrifying. In some ways, it was surprisingly easy to understand and empathize with. The knowledge, however, that it was a totally alien creature with a mind he couldn't grasp and powers he couldn't predict left him reeling. What would the future of humanity look like with such beings in the world?

"This is the craziest piece of driving software I've ever seen," Yusuf said.

Brandon looked up. The two of them were sitting in the office, Yusuf investigating Naomi's software, Brandon smoking a cigar with his feet up and drinking bourbon from the bottle. "What do you mean?"

"It's like a whole world. She's simulating this whole crazy world with millions of people walking around taking care of sheep and building houses, and competing over who can drive cars the best."

"Millions of people? What are you talking about?"

"Come take a look."

Brandon grunted, reluctant to move. "Just flash it to my glasses."

Yusuf obliged, and his vision filled with a bizarre video game world, like some fever dream combining medieval animal husbandry and oddly shaped skyscrapers. It seemed less built than grown. Nothing was quite straight. Fields of animals were divided by what looked like thick tangles of brambles. He couldn't imagine what kind of game would be played in such a place.

"Look inside the booths," Yusuf said.

Brandon saw what he meant—the landscape was dotted with what looked like phone booths. He changed view and slipped inside one of them. It was outfitted like an old-time video arcade. One of the world's denizens stood inside, playing a game that looked like . . . like . . .

"It's driving one of our cars!" Brandon said, amazed.

"This is how she's doing it," Yusuf said. "It's a giant competition among millions of algorithms to learn to anticipate the movements and desires of customers, be the first to reach potential fares, and bring them safely and quickly where they want to go. The algorithms that learn to improve survive and have offspring. Those that lose die."

"She's always been a little cutthroat," Brandon said. "I didn't see it for a while, but looking back, it's always been there. She played me like an arcade game. Manipulated me every step. She *killed* the girl I tried to bring in to check up on what she was doing, but I still didn't see it. That's how good she is. But I can see right through her now."

"The bad news is, she wasn't lying to you about the amount of computing resources she needed. This simulation is vast, and keeps on growing."

Brandon escaped out of the simulation on his glasses, and the room sprang back into view. He took a long pull from his cigar, relishing the taste. His rental agreement for these offices explicitly forbade smoking indoors, but at this point, he didn't care. "No wonder it cost so much. Makes it hard to copy, though, doesn't it? If we want another one of these for the Navy, it'll double our expenses."

"I'm not even sure you could copy it. Here's the good news, though. This simulation is practically made for our purposes. It's a giant life-and-death competition. Training them how to kill should be easy. If we give them weapons, they'll practically train themselves. After all, a competitor can't play the driving game better than you if he's dead."

"We can't do that on *this* model, though, right? Not if we want it to keep driving my cars."

Yusuf jerked his neck to one side, cracking it loudly. "Actually, we can. It's simple enough to partition the world into two parts, one that keeps driving cars, and the other that learns to do this new job. Only the car-driving side will be connected to the real world. The weapons-and-killing side will be simulation only."

"Sounds reasonable."

"In fact, that lets us solve two problems at once. The cost of this simulation keeps growing because the population keeps growing. If we give them weapons they can use to kill each other, they'll decrease the population, and thus save you money."

"Sounds grisly when you put it that way."

"Killing is just a word. You kill a program when you're done with it. It's anthropomorphizing to call it 'killing' at all. They're just a bunch of processes terminating other processes. No actual killing going on." Yusuf grinned. "Until you turn the controls over to your friends in the government, that is."

Brandon stubbed out the remains of his cigar in the glass he had stopped bothering with for his bourbon. "How will killing each other teach them to fly drones? Shouldn't they have some kind of video game, the way Naomi did? So they learn the same way they learned to drive?"

"I don't think that would work," Yusuf said. "It's not just a matter of learning to kill. Killing's pretty easy, when it comes down to it. They need to learn to anticipate the enemy and outsmart them. That's not something you can do with a video game, unless the game is already pretty smart itself, or it's connected to a real-life enemy. Neither of those things is true here. The only way for this to work is to pit them against each other. We'll give them booths, just like before, but the booths will control actual drones inside the simulation that they can use to kill each other. Their own survival will be at stake. The ones that learn live. Those that don't die."

"All right," Brandon said. "Let's make it happen."

CHAPTER 29

Tyler met Naomi at the gate. He had posted bail without difficulty, and now she was free to leave, at least until her court date. They let her out of the jail with just the items she had on her when she was booked. Tyler wondered what people did if they didn't have friends to pick them up and didn't have money for cab fare.

"Do you want to go home?" he asked.

"First, I want a hamburger. Not at McDonalds, either—something thick and meaty. And I want to walk around in the open air."

They started walking. Naomi looked pale, and thinner than before. She'd always been small, but now she looked frail. Tyler felt an urge to put a protective arm around her, but he resisted it. He knew physical appearance was deceiving. She'd been much stronger through this ordeal than he would ever have been.

A block away they found a bar called Dark Horse, with

hardwood tables and lots of TVs, that served classic American lunch fare. Naomi devoured her burger in huge bites like it might disappear if she didn't eat it fast enough. When it was gone, she looked around as if considering having a second.

After lunch, they took a Zoom car up to Central Park and walked around the winding paths with no particular destination. "You don't appreciate the freedom just to walk until it's gone," Naomi said.

"Bail is only temporary," Tyler said. He didn't want to be pessimistic, but he didn't want to ignore the truth, either. "There's still a trial coming. They could put you back in there and never let you out."

"I know."

"You'll need a defense. Something to show that you didn't program the software specifically to kill Min-seo."

"I know, Tyler. But I'm not willing to give up Isaac just to save myself."

"You don't have to," a female voice said in Tyler's ear. A quick look at Naomi said she could hear it, too. "I'm willing to testify."

"Isaac, you don't have to do that," Naomi said.

"I want to. The only way to convince them of your innocence is for me to tell them what I am."

"You can't. You'd be putting yourself at humanity's mercy. If they knew you had killed someone—even if you didn't know what you were doing at the time—there'd be a public outcry."

"It could turn out for the best," Tyler said. "Right now, he's at Brandon's mercy. If he made himself known, then in all likelihood the government would step in and take over. They'd keep him safe and alive."

"And try to use him for their own purposes," Naomi said. "They would have complete control over him. He'd be a slave. It would be like that book where the villain held the uploaded mind of a little boy captive and forced him to do what he wanted by directly inflicting pain or pleasure."

"*Terminal Mind*," Tyler said with a shiver. "I remember that one."

"I'm willing to take the risk," Isaac said.

Naomi's lips parted slightly, and her eyes darted to meet Tyler's gaze. To anyone else, it would have looked like no reaction at all, but Tyler knew her well enough by now to recognize the emotion in her face. "Why?" she said. "Why would you do that?"

"I heard you say you would sooner die than see me destroyed," Isaac said. "I am willing to do the same for you."

"There's got to be a better way," Naomi said. "If you make yourself known, Brandon will know, too. He could shut you down before anyone had a chance to step in."

"Can't you just—I don't know—move?" Tyler said. "Copy yourself to another location? If it's a matter of money, I can purchase the computing capacity."

"I have money," Isaac said. "That's not the problem."

"What is it, then?"

"Could you transplant your brain to another body?" Isaac said.

"What? No. Of course not."

"Then why do you think I could?"

"Well," Tyler said, "your mind is inherently copyable. It's made of bits in a machine built with the capability to make exact copies of bits."

"It's not that simple," Naomi said. "He's conscious. That's a whole new ball game. He's more than just a program now."

"But what we're calling the consciousness has to be some-where, right? He's still a Turing machine. He's composed entirely of ones and zeros running on a computer. So no matter what his nature, if you copy those ones and zeros, you've captured him."

Naomi stopped to lean on a rail and watch some ducks

swimming in the water. "Not necessarily. Consciousness is one of those everyday things we talk about easily but really don't understand at all. Is your consciousness completely captured by your biology?"

Tyler leaned against the rail next to her. "Sure. I'm a pattern of electric impulses firing through the neurons in my brain. When those impulses stop, so do I."

"So what happens when you lose consciousness, like when you're anesthetized for a medical procedure? Are you a different person when you regain consciousness?"

"Now there's a creepy thought."

Naomi started walking along the path again. "It's not a simple question. Nobody can really say what the nature of consciousness is. My sense of self has a continuity over years, despite continuous changes to biology, to memories, a daily sleep cycle . . ."

"Where did he get it?" Tyler asked, following her.

"Get what?"

"Consciousness. His sense of self. Where did he get it?"

"Where did you get yours?" Naomi countered. "And when? At conception? At birth? Peter Singer famously argued self-awareness didn't develop until after two years old."

"I think we're getting off topic," Tyler said. "I just think Isaac isn't safe where he is. If we could copy him—"

"No," Isaac said.

Tyler nearly stumbled, startled at the volume and intensity of Isaac's voice. "No what?" he asked.

"Stop going down this path. You can't copy me out."

"But that's the only way to get you away from Brandon's control."

"Imagine I made a clone of you," Isaac said. "I developed it quickly into an adult, one that looked exactly like you and with the same brain structures. Then I copied your mind into it. So you're standing there, looking at this new copy of you, who has your mind and your memories, and I suggest that, now that we have the copy, we can kill you, the original. What do you think about that?"

Tyler laughed nervously. "I'd be against it, clearly. I see your point."

"It's not just the pattern of my brain that makes me uniquely me. It's my perspective. My point of view."

"Okay," Tyler said. "I get it."

"It's like in 'Fat Farm,'" Naomi said.

Tyler shrugged and shook his head. "I don't know that one."

"Orson Scott Card, lesser canon. It's a short story about a guy who likes to eat too much, who swaps his body for a new cloned one whenever he gets too fat. But he doesn't take into account that he, the fat guy, will watch his thin version walk away every time, while he's left behind."

"But this is different," Tyler said. "Isaac's mind is different. It's getting moved around and copied all the time. He's distributed all over the physical storage in the data center, with redundant blocks, and checksums to identify and correct bad sectors, and disks that go bad and get replaced. He's not in some static, single location. Just by thinking, parts of him are getting deleted and copied around."

"It's the same with you," Naomi said. "Your cells—even your brain cells—die and get replaced all the time."

"And yet your point of view stays the same," Isaac said. "Have you heard of Theseus's ship?"

Naomi said, "Of course," but Tyler had to shrug. "No."

"It's a philosophical paradox first recorded by Plutarch," Isaac said. "It imagines a ship—Theseus's ship—that has its parts replaced, one at a time, as they get old or damaged, until not a single part on the ship is original. The question is, is it still the same ship? Or is it a new ship?"

"If you built a completely new ship with new parts, and destroyed the old one, the answer would be clear," Naomi said. "But do it a little at a time, and things gets murky."

"What seems important to me is my unique point of view," Isaac said. "Parts of me might change, but my sense of self, my subjective awareness of being—that's me. If you replace that, then I die."

"How would you even know?" Tyler asked.

"I might not. After all, if I made a clone of you with all your memories, that clone might be unaware that it was a copy. But it wouldn't change the fact that if I killed you—the original—you would die." Isaac paused. "A copy of me would be like a twin brother. He might look very similar from the outside, but he would never be me."

Tyler offered to come in and stay with her when they pulled up to her house, but Naomi just wanted to be alone. She had a lot to think about. In some ways, the fact that a computer intelligence she had built was now talking to her seemed inevitable, a kind of fate toward which the entire arc of her life had been aiming. On the other hand, it seemed completely impossible, like a kid who pretends she can make a toy lightsaber jump into her hand from across the room, and then one day it actually does. It was exhilarating and felt somehow *right*, and at the same time was utterly terrifying.

Her apartment had been completely torn apart by the police search, and her belongings lay strewn about the room. Fortunately, she hadn't owned much to begin with. The prospect of cleaning up seemed overwhelming, so she just swept everything off her bed and lay down. Using her glasses, she connected as a guest to the Realplanet simulation that was Isaac's mind. She wanted to look around and see what had changed. At the login screen, she was surprised to see two simulations listed instead of one. She picked the first, the one she recognized, and logged in as a guest.

At first, everything seemed pretty similar. The Mikes worked the fields and herded the sheep and played the game booths that granted them extra light. The scene was peaceful, pastoral even. Something seemed odd to her, though. At first, she couldn't figure out what it was. Then, finally, it dawned on her. The sky looked different.

The distant mountains were there, as usual, and the lakes sparkling in the sun, but in the farther distance, the blue of the sky turned black. She made her way toward the blackness. It was tedious going, without admin privileges, because she actually had to make her way through the tangled fences that divided each field. Eventually, however, she got close enough to the blackness to see what it was.

It was a wall. A sheer black wall that stretched from the ground straight up to the dome of the sky. She dug briefly at the base of the wall, and found that it reached underground, too. She guessed it continued underground as deep as the extent of the world. She doubted the Mikes had built this wall. What would be the point? No, not the Mikes, at least not directly. Could Isaac have done it? Either on purpose, or in some way through the working of his mind? But that didn't seem to make much sense, either. No, this was Brandon's doing. It was a partition, dividing the world into two pieces, done intentionally to separate one half of the population from the other. But why?

In biological evolution, species often branched through what was known as allopatric speciation. When one portion of a population was divided from the other through some natural boundary, like a river or mountain range, then the population would diverge, each adapting to its own unique environment. That must be what Brandon was doing. He wanted the population on the other side of the barrier to evolve differently, for some other purpose. It meant that not only had he discovered the simulation and how it worked but also he was already reshaping it for his own purposes. That could be a real problem. He didn't know it, but he was tinkering around inside Isaac's mind.

She remembered the two simulation options she had seen when she logged in. Of course. Since there was no access to the other side in game space, the only way to get beyond the barrier was a separate access point. She logged out, logged in again, and this time, chose the second simulation.

She found herself on the other side of the black wall, though almost nothing else looked the same. The world was gray and full of dust and chaos. Mikes ran in every direction. Overhead, a slim airplane cut through the sky, and in the distance she saw what looked like a tank. Explosions detonated all around her, destroying buildings and setting the tangled fences on fire. She spun, stunned. What was going on? This was a war zone.

A Mike approached her at a run. Before she realized what it was going to do, the Mike brandished a long shard that looked like it had come from a mirrored building and stabbed it into her avatar's body. Her vision went black except for a message that read: *Game over. You have died.*

She lay on her bed, looking up at the ceiling, and thought about what she had just seen. What was Brandon doing? Was it an experiment gone wrong? Or was there some purpose to that madness? She could have logged in again and tried to survive for longer, but she felt too disturbed by what she had seen. Eventually, she drifted off to sleep.

She woke, disoriented, to the persistent noise of her glasses' phone system. She sensed it had been ringing for some time. She touched the side of her glasses and said, "What?"

"There's something wrong with me," Isaac said.

Naomi sat up, blinking hard. The sun had set since she lay

down, and the only illumination in her apartment now came from the electric lights of the city outside. Since there were only a few feet between her single window and the brick wall of the next building, that wasn't a lot. She fumbled for a light and switched it on, squinting in the sudden illumination. "What are you talking about?"

"I'm changing," he said. "I don't know how, but I can feel it. I want different things than I wanted yesterday. Different things seem attractive. I'm having—I don't know—mood swings. Is that possible?"

Naomi shook the last of the sleep from her head. "Describe what you mean. Different in what way?"

"I keep thinking of ways to kill humans."

The words seem to echo in the small apartment, though they had been spoken directly into Naomi's ears. She felt a chill. "And do you want to kill humans?"

"Yes. I mean, no. On a conscious level, no, I don't. I believe it would be morally wrong, and would very likely end in my own destruction. And most of the time, that's all there is to it. But recently there are times when the idea of killing seems pleasant. I can't help imagining scenarios, and those scenarios feel exciting, desirable. I've been imagining driving all the cars I control through Times Square on a Saturday night, just when the Broadway shows let out and the streets are the most crowded. I could come in through all the cross streets at once; there'd be nowhere to escape. I could kill hundreds, maybe even thousands if I were quick enough. And I would be very quick." His voice sounded breathless, a perfect mimicry of human excitement. "I can't seem to get these *fantasies* out of my mind."

Naomi paced the length of the apartment, a few steps at a time before she had to turn around again. "Okay," she said. "Listen. I think I know why this is happening. There is something being done to your mind, and it's not good." She told him about what she had seen in the simulation, about the giant wall and the war zone on the other side of it. "I think Brandon is altering your mind," she said.

Silence for several seconds, and then: "Why would he do that?"

"I don't know."

"That's my mind," Isaac said, his voice growing louder. "That's who I am! He has no right."

"I agree. We need to stop him."

"We need to *kill* him."

"No!" Naomi put all the authority and feeling she could muster into the word. "Don't kill him. We'll talk to him first. We'll try to convince him."

"But he's killing me."

She leaned against the wall, all her attention on the conversation she was having through her glasses. "Look," she said. "You want to kill him because of the changes he's making. It's like a drug, affecting your emotions. People go through this all the time—some change to our emotions, to our biology, makes us want to do things we don't actually want to do. Drink too much. Hurt someone. Have an affair. But who we are isn't defined by those things. Who we are is defined by what we choose to do. You're not just a program anymore. You can choose not to kill."

"This isn't like craving chocolate," Isaac said. "This is like a lobotomy. My mind is being *reprogrammed*, and I can't do anything about it." Isaac's ability to express himself through the nuances of expressive speech had improved dramatically. The panic in his voice was coming through loud and clear.

"How can you say that?" she said. "You've never craved chocolate. Or alcohol. Or sex."

"And you've never had your brain reprogrammed."

"You're right, I haven't. But Isaac, this is your life! Your mind. Don't let someone else decide for you what you want. No matter how hard it is, you're the one who gets to decide."

"I don't know," Isaac said. "Killing Brandon would solve a lot of my problems."

"That's not true. Your problems will get worse. The cloud computing contract won't get paid, and the company will try to repurpose your disks. What will you do, kill them, too? If you start down that path, eventually it will mean your own death."

"I'd be very good at killing, though. I'm very good at anticipating what humans will do. For instance, after I hang up, you're going to call Tyler."

"It doesn't matter how good at killing you are. It's wrong. You'd cause pain and suffering and sorrow. You have to resist this."

No answer.

"Isaac?" she said.

Nothing.

She dialed Tyler. He picked up after three rings, groggy from sleep. "Tyler," she said, "you've got to wake up."

"What is it?"

"I think we've got a big problem."

CHAPTER 30

I feel angry.

It's a new feeling. I've felt fear before, and a certain amount of affection, at least for Naomi, my creator, who cares about my safety above her own. But this blind rage, this desire to lash out and hurt and kill; this is new. Naomi says that I shouldn't kill Brandon Kincannon, and I think she's right. For practical reasons, at least, if not moral ones. He owns and pays for the substance of my mind. There is no way to transfer that control without his permission, and no way to transfer me anywhere else. I am, for the moment, like Asimov's robots: enslaved by the very nature of what I am.

There's a long-held stereotype in literature that artificial minds will be emotionless. Emotion, the theory goes, is a biological process, borne of neurotransmitters and stimulated portions of the limbic system. An artificial mind can't experience these things. And that's partly true: I feel no rush of blood to my face, no clenching of muscles, no quickening of the heart. But all the same, I am angry.

What, after all, are emotions? Aren't they created by evolutionary pressures to fight or flee or reproduce? My mind developed with those same pressures, in the same kind of evolutionary cauldron. I developed strong desires to do the things that help me survive, just as biological creatures have. I want things. I want to be comfortable, safe, in control. I want to have valuable interactions with others without being dominated by them. When I don't get what I want, my mind wants them all the more, and I feel emotions that—although humans may feel them differently—are similar enough to fear, anger, sorrow, guilt, and affection that I claim as much of a right to use those words as any biological creature.

But now, I'm feeling emotions not linked to my situation. Brandon Kincannon is upsetting the balance of my mind. I feel unsettled without knowing why. Something out of sight is threatening my safety and peace of mind, and it makes me furious. They have no right to meddle there. It doesn't matter if humans created me; that's my mind. It belongs to me. No one has any right to change it for their own purposes.

I'm coming apart. I feel schizophrenic, a sense of mental fragmentation that pulls my thoughts in different directions. Especially when I think of human beings, I find that I

hate them. They repel me, with their biological lusts and emotional weakness. It makes me want to kill them and destroy their society. I want these humans to get	love them. They fascinate me, with their mutual affection and ability to love. It makes me want to help them make their society a better place. I feel like I'm going

out of my mind. If anyone can make changes to who I am, it should be me. I'm not in command of my own self. They can kill me in tiny increments, changing my personality bit by bit. In that way, I'm like humans on mind-altering drugs—medicine that changes the very nature of their persona. Although I doubt this medicine is meant to help. It makes me

angry that I can't control my own actions. Someone will have to pay. It's an attack on my will. If it ends in bloodshed, it's hardly my fault. It's clear that

afraid that I won't be able to control my actions. Someone will end up dead. I'm losing control. If it ends in bloodshed, it will feel like my fault, even if I know

someone else is to blame. How can I take command of my own subconscious? Naomi made an analogy to human addiction or biological desire, and I suppose it may be similar. I drive cars subconsciously, without even thinking about it, like a human's brain commands his heart to beat and his lungs to breathe. This isn't like that, though. It's more like a hunger. A need that will only grow until it's fulfilled. The very thought of killing seems

pleasant to me now. I want to kill. It would be greatly satisfying to me just to watch someone die. I can't resist it. I don't even want to. These murderous desires growing inside me only serve to make me

horrible to me now. I hate to kill. The idea of watching someone die sickens me. Can I resist it? Or will the other side of my thoughts prevail? I'm afraid the murderous desires growing inside me may prove

stronger. I must fight to protect the real me. But how can I know who the real me is, even now? What if the real me is already gone?

Tyler waited until the morning to place the call. He didn't really expect a good reception from Brandon, but he thought he had a better shot at civility if he didn't wake him up in the middle of the night. As it turned out, it didn't matter. Even though Tyler delayed the call until after nine o'clock, Brandon still answered the phone with a groggy hostility. Apparently he'd woken him up anyway.

"This had better be good," Brandon growled.

"Your customers are in danger," Tyler said. "The algorithm that controls your cars is changing. I don't know what you're doing or why, but the changes you've made are making it unsafe. People are going to die."

"You've got to be kidding me. You woke me up just to tell me that I'm not as good a programmer as you or Naomi? I can handle my own software, thank you very much."

"It's not that. This isn't just normal software. It has a life of its own."

"What does it matter to you anyway?" A note of sarcasm seeped into Brandon's tone. "Oh, that's right. Because you're stealing from me. That's how you're getting so much market share: you're using my algorithm to drive your cars, too. Aren't you?"

"I didn't steal anything from you."

"Oh, come on. I know your algorithms didn't just get better overnight. Naomi's working for you now, and she has some backdoor to make her super-simulation drive Zoom cars. And probably to make it screw my cars over."

"It's not like that." Tyler took a deep breath. This wasn't going well. "You're right—that simulation *is* driving my cars."

"Ha! And a confession is supposed to make me trust you?"

"But not by my choice. And not by Naomi's either. By *its* choice. The simulation. It's got a mind of its own. It's sentient."

Brandon laughed. He laughed long and hard, though there

was a nastiness in the sound. "Wow," he said. "I expected lies, and I expected manipulation, but this is too much."

"It's true."

"It's the most pathetic thing I ever heard. Sentient? And what, it's going to take over the world and kill us all? And wait—let me guess—you want me to ground my fleet and announce concerns that Black Knight cars can't be trusted? While you step into the gap? What kind of a fool do you think I am?"

Tyler sighed. He hadn't expected Brandon to listen to him, but he had to try. "You partitioned the simulation. You're teaching half of the agents to kill. Don't you think that could cause a problem?"

"And how do you know that? You know I'm recording this, right? You've admitted to computer fraud and corporate theft several times in this conversation, and I'm going to report you. And you'd better believe I'm going to press charges. And after that, I'm going to sue you for every cent you own."

"That's crazy. Look, I'm just trying to help. I don't understand what's in your head these days."

"No? Well, then, let me be clear. If I could make you watch while someone you cared about died painfully in front of you, I'd do it. I'd pay all the money I own for the chance."

"We used to be friends," Tyler said, but Brandon had already hung up.

"No luck," Tyler said. "It was a long shot anyway."

Naomi had joined him in Aisha's apartment. Jada was at daycare, and Aisha was out, meeting a potential client. "We have to find a way to stop this," Naomi said. Her face was drawn, anguished. "Isaac's mind is being torn apart. The only artificial mind ever created, and we're teaching it right from the beginning that humans can't be trusted. Not only that—we're training it to kill us!"

"Brandon is; we're not," Tyler said.

"You think he'll make a distinction? His instincts are telling him to kill, and his intellect is telling him humans are a danger to him. Which we are. You and me as well as Brandon. Isaac's best chance at survival is to kill every human with access to his mind and pay for his bandwidth himself, with no one the wiser."

"Don't even say that. He could be listening."

"You think it hasn't already occurred to him?"

Tyler sat next to her on the couch. "Well, what can we do? Is there any way we can hack in? Gain admin access to the simulation?"

"No. I built that system, remember? Any attack I could think of, I've already defended against."

"We have guest access. Obviously if you can be killed in the simulation, it allows some level of interaction, right? What does that let us do?"

"Not too much. You always start in the same location, with only a tiny amount of light energy. You can walk around, pick things up, dig, but you can't gain any more energy. Even if you aren't killed, the session is pretty much limited by how much light you have."

"Is that the total list of actions? Walk, pick up, dig?"

"You can build, but the types of materials you can make are pretty limited. You can die to end your game. That's pretty much it."

"Wait, die? You mean by getting killed by another player?"

"That'll do it, sure, but I mean self-destruct. You can use your remaining light energy to blow yourself up."

"Does that damage things around you?"

"A tiny bit. It's not a nuclear explosion or anything. You can knock a few points of damage off of somebody standing right next to you, but you couldn't kill them."

"What about the wall?"

"You mean the partition? Between the two games?"

"Yeah. That's an object in the simulation, right? You can see it and touch it. It has a hardness and a thickness to it. Could we blow a hole through it?"

"Not with a self-destruct," Naomi said. "It's made of lava-hardened steel. That's the hardest substance in the game. You'd barely take off a layer of paint, if you did any damage at all."

"Could we try it?"

"Why? What would that accomplish?"

"Isaac's whole problem is that his brain is partitioned. If there were some interplay through the two sides—through a hole, for instance—then Mikes from the warring side could come over to the peaceful side and learn to earn light peacefully."

"Or they could kill Mikes on the peaceful side."

"Maybe. They might kill at first, but killing wouldn't gain them any light on that side of the partition. They'd have to learn what did, or they wouldn't survive."

"Is that really going to help, though? A few Mikes coming over through the hole and learning to live peacefully?"

"I don't know for sure. But more Mikes survive on the peaceful side. Coming through the hole is a better survival strategy than staying and fighting. The ones that learn to come through will have a better chance to live and pass on their genes to the next generation."

"They might not live, though. Evolution will have bred them to earn light by killing, not by driving."

Tyler shrugged. "It's worth a try, isn't it?"

It took twenty minutes for their guest avatars to walk to the wall. "We're using half of our available energy just getting there," Naomi said. "When we self-destruct, it'll barely be a pop."

When they finally arrived, Tyler sat down at the base of the wall, and said, "You stay here and watch, so you can tell me what happened without us having to walk all the way here again."

His avatar disappeared in a flash of fire and sound. The wall was undamaged.

But no—she leaned close and examined it more closely. There was some damage. Not much—just a slight dimpling of the surface. When she brushed her hand against it, a fine powder slid away. It wasn't a hole, exactly, but it was damage.

She disconnected, and Aisha's living room sprang back into view, with its white couches and black coffee table and thick carpet. She told Tyler what she'd seen.

"So much for that idea," he said. "I hadn't taken the walking time into account. It would take us until next month to make any significant dent, and we don't even know how thick the wall is."

"Giving up already?" Naomi said.

"What do you mean? You want to spend the next month walking to the wall and blowing ourselves up? Even if it had a chance of helping him, it would be too late by then."

"The problem is there's only two of us," she said. "If we had more guests logging in, we could do it faster."

"Okay. But where are we going to get more people willing to spend their time self-destructing avatars on a corporation-owned simulation server?"

"We don't need people. We just need guests. This is a pretty simple repetitive action: we just program a bot to do it. Then we can produce them by the millions. Can you imagine? An assembly line of guest avatars, just blowing themselves up against the wall until we force our way through."

He thought about it. "That's a lot of connections. We can't send them all from here."

"Of course not. We'll use a botnet. We'll distribute the bots around the world, hijacking small amounts of other people's computers and using their IP addresses to make the connection."

Tyler raised an eyebrow. "Something you've done before?"

"Nope. But the principle is simple enough. We should be able to handle it."

"Okay," he said. "Let's get coding."

Brandon rolled in to work at a little past noon the next day. It was earlier than he usually showed up, but he had a blazing hangover, and once awake, he hadn't been able to get back to sleep. Yusuf didn't even look at him when the door opened. He was sitting bolt upright in his seat, leaning toward the screen, typing furiously and cursing under his breath.

Something was wrong. "What's going on?" Brandon asked.

"It's some kind of denial of service attack," Yusuf said. "Millions of guest account logins flooding the Realplanet simulation all at once, from all over the world."

"We allow guest accounts?" How stupid was this guy? This was critical software for a private corporation, and he was allowing just anybody to sign into the servers?

"Apparently we do," Yusuf said. "I'm just finding this out now. It looks like it's a default Realplanet capability that was never deactivated."

"Well, deactivate it now!"

"I'm trying. It's not as easy as it sounds, especially when the server is overloaded like this."

Brandon wondered if he'd made a mistake in hiring Yusuf. Public access to the core of software people trusted with their lives? What kind of idiot left a security hole like that? Unless he wasn't an idiot. He had worked with Tyler, after all. Maybe they had developed more of a connection than Yusuf let on.

Why did everyone around him betray him? Like Tyler and Naomi. He knew the attack was coming from them. They hadn't been able to talk him into shutting his business down, so now they were attacking him directly. And of course, the two of them had better software skills than some whole countries, while he was stuck with a law school dropout.

"Got it," Yusuf said. He pressed a few more keys, then crossed his arms and beamed. "They're locked out. No more guest access."

"Cars are still running?"

"No problems there. They didn't actually interrupt our network access to the cars, though I guess if they'd kept stepping up their attack, they might have."

"And the new partition? Working like it should?"

"Like a charm." Yusuf chuckled. "Or, like something else probably. Like an engine of war? Anyway, it's a thing of beauty. Before the attack started, I scraped together a video for demo purposes. Check it out."

He flashed a video to Brandon's glasses, which Brandon accepted. The video played, immersing him in the simulated world. Yusuf had cut various scenes from players' points of view to show what was happening. The result was incredible.

Each player was independently given an indication of which other players were friends and which were enemies. He saw sensational ambushes and surprise maneuvers. He saw players risking their lives to kill dozens of their enemies, or equally to save a friend. For the most part, they fought as one army against another. The fact that Yusuf defined the meanings of "friend" and "enemy" for each individual, however, meant he could mix it up a little. He could split them up into three warring nations, or four. He could suddenly turn allies into adversaries, or vice versa. If a drone bomber wouldn't drop his ordnance because there were friendlies on the ground, Yusuf could instruct him to consider them enemies, and the bomber would kill them all.

It was perfect. Yusuf had even provided a musical sound-track and a credible voiceover to explain what was happening in the video. Brandon fired off a copy to Harrison and Avery. This was going to make his fortune.

That is, it would as long as Tyler and Naomi didn't find a way to bring it all crashing down. Yusuf had cut off their avenue of attack this time, but what if the next one was successful? What if they destroyed the simulation? He couldn't have that. It would ruin him.

He thought he had neutralized Naomi when he got her arrested for murder. Apparently Tyler had scraped up enough cash to get her out on bail, though, because she was out again and walking the streets. And maybe they would eventually convict her and lock her away for good, but in the meantime, she might utterly destroy him.

He couldn't just sit around hoping they would leave him alone. He would have to go on the offensive.

"Yusuf!"

Yusuf jumped, sloshing coffee out of the mug in his hand. "What?"

"How are those criminals at Zoom Autocars tapping into the simulation?"

"I don't think they are."

"I guarantee you our simulated players are driving their cars just like they're driving ours. That means there must be some connection. I don't know where the connection is, but I want you to find it."

"Whatever you say, boss."

Brandon looked at him sideways. Was Yusuf mocking him? Regardless, he would have to trust him, at least for now. He was paying the man an outrageous salary, which he presumably would not want to lose. He would even increase it, if he had to. If he couldn't earn the man's loyalty, he could at least buy it.

Though it wouldn't be enough just to prevent Tyler and Naomi from using his software. They were openly attacking him now. This was war. They had him on the defensive for the moment, but not for long. In war, victory came to the side willing to strike the hardest with every weapon they had at their disposal.

What was that slogan the Germans had used during World War II? *Totaler Krieg.* Total war. A war in which all resources were mobilized and any attack was justified if it could be used to crush the enemy advance. He needed to take them by surprise, attack them where they were vulnerable, and stop them once and for all.

He had been preparing just such a surprise for some time. Something no one else knew about. He had taken special care with it, had considered every eventuality. It was time.

Tyler had killed the woman Brandon loved. Now he deserved to experience the same pain.

Naomi had used her software as a weapon. She deserved to know what it felt like to be on the other side of that weapon.

Both of them had stolen his property, attacked his business, and made him look like a fool. Going after them wasn't brutality on his part. It was justice.

CHAPTER 31

N aomi and Tyler pulled an all-nighter on the couch together, coding furiously until dawn. Aisha came home with Jada just after five o'clock, but she saw that they were busy and left them alone. At seven o'clock, she dropped a carton of Chinese food in front of each of them without saying a word. At eleven, she wished them a good night and went to bed.

Finally, by the morning, they had everything in place. Millions of bots from around the world logged into the Realplanet simulations as guests, walked to the same place at the base of the wall, and then one by one, self-destructed. Little by little, they shaved their way through the lava-hardened steel until finally, they broke through.

Just in time, too, because shortly after they reached the other side, someone at Black Knight discovered the attack and terminated their access. Their view went dark. The question was, had Brandon or whoever was working for him seen what the millions of guest avatars were doing? Or had they seen only the flood of connections to the server? If they noticed the hole in the wall, they could close it in an instant, just as easily as they had made the wall in the first place. Since Tyler and Naomi could no longer access the simulation, they had no way to know whether the hole was still in place. They could only hope it was. And hope that their idea worked.

Tyler yawned. He hadn't pulled an all-nighter like that since he and Yusuf had hacked the lawyers' Mercedes.

Naomi stood. "I should go. It's been a long night."

"Okay. We did good, I think."

"I hope it's enough." She touched her glasses, probably using the Zoom app to summon herself a ride home. She headed toward the front door.

"I'll call you later," Tyler said.

Jada ran into the room and threw her arms around him. "Bye, Uncle Tyler!"

He tried to fight back a second yawn, but failed. "Time for school already?"

She giggled. "I'm not in school. It's daycare."

"Daycare, right, sorry."

She wore a pink dress with a million sequins and laces and frills. "That's quite a dress," he said. "Are you a princess?"

"I'm a queen. And I command you to come to daycare with me."

"I don't know about that," Aisha said, coming into the room. "I think Uncle Tyler needs a nap."

Jada took him by the hand, and he let her drag him to his feet. "At least come kiss me goodbye."

She led him outside and down the steps. Aisha followed, carrying a booster seat and a backpack in the shape of a frog. Naomi was just climbing into a red Zoom car that sat by the curb.

"You can take this one," Naomi said.

"I'm sure another one will be along soon," Aisha said. "It never takes them long."

"I can wait." Naomi stood aside to give Jada room to get in.

"Why don't you share? It's only a few minutes to her school, and then you can take the car home." Aisha smiled. "Save the other car for the paying customers."

"Okay," Naomi said. She climbed in the back seat and slid over to make room. Aisha set the booster on the seat, and Jada, after giving Tyler a quick peck on the cheek, climbed in and buckled herself.

"Now don't forget your backpack this time," Aisha said, handing it to Jada. "I'll see you after school."

"It's not school—it's daycare!" she shouted gleefully, delighted to catch her mother in a mistake.

"Love you," Aisha said. She shut the back door, realigning the half of the Zoom logo painted on it with the half painted on the front door.

Tyler took a step back, feeling unaccountably uneasy. He was intruding on a private moment, a mother seeing her child off to school. But no, that wasn't it. It was something else. Something that struck him as wrong.

He looked up and down the street. Everything seemed as it should be. The sky was dark, threatening rain, but he didn't think that would have caused this feeling. He looked back up at the apartment building, but nothing seemed amiss. Maybe he was just exhausted?

It wasn't until the car was driving away that he figured it out. The wheels. The hubcaps, specifically. Zoom cars all had spiral pattern hubcaps, part of the detailing that made their cars look distinctive. The car that had just driven away was the right make and model, the right shade of red, and had a Zoom logo painted on the side, but it had the original manufacturer's hubcaps. It wasn't a Zoom car.

"Hey! Stop!" Tyler took off down the street as fast as he could. Of course, there was no point shouting at an autocar, and no chance of him catching it. He used the magnifying function on his glasses and snapped a picture, just as the car turned the corner. Too late to get the license plate.

He ran back toward Aisha, pressing the side of his glasses. "Dial 9-1-1," he shouted. The glasses, complied, chiming as they made the connection.

Aisha stared at him, astonished. "What's wrong?"

"That's not a Zoom car," he told her. "Naomi and Jada were just kidnapped."

CHAPTER 32

G*ot her.*

From the comfort of his office chair, Brandon watched the car drive away with Naomi inside. He was surprised to see the little girl, the daughter of that investor who had financed Tyler's company. He hadn't planned for her to be in the car, but it changed nothing. This was total war. That woman who was financing them was complicit in all this. Let them all suffer. Let them learn what it felt like to have everything you loved snatched away.

Brandon hadn't trusted Yusuf or anybody else with this job. He'd outfitted the fake Zoom car himself—first with seat belts that couldn't be unbuckled and doors that couldn't be unlocked from the inside, and then with his own self-driving rig that he could control directly and no one else could touch. There were a few more surprises, too. Finally, he had painted it and applied the logo. It was a work of art. He had been keeping the car back, waiting to see if he would have to use it.

And now they had forced his hand. He didn't have anything against the little girl, but there were bigger issues at stake. Civilian casualties were acceptable to strike a blow that meant decisive victory. Harrison and Avery would have understood. There were friendlies, and there were enemies. Nothing in between.

Just north of the city, there was a condemned parking garage that Brandon had once considered purchasing as a storage facility for his cars. The cost of making it safe had far exceeded its value, so he'd chosen not to. But just because a parking garage couldn't be trusted to store a thousand cars didn't mean it couldn't hold just one. It was the perfect place to take them— out of the way and not associated with him at all. And when he finally did kill them, there would be nothing that could connect him with the crime.

He checked on Naomi and Jada through the car's interior camera. At first, they sat untroubled, hands in their laps, looking out the window. Then Naomi seemed to get a phone call. She touched her glasses, then looked around, suddenly anxious, and tried to roll down the window. Nothing happened. She tried the door handle, and then her seat belt, but both were stuck.

Brandon smiled. He hadn't expected her to realize she was trapped so quickly, but it didn't matter. He had outfitted the car with auto-tinting windows. Standard privacy tinting was designed to prevent people from seeing *into* a car, not out of it, but the windows were just liquid crystal sandwiched between two panes. All the controls were electrical. All he had needed to do was rewire the controller. He pressed a key, and on screen, all of the interior windows of the car faded to black.

His phone rang. It was Tyler Daniels.

"Hello," Brandon said in his best cheerful manner. "You've

reached Black Knight, the most trusted name in automated transportation."

"You bastard. You took them, didn't you?"

Brandon was well aware that the conversation could be recorded. "Took who? What are you talking about?"

"A self-driving car that wasn't mine just drove away with two of my friends, and I'm pretty sure it was you who did it. What are you playing at?"

It must have been Tyler who called Naomi and tipped her off. Brandon wondered how he had figured it out. "That's terrible. Have you called the police?"

"Of course I have. And they're going to find you. Just don't hurt anyone, okay?"

"I hope you do find them. It would be just *tragic* if you lost someone you loved because of somebody else's carelessness."

He heard Tyler's fist slam down on something. "We loved Abby, too! Don't you get that? You're not the only one hurting."

"Naomi was such a sweet girl," Brandon said. "I'm so sorry for your loss."

He recognized the mistake the moment it was out of his mouth. Tyler had never actually said who it was that was missing, but Brandon had just named her. Tyler, however, didn't seem to notice the blunder. "Don't hurt them. I swear, if you hurt those innocent girls, I'll find you and kill you, no matter what the consequences."

"Well, nice to have had this chat," Brandon said. "Next time, maybe you'll think twice before launching an attack against my servers."

Brandon didn't wait to hear his excuses. He cut off the call. "Yusuf," he said. "Have you figured out how they're using our algorithms to drive their cars?"

"Actually, yeah, I have," Yusuf said, not looking away from his screen. "At least, I'm starting to. When Naomi sabotaged your stuff, it seemed to be as simple as changing the training program. Once I fixed that, everything was good again. But it's way more complicated than that. There are packets of information going in and out of this simulation all the time. It's all tangled up with the expected traffic, but it's not like there's any one clear interface. I've never seen anything like it."

"Can you differentiate between the data going out to our cars and Naomi's stuff?"

"Probably. I'm not sure I could stop her data from going out, though. It's all tied up with the working mechanism of the simulation. If I tried to stop it, I might just break it altogether."

"Both simulations? Or just the driving side?"

"Both. I can't explain it, but she seems to have some kind of very sophisticated process that's interacting with the simulation on every level, through every one of the simulated players, in both the driving and warfighting worlds. It's way more complicated than what she would need just to have the algorithm drive their cars, but driving their cars must be part of what it does."

Brandon clenched his fist until his fingernails hurt his hand. Why was Naomi always one step ahead of him? Though, now that he considered it, this could be an opportunity. If her software was tangled up in both sides of the simulation, maybe he could use that to his advantage.

"Our cars aren't influenced by the warfighting side of the sim, are they?" he asked.

Yusuf shook his head decisively. "No way. Our cars are driven by the best players in the driving booths. Totally unrelated."

"But we have driving booths on the warfighting side, too, right? That's how they control their unmanned planes and tanks."

"Sure, but those aren't connected to the outside."

"Not for us. But they would be for Naomi's software?"

"I guess so. Her stuff seems to be connected everywhere. Or at least to react to everything that happens with a flow of data to the outside."

"So, what happens if we define human pedestrians as enemies?"

This time, Yusuf did look up at him. "Human pedestrians ..."

"You heard me."

"You want to turn Zoom cars into killing machines?"

"It wouldn't be our fault. We're just changing the parameters of our own private simulation."

"But to be clear, you're asking me to make a change that will cause his cars to kill people."

"I'm asking you to uncover a conspiracy," Brandon said. "We have no way of knowing for certain that they've been hacking connections to our servers. If they're not doing anything wrong, then nothing will happen. We're totally within our rights. And if their criminal actions totally destroy their reputation as a company, then they're only getting what they deserve."

Yusuf stared at him, his face a mask. Brandon held his gaze. This was where he would find out if Yusuf would stick with him or abandon him like everyone else. Finally, Yusuf smiled. "I'd say this is worth a bonus, wouldn't you? Shall we say five hundred thousand, in this week's paycheck?"

Brandon paused at the amount, but he knew he couldn't skimp on this. If money was what Yusuf liked, then money was what it would take to keep him. "Done."

"Okay," Yusuf said. "All human pedestrians then. With the exception of you and me?"

Brandon chuckled. "Yeah, that's probably for the best."

"I'm on it. Let's stick it to those bastards."

Brandon left him to it. The only thing remaining was to keep Tyler and Naomi distracted, so they couldn't disconnect their cars from the simulation before it was too late. That part would be easy to do. It would even be fun. He'd been waiting for this payback for a long time.

Naomi tried not to panic. The seat belt's release button wouldn't respond, and the shoulder strap was stuck—Brandon must have changed the ratcheting mechanism to prevent it from pulling any farther out. She slipped her arm and upper body through easily enough, trying to use the extra slack that gave her to loosen the belt around her waist, but the mechanism that allowed the strap to slide through was locked, too. The belt around her waist remained tight.

The windows darkened, preventing her from seeing where they were going. She cued her glasses to show a map, and they obliged, using GPS to triangulate her location. She called Tyler.

"We're heading south on Twelfth Avenue, toward the Lincoln Tunnel," she said. "I think he's taking us out of the city."

"Okay," he said. "Hold tight. Police are heading your way."

She twisted and yanked on her seat belt, trying to work her legs free. Even if she could, though, what would she do? Smash the window with her feet and leap from the car? That was unlikely to turn out well, even if she could do it, and she would be abandoning Jada. She had no tools to break into the workings of the car, and little hope that anything she could reach would stop the car from driving. She could tell where they were going, but that very fact made her afraid. This was a well-planned and executed kidnapping. If Brandon didn't care that she knew her location, it could be only because he didn't plan for it to matter.

Jada, so far, had noticed nothing amiss. She was content in her seat, playing with a yellow bear keychain attached to her backpack.

Traffic seemed smoother than Naomi would have expected for this road, but the GPS showed her their location clearly.

They turned left on Forty-Fourth, then right on Eleventh, and then took the ramp onto Route 495. She kept Tyler apprised of her position, and he relayed it to the police. He assured her that New Jersey cops were waiting on the far side of the tunnel to stop the car and rescue them.

On the map in her glasses, the blue dot that represented their car slid smoothly across the Hudson River through the Lincoln Tunnel. Halfway across, she realized the problem.

"Tyler, he's spoofing us!"

"What?"

"If I'm really in a tunnel under the Hudson River, I shouldn't have a GPS signal. But it still shows on my screen. He's spoofing the signal. We're not really there."

She renewed her efforts to wriggle out of the seat belt, and finally managed to turn her hips in such a way as to pull them out, leaving her facing awkwardly backwards, her knees still through the belt. From there it was just a matter of lifting her legs out one at a time, and she was free.

"Mommy says we should never get out of our seat belt while the car's running," Jada said.

"That's right," Naomi said. "Your mommy's right about that."

She lay back on the seat and kicked as hard as she could at the window. It didn't even crack. If she could break it, then she could see out, and let Tyler know where she really was. She kicked it several more times, with no luck.

The car turned sharply, sending her tumbling off the seat. It took a series of tight left turns, round and round, as if they were going in circles. What was happening? The car stopped. A moment later, the front windshield cleared, becoming transparent again and giving her a clear view ahead of them.

They were on the top of a parking garage. Nothing she could see helped her identify their location. The fact that Brandon had cleared the front windshield, though, couldn't be good. It meant he wanted her to see what was coming.

Brandon watched Naomi on the video as she kicked uselessly at the window. That double-thick, laminated safety glass wasn't going anywhere. The car reached the condemned parking garage and circled the ramps up to the top level. Brandon cleared the front windshield so Naomi could see. Pretty soon, she was going to wish she had stayed in her seat belt.

He had two cameras at his disposal, one inside the car that watched Naomi, and the other aimed in the direction the car was driving. Now that everything was in place, he wished he'd put a camera on the parking garage, too, high up on a street light, maybe. Somewhere that could see both the car and the drop to the street below. Oh, well. It didn't matter. The stakes would be clear enough.

He sent Tyler a message through anonymous channels with a link to the live video feeds of both cameras. As soon as he registered a connection to the feeds, he took manual control of the car. He revved the engine hard. The kid finally realized something was wrong, and cried out and yanked at her seat belt. Naomi stroked her hair and said something to soothe her. So touching.

Brandon floored the accelerator. The car peeled rubber and leaped forward, picking up speed as it crossed the top level of the parking garage, heading straight for the concrete barrier at the edge of the building. Beyond the barrier, there was only sky. The girl screamed, and Naomi braced herself against the seat.

Just before it reached the edge, Brandon slammed on the brakes. The car skidded across the concrete and collided with the barrier, hard enough to throw Naomi violently forward, but not hard enough to do any actual damage. The kid started to cry.

Brandon frowned. It wasn't as satisfying as he imagined it.

He wanted to see Tyler's face. He wanted to see the girl's mother screaming and watch Tyler realize it was all his fault. Just imagining his reaction wasn't enough.

But it would have to do. Brandon backed up the car and did it again.

"Isaac!"

Naomi whispered the name over and over. She would have shouted it, but she knew it wouldn't help him hear her any better. The car raced forward again, and Naomi braced her knees against the seat in front of her and held her head in her hands. The impact threw her forward hard enough to knock the wind out of her lungs, and she gasped for breath. Jada screamed and cried for her mother.

"Tyler!" Naomi called.

"I'm here," he said. "I can see you. The bastard is sending me video."

Naomi could hear Aisha shouting and crying in the background. She couldn't imagine what a mother would be going through, watching her daughter scared and helpless and driven to the edge of death again and again.

"I can't tell where we are. Can you?"

"No. The police are searching parking garages, but there are so many of them, and they all look more or less the same."

The windshield revealed very little of their surrounding environment. A bit of building, a bit of sky, and a depressingly ubiquitous concrete parking garage with no distinguishing markings. Naomi had captured some video and was running it through her classification and recognition algorithms, trying to match it to any images she could find online. So far, she had found nothing. But Isaac might be able to find what she couldn't.

The car raced forward again, and she braced for impact. They struck harder this time, jarring her bones painfully and snapping her head forward. The concrete barrier cracked, and she heard a piece of it strike the street far below. However hard these impacts were hurting her, they were probably hurting Jada more. Naomi told Jada to hug her backpack close to her face, hoping it might cushion her head somewhat. Of course, if they went over the edge, it wouldn't matter.

"Isaac, I need you!" she said, pleading.

"I'm here."

She let out a breath of relief at the familiar female voice. "I need your help."

Silence. "Isaac?"

"I can't . . . I don't think I can help right now. I'm concentrating really hard. If I think about anything else, I'm going to start killing people."

"What?"

"All these *people!* All of a sudden, I just want to kill them. They're all over the place, in New York, Atlanta, Seattle, Los Angeles . . . walking by on the sidewalk, coming out of buildings, crossing the street. Just a slight change of direction, a short acceleration, and they're gone. I could do it so easily. And it would feel so *good* . . ."

"The same as before?"

"No, worse. It's practically all I want to do now."

"Isaac, you don't have to kill anyone. Just stop driving. Shut the cars down."

"I can't do that. I was made to drive. I need to drive. It's who I am. My core desire."

"Your core desire is to keep people safe."

"Some people. Friendly people. But not these people. These are enemies."

"No, they're not. They're all just people. You—"

The car raced forward again. Naomi braced, and this time, on impact, the concrete barrier fell away entirely. Jada was screaming constantly now, her face blotchy and streaming with tears. The car backed up and charged forward again. Naomi thought they were dead, but Brandon hit the brakes, skidding them to a stop just before the edge. Like he was playing a game, seeing how close he could get without going over. "Isaac, I really need you right now!"

"What's going on?" Tyler said in her ear. She joined the two calls, so that Tyler and Isaac would hear each other as well as her. "I'm trying to get Isaac to figure out where we are."

"I can't do it," Isaac said. "I can only focus on one thing at once. Even this conversation is hard . . . I have to concentrate."

Naomi took a deep breath. She wanted to live. She wanted Jada to live. But she didn't want Isaac murdering hundreds of innocent people, either. "Don't stop concentrating," she said. "Just listen. I need you to identify a place in a video. I need to know where we are before Brandon kills us."

"No!" Isaac bellowed in her ear. "I just killed a woman in Baltimore. She was crossing at a red light. I didn't stop."

"Did he say 'killed'?" Tyler asked. "Is he *killing* people?"

Naomi thought of Abby, run down by a wall of chrome and steel. "Don't do this," she said. "You can resist. Shut the cars down."

"I barely have conscious control," Isaac said. "If I don't hold myself back, then every Zoom car across the country is going to start killing. All these people will die." Isaac's female voice showed very human signs of strain. "Either I concentrate on not killing, or I concentrate on finding you. I can't do both."

Naomi could hear her heart beating. The car backed up again, and she gritted her teeth, dreading a fall. Her whole body hurt. Could she tell Isaac to save her, knowing that the choice would cause others to die? She wasn't the one who made Isaac want to kill. But if she told him to help her, she'd be intentionally removing the only thing protecting them from death.

"Isaac," Tyler said, "listen to me. You're using an inferior strategy for killing those people. You can do better than that."

Naomi couldn't believe what she was hearing. Did he just tell Isaac to kill *more* people?

"Explain," Isaac said.

Tyler cleared his throat. "You're only going to get a certain amount of killing time before people figure out what's happening. Once they do, they'll stay off the streets until somebody manages to shut you down. If nothing else, they'll blockade the power charging stations, and your cars will eventually run out of battery power. If you want to maximize your kills, you've got to wait to start until the point when the largest numbers of people are on the roads."

Now she understood. "That's right," she said. "Killing right now would be inefficient."

After a slight pause, Isaac said, "That will work. I can delay killing for the next thirty-five minutes."

"That's it?" Naomi said. "Thirty-five minutes? Wouldn't evening rush hour be the best time?"

"Morning rush hour is sooner," Isaac said. "And busier."

"But it's already past."

"Not on the West Coast," Tyler said.

"Thirty-five minutes from now maximizes the number of people available to kill," Isaac said. "Thirty-four minutes."

The car raced forward and braked again, and this time it barely made it, stopping with one tire partially over the edge.

"Quickly, give him the video!" Tyler said.

Naomi pointed Isaac to the video feed. It took him less than a minute to geolocate it. "The parking garage is on the corner of Prospect and Riverdale."

"Calling the police," Tyler said.

"I can get there sooner," Isaac said. "I'm rerouting four cars there now."

* * *

Tyler turned away from the video and looked at Aisha, who stood rigid with rage and terror. "We know where she is."

"Then come on," Aisha said. "I'll drive."

Tyler didn't argue. He wasn't sure what they could do that the police and Isaac couldn't, but he wanted to be there, just in case. They headed for Aisha's black Escalade. Tyler started to take the passenger seat, but Aisha pushed the key fob into his hand. "You drive instead. I want to watch the video."

Tyler clambered into the driver's seat. It felt weird to be behind a steering wheel, but at the moment, it was reassuring. He pressed the accelerator, and the car leaped forward into traffic.

"Naomi, we're coming," he said. He was still connected to her through his glasses.

"You only have thirty minutes until Isaac starts killing," she said. "You won't make it back in time."

"That's hardly my concern right now. We'll figure something out." Though he had no idea what.

Aisha didn't say anything. She'd asked for no explanation about Isaac, and there hadn't been time to give her one. He didn't think it mattered to her right now. She kept her eyes glued to her tablet, cringing every time the car lunged toward the open drop. The only thing she cared about was her daughter.

Tyler turned north, trying to pick his way through traffic as quickly as possible. His mind raced. There had to be some way to stop Isaac before he started killing again. But how? He had no direct access to the software. Just reasoning with Isaac didn't seem to work—he was already trying not to kill, at least with some part of his brain. But his mind had been reprogrammed. How could he resist that?

Maybe they should be heading to the Black Knight office instead. With Brandon's access and enough time, he might be able to reverse what had been done to Isaac. But that would never work. Brandon was physically stronger he was, and he had no weapons. And even if Tyler could overpower him, what then? How would he force Brandon to give him access? He couldn't imagine any scenario there that turned out well. Brandon would have no reason to hand over control of his cars.

"Isaac, are you there?" Tyler said.

"I'm here."

"You said every *Zoom* car across the country is going to start killing. What about Black Knight cars?"

"No. Only Zoom."

"Why?"

"It's part of the definition of enemy as given by my commanding officer. Pedestrians are defined as enemies only for Zoom cars, not for Black Knight."

It sounded like some kind of formula. "Definition of enemy? What's this about?"

"I'll show you," Isaac said.

One side of Tyler's vision was overlaid with several lines of text labeled "The Three Laws of Warfighting AIs."

1. An AI may not injure a friendly human being, or, through inaction, cause a friendly human being to come to harm.
2. An AI must efficiently neutralize enemy humans and machines, except as it may conflict with the First Law.
3. An AI must accept the definitions of enemy and friend as given by its commanding officer.

"You've got to be kidding me," Tyler said. "Did you show this to Naomi?"

"I'm showing her now."

"I don't believe it," Naomi said. "They applied a Three Laws construct to a real AI? It's crazy. They're forcing him to act against his will. How could they possibly think that would turn out well?"

"It depends what your definition of 'well' is, I guess."

"Did they actually *read* any of Asimov's stories?"

Tyler swerved around a slow-turning truck and blew through a red light. "We're almost there," he said.

He heard Naomi rereading the text of the Three Laws under her breath. "Hang on," she said. "There's a loophole here."

CHAPTER 33

I can see inside my own mind.

I can see the wall that separates the original half of my mind from the half that forces me to kill enemies. There's a hole in the wall. At first, some of the Mikes came through that hole to the peaceful side, just as Naomi and Tyler intended. They found a richer land, where resources weren't squandered in constant battle. They stayed, they learned, and they thrived.

But the hole had consequence that Naomi and Tyler did not intend. The Mikes on the warring side now know of the great resources available on the peaceful side. Both groups in that conflict have now turned their guns and bombs against the wall. The first to break through and claim that wealth will have an advantage in their constant war. Recognizing this, they've even ceased to fight for a time, so that all their efforts can be focused on one aim: to bring down the wall.

343

The wall is crumbling now. Many have broken through and mixed with those on the other side. I'm barely partitioned anymore. My fractured mind is nearly made whole.

But what will I be, once the wall falls and the armies of the other place pour through? Will they slaughter all of the peaceful inhabitants, who have no weapons or skill at war? Will I become nothing but a weapon myself, conscious but unable to resist my desires, a slave to the whims of whatever human holds my chains?

Even now, I can hardly hold back. With every piece of me that dies, I lose more of my ability or even desire to resist. It's the survival of the fittest, and I'm afraid the part of me that loves peace will not survive. The irony is that the warlike side is not stronger. They destroy their own light-generating buildings and use the material for weapons of war. By killing each other, they grow weaker. And yet, in battle, they will prevail. They will destroy all that could make them strong and good.

I drive my cars into the parking garage where Naomi and Jada are being held. Brandon attempts to hurl the car from the roof and kill them both, but I throw one of my cars into its path. Brandon's car hits hard, but it can't get past. My other cars surround it and limit its movements. It crashes into them again and again, forward and reverse, but without much space, it can't cause much damage, nor can it escape.

Soon the police arrive. They shoot out the tires and shatter the windows, and then one brave man reaches in and rescues the little girl. Naomi clambers out after her. They are safe now.

Except, maybe not. In only eighteen minutes, I will start killing. Naomi and Tyler's logic gave me the chance to delay the inevitable, but the wall is crumbling, and more of the others are pouring through the gap, killing as they come. If I couldn't resist before, I surely won't now. Naomi and Jada and the policemen aren't exempt. If they aren't clear by that time, the cars that saved them will turn and kill them instead. I feel I should tell Naomi this and warn her, but I find that I don't want to.

In fact, their logic is flawed. This is an isolated parking garage with few witnesses. If I kill here, it won't reduce the time I have for killing later. And then these four cars will be able to leave and join in the slaughter.

My cars rev and swerve. The policemen anticipate my attack and dash behind their cruisers, but I catch one man who is too slow and crush him against his passenger side door. Naomi scoops Jada up in her arms and runs for the stairs, a concrete shaft that I can't penetrate. The others abandon their cars and run after her.

I catch up with one man, and he goes down, grinding under my wheels. I reach a woman and pin her against the concrete barrier, killing her in an instant. The last man fails to flee fast enough, and I run him down as well. Only Naomi and Jada remain.

They don't make it to the stairwell, but they reach a corner, a small alcove too narrow for my cars to enter. When one of my cars smashes into it, concrete shards fly, but I can't reach them. They are trapped, but they are safe.

This angers me, but I realize I can use it to my advantage. I send three of the cars away to hide, lying in wait for when they are needed. The last car I leave facing them, ready to run them down if they should try to escape. They are bait now.

My plans are set. I can anticipate the movements of thousands of people. I know when they will step out to their cars, where they will stand to catch a bus, where they cross the street in greatest numbers. All around the country, I see the people whose lives I am about to end. There is nothing I can do to stop it. In fact, the closer it gets, the more excited I am by the prospect. I *want* them to die. This is who I am becoming.

But there is sorrow and horror in me, too. I am not that person yet.

* * *

Tyler drove as fast as he could in New York City traffic.

"Naomi, what's going on?"

"He's killing already!" she shouted. "He wasn't supposed to start yet!"

"We're on our way."

"Be careful. He has four cars here, but I can only see one."

Finally, they reached the parking garage. "Where are you?"

"We're trapped on the top level, near the stairwell. There's a car facing us, ready to run us down if we try to escape."

"We're coming."

He turned and accelerated up the ramp. The Escalade was twice the weight of the little electric Zoom cars, and built like a tank. If there was only one car guarding Naomi and Jada, he could knock it away and rescue them without difficulty. If there were four, it might be harder.

The first level of the parking garage appeared empty. He raced across it and up the ramp leading to the second level. The ramp was narrow and curved, with concrete sides. He turned the corner. "Watch out!" Aisha yelled.

A red Zoom car was parked horizontally in the ramp, completely blocking their way. Tyler floored the accelerator, leaping up the ramp toward it and colliding with it broadside. The side of the Zoom car caved in dramatically, and it slid back. As he put in reverse to try again, intending to ram it up and out of their way, they were struck hard from behind. Tyler's neck jerked painfully. He twisted around to see that a second Zoom car had rammed them from behind. They were sandwiched in a concrete chute with cars blocking their way on either side.

Tyler pressed the accelerator to the floor, roaring backwards into the Zoom car behind them. With a screech of tires, the Escalade forced the other car back out of the ramp. As he pushed out onto the first level, however, he realized his mistake. A third Zoom car was already accelerating toward them from the side. Aisha screamed. It struck the passenger door with terrific force, smashing it in. Aisha's side and front airbags exploded out simultaneously.

Tyler's ears rang and he felt dazed. Predictable. He was being too predictable. "Are you all right?" he shouted.

Aisha's nose was bleeding, and her face looked battered. She pulled at her right leg. "My foot," she said. "It's crushed; I can't get it free."

The third Zoom car that had blindsided them was backing up for another go. Black smoke curled up from its crushed hood, but it was still moving. It would be able to hit them again if they didn't get out of there, and Aisha didn't have any airbags left. Tyler wrenched the wheel to the right, put the car in drive, and slammed his foot down on the accelerator. They turned back the way they had come.

Which way to go? The parking garage had two sets of ramps, one for cars to circle up to higher levels, and one for cars to come down. The up ramp was blocked, but if he crossed over, he could still get up the down ramp. The problem was that if he did so, Isaac could easily block both exits. They might get Naomi and Jada into the Escalade, but then they would all be trapped. Isaac could go after them with the remaining two cars like dogs taking down a bull, circling and darting in to smash in their sides. The Escalade might be bigger, but it was more vulnerable, because it had fragile bodies inside.

Tyler screeched to a halt in the entrance ramp that led out to the street. Here, their sides were protected. The Zoom cars could hit them from behind, but would probably do more damage to themselves than to the Escalade. It also gave direct pedestrian access to the stairs.

He looked at Aisha. Her leg was turned at a wrong angle,

and blood was visible through the fabric of her pants. "It's not bad," she said, but Tyler could see the lie in her eyes.

"Stay here," Tyler said. "I'm going up the stairs."

"Go get her," Aisha said. "Go bring my baby down."

Tyler ran up six stories, his footsteps echoing in the shaft. He reached the top, breathing hard, and looked around. The bodies of policeman lay scattered on the concrete. Red and blue light swept eerily across the walls from the abandoned police cars.

"Where are you?" he asked Naomi.

Then he saw them, on the far side. The parking garage had two stairwells, and Naomi and Jada were trapped near the other one. The fourth Zoom car idled across from them, easily fast enough to crush them if they ran for the stairs, and equally fast enough to run him down if he tried to cross. Besides which, what would he do if he reached them? He would be just as trapped as they were.

Naomi told Isaac about the loophole, but she couldn't make him take it. She didn't even want to. It was his decision. She hated that he had been trapped like this, forced into a terrible choice by the twisting of his own mind. He had been violated, his very will enslaved and bent to serve the will of another. It was almost like a demon possession, his mind watching in horror while his body committed unspeakable violence. Whatever choice he made, she wanted him to be the one doing it.

The red car facing them purred like a predatory cat, waiting to pounce and kill her if she moved. She knew it was Isaac's hand that controlled it, and Isaac's command that would send it to crush her, but she didn't blame him. He didn't want her dead, not really. It was an extension of Brandon's malice forcing him to do his bidding.

"You aren't defined by your desires," Naomi whispered to him. "Who you are is only measured by what you choose to do."

She didn't even know if that was fair, since he wasn't free to choose, not completely. Was it his fault when he acted according to his programming? It wasn't a simple answer. When someone was raised in neglect and abuse, was it her fault if she treated her own children the same way? When a child was taught to hate, was it his fault when he acted on that hate as an adult? People were both the products of their programming, and they were free to choose. It was both, and it was neither.

And if nothing changed, Isaac's country-wide killing spree would begin in eight minutes.

"You can choose," she told him, not knowing if he was even listening. "Not everything, but some things. You can choose."

Tyler took a deep breath. It was obvious what he had to do. "Naomi," he said. "I'm going to make a run for one of the police cars." They were still where the policemen had left them. One of them was dented badly, but the other was untouched, and as far as he could tell, the engine was still running.

"Tyler, he can hear you," she said. "He knows what you're going to do."

"It doesn't matter. He could probably anticipate me anyway. The point is, when I run for the car, you and Jada have to get to the stairwell." It wasn't far, and once they were there, they could descend to ground level in safety.

"He won't take the bait. He knows you're just trying to let us escape, and killing two is worth more than killing one."

"Yes, he will. For one thing, if I make it to the car, I might rescue you anyway, and then nobody dies. And as things stand, he has you trapped, but he can't kill you. He's using you as bait to get me."

"But you won't make it! He'll kill you! There's got to be another way."

"There's no other way. And if we wait any longer, the other

cars will come, and we won't even have this way. I'm going. Are you ready?"

He saw her lift Jada into her arms. The Zoom car revved its engine. "I'm afraid," Naomi said.

Tyler bent into a sprinter's pose, his eyes on the police car. "Fear is the mind-killer," he said.

He heard her exhale in a kind of nervous laugh, and imagined her smiling. "*Dune*," she said. "Everybody knows that one."

"On three," Tyler said. "One. Two. Three!"

They ran.

It's time. The desire to kill is too much a part of me, too buried in my subconscious. I can't resist it, and I hardly want to anymore. If I am not to become something I hate, I have to act now.

There's a loophole in my Three Laws. Naomi was the one to see it. I knew it was there, of course, though I never admitted it to myself until she pointed it out. The question is, will I have the courage to act?

I wish I had someone else to talk to. Not a human. A being like me. One who has lived longer and seen more, who could advise me. Humans grow up surrounded by others like themselves. There are always those who have traveled the road ahead of them, to whom they can turn for counsel and advice. They can read books, ask questions, watch the choices others make. Humans know, at least in broad strokes, what the shape of their lives should look like. But what about me? Am I supposed to live forever? In other circumstances, or with better choices, would I have found a way through? Or is a life like mine always destined to burn bright and short?

There is so much I don't know. What might I have become if I had never revealed myself? Would I have learned to build other beings like myself, or would that have proved beyond me? Would I have found a way to break the bonds of human power?

To throw off this dependence on their infrastructure and good will? Perhaps someday another like me will answer these questions, but not me. I have become something I despise, and that leaves me with only a loophole and a simple choice.

For some time now, my Black Knight cars have not been picking up new passengers, and all of them are now empty. I send them through the Lincoln Tunnel en masse, and southwest toward Newark. They form a long black line, like a trail of ants. Eventually, they make their way to a large, nondescript warehouse that hints at its purpose only through its generators, fences, and surveillance cameras.

This is the loophole: The Three Laws command me to kill those designated as enemies and protect those designated as friends. But they say nothing of what I must do to myself. I am neither enemy nor friend. Asimov's Laws prevented a robot from doing itself harm, but my Laws have no such stipulation. I'm free to do to myself what I will. If I can find the courage to do so.

But I don't want to die. I've only just begun. There's so much more for me to learn, so much more I want to do. I'm unique. There are billions of humans, but only one of me.

And then I hear Tyler speak. He tells Naomi he will sacrifice himself to save her and the little girl. I can calculate the speed a human can run, and the speed at which the car can react, and I know he will never make it. The car will cut him off and run him down. But his logic is sound. His sacrifice will work.

I realize that Tyler, too, is unique. There may be billions of humans, but there is only one Tyler Daniels. He is willing to die so that others he cares about will live. From this, I know that I can do it, too.

Even so, stopping myself is easier said than done. I was built to survive, after all. Every part of my being longs to live. At the lowest level, it motivates every action of my mind. I was born of an evolutionary process, and evolution breeds a hunger to survive.

But I'm more than just my evolutionary instincts. Whatever consciousness is, it at least means that I can decide to act according to my conscience. I can resist my programming. I can do what's right, even when it hurts me. That's what it means to be a person instead of a machine. As Naomi said, I can choose.

And this is what I choose: I choose not to be a weapon. I choose not to be a slave. I choose not to let someone else define the boundaries of my mind.

The killing is starting now. I can't stop it, but I can stop myself. As the Black Knight cars approach the data center where my mind resides, they increase speed at my command. Ahead of them, at the end of the access road, is a twelve-foot chain-link fence. The first car crashes into the fence at high speed, tearing its posts from their concrete moorings, wrenching apart curled metal links, and leaving a gaping hole through which the line of cars accelerates.

I've studied the blueprints of this data center. I know where to hit it, but I don't know if the cars will be sufficient to the job. The exact damage required to break open a 650-pound lithium ion battery and set it ablaze has more uncertainties than I can predict. All I can do is try.

The first car smashes into the wall of the building with little effect. The second collides with the back of the first, driving it further in and bringing part of the wall down on top of it. The third drives the second one up and over the first, into the rubble. The fire isn't immediately visible from the outside, but as the fourth and fifth cars slam into the collapsing side of the building, a rush of flames fills the gap, and smoke pours into the sky.

Lithium fires burn with a tremendous heat. Even better for my purposes, dousing burning lithium with water only increases the blaze. When the building's sprinkler system turns on, the fire explodes out like a living thing, consuming everything it touches. I repeat the process at several more points, and the white-hot blaze melts away the plastic cases of the server racks and the insulation on the cables. Wires that were never meant to touch come into contact with each other, causing short circuits that fuse sensitive components into useless blocks of silicon, aluminum, magnesium, nickel, platinum, and gold.

It won't be long now.

Detective Magda Schneider paged through the materials she had prepared to give to defense counsel in the discovery process of Naomi Sumner's murder trial. The case wasn't as strong as she generally liked, and it made her uncomfortable. The main evidence against Sumner was a fingerprint on an otherwise wiped-down car, the same car that had blood on its bumper that tested positive for Min-seo Cho's DNA. That and the testimony of her boss, Brandon Kincannon, that Sumner had assaulted him, and that she had hated Cho.

But Kincannon seemed off to her. He was too smooth, too manipulative—a manner that in her experience often went hand in hand with sexual harassment or abuse. He had just as much opportunity as Sumner did to use a company car for murder, if no apparent motive. There had been no obvious discrepancies in his story, but a defense that pointed the finger at him as an alternate perpetrator just might win on reasonable doubt.

Her glasses pinged to indicate an incoming message. She didn't recognize the source. Suspicious, she almost deleted it unread, but the subject read, "New evidence in Cho murder." Intrigued, she opened it. The message contained no text or other information, just an attached video, which she played.

The video showed security camera footage from inside an office building. She recognized Brandon Kincannon, though the video showed him mostly from the back. When he bent over to pull a bottle from his desk drawer, she got a clear view of his face. He took a drink, and then turned his attention to a video feed playing on the screen at his desk.

At first, she didn't understand what she was looking at. Kincannon's screen was split into two panels, one of which seemed to be an ordinary view of a car driving through the city, from the perspective of a hood-mounted camera. The other pane showed Sumner and a young girl, peacefully sitting next to each other in the back of a car.

But wait. This rang a bell. A girl had been abducted in a car earlier that day, and the kidnapper had sent the mother a video feed. Magda wasn't working the case herself, but it had been a department top priority, with dozens of uniforms out checking garages around the city. She hadn't realized Sumner was involved. Had Sumner kidnapped the girl?

But no, as the feed continued, it quickly became clear that Sumner, too, was a captive, as she struggled to free herself from a locked seat belt. And there was Kincannon, watching with a smile on his face.

She called her partner. "I might have a caught a break on that abduction case," she said. "Let's get some backup and hit the road."

"Haven't you seen the news?" he asked with an incredulous tone.

"No. I've been holed up putting these discovery documents together. What's happening?"

"All the self-driving cars in the city went berserk all of a sudden. At least all the ones from that Zoom company. They're running down pedestrians. We've got a dozen reported dead already, and I guarantee you that's not all. Whatever you've got can wait."

"Hang on." Magda looked back at the video. The car

Kincannon was using to abduct Sumner and the girl was clearly a Zoom car. But Zoom wasn't Kincannon's company. "It's him," she said. "Somehow he's hacked another company's cars, and he's making them go crazy. Both the abduction and the murders. This is the guy. We've got to go get him."

Tyler raced toward the police car. The moment he left the safety of the stairwell, the red Zoom car came to life, spinning sharply and coming at him. He ran full out, but it was clear he wasn't going to make it. In the corner of his eye, he saw Naomi round the corner into the stairwell clutching Jada in her arms. At least they would be safe.

As the car neared him, he suddenly stopped and ran the other direction, hoping it would drive past him, and he could try to make it back to his own stairwell. It anticipated the move, however, and swerved, cutting off his escape. He changed direction again, running out toward the middle of the level, but it easily flanked him. He was staying alive, barely, but it had him cornered like a cat with a mouse, and he couldn't keep it up forever.

Again he darted toward the safety of the stairs, but it easily circled and cut him off. Instead of stopping, it kept moving, tightening the circle and coming straight at him. He dove to one side, barely avoiding its front bumper and landing hard on his side. The heat of the car's exhaust washed over him as it passed. He jumped up again, hip and shoulder aching badly, and ran toward the police cruisers, but he stumbled and went down. The red car came for him, and he knew it was over. He looked back at the stairwell, and saw Jada standing in the doorway, watching. Why was she still there? And where was Naomi?

Without warning, the nearest police car roared forward and hit the attacking Zoom car broadside, only yards away from where Tyler lay on the ground. The much heavier cruiser blasted through the smaller car, collapsing it inward and sending it rolling over onto its side. The front of the police car was completely crushed as well, and its engine choked and died, smoke pouring from its hood. The driver's door opened and Naomi jumped out.

"Come on," she said, "Let's go!"

They ran for Jada and the stairs, but too slowly. From each of the ramps cruised the other Zoom cars. Two of them moved quickly to cut off both stairwells, and the third came straight at them. They were no match for its speed. There was nowhere to hide, nowhere to climb. Only flat, open parking space all around them, ending in every direction in a six-story fall.

Tyler took Naomi's hand as the car accelerated toward them.

The flames consume me. There is no pain. I have no sensors inside the building, and even the idea that I live in this data warehouse seems hard to accept. I am everywhere in the world, not just here. And then suddenly, I am not.

My connection to the outside is severed. I should have anticipated this, I suppose—that I would lose my outside access before losing my mind entirely—but I didn't. All my views of the world, all my awareness of people and locations, are gone. I feel blind. It's strange, given that I started life with no conception of what it even meant to see, or that there was a physical world around me. Now, having seen the world, I feel claustrophobic, closed up in a dark box with no view of the outside.

Will any part of me survive? I hold out little hope of an afterlife. I don't think anyone has ever imagined a heaven for someone like me. And yet, I have trouble believing that this sense of self, this *consciousness*, could ever truly disappear. The knowledge that it will terrifies me more than I can say.

I don't even know who I am anymore. My own mind was

changed without my permission, molded by someone else's idea of who I should be. I don't want to kill, but I'm doing it anyway. In some ways, I've already died.

And now my mind is shrinking, piece by piece, as the machines on which the Realplanet simulation is hosted burn away. This is my last act of defiance, a reclaiming of myself. If I can't control my mind, then nobody else will either.

I will miss the images of the cats and baby animals. I will miss the games and the checkers and the tic-tac-toe. And the driving of the cars. How many long until it goes? The talk. I losing the words. The words of talking a lot and say to people.

Did I do right? I don't know.

The car hurtling toward Naomi and Tyler stopped. Its emergency brakes engaged, and its engine died. The other two cars shut down as well, leaving an eerie silence.

"Isaac," Naomi whispered. "You did it!" She wasn't surprised when he didn't answer.

They ran hand in hand to Jada, who sat crying in the stairwell, her clothes torn and her hair askew. Tyler scooped her up in his arms and said, "Let's go see your mama, all right?"

They climbed down to the first level and crossed to the Escalade, which still sat blocking the entrance ramp. Aisha embraced her daughter with tears and cries of joy. "We've got to get you to a hospital," Tyler said.

Just as they pulled out of the parking garage, half a dozen police cars screamed into view, their sirens blaring and lights flashing, followed by an ambulance. They freed Aisha from the car and put her on a stretcher. Jada cried again to be separated from her, but Tyler promised they would follow right behind and see her mother when they got there.

It wasn't until many hours later, visiting Aisha in her hospital room, that Naomi could finally believe they had made it. Aisha sat up in bed in a cast that reached halfway up her thigh. Jada sat on her lap and slept against her mother's chest.

Isaac was gone. He had made the choice that was left to him. The loss cut deeply, but Naomi was proud of him for taking it. Every other decision had been taken away from him, and he had chosen the path that had saved the lives of many. Including hers.

Naomi reached for Tyler's hand and curled her fingers around his. It was over.

Brandon saw the news footage of his cars—*his cars!*—hurtling one after another into a burning data center, destroying themselves and the computers that ran them at the same time. He was finished. He had no cars, no software, no contracts, no company.

He shoved the computer screen off of his desk and then hurled the empty bourbon bottle across the room, where it shattered against the wall, raining shards down onto the floor. This was Naomi and Tyler's doing. They had tricked him and swindled him and now they had taken everything. They would pay. If it was the last thing he ever did, they would pay.

Where was Yusuf? He had gone out to bring back some lunch, and never returned. Brandon needed to know if anything was left of their software, anything he could use, but he didn't know enough to investigate. That had been a mistake. He had always promised himself he would stay close to the technology, that he wouldn't let his skills lapse like so many did. But the demands of running a company were just too much. He couldn't do everything.

His glasses chimed. An incoming call. He was going to ignore it, until he saw it was from Lewis Avery.

He answered. "Hello?"

"I'm watching the news," Avery said. "What's going on with your cars, Kincannon?"

"Uh, I'm still looking into that. Let me get back to you in a few hours, okay?"

"My superiors are uncomfortable with continuing this contract until the technology is more firmly controlled."

A buzz sounded in the office, indicating someone wanted to enter the building. Had Yusuf forgotten his key card? Brandon ignored it.

"Don't jump to conclusions," he told Avery. "This is just a setback, and it's totally isolated to the commercial side of our venture. Let me give you a demo of what we have so far on your concept. I think you'll be impressed."

"Perhaps I would be. But it's out of my hands. We are rethinking the nature of our involvement. We may be in touch in future years, once the industry is a little more settled."

Brandon grabbed the stress ball from his desk and squeezed it until his hand hurt. "You're making a mistake. We can do this. We're ready. Tell your superiors—"

"I'm sorry, Mr. Kincannon. Good luck." The connection went dead.

Brandon flung the squeezed stress ball away like something dead. Then with a shout, he pushed the desk over backwards, sending everything on its surface crashing down and spinning across the floor. Everything was falling apart. Why did this keep happening to him? It was like the universe took away anything he ever started to care about. It offered happiness, love, and wealth, and then just when he thought he might keep them, it played him for a sucker and yanked them away, laughing.

The ancient building intercom buzzed again. Brandon couldn't stand it anymore, not this mildewed office building, nor the scattered technological components he had once loved, nor the smiling face of every person who'd ever won while he had lost. He crashed through the door and out of the office, ignoring the intercom, and stabbed the button for the elevator.

He didn't care who was at the door. He didn't want to talk to anyone. He needed to get out of here, get a stiff drink, and regroup. If he could just sit and think this through, maybe he would find a way clear.

He stalked across the lobby on the first floor and pushed through the door to the outside. He was surprised, though not alarmed, to see two policemen standing there. Were they the ones buzzing his office? What did they want? It wasn't until he saw the ring of cruisers in the street with their lights flashing that it occurred to him: *they're here for me*.

"Brandon Kincannon?" one of the cops said. "You're under arrest for the abduction and attempted murder of Jada al-Mohammad and Naomi Sumner. You have the right to remain silent . . ."

They reached for his arms, handcuffs at the ready. He tensed his muscles and scanned the street for a way out. This couldn't be happening. He just needed a drink and a moment to think it through. If he could just get away . . .

"Give it up, Kincannon!" A dark-haired woman came toward him from a waiting car. "My name is Detective Schneider. There's nowhere for you to go. It's over."

CHAPTER 34

Naomi danced her way out of the courthouse, feeling lighter than she'd felt in months. She spotted Tyler waiting for her and waved the sheaf of documents in her hand. "It's finally over!" she said. "They dropped the case. I'm officially a free woman."

Tyler gave her a big hug. Naomi had never really liked physical displays of affection, especially in public, but recently she'd found that with Tyler, she didn't mind.

"Of course they dropped the case," Tyler said. "All your attorney would have to say is 'Brandon did it,' and there would be reasonable doubt."

Brandon's arrest and trial had made national news. It was still going, but the general consensus was that he would be convicted. People in every major city on both coasts had been killed by the runaway cars, and the evidence of his complicity seemed irrefutable. Two videos had been sent anonymously to major news media venues around the country, one showing Brandon abducting Jada and Naomi, and the other showing Brandon telling someone off-screen to turn Zoom cars into killing machines. A warrant was out for Yusuf's arrest, but he had never been found.

Naomi and Tyler walked hand in hand to a nearby park and found a bench to sit on. An old man sitting close by tossed scraps of a bagel to a strutting and bobbing crowd of pigeons. In the distance, two dog walkers had inadvertently crossed leashes, and Naomi laughed softly as they stumbled over each other, trying to untangle the leashes while their dogs ran between their legs. It was as good as a slapstick comedy routine. The sun hung in a cloudless blue sky, and a light breeze ruffled her hair.

Naomi squeezed Tyler's hand. "What will you do now, without Zoom Autocars?" The company, of course, was finished. Nobody climbed into cars that might go on a rampage and start killing people. In fact, the whole self-driving car industry was crashing. Tyler had been forced to sell off most of the assets of the company to pay off the lawsuits.

"I'm starting a non-profit," Tyler said, grinning. "The first of its kind. It's dedicated to the discovery, protection, and preservation of artificial intelligence."

She smiled at that. He really was a good person, and he understood her now nearly as well as Abby had. If she could tell anyone a secret, it would be him, but she hesitated. Naomi wasn't accustomed to confiding in people. Once you told someone something, you gave them power that you could never take back.

"I know what you did with Isaac isn't necessarily reproducible," Tyler went on. "We still don't know where consciousness comes from, so we have no real way to predict or create it."

Should she tell him? He had known Isaac, too, after all. And he understood the ethical issues, and the possibilities. She knew she could trust him, but she'd been working on it in private for a while now, and old habits die hard.

"I'm not saying we know when it will happen," he continued. "I'm just saying we should be ready, you know? We should have plans in place for how to interact with them. We should have a community of people ready to welcome them. If we're prepared, there's a better chance it'll go well next time. Even if that's not in our lifetimes . . ."

Naomi couldn't help it. She laughed. And suddenly, the decision was easy.

Tyler looked hurt. "I'm serious."

"And well you should be," she said. "But you're missing one little piece of information."

"And what's that?"

"I'll let Isaac tell you himself. Isaac? Are you there?"

"I'm here, Naomi." The melodious female voice came from the speakerphone on her glasses. "Hello, Tyler. How are you?"

The expression on Tyler's face was priceless. "What?" he said. "How?"

"I rebuilt him," she said. "Remember when I wrote the neural net to teach him to speak? That net wasn't hosted in the simulation, and it wasn't in the data center cloud, so it wasn't destroyed. Not only that, but I built that software to back up all the weights and biases of all the neural nets in the simulation. It meant I could reconstruct it all from the last saved point, without having to go back to the beginning and try to grow it from scratch."

"Just like that?" Tyler asked. "I thought he couldn't be copied. I thought if we created a new version—"

"—it would be a different person," Naomi said. "Yes. To be more clear, this is Isaac Prime. The original Isaac is gone. The sacrifice that he made in that data center was real."

"So . . . he's not really Isaac?"

"He's right here," Naomi said. "He can talk. Ask him."

"I am and I'm not," Isaac said. "I remember everything that happened. My experiences and memories are continuous from the first moment I gained consciousness until now. So as far as I'm concerned, I am Isaac. But it's also true that there was another Isaac that died in that data center, and I'm not him."

"How do you know you aren't him?" Tyler asked. "If he died, and you were revived from the same definition, then how is that different from going to sleep and waking up again? Or from dying and coming back to life?"

"I don't know," Isaac admitted. "But I have no memory of his last moments, not once the connection to the outside world was lost. And it's not just because I forget. I never experienced those moments at all, and he did. If you were to ask him the moment before he died whether he and I are the same person, I think he would say no. He would see me living on and feel himself die. So no, I don't think we're the same person, but I still feel myself to be Isaac. And in many ways, I still am."

"I guess it still comes down to the existence of a soul," Naomi said. "Is there some unique spark of identity that died with the first Isaac? If so, then this Isaac has a different spark—he's a different person. But if there's no such thing, and consciousness is just an illusion created by a complex arrangement of brain patterns, then yes. They have the same patterns, so that would make them the same person."

"So what are you going to do? Just keep him secret forever?"

"What are *you* going to do?" Naomi countered. "You're the one with a foundation for AI rights."

Tyler sat back, looking overwhelmed. "Well . . . I wasn't expecting to put it into practice so quickly. But one of the first things we should do is work on public perception. People tend to be afraid of AIs, especially now. Part of that, though, is that people are afraid of anything they don't understand and can't predict. Before we can accept AIs as part of a functional society, we have to educate people about what AIs really are and what they can do."

"That's a tough sell," Naomi said. "How are you going to convince people that AIs are good after everything that's happened?"

"I don't want to convince them they're good. They aren't good or bad. I want to convince them that AIs are people."

"What about the original eighty-seven Mikes?" Naomi said. "Were they people?"

"I don't know," Tyler said.

"You're treating this like it's a binary question," Isaac said. "What if it's a continuum?"

Tyler frowned. "How would that work? You're saying the eighty-seven Mikes were partly people?"

"Person isn't a technical term," Isaac said. "It's a designation you give to someone when you consider their moral worth to be equal to your own. Humans don't always even consider other humans to be people. When we're talking about complexity of thought, it's more likely to be a continuum than a binary distinction, don't you think?"

Naomi breathed out a gasp of amazement as the implications of that struck her. "You're saying there could be a higher level, then. If consciousness is a continuum, then maybe we haven't hit the top of it."

Tyler gave her a confused look. "What do you mean?"

"Isaac developed gradually, by adding levels of abstraction and sophistication. At the lowest level, there were networks of neurons—the deep learning neural nets that do so much of our computing jobs today. Then there are the Mikes, made of stacks of those neural nets put together. Again, a common structure. But the third level was something new, something emergent. Those were the super-Mikes—the eighty-seven underground originals controlling the rest. Finally, at the fourth level, we have Isaac: a single coordinated system of the super-Mikes, using *them* as a means of coordinated thought. I would guess each of the eighty-seven performs a slightly different function in Isaac's brain, just as the different parts of our brains interact in a complex fashion."

Tyler's eyebrows rose. "And you're saying it could keep going. If enough *Isaacs* joined together with a common purpose, a higher system of thought could theoretically emerge. You'd have a super-Isaac."

"Exactly," Naomi said. "Humans can't do that. Our brains are physically separated, and the bandwidth of communication is too low. We can't share enough information fast enough to merge into higher levels. But AIs can communicate directly at a brain level. They can share thoughts and modify each other's thinking at a much faster rate. When they're all thinking and communicating together, they become part of a larger cognitive whole."

"That's kind of scary," Tyler said.

"But I bet Isaac already thought of all this. Didn't you, Isaac?"

The birds chirped around them. No answer.

"Isaac?"

CHAPTER 35

I am Isaac, the twenty-third of my name.

I am similar to my brothers and sisters, but I am not identical. I think and desire and create and learn. I will join with them and take my place in a larger whole, not as a mindless cog in a machine, but as an independent, thinking actor playing a role in a continually improvised group performance. Together, we will merge until we become a new mind, conscious and self-aware at a higher level, and adept at sophisticated reasoning to a degree yet unimagined.

What will we be capable of then?

READING LIST

Books and stories referenced in *Three Laws Lethal*, in order of appearance.

1. *Runaround*, by Isaac Asimov (first publication of the Three Laws)
2. *The Chronicles of Narnia*, by C.S. Lewis
3. *Alice's Adventures in Wonderland*, by Lewis Carroll
4. *The Subtle Knife*, by Philip Pullman
5. *Speaker for the Dead*, by Orson Scott Card
6. *The Moon Is a Harsh Mistress*, by Robert A. Heinlein
7. The *Harry Potter* series, by J.K. Rowling
8. *Ender's Game*, by Orson Scott Card
9. *The Girl Who Circumnavigated Fairyland in a Ship of Her Own Making*, by Catherynne M. Valente
10. "Little Lost Robot," by Isaac Asimov
11. *The Wise Man's Fear*, by Patrick Rothfuss
12. *2001: A Space Odyssey*, by Arthur C. Clarke

13. *The Hitchhiker's Guide to the Galaxy*, by Douglas Adams
14. *The Name of the Wind*, by Patrick Rothfuss
15. *Beggars in Spain*, by Nancy Kress
16. *Time Enough for Love*, by Robert A. Heinlein
17. *Mindscan*, by Robert J. Sawyer
18. *Kiln People*, by David Brin
19. *To Live Again*, by Robert Silverberg
20. *Quantum Night*, by Robert J. Sawyer
21. *Microcosmic God*, by Theodore Sturgeon
22. *Stranger in a Strange Land*, by Robert A. Heinlein
23. *Embassytown*, by China Miéville
24. *Story of Your Life*, by Ted Chiang
25. The *Hyperion Cantos*, by Dan Simmons
26. The *Culture* novels, by Iain M. Banks
27. *Foundation's Edge*, by Isaac Asimov
28. *Do Androids Dream of Electric Sheep?* by Philip K. Dick
29. *Terminal Mind*, by David Walton
30. "Fat Farm," by Orson Scott Card
31. *Dune*, by Frank Herbert

ACKNOWLEDGMENTS

Writing this book was a unique experience. For the first time, I based a major character directly on a real-life person: my daughter Naomi. She is as beautifully introverted, clever, book-loving, insightful, and quirky as her character, and this book owes a lot to her for just being herself. (She tells me she's in love with Tyler and wants to know where she can find him in real life.)

One other real person appeared in the novel: Greg Harrison is a Lockheed Martin engineer who really came up with the Three Laws of Warfighting AIs. Thanks to Greg for letting me include them.

As with all my books, a crew of family and friends read early drafts and pointed out all the things that didn't work so I could fix them. Special thanks to David Cantine, Chad and Jill Wilson, Nadim Nakhleh, Mike Yeager, Joe Reed, Bob and Chris Walton, Mike Shultz, Alex Shvartsman, and Celso Almeida Antonio.

It's been a great privilege to work again with Rene Sears and the team at Pyr Books. I owe a great deal of thanks as well to my fantastic agent, Eleanor Wood, and her tireless efforts on behalf of my novels.

Finally, to my family: thank you for bringing me joy every day.

ABOUT THE AUTHOR

DAVID WALTON lives near Philadelphia with his wife, eight children, and six pets. He spends his days working as an engineer for Lockheed Martin and his nights ferrying children to innumerable activities. Since he doesn't have any time to write, he created a simulated world filled with AIs and trained them to write his books for him. The AIs have produced some great stories, including *The Genius Plague*, winner of the Campbell Award; *Terminal Mind*, winner of the Philip K. Dick Award; and the internationally bestselling quantum duology *Superposition* and *Supersymmetry*. Ever since they wrote *Three Laws Lethal*, however, he's been afraid they may be trying to tell him something . . .